D1246295

A Baby to Call Ours
Front Porch Promises
Book 5

By

Merrillee Whren

Blessings!
Merrillee
Whren

If we confess our sins, he is faithful and just and will forgive us our sins and purify us from all unrighteousness.

—1 John 1:9 NIV

CHAPTER ONE

"Jimmy, thanks for coming in to talk to me."

"My pleasure, sir." Jimmy Cunningham shook his uncle Graham's hand.

"Have a seat." Graham Cunningham motioned toward the black leather chair next to his massive mahogany and cherry desk.

"Thanks." Jimmy settled in the chair, hoping this meeting meant more business for his painting company. His uncle had real estate dealings in the area and could probably use a good painter. When Jimmy was younger, he'd let his uncle intimidate him, but he wouldn't let that happen today.

Graham eased into his chair and steepled his hands as he propped his elbows on his desk. "I have a business proposition for you."

"Yes, sir." Jimmy couldn't contain his smile. "I'd like to hear about it."

Eyeing Jimmy, Graham eased back, his hands still steepled as he rested his elbows on the arms of his chair. "You know ever since Mitch got his MBA I've been begging him to get involved in some of my business holdings, but all he wants to do is run that garage."

"Yes, sir. I know how much Mitch loves to work on

cars." Jimmy never understood his cousin, Mitch, Graham's older son. Jimmy would've given anything to have been in Mitch's shoes growing up. Mitch's family was the toast of their little Tennessee town, Pineydale, while Jimmy and his family were the also-rans. Despite the times Jimmy had bested his cousin in their ongoing rivalries, Jimmy had always envied Mitch. "And he has a fine business of his own there."

"That's true, but I need to train someone to take over the business here in Pineydale when I retire in a couple of years. Alec is already running things over in Johnson City." Graham leaned forward again. "What do you think about stepping into those shoes? I've seen the way you've run your painting company and expanded it over the years. I think you would do a good job working for me."

Jimmy could hardly believe what his uncle was saying, but Jimmy didn't dare show his shock or too much enthusiasm for the idea. Taking a slow breath, he quickly formulated a positive but cautious response. "That sounds very interesting. Can you give me more details?"

Graham smiled as he nodded. "You'd be put in a type of internship role."

Jimmy didn't like the sound of the internship. "Does this mean I'm on trial, and if I don't perform according to your liking, then I'm out? Or would this be more of an apprenticeship, where you mentor me and bring me along to your satisfaction?"

"I'll be mentoring you, but there are no guarantees with this." Graham's eyes narrowed. "I like to see results before I make any decisions about the permanency of this position."

Jimmy didn't dare squirm in front of his uncle. The

man always drove a hard bargain. "And how long is this trial period?"

"Six months to a year. I like to leave things flexible." Leaning forward, Graham narrowed his eyes even further. "There are two stipulations for this job. One, you need to finish your college degree. Two, you need to find a wife. I want my executives to have a steady family life as well as a college degree."

Jimmy used every bit of his willpower not to overreact to his uncle's over-the-top demands. Getting a college degree was within reason, but getting married was another can of worms. He didn't even have a steady girlfriend. Going into this meeting, he'd promised himself he wouldn't be daunted.

"Uncle Graham, I'm for getting my college degree, but you can't expect me to get married just to have this job."

Graham lifted his chin as he eyed Jimmy. "That's exactly what I'm expecting. You have proven your work ethic with the painting business, but your personal life is something you have to address. Having a wife and a settled family life will make a difference."

His uncle was being unreasonable, but was there any wisdom in arguing with him? He was probably thinking of the mess Jimmy had created when he'd come between Mitch and his fiancée. "I can make good on my personal life without getting married."

"You don't have to get married immediately, but if you take the job, I have to see some progress on that front." Graham's gaze bored into Jimmy.

Jimmy stared back. "Uncle Graham, I understand why you might think I need a more stable personal life, but even if I don't have to be married right away, you can't expect me to get married just to have this job."

"So you're saying you don't want the opportunity?"

Jimmy wouldn't let his uncle see him sweat. Was it possible to make Uncle Graham see the fallacy in his marriage requirement? "I find the prospect interesting, but I can't create a love interest out of thin air."

A superior smile claimed his uncle's face as he stood. "If you want the job, marriage is one of the requirements. Take it or leave it."

"I understand." Jimmy manufactured a smile as he stood. "Thank you, sir, for considering me. I'll think it over. I would have to find someone to run my painting business if I decide to accept your offer."

Graham joined Jimmy on the other side of the desk. "You let me know what you've decided a week from today. We can go from there."

Jimmy extended his hand. "Thanks again. I'll let you know my decision in a week."

"You're welcome." Graham grinned, as if he knew what Jimmy was thinking. "I look forward to hearing from you."

With a nod, Jimmy left his uncle's office with a slow, deliberate pace. What had seemed like a golden opportunity to become part of his uncle's company had turned into fool's gold, or at least, that was the way it seemed to Jimmy as he hunched his shoulders deeper into his coat to ward off the wind of a late-winter day. With a sense of foreboding, he slid into his company van. He wanted to prove himself to Uncle Graham—show the man what Jimmy Cunningham was made of—but would it turn out to be chasing after an impossible dream?

Jimmy drove down Main Street until he reached the

lumberyard. He turned left and slowed the van to a crawl. He wanted to talk to his cousin Mitch but wasn't sure it was a good idea. After all, Jimmy and Mitch hadn't always been on the best of terms.

After stopping the van in front of Wilbur's Garage, an all-white block building, Jimmy sat there still holding the steering wheel with a death grip, as if it could save him from a wrong decision. Wilbur had been Jimmy's great-uncle who had owned this garage until he died from cancer several years ago. Now Mitch ran the place. With a loud sigh, Jimmy exited the van and trudged to the door. Maybe Mitch was already aware of his dad's plan. Even if Mitch knew, Jimmy needed to have this conversation to make sure Mitch was on board.

"Hey, Johnny, how's your day going?"

The man behind the counter with the thinning brown hair looked up. "Hey, Jimmy. Day's going great! What brings you by? Got trouble with your van?"

Glancing around, Jimmy shook his head. "I'm here to talk to Mitch. Is he here?"

"He's out back working on one of his restorations." Johnny cocked his head in that direction.

"All right if I go back to talk to him?"

"Sure."

"Thanks." Jimmy went through the door at the back of the waiting area. His breath created a cloud in the cool air as he approached the small block building at the back of the property.

He opened the door. "Mitch. You here?"

"Yeah." Mitch appeared from the far side of the red sports car that gleamed in the light beaming through the window on the far wall.

"Wow! Amanda's car looks fantastic!"

Mitch knit his eyebrows. "You haven't given away my secret, have you?"

"Nope."

Mitch smiled. "Good. I want this to be a wedding surprise."

"Amanda will definitely be surprised. She probably thinks you sold this long ago." Jimmy eyed Mitch. "Ready to give up the bachelor life?"

"Ready as can be. I can hardly wait to make Amanda my wife." Mitch rubbed the back of his neck. "I know you and I haven't always gotten along, but I wanted to say you did me a favor when you came between Whitney and me. Marrying her would've been a big mistake."

"Thanks for that." Jimmy thought about the messy business with Mitch's former fiancée. "She wasn't good for either one of us."

"You can say that again." Mitch raised his eyebrows. "I need to ask a favor of you."

"Sure." Jimmy couldn't imagine how he could help his cousin.

"I was planning to have Alec drive this car up to the country club during the reception and surprise Amanda when we leave, but I forgot he doesn't know how to drive a stick."

Jimmy laughed. "You mean your little brother never learned to drive a car with a manual transmission?"

Mitch shook his head. "Yeah. He couldn't be bothered."

"Be glad to do it. Just let me know the details." This friendly talk made Jimmy reluctant to bring up the conversation with Mitch's dad. Jimmy didn't want to ruin the camaraderie, but he had to know what Mitch thought of his dad's job offer. "By the way, I had a talk with your dad today about doing some work for him."

"That's great. Are you painting some houses for him?"

"Not exactly." Jimmy hesitated. "He said you weren't interested in taking over the business dealings in Pineydale and asked if I'd be interested in an internship to learn the business."

If Mitch was surprised, his expression didn't show it. "What did you say?"

"I didn't make a decision, but I have to give him my answer a week from today." Jimmy eyed Mitch. "I just want to make sure this is okay with you."

Mitch clapped Jimmy on the back. "If you want to deal with my dad, be my guest."

"So you actually don't have any desire to be part of your dad's business?"

Mitch motioned toward the area around him. "And give up all this? Never. I love my dad, but his demanding business approaches rub me the wrong way. I'm happy right here."

"Yeah, talk about demands. Your dad says I need to get my college degree and find a wife."

Shaking his head, Mitch laughed out loud. "Welcome to Graham Cunningham's world."

Jimmy wasn't sure he could trust his cousin's advice, but he had to ask. "So do you think I'd be crazy to take him up on his offer?"

A wry smile painted Mitch's expression. "It's up to you. I'd say the degree is a slam dunk, but the wife thing is another matter. Got any prospects?"

Jimmy let out a halfhearted laugh. "Not many

prospects around this town unless they drop in out of nowhere, like Amanda did for you."

"Yeah, she's a gift from God. If her car hadn't broken down here, we would never have met." Mitch rubbed his chin. "Maybe you should pray about it."

"Were you praying to find a wife when that happened?"

"Got to admit I wasn't, but Aunt Charlotte was."

"Maybe I should get Aunt Charlotte on my team."

Mitch nodded. "She's already on your team. I'm pretty sure if you ask her, she'll tell you she's been praying for you to find the right woman ever since you were old enough to think about girls."

"For real?"

"Yep. If there ever was a praying woman, it's our great-aunt Charlotte."

Jimmy put a visit to his great-aunt on his to-do list. "Maybe she can give me some advice."

Mitch shrugged. "Maybe. If not advice, some prayers. Ask her to pray for warmer weather for the wedding."

Jimmy laughed. "You could've waited until summer to get married."

"If I'd had my way, we would be married by now no matter what the weather, but Amanda wanted her sister, Kelsey, in the wedding. So we're getting married while she's on her spring break from college."

"Yeah. I remember Kelsey from last fall when she came to see Amanda perform at the Ryman in Nashville."

Mitch raised his eyebrows. "As I recall, you two hit it off. Too bad she doesn't live closer. She might be a good wife prospect."

"Yeah, she's a fun girl." Jimmy extended his hand to

Mitch. "Thanks for your input about your dad."

"Anytime." Mitch shook Jimmy's hand. "I'll be in touch about the car, and you shouldn't let my dad steamroll you about anything."

"I'll try to keep that in mind." Jimmy waved as he departed, still not sure how he should deal with the job offer. At least he had Mitch's blessing.

Minutes later Jimmy stopped his van in front of Charlotte's house, a century-old foursquare that sported a big front porch with rockers and a swing. Charlotte and her late husband, Wilbur, had had no children of their own, but they had welcomed their nieces and nephews to their home. Over the years Jimmy hadn't availed himself of their hospitality as much as Mitch had. Great-uncle Wilbur and Mitch had had a special bond.

Jimmy took the front steps two at a time. Before he could ring the bell, Amanda answered the door. "Jimmy, you're early for supper."

"I didn't know I was invited." He stepped into the front hall.

"You know if you visit near suppertime, you're sure to get invited." Amanda grinned. "You have business with Charlotte?"

"Maybe." Jimmy wasn't sure he wanted Amanda to be privy to what was on his mind. "Is Charlotte around?"

"Yeah, she's cooking up something perfect for a blustery day in March." Amanda motioned toward the kitchen. "I'm off to meet Mitch. We have to see the caterer about some last-minute stuff for the wedding."

"See you later."

Amanda grabbed her jacket from the hook near the front door. "We'll be back for supper."

Glad to have Charlotte to himself, Jimmy sauntered to the kitchen. "Do I smell something delicious?"

"White chili." Charlotte looked up from the pot she was stirring, a slow smile emerging as she looked his way. "Jimmy, what brings you by?"

Jimmy gave his great-aunt a kiss on the cheek. "Need advice, and I thought of you."

Charlotte's smile broadened as she put the spoon on a little tray next to the stove. She motioned to the barstools at the counter. "Let's sit down, and you can tell me what this is all about."

Hoping this was a good idea, Jimmy pulled out a stool from under the island countertop and straddled it. Then he proceeded to recount his conversation with his uncle. After Jimmy finished, he raised his eyebrows. "What do you think?"

Charlotte frowned. "Sounds like Graham's trying to manipulate lives again."

"Yeah. That's what I thought, and I'm not sure I want to jump through his hoops."

Charlotte waved a gnarled finger in Jimmy's direction. "But do you want the opportunity?"

"I do. I honestly do, but I don't know what to do about that wife part." Jimmy frowned. "That certainly is controlling."

"It is, but if you want the position, you will eventually have to find a wife."

Jimmy's shoulder sagged. "Guess I'll have to bow out."

"So you're saying no one will ever fall in love with you and marry you?"

Jimmy shrugged. "Could be. I don't exactly have a

stellar reputation with the ladies around here. Besides, Graham's demand sounds so calculating. Not the reason to get married."

"True." Charlotte eyed him. "But that doesn't mean you can't be on the lookout for a wife. Something tells me that Whitney broke your heart and you've never gotten over it."

Was that true? Jimmy had pretty much avoided thinking about Whitney. She made him feel guilty, despicable, and inadequate. He had tried to wipe her from his thoughts. Even Mitch's confession about her today didn't make Jimmy feel any better.

Jimmy narrowed his gaze. "What makes you think that?"

"You've never had a serious girlfriend since."

"I've been too busy to think about a relationship. Besides, there aren't many available women my age in Pineydale."

Raising her eyebrows, Charlotte tilted her head. "So that's your excuse."

Jimmy rubbed his forehead. Talking about Whitney gave him a headache as well as a heartache. She'd been his girl until he'd partied too much, dropped out of college, and joined the army. She had her sights set on someone with more ambition than him. She thought Mitch fit the bill until he chose the garage over his dad's business.

Even though Jimmy was positive Whitney had always loved him and not Mitch, Jimmy hadn't been good enough for her. He'd come up short. That haunted him still. Was he chasing after this job offer because he wanted to show people he was somebody, not just a college dropout who painted houses for a living?

"You're pretty quiet. Got no response?" Charlotte eyed him.

"Aunt Charlotte, I've got no excuse or response." Jimmy released a heavy sigh. "Maybe I should just stick to painting houses. I'm good at that."

"It's your choice, but maybe you should consider challenging yourself. Don't sell yourself short. There's a young woman out there who will love everything about you. The good and the bad. Get out there and find her."

"I wish I had your confidence." Jimmy never let anyone see his vulnerable side, but here he was putting it on full display for Aunt Charlotte. "I'll consider it. I have a whole week to think it over."

"And I have a whole week to pray about it, and so should you."

Nodding, Jimmy chuckled. "Mitch said you'd be doing that."

Charlotte hugged Jimmy. "I was blessed to marry into the Cunningham clan, and I've been praying for Wilbur's kin since then."

Jimmy returned his great-aunt's hug. "And we're blessed to have you. Thanks for listening."

"Anytime." Charlotte patted him on the back. "You stay for supper."

"Thanks for the invite, but I've got a lot of thinking and praying to do on my own." Jimmy saluted her. "See you at the wedding."

Charlotte clapped her hands. "You sure will. I can hardly wait."

"I'm happy for Mitch and Amanda. They're good for each other."

"You can say that again. Now we have to find someone

for you." Charlotte wagged a finger at him. "The Lord has the perfect woman picked out for you already."

"If that's the case, I hope He lets me know who it is sooner rather than later." Jimmy gave Charlotte a peck on the cheek. "Now I've got to get going."

Jimmy waved to Charlotte as he raced to his van. He wanted time alone to think about the advice he'd been given. And he needed to pray, but he hadn't done much praying in recent years. He had straightened out his life to some degree, but he had a long way to go. Having a conversation with God was a good place to start.

***

Organ music drifted into the room at the back of the church, where Kelsey Reynolds helped her sister, Amanda, with the last-minute preparations before she walked down the aisle. Kelsey took a calming breath and fought back the nausea, which she'd been experiencing most of the day. She prayed she wouldn't get sick and ruin her sister's wedding, but Kelsey wasn't sure God would hear her prayers. Maybe for Amanda's sake, He would.

"How are my two girls?" Wearing a kilt for the Scottish wedding, Grady Reynolds stepped into the room.

"Ready to get married." Amanda rushed over to her dad and hugged him. "Dad, you look handsome in your kilt."

Grady smiled as he brushed a hand down the Cunningham tartan, then straightened his dark jacket. "I'm not sure about wearing this thing, but I'm ready to give you away."

Amanda laughed. "I think you've been saying that

since I was thirteen. And you look absolutely fabulous in a kilt."

"If you say so."

Amanda laughed again. "I do."

"You have given me a few sleepless nights, but you girls make me proud." Grady stretched out his arms and drew his daughters close. "I love you more than you know."

Amanda hugged her dad back. "And we love you."

Kelsey didn't say anything. She just wanted to get through the wedding without making a scene. She turned and grabbed her bouquet. "Time to take my place. See you at the altar."

Amanda hurried over and hugged Kelsey. "I love you, little sis."

"Me, too. You look beautiful." Kelsey blinked back her tears. "Now I'd better get going."

Kelsey stood in the entrance at the back of the church. People of every age filled the dark wooden pews with the white trim. The setting sun shone through the stained-glass windows on the west side of the church and cast an iridescent glow through the sanctuary. White flowers and lighted candles decorated the platform.

Dressed in their dark jackets and kilts made with the red-and-black Cunningham tartan, Mitch and Alec, the best man, stood at the front with the pastor who would perform the ceremony. Kelsey had to walk down the aisle just like in the rehearsal. She could do this. She would pass by the smiling faces and pretend everything was perfect—everything but her.

As the bagpipes signaled her entrance, she ran a sweaty hand down the skirt of her red dress, which matched the

Cunningham tartan. The filmy material beneath her fingers did little to calm her nerves. The dress only served to remind her of the day she'd picked it up in Spokane and made a discovery that spun her world out of control.

Pasting on a smile, she took that first step. Put one foot in front of the other. That was all she had to do, but the aisle seemed a mile long, and for a second everything swam before her eyes. She couldn't faint. That was supposed to happen to the bride or groom, not the maid of honor.

Mitch smiled at Kelsey as she took the next step. She adored her future brother-in-law. Amanda had made a good choice. Kelsey wished she'd done the same. She smiled back and determined she would make the best of this day. She had to for Amanda.

When Kelsey reached the front, Mitch gave her a subtle thumbs-up, then turned his attention to the back. Amanda stood there, her arm looped through Dad's. She was all smiles and beauty in white. The expression on Mitch's face told everyone in that church that he was a man in love. Kelsey wondered whether a man would ever look at her that way. She feared not, but this day wasn't about her. It was her sister's day. Kelsey put that thought squarely in her mind as the folks in the pews stood.

While the bagpipes played, Amanda made her way down the aisle until she stood beside Mitch, who smiled down at her. Despite her own troubles, Kelsey was happy for her sister.

Like an automaton, Kelsey made her way through the rest of the ceremony—the vows, the exchange of rings, and the unity ceremony. Then the kiss sealed them all.

Accompanied by the sound of the bagpipes, the bride

and groom held hands as they hurried to the back of the auditorium. Kelsey breathed a sigh of relief. She had made it through the wedding without incident. Maybe the worst of the nausea and dizziness were behind her. She could only hope as she prepared to stand in the reception line and greet a lot of people, mostly strangers. She shook hands, smiled, and made small talk as the guests filed out of the church.

Finally Kelsey spied a familiar face as her stepcousin, Max, and his wife, Heather, drew closer. "Max and Heather, it's so good to see you. I'm so glad you made it."

"So are we." Max hugged her. "We wouldn't miss Amanda's wedding."

Heather hugged Kelsey. "Are you okay? You look a little pale."

Kelsey forced a smile. Even though Heather was a nurse, there was no way she would know what was wrong. "Too many late nights studying for exams before I came."

"That'll do it." Heather patted Kelsey's shoulder. "You'd better get some rest after this is over."

"I intend to. That's why I'm housesitting for Mitch and Amanda while they're on their honeymoon." Kelsey hoped a week to herself would help her sort out her life.

"Yeah, a week of relaxation is probably just what you need." Max hugged her again before he and Heather proceeded to shake hands with Alec.

As Kelsey looked toward the folks waiting to greet the wedding party, Jimmy Cunningham sauntered her way, a grin splitting his handsome face. "Well, well, if it isn't the prettiest maid of honor I've seen all day."

Kelsey couldn't help grinning back even though her stomach roiled again. She sure didn't want to barf on his shoes. "Should I take that as a compliment? I believe I'm the only maid of honor."

He leaned closer. "That's a compliment for sure. I hope you're saving a dance for me."

"I'll see if I can fit you in. You know the maid of honor is in high demand as a dance partner." Kelsey remembered how much fun she'd had with Jimmy when she'd been in Nashville last fall for Amanda's concert. But he was a smooth talker just like that lowlife Brandon, who'd broken her heart and left her life in a shambles.

"High demand or not, I expect a dance." Jimmy winked as he moved on.

While Kelsey tried not to think about any man, especially charmers like Jimmy and Brandon, Mitch's great-aunt Charlotte grasped Kelsey's hand with her gnarled fingers.

"What a wonderful wedding. You and your sister look lovely."

Kelsey resisted the urge to embrace the older woman and just hang on for dear life. Something about Charlotte's presence gave Kelsey a sense of peace. Charlotte had a way of turning gloom into sunshine. "Thanks. Amanda deserved this day, and the weather has been perfect."

"Splendid. Warmer than normal." Charlotte squeezed Kelsey's hand again. "We prayed for just such a day, and God granted our prayer."

Kelsey nodded as Charlotte reached out to Alec. Charlotte's statement reminded Kelsey that God had also granted her request to get through the wedding, but she still had to survive photos and the reception. *Lord, please get me through the rest of these activities so nothing will distract from Amanda's day.*

The photographer made quick work of the wedding party and family photos, much to Kelsey's relief. She rode with her dad and stepmom to the Pineydale Country Club for the reception, while the bride and groom stayed behind for more photos.

When they reached the country club, Kelsey hurried off to the restroom. But the nausea never came while she stood in the stall. She closed her eyes as she leaned her head against the cool door. If she was going to be sick, why couldn't it be now? She should be thankful that the sick feeling had fled, but she worried that it would return at the worst time.

Kelsey washed her hands and studied her reflection in the mirror. She was pale, just as Heather had said. No one else had mentioned it. Kelsey pinched her cheeks and hoped that would give her face a little color. She joined her parents as they talked with Mitch's parents while a DJ played soft music in the background. All she really wanted was to go somewhere and hide, but she had a dinner to get through and a toast to give.

The bride and groom arrived with great fanfare, and Kelsey took her place at the head table with the rest of the wedding party. Soon servers brought food to the tables. Kelsey swallowed hard as she stared at her plate. Did she dare eat? Just the smell of the food was making her stomach churn. She cut a piece of the chicken but pushed it around with her fork.

Amanda leaned Kelsey's way. "Don't tell me you're trying to lose weight again."

"No." Kelsey smiled. Thankfully, Amanda didn't have a clue what kept Kelsey from eating. "Just a little nervous about giving the toast."

Amanda put an arm around Kelsey's shoulders. "Don't worry about the toast. It's all for fun. Whatever you say will be fine."

Kelsey offered a slight smile. "I just want your day to be perfect."

"It doesn't have to be perfect. It just has to be fun." Amanda raised an eyebrow. "Mitch and I just want to share this with the people we love."

"Yeah. That's the important thing."

"Now eat." Amanda motioned toward Kelsey's plate. "You need your energy to give that toast and catch the bouquet."

"I've got plenty of energy. I'm fine." Kelsey wished she was fine, but she couldn't share her problems with her sister or her family. She didn't know what to do about the mess she was in.

When the server whisked her plate away, Kelsey had no complaint. She leaned back in her chair and tried to relax. She fingered the little note card on which she'd written a few reminders about what she wanted to say during the toast. She looked over at Amanda, who laughed at something Mitch had said. For the first time ever, Kelsey envied her sister.

Growing up, they'd often been at odds. Amanda had been the rebellious one, and Kelsey had been the parent pleaser. Now everything was falling into place for her sister, while everything was falling apart for Kelsey.

CHAPTER TWO

Conversation and laughter floated through the country club dining room as Jimmy watched Kelsey at the head table. A pretty girl with dark hair falling in waves around her shoulders, she hadn't smiled much tonight. She didn't seem like the same young woman who had laughed at his crazy jokes and made him feel important and full of life that night last fall after Amanda's concert.

At the time he'd thought she might be a little young for him. She was nearly eight years younger, but he shoved that worry aside. Despite the age difference, they'd still had a good time and could do that again tonight. He looked forward to dancing with her.

When they'd spoken in the reception line, he'd sensed a troubled look in her blue eyes, despite her congenial greeting. He didn't know her well enough to know the meaning behind that look. He'd like to get to know her better, but she was here for a week, then gone.

While he sat there thinking about Kelsey, the DJ announced the toasts from the best man and the maid of honor. Alec went first with his toast, as he had the guests laughing at his stories about Mitch. Alec ended with a touching tribute to Mitch and Amanda, causing a few guests to reach for a tissue to dry their eyes.

When Kelsey's turn came, Jimmy studied her

expression. He couldn't figure out whether she was happy or sad. Among other things, she told the story about how she and Amanda got lost in the woods and had a search party looking for them because they were trying to bring about a match between their dad and their stepmom, Maria.

Looking at Amanda and Mitch, Kelsey held her glass high. "Now Amanda has found her own wonderful match in Mitch. Congratulations, you two."

A chorus of cheers followed Kelsey's toast, then the DJ announced Mitch and Amanda as they stepped onto the dance floor for their first dance. The father-daughter and mother-son dances followed. Then the DJ opened up the dance floor to the other guests. Just when Jimmy thought he had a chance to ask Kelsey to dance, Mitch appeared at his side.

"Hey, Jimmy." Mitch surreptitiously handed Jimmy the keys to Amanda's car. "This would be a good time to get the car and park it near the front door."

"Will do." Jimmy pocketed the keys.

"Alec will meet you in the parking lot and drive you over so you'll have a vehicle here when this is all over."

"Good thinking." Jimmy nodded. "Are you sure out front is fine?"

"Yeah. Amanda won't be going out there until we're ready to leave." Mitch glanced toward Amanda, then returned his gaze to Jimmy. "I really appreciate your help."

"Anytime." As Jimmy left the country club, he wondered if this started a new chapter of goodwill with Mitch. Jimmy hoped he could prove himself to Mitch and Graham. Respect, that was all Jimmy hoped for.

But where would he find a wife? And how soon did he have to find one?

"I hear that you might be joining the business." Alec maneuvered his car onto the main road leading into town.

"I'm giving it some serious thought."

"It's a good opportunity for you." Alec pulled into the space in front of the garage.

Jimmy nodded. "You might be right, but I have a few things to work out before I decide."

"I hope you'll join us." Alec motioned toward the garage. "The car is parked out back. I'll see you in a few minutes at the country club."

"Sure thing." With a salute, Jimmy hopped out of Alec's car.

As Jimmy walked around the back of the building, he had a rising sense of hope that things would work out with this job. With Alec in his corner, Jimmy figured he could maneuver around Graham's demands. Did Alec know about the job requirements?

Alec's knowledge or ignorance shouldn't weigh on Jimmy's decision. He was the one who had to decide whether he wanted to tie himself to another man's whims. He wished the answer was clear.

Letting out a loud sigh, Jimmy parked the sports car at the curb near the walk leading to the front door of the country club. As he got out of the car, he gave the roof a little tap. Amanda would enjoy her surprise. Now he had to collect a dance from Amanda's sister.

With a spring in his step, Jimmy entered the dining room and searched for Kelsey. She was on the dance floor with his little brother, Jeremy, moving to a song with a fast beat. A flash of jealousy zipped through Jimmy's mind. Jeremy was closer to Kelsey's age. Maybe she preferred that. Jimmy wanted to cut in, but he thought better of that strategy. He would wait until this dance ended.

But before Jimmy could make his move onto the dance floor, Jeremy pulled Kelsey close as the sounds of a slow song floated through the air. While Jimmy stewed, Mitch strode across the room.

His eyebrows raised, Mitch stopped in front of Jimmy. "Get the job done?"

"Yeah." Jimmy handed Mitch the keys.

"Great." Mitch motioned toward the dance floor. "Amanda's gearing up to throw her bouquet. Then I get to do the garter. You need to get in line for that."

Jimmy laughed. "Yeah. Like that's going to help me find a wife."

"You never know." Mitch smirked as he hurried off to join Amanda.

A few minutes later, Jimmy leaned against the wall at the back of the room while the single women took to the dance floor, most of them related to him in some way. He watched the proceedings with a smile. Someone had even convinced his great-aunt Charlotte to join the fun.

But Amanda must have put out the word that Kelsey was supposed to catch the bouquet, because the group shoved Kelsey to the front. Her expression said she didn't want to be there. Amanda let the bouquet fly, and Charlotte caught it. Everyone laughed and applauded as she took a bow.

Then Charlotte turned and handed the bouquet to Kelsey. "I think this was intended for you."

Kelsey hugged Charlotte but insisted the older woman keep it. Kelsey hurried off the dance floor and stationed herself near the expansive sliding doors that led to the patio just off the first tee box on the golf course. She crossed her arms and looked as though she wished she could shrink into the wall.

While Jimmy speculated about Kelsey's demeanor, several guys dragged him onto the dance floor to join the other single men who lined up to catch the garter. Mitch flashed him a knowing look as he slipped the garter off Amanda's leg. He twirled it around his finger as he surveyed the group of guys. When Mitch's gaze landed on Jimmy, he decided he might as well make an effort to catch the thing.

Like a slingshot, Mitch sent the garter flying. Jimmy reached out and snagged it, grinning the whole time. Laughter and applause filled the air as the other guys clapped him on the back. They joked about finding him a wife. Little did they know that particular subject had consumed his thoughts in the last couple of days. Come Monday Jimmy would have to decide about the job. Saying yes meant getting married sometime in the not-so-distant future. Maybe he should just say no and be done with the whole crazy idea. Uncle Graham's stipulation went too far, but Jimmy wanted the job. Did he want it bad enough to put himself out there and risk his heart again?

The time had come to finally get that dance with Kelsey. Jimmy walked toward the side of the room where she stood, her arms crossed as she stared into space. He slipped a hand through the garter and pulled it up his arm as if it were a badge of courage. As he drew closer to her, she looked at him, misery evident in her gaze. If he asked her to dance, could he change that expression? He hoped so.

"Hi." For some unexplained reason, his pulse raced when she smiled.

"Hi." She uncrossed her arms as her smile turned into a grin. "Looks like you're going to be the next groom."

"If that superstition can be believed." He held out his hand. "Would you like to discuss it while we dance?"

She stepped closer. "I might be persuaded."

"Good." Jimmy put an arm around her waist as the DJ played a slow song. *Perfect.* The words flitted through his mind as he held her close.

They barely moved from the spot where they stood as they swayed together to the slow beat of the music. Without warning, Kelsey wrenched herself from his arms and raced out the nearby door.

"Kelsey, what's wrong?" Jimmy chased after her.

"Please go away." Leaning over, she vomited.

"Are you sick?" Stupid question. Of course she was sick.

"Just go." She waved a hand as she turned away from him, a little sob sounding into the night air.

Jimmy hesitated, not knowing what to do. He had to help her. He went back inside and headed to the men's restroom. He grabbed a bunch of paper towels and held several under the faucet, then squeezed the water from them until they were just damp. He took more dry towels and filled a plastic cup with water.

He made his way outside through the door near the kitchen. He didn't want to draw attention to himself or to Kelsey, who was obviously embarrassed to be caught barfing in the bushes. Probably the pained look he'd seen on her face most of the day was a result of her not feeling well. He hoped she wouldn't refuse his help.

Trusting she was still where he'd left her, he hurried toward the spot. He slowed his pace when he spied her silhouetted against the light from the full moon. Her head lowered, she stood there with her arms wrapped around her torso as she rubbed her hands up and down her arms. Despite the warmer-than-normal temperatures of the mid-March day, the nighttime had brought a chill to the air.

Jimmy hoped calling out to her wouldn't scare her. "Kelsey, it's Jimmy. I brought something for you."

She turned. He couldn't read her expression in the dark, but the way she straightened her spine indicated she wasn't happy he was here. "I told you to go away."

"I know, but I thought you might feel better if you had something to wipe your face and a little something to drink." He took a step closer and held them out to her.

Like a wary wild animal tempted by a scrap of food, she reached for the paper towels, her eyes downcast. She wiped her face and hands. He took another step toward her as he offered her the cup of water.

She took a sip, then finally looked at him. "Thank you."

Jimmy stared at her in the dim light. "Are you okay?"

"No." Kelsey buried her face in her hands as another sniffle escaped. Her shoulders shook as she tried to stifle the sobs with her hands.

"Please let me help you."

"You can't help. There's nothing you can do except go away." Kelsey glared at him.

"There must be something I can do." Why was she refusing his help?

"You can't make this better. I'm pregnant." Misery capturing her pretty features, Kelsey looked at him. She slapped a hand to her mouth. Her eyes grew wide as she shook her head. "I can't believe I told you. No one else knows."

"Probably because I'm a good listener, and I've got a broad shoulder for you to cry on."

She burst into tears, and Jimmy gathered her into his arms and held her as she wept. Even though she was upset, she didn't resist his comfort. He was thankful for that even though he had no clue what to say, despite the dozen questions flooding his brain.

He patted her shoulders. She felt small and fragile in his arms. A protective feeling toward her inundated him. Crazy.

When she stopped crying, he took a step back and held her at arm's length. "What do you plan to do about your pregnancy?"

She refused to look at him as she put one hand to her forehead. Her breath hitching, she shook her head but didn't say a thing.

Jimmy waited for some kind of response, but none came. Maybe she wished he'd go away. "Guess you'd like me to leave."

Kelsey finally looked up at him, tears on her cheeks. "Don't go, but don't judge me."

Jimmy smiled wryly. "I'm not in any position to judge anyone. Didn't Jesus say the person who is without sin should throw the first stone? My life is far from perfect, so I won't be throwing any stones."

A little smile fought with the tears as she shivered. "Thank you."

"You're cold. You want to go inside?"

Kelsey shook her head. "No. I can't go in until I pull myself together."

Jimmy shrugged out of his jacket. "Then put this on."

Without any resistance, Kelsey let him put the jacket around her shoulders. He led her to a bench in a sheltered area near the building. He sat down, bringing her with him. They sat there for a moment as the muted music filtered out to where they were.

"What about the father? Does he know?" Jimmy immediately wished he could take the question back.

Kelsey's big blue eyes filled with tears again. Her shoulders shook as the waterworks spilled down her cheeks, but not a sound came out of her, as she held a hand in front of her mouth. Her silent cry shattered his peace.

"I was so stupid. He's a horrible man." She closed her eyes.

Jimmy stared at her. He touched her arm. "Why do you say that?"

Kelsey opened her eyes and stared back at him. "He lied to me about everything."

"You want to tell me about it?"

"What good would it do?"

"It might help you figure out how you're going to handle this."

She looked doubtful, but she said, "Okay. I really should explain so you don't think I'm this...this..."

"I'm not going to think anything. Remember—you asked me not to judge."

Despair imprisoned her expression. "I know, but I'm judging myself and not finding much to like right now. I didn't intend to tell you or anyone, so I want you to understand what happened."

"How did you meet this guy?"

Pain radiated from Kelsey's eyes. "I worked part time for my dad last summer at the long-term care facility where he's the administrator. Brandon delivered medical supplies there. He asked me out, and we dated through the summer. We'd go out on Friday's after he finished his deliveries. I should've gotten a clue when that was the only time we went out."

Jimmy knit his eyebrows. "Why do you say that?"

"He lived in Spokane, but he never took me there for a date." Kelsey pressed her lips together as if she was going to cry again, but she took a deep breath and squared her shoulders. "There's a lot more to do in Spokane than in Pinecrest. I kept telling myself that it was just inconvenient for him to have to drive me to Pinecrest, then drive back to Spokane."

"That's a reasonable thought."

"Yeah." Kelsey twisted her hands in her lap and lowered her gaze. "Then I went back to college in the fall, and the drive was even further between Spokane and Pullman, where I go to school at Washington State University. I kept trying to convince him to come to Pullman for a football game, but he said he couldn't get away."

"Was he lying about that?"

Looking up, Kelsey blinked back more tears. "I should've recognized his lies when he refused to go to a game that was actually held in Spokane, but I believed him when he said he had to work."

"Why did you continue to believe him?"

"Because I thought I loved him." Misery carved a frown across her face. "But he broke up with me. He said the long-distance romance just wasn't working out."

Jimmy frowned. "If you quit dating, how did the pregnancy happen?"

Kelsey hung her head. "My idiocy."

Jimmy wasn't sure what to say. People in love often did stupid things. Like the way he'd acted when it came to Whitney. He hadn't gotten her pregnant, but his careless behavior had fostered a feud with Mitch that was finally coming to an end. He'd hurt Mitch, Whitney, and himself with his actions.

"You want to explain that?"

Shrugging, Kelsey looked at him as if she'd just realized she was telling her secrets to a man she barely knew. "I've told you this much. I might as well tell you the whole sorry tale."

Jimmy held up his hands. "Your call. You don't have to tell me anything you don't want to."

"You're easy to talk to. I thought that from the moment I met you last fall."

Her timid smile and compliment turned his heart inside out.

"Brandon had just broken up with me right before I went to Nashville. You made me feel a whole lot better that night."

"I'm here to help." Jimmy didn't want to admit that her praise was a big boost to his ego.

"And you have helped." Kelsey touched his arm. "I didn't realize how good it would feel to actually tell someone what's happening with me."

Jimmy swallowed hard as he tried to tamp down these crazy romantic feelings. She was pregnant with another man's child, and here he was wishing he could kiss her. He had to get a handle on his wild thoughts. She didn't need another guy coming on to her. "Glad to make you feel better."

Kelsey's sad expression belied her smile. "I thought I was over Brandon. Everything was going well at school. I went home Valentine's weekend so I could babysit my little brother, Noah, while Dad and Maria went out on Friday night. My twenty-first birthday was the next day, and after a family dinner, I went out with some of my high school friends."

"And I'm guessing there might have been a little alcohol involved in the celebration?"

Kelsey let out a halfhearted laugh. "Yeah. My friends took me to the local steakhouse and insisted that I have a drink."

"And that's all?"

"That was all until Brandon showed up unexpectedly."

"I thought you said he lived in Spokane." Jimmy did some mental calculations and figured she must be barely a month pregnant.

"Yeah, he does, but he said he had to make Saturday deliveries to Pinecrest because his route had changed and he'd stopped to grab a bite to eat before he headed back to Spokane."

"Another lie?" Jimmy asked.

"That part might have been true." Kelsey's breath hitched again. "My friends insisted that he join us, then found excuses to leave. And Brandon said he'd drive me home. They knew how much I liked him, and they thought they were doing me a favor by leaving us alone. It didn't turn out that way."

"So what did he do?"

Shaking her head, Kelsey closed her eyes, as if trying to shake away a bad memory. "He told me just what I wanted to hear. That he'd made a mistake when he broke up with me. He wanted to start over."

"So wasn't that good, or was that another lie?"

"Yeah, he wanted to start over—start over by telling me he still loved me—a complete and utter falsehood." Kelsey's voice broke. "If I keep crying, I'll never be able to go back inside. I hope Amanda doesn't miss me and come searching."

"You don't have to continue if it's going to upset you."

Kelsey sat up straighter. "I want to tell you so you won't think I'm an awful person."

"Okay." Jimmy wanted to tell her he didn't think she was awful, but right now he just needed to listen.

"First, he ordered me another drink."

"Are you saying he tried to get you drunk?"

"I'm not sure." Kelsey shrugged. "Just as I finished the drink, I got a call from my dad. Noah had suddenly spiked a really high fever, and Dad and Maria were taking Noah to the hospital. I was upset and told Brandon I wanted to go to the hospital."

"So he drove you there?"

"Yeah, and waited with me until the doctors decided to admit the baby. Maria and my dad intended to spend the night and told me to go on home. So Brandon drove me home and insisted he walk me to the door. I slipped on an icy spot in the driveway, and he reached out to save me from falling, but we both went down. I scraped my knee and got a big hole in my pants. He helped me inside."

Jimmy got the picture. This Brandon character had seen his opportunity to get Kelsey alone and took full advantage of it. Jimmy remained quiet and just let Kelsey talk. She needed a sounding board.

Kelsey twisted her hands in her lap. "I changed out of

my torn pants. Doctored my knee and hand. When I came back into the kitchen, where Brandon had waited, he had made us some hot chocolate. He led me to the couch in the living room, where we sat and talked. He said all the things I longed to hear, then started kissing me. It was like I had no power to resist him."

Kelsey closed her eyes as she pressed her lips together.

Jimmy wondered whether the man had put something in Kelsey's hot chocolate. Jimmy reached over and held her hand. "You don't have to go on. I understand."

"But that's not all."

"Did he force himself on you?"

She took in a shaky breath. "I don't remember saying no, but I'm afraid I was a bit tipsy. I'd never drunk alcohol before. I was always the good girl who followed the rules. So a couple of drinks certainly made me less in control. The drinks, the warm room, and his persuasive words definitely lowered my resistance to his advances."

"When do you plan to tell him about this baby?"

"I'm not."

Her expression told Jimmy he shouldn't argue, but he didn't want her to make another mistake. "Are you thinking of terminating your pregnancy?"

She covered her mouth with one hand and stared at him, her eyes wide. "Why do you care?"

"I used to not have an opinion one way or another about abortion. But after seeing my sisters' ultrasounds, I know it would be wrong to make that choice. I don't want you to do something you'll regret and make you feel worse than you do now."

Kelsey stared at him in the dim light. "You don't have to worry. I considered that option only for a day or two after I found out Brandon is married."

Jimmy had to count to ten to keep from shouting. It was a good thing this Brandon guy was nowhere near, or he might have a black eye. "Married? He certainly is a liar."

Kelsey hung her head. "That's why I was so devastated about being pregnant and considered ending the pregnancy, but in the end I realized it would just compound my problems."

"How did you find out he was married?"

"I had no clue. He had sent me flowers and texts at school, telling me how much he cared about me. I was feeling really happy about our relationship. The first Saturday in March, I had to go into Spokane to pick up my dress for the wedding. When I stopped to get lunch at this pizza place, I saw Brandon sitting there with this woman and a baby. I thought it was his sister because he'd mentioned having a sister. I walked over to say hi."

"What did he do when he saw you?"

Kelsey frowned. "The look on his face was one of pure terror. I knew immediately this woman wasn't his sister. Then I saw the wedding ring that he never wore when we were together."

"What did you say to him?" Jimmy could just imagine the devastation Kelsey had felt.

"I tried to be as calm as I could be and said hi. His wife introduced herself and their little girl. I could tell he was just waiting for me to get angry and reveal his secret life to his wife. But I saw this happy woman with her sweet baby, and I couldn't ruin her life with this information. I hope he straightens out and takes care of his family. That's why I don't want to tell him about this baby. I don't want to tell anyone."

"But you told me."

Sadness filled her eyes as she shrugged. "I wasn't intending to, but it just came out. Guess I had to tell someone…someone who isn't family. I don't know what I'm going to do. I just can't tell my dad. He'll go ballistic. I've always been the one who followed the rules. Did all the right stuff, while Amanda was the troublemaker."

"So you're feeling like you've let everyone down?" Jimmy wanted to gather her into his arms again and tell her everything would work out okay, but he couldn't make that promise. He had no idea why he was feeling this way toward her. Maybe because he was the only one who shared her secret.

Kelsey nodded. "Let's just not talk about this anymore. I want to go back inside and dance the night away and pretend just for now that my life is normal. Not the mess it is."

Standing, Jimmy took Kelsey's hand. "Then let's go dance. I'll be glad to be your partner."

Kelsey popped up. "I'm feeling much better, thanks to you. I'm all yours."

Although Kelsey's statement was only an expression, it made Jimmy's heart twist. He had this crazy feeling that he wanted it to be true. She wasn't his in any sense. They barely knew each other. But he'd let her confession and her compassion for Brandon's wife and little girl go to his head and his heart.

As they stepped into the room, Amanda rushed over and gave Jimmy a speculative glance before taking Kelsey's arm. "There you are. I couldn't find you anywhere. We're about ready to cut the cake."

Kelsey smiled over at Jimmy. "We were just getting some fresh air. It's a beautiful night, but I'm ready to watch you cut that cake. You don't need my help, do you?"

Amanda propelled Kelsey forward. "No, but I want you to be here."

"I'll be standing right here next to Jimmy." Kelsey looped her arm through his as she smiled up at him.

"Okay. That's great." Amanda hurried off to join Mitch.

His pulse zinging, Jimmy looked over at Kelsey. "You didn't have to stay here with me."

She turned her head toward him. "You said you'd be my partner, and I'm holding you to that."

"It'll be my pleasure." Jimmy bowed.

Arm in arm, Jimmy and Kelsey watched as Mitch and Amanda cut the cake and had a little fun feeding each other. The DJ then invited everyone to have cake and do some more dancing.

Jimmy motioned toward the cake table. "What's your pleasure? Cake or dancing or both?"

"Dancing. You know what might happen if I eat something."

"You do have to eat." Jimmy took her in his arms as a slow song played over the loudspeakers.

"I know, but I'm afraid to right now."

"Have you seen a doctor?"

Kelsey shook her head. "I thought we weren't going to talk about that subject."

"Okay." Jimmy pulled her close as they swayed to the music.

He liked the way she felt in his arms. Could he help her somehow? At that moment, he saw Graham Cunningham smiling in their direction. Realization popped into Jimmy's mind. He had the perfect solution for Kelsey. He banished the crazy notion. Then snatched it back just as quickly.

What would her reaction be if he asked her to marry him? He needed a wife, and she needed a father for her baby. When he'd met her last fall, he'd wished she lived closer so they could get to know each other better. She'd punched all the right buttons for him. Fun. A good sense of humor. Smart. Could hold a conversation without dominating it. And she was good looking as well.

As far as wife prospects went, she scored at the top.

He'd been brought up to believe marriage was for life. Would a marriage like this work, or was he completely out of his mind for thinking such a thing? Would he be using her just like Brandon? No. They would be helping each other. At least that was how Jimmy wanted to frame it.

There was one way to find out. Ask her. But she didn't want to talk about it anymore tonight. He would talk to her tomorrow. Besides, sleeping on the idea was probably best. Tonight he would help her forget her troubles. He would deal with reality tomorrow.

CHAPTER THREE

The flowers from Amanda and Mitch's wedding still adorned the platform in the church. They were long gone on their honeymoon to Florida, while Kelsey sat in the pew next to her dad and Maria. Her mind was not on the sermon but full of the things that had happened last night.

Kelsey had no idea how she would face Jimmy, who was here somewhere. Even though he said he wouldn't judge her, how could he not when she'd blurted out her tale of woe, then blubbered all over him?

She didn't want to talk to him. She wanted to go far, far away and hide from the people she knew. But she couldn't hide from God. She had failed to follow His principles, and now she was paying the price. She would have to figure out when and how to tell her dad about the mess she was in. So far today, she'd managed to conceal her morning sickness from her dad and Maria, who were also staying at Mitch's place, but she couldn't hide her pregnancy forever.

As soon as the church service ended, Kelsey excused herself and raced to the ladies' room. She wet some paper towels and took them into the stall. She leaned against the side wall as she let the nausea pass. How long would she feel as though she would throw up at any moment? How soon before someone close to her figured out her condition?

When she came out of the restroom, Jimmy stood there smiling at her.

"I thought I might find you here." He stepped closer.

Kelsey didn't know whether to be annoyed or happy. That second emotion surprised her. He knew too much. "How are you this morning?"

"That's probably what I should be asking you."

"I'm fine."

"Good. Do you have time to talk?"

Kelsey looked around for her dad. She spied him conversing with Mitch's parents. "Not really. I have to drive Dad and Maria to the airport."

"Then when you get back."

"How did you know I'd be back?" She narrowed her gaze.

"You've lived in a small town. You know everyone knows everyone else's business." Jimmy grinned. "Mitch told me you'd be staying in their place to look after their puppy."

Kelsey rolled her eyes. "Yeah. I can't believe they got a dog just weeks before they got married."

"How are you and the dog getting along?"

"Fine." What would Jimmy say if he knew the dog had been her confidante before he was? He'd probably laugh. He had a way of cheering her up that she couldn't explain.

"That's good since you'll be taking care of her for a week."

"I just hope this warmer weather holds. It's really cold back in Pullman."

"I ordered this weather just for you."

Kelsey lifted her eyebrows. "Like you can control the weather."

"I didn't say I controlled it. I said I ordered it. I'm just happy that the order came through."

Kelsey laughed. She couldn't help herself. She was pretty sure she knew what he wanted to talk about, but she would ask anyway. "So what do you want to discuss?"

He raised his eyebrows. "I think you know, and I figured you didn't want me to say it out loud, right here?"

"Okay. Yeah, I got it." Kelsey pressed her lips together. Talking about the weather and sharing a laugh wouldn't change her circumstances. But what could he say that would help in any way? She just didn't want to talk about it. "I don't think we have anything more to say on the subject."

"I do, and I hope you'll listen."

"I'll think about it and give you a call when I get back from the airport." Kelsey retrieved her phone from her purse. "Give me your number."

"Sure." Jimmy took her phone and input his contact information. "See you later."

"Maybe."

He gave her a no-nonsense look. "Whether you want to talk to me or not, I'm sure I'll see you around."

Kelsey stood there and watched Jimmy walk away. She should hear him out. He'd been a real help last night. She'd been embarrassed to talk to him today, but that didn't give her an excuse to be rude or dismiss him. Whether she talked to him about her pregnancy or not, she had to see him and apologize after she got back.

Kelsey's dad approached. "We'd better get going. Maria and I certainly don't want to miss our plane. You never know about security in the airports these days."

Kelsey hurried after her dad, then helped Maria get Noah into his car seat in the back. With her dad driving and Maria in the front, Kelsey sat in the backseat with her little brother, who was nearly four months old.

She couldn't help thinking that in a year's time, she would have a baby about this age. The prospect seemed unreal. Everything about her life felt like it should belong to someone else, not her. She didn't want to think about what the future held, but being with her sweet baby brother only served to remind her that she carried her own child. She wanted the best for that child. What would it be?

The drive to the airport went quickly as they ate the sandwiches that Charlotte had packed for them. Kelsey was thankful she had no nausea.

After they pulled up to the departures lane, she hugged her dad, Maria, and Noah goodbye. "I'll see you in a week."

"Have fun babysitting that dog." Grady winked. "I hope you don't get lonely in a strange town."

Maria gathered her things. "I don't think she'll be lonely. There was a certain young man who seemed very interested in your daughter."

Grady frowned. "That's what I'm afraid of. Don't have too much fun."

Kelsey tried to smile. "Thanks for the advice, Dad."

He hugged her again. "We'll pick you up at the airport next Sunday. Love you."

"Love you, too." Kelsey hopped back into the car before things got too mushy. She so didn't want to disappoint her dad, but there was no getting away from the fact that she would.

On the drive back to Pineydale, Kelsey tried not to cry. She had a week to figure out how she was going to break the news of her pregnancy to her dad. Should she make sure Maria was present so he wouldn't yell too much? Was that fair to Maria, who had often run interference between her husband and her stepdaughters?

As Kelsey neared Pineydale, she formulated her apology to Jimmy. Was he really interested in her, as Maria had said, or was he just being kind? The answer was obvious. What man would have an interest in some woman who was pregnant with another man's child? But she couldn't forget how he'd singled her out last fall. They'd had a great time together that evening.

After she arrived back at the house Kelsey would call home for a week, she let the dog out into the backyard. The golden retriever puppy, who was all feet, romped around on the grass.

"Come here, Dolly."

The puppy stopped for a second and looked at Kelsey, but a moment later Dolly took off in a crazy circle around the bare-branched trees. Kelsey laughed and called the dog again. She came and sat at Kelsey's feet. "Good dog."

The puppy barked and took off again. A leash would be a good idea. Kelsey quickly found one in the enclosed back porch. She grabbed a jacket and managed to snap the leash onto the wriggling pup's collar.

"Okay, Dolly, we're off for a walk."

Kelsey remembered seeing a park near the church. That would be a good place to walk the dog and to meet Jimmy. After she reached the park, where daffodils marched their golden trumpets across the landscape, she called Jimmy.

He answered on the third ring. "Hi. Back from the airport?"

"Yeah, I'm at the park, if you still want to talk."

"Where in the park?"

"I'll meet you at the big statue in the center."

"Be there in a few minutes."

Kelsey hung up and looked toward the monument as Dolly tugged on the leash. The dog was eager to get to their destination. Kelsey wasn't so sure she was ready for this conversation. She wandered over to the concrete structure where the Stars and Stripes fluttered in the breeze. She read the inscription that honored veterans of several wars.

A few yards away a man and woman played with two little girls on the slide and swings. The sight made Kelsey think about her child. Would it be a boy or girl? Would she be a single mom or give the baby up for adoption? Could she bear to part with her own child? Would the baby have a better life with two parents rather than a single mother? There were too many questions she didn't have answers for.

A bench sat on one side of the monument, and Kelsey plopped herself there to wait. The pup settled at her feet, as if she knew Kelsey's mind was filled with troubling thoughts. She leaned over and patted Dolly on the head. "Good girl. No barking when Jimmy shows up. He's our friend."

A gray sedan pulled up to the curb on the far side of the park, the bright sun glinting off the windshield. Kelsey shaded her eyes in order to see the driver as he exited the car. Jimmy.

He had his hands stuffed into the pockets of his khaki

jacket as he loped across the mostly brown grass in the park. The serious look on his face made Kelsey nervous. What was he going to say? She hoped this meeting wouldn't be a mistake.

Her tail nearly wagging her body, Dolly leaped up as Jimmy drew near.

"Hi." Jimmy barely looked at Kelsey as he leaned down and held out his hand for Dolly to sniff. Then he patted the dog's head.

Looking at him, Kelsey swallowed the lump in her throat. "Hi."

He settled beside her on the bench. "Have a good trip to the airport?"

"Yeah. Plane was on time, and everything was good."

"Great."

This conversation was stilted and too polite. She wanted to get right to the point and find out what he had to say. "So what did you want to talk about?"

"I've got a suggestion for you regarding your situation." His Adam's apple bobbed, and he didn't look her in the eye.

Kelsey leaned back on the bench. He appeared more nervous than she was about this conversation, which surprised her. He always seemed so cocky, so sure of himself. "What's your suggestion?"

He continued to look anywhere but at her. "Marry me, and I can be a father for your child."

Stunned, Kelsey let his statement soak in. A dozen questions ran through her mind, like children in the park chasing after the same ball. She took a deep breath. "Why would you want to do that?"

"Because I want to help you." He finally looked at her,

then held up a hand. "Hear me out before you dismiss the idea."

"Okay." Kelsey gripped the dog's leash tighter, as if doing so would steady her thoughts.

"I know this is a little crazy, but you don't want to tell your family you're pregnant, and I need a wife."

"You need a wife? Whatever for?" Kelsey frowned.

"So I can fulfill one of my uncle's job requirements."

Kelsey narrowed her gaze. "Graham Cunningham is saying you have to get married to have a job?"

"Not exactly." Jimmy went on to tell Kelsey about the discussion with Graham. "I have to give him my decision tomorrow. The college degree is something I want, and part of the compensation for the job includes college tuition. I messed up the first time I went to college. Partied too hard and flunked out. I've grown up a lot since then. I don't have to have a wife on day one, but I don't know where I'd find one in this town in the next year. Then you show up, needing a little help. It's up to you. If we get married now, your pregnancy shouldn't raise any eyebrows. I'm throwing it out there as an option if you want to take it."

Kelsey couldn't imagine accepting this offer even though it would solve the problem of not having to tell her family about the child she carried. Maybe. Would people eventually guess that she was pregnant before they got married? "How can we think about getting married when we barely know each other?"

"We've got the rest of this week to get to know each other."

"Are you serious?"

"Yeah. The idea came to me last night when we were

dancing. I decided to sleep on it. When I woke up this morning, it still seemed like a good solution to both of our problems." Jimmy raised his eyebrows as he gazed at her.

Her heart did a little flip-flop at the prospect of being married to this man. How could she rush into a marriage for her own selfish reasons? Marriage was sacred, intended for people who loved each other. At least, that was what she'd always thought. People in other cultures got married for reasons other than love. Would that work for her and Jimmy?

But there was no way she could consider a real marriage. She just couldn't be with a man—share a bed with him—when she didn't love him. She'd already let love lead her into a big mistake. She didn't want to make another one with a man she barely knew and certainly didn't love. "I can't give you an answer now."

"That's fair." Jimmy placed an arm along the back of the bench. "I can understand your reluctance."

"I don't think you can begin to comprehend half of the doubts I have." Kelsey stared straight ahead. "I can't drop out of school. My dad would have a fit."

"Sounds like your dad will be upset no matter what you do."

Kelsey turned and looked at Jimmy. "Are you dumping on my dad?"

"Whoa. I'm just stating the obvious." Jimmy held up his hands in a defensive gesture, then stood. "Maybe I'd better go. Your objections make it clear you aren't interested in my suggestion. I won't bother you again."

Dolly whined as Jimmy walked away. Kelsey's heart sank to her stomach. Had she just thrown away a chance to make a better life for her unborn child? Would Jimmy make a good father? One thing she did know. She had never apologized, as she had intended in the first place, and now she owed him another apology for shoving away his offer to help.

"Jimmy, wait." Kelsey chased after him, Dolly barking at Kelsey's heels.

He turned just before he reached his car, his expression grim. "Did I forget something?"

She stopped feet away from where he stood. "No, I did. I forgot to apologize for my behavior this morning, and I did it again just now. This whole thing is making me a bad person. I'm sorry. Can we start over?"

Jimmy took a step closer. "You aren't a bad person. You're just concerned about your future and have some big decisions to make. If you're sure you want to start over, we can do that."

"I'm sure. Thank you."

"If you want, I'll drive you home and we can discuss your reservations." Jimmy opened the door for her.

"Okay." Kelsey looked at Jimmy, then his car. "Is it okay for Dolly to ride in the back?"

"Sure. Let me help her into the car." Jimmy held his hand out for the leash.

With Dolly settled in the backseat, Kelsey buckled her seat belt. She prayed this meeting would hold some solutions, not more mistakes. She should have been praying before, but God might not be listening.

***

Jimmy pulled his car to a stop in front of Mitch and Amanda's house, then helped Kelsey get Dolly out of the back. He wished he were more confident about the outcome of this discussion. She had shot down his idea, and his ego had taken a big hit. He should've known his suggestion wouldn't make her jump up and down with joy. But he had hoped it would give her a safe place to land.

They walked to the front door without saying a thing as Jimmy held Dolly's leash. After they were inside, the awkward silence continued as he stood there, his hands stuffed into the pockets of his jacket.

"You can sit down." Kelsey motioned to the nearby chair, covered in a medium-brown fabric.

Jimmy plopped onto the chair, still afraid to say anything. He wanted to go through her concerns, but he didn't know where to start. He was hoping she'd take the lead and ask a question. He had to get this thing going, or they might stare silently into space or talk about the dog.

"Tell me what bothers you about my proposal." He held his breath while he waited for her answer.

"Everything." She sat on the couch, perpendicular to the chair.

Shot down again. "That's pretty broad. Can you narrow it down just for discussion's sake?"

Her eyes filled with tears. "I don't know where to start."

"That makes two of us." Jimmy didn't want to make her cry. He only wanted to help, but maybe he was making things worse.

Kelsey blinked rapidly. "Would you expect this to be a real marriage?"

A real marriage. He hadn't thought that subject through. Was she saying she wasn't interested in consummating the marriage? He was pretty sure that was what she meant, but he was afraid to ask. He rubbed a hand across his chin. "We don't have to decide that now."

"Maybe not this moment, but it has to be part of the decision."

"Sure." Here he'd thought he'd considered every aspect of his proposal, but he certainly hadn't considered that one. This whole thing was going downhill fast. Maybe he'd thought she was more desperate to keep her pregnancy under wraps than she'd first indicated. Where did he go from here? "You mentioned finishing school."

"Yeah, how am I supposed to do that if we get married now?"

"You can. We'll get married, and you'll go back to school just as you planned. When the semester ends, you can move to Pineydale and finish up your degree at ETSU over in Johnson City."

"What's ETSU?"

"East Tennessee State University. That's where I'll be finishing my degree, too."

"But what if they don't have the same course of study I'm pursuing?"

"Let's look it up."

"I'll get my tablet." Kelsey disappeared into the hallway.

His spirit a little lighter, Jimmy waited for her return. At least she was interested enough to check out the offerings at ETSU. She walked back into the room, her eyes trained on the tablet as she tapped the screen.

She sat back on the couch, then looked up at him. "Come sit by me."

Jimmy smiled as he joined her. Maybe she was warming up to the idea. "What did you find?"

"My major is communication. ETSU has an advertising and PR major that looks similar. I'm sure to lose some credits, but maybe not too many." She looked at him, her expression swimming with doubt.

"Maybe you can talk to someone in admissions to find out."

"I suppose." Kelsey shrugged. "Aren't people going to think we're crazy for jumping into marriage when we barely know each other?"

"They are."

"Isn't it all going to be a lie?"

"We'll have a piece of paper that says we're married. What's the lie?"

"People will think we're in love. That won't be true. When it's obvious that I'm pregnant, people will think the baby's yours. That won't be true. I don't want to live a lie."

Jimmy couldn't dismiss her concerns. "Everything you've said is true, and I understand not wanting to live a lie. So that leaves you with having to tell your family that you're pregnant. If that's what you want to do, I'll go now."

"I don't know what I want." Kelsey's voice came out in a strangled cry, and she buried her face in her hands.

"I seem to have made things worse." Jimmy put an arm around her shoulders and pulled her closer. He wished he could take away her pain and confusion. Something about her vulnerability created a soft spot in his heart.

She looked up at him, her eyes filled with anxiety. "No, don't leave. I've made my own mess. Maybe I should just own up to it and suffer the consequences."

"You could do that, but doesn't your baby still need a father?"

"Why would you want to be a father to a child that isn't yours?" A little pucker appeared between Kelsey's eyebrows as she stared at him with those blue, blue eyes.

"Because I'm a good guy." He grinned. "And I need a wife."

Kelsey ran a hand through her hair. "I forgot about that part. But I'm sure you want a real wife, don't you?"

A real wife. A real marriage. So they were back to that. Yeah, he wanted real, but maybe he would have to settle for convenience now with the hope of real later. Was that crazy? Had his uncle's job offer made Jimmy reach for impossible dreams—dreams of a great job, a pretty wife, a baby, and respect in this community?

He wanted those things, but most people in this town still looked at him as someone who had frittered away respectability with reckless living. He'd ruined Mitch's relationship with Whitney and damaged any hope of keeping her love while he'd earned a reputation for wrecking everything he touched. He'd finally made good with his painting company, and now he would give that up for a chance to prove himself in his uncle's business.

"Well?" Kelsey lifted her chin.

Jimmy stared at her. How could he answer that? With honesty? Yeah, with honesty. "You're right. I had counted on this being a real marriage."

"I can't. I'm sorry, Jimmy. I don't love you. I don't know you, and I just can't be a real wife. It wasn't a good experience with someone I loved, so how could it be good with someone I don't love? And then this…" Kelsey shook her head, misery marring her pretty features as she held her hands out in front of her and looked down at her belly.

Jimmy wiped a hand down his face. He wanted to

smash that Brandon character's teeth in. Maybe the guy hadn't actually raped Kelsey, but he'd taken advantage of an innocent young woman and made her first sexual experience something terrible. Jimmy couldn't undo that, and he didn't want to make it worse. "I wish I could—"

Kelsey put a finger to his mouth. "You can't wish for the impossible."

Her touch made him wish for the impossible, but she had made his ego a punching bag. She was turning him down flat. Why couldn't he let this go? Couldn't he find a wife somewhere else? Maybe if he tried hard enough, but he'd dated the few eligible women in this town, and none of them had suited. With a new job and school, when would he have time to develop a relationship, especially if he had to broaden his territory to surrounding communities?

Was marrying Kelsey an easy way out? No, but with Kelsey, he could start fresh. She didn't know about any of the baggage he carried. He could do this right and show her that he could be a good husband and a good father and an upstanding man in the community. He would show his uncle that he wouldn't be sorry he had hired Jimmy Cunningham, and Kelsey wouldn't be sorry if she married him. And maybe, just maybe they would actually fall in love. He could definitely see that happening, at least on his part.

Jimmy took both of her hands and his. "I'm willing to take a gamble on you on your terms if you'll take a gamble on me."

"But what if we never fall in love? I don't want that for either of us."

"What's not to love about Jimmy Cunningham?" He

spread his arms open.

Kelsey laughed. "You do make me smile."

"That's a good start." Jimmy remembered how his dad and mom had laughed together on so many occasions. His parents had laughed and loved a lot. Even now, Jimmy could see that happening with Kelsey. "What do you say? Can we at least give it a week before we dismiss the idea completely?"

Kelsey sighed. "Okay. I'll give it this week."

Jimmy couldn't contain his smile. "And I think we should start with you meeting my family."

"Meet the parents already?"

"We only have a week, and it'll be meet my mom and my siblings and their families. My dad passed away several years ago from a heart attack."

"I'm so sorry. I didn't know." Kelsey grimaced.

"That's okay. You probably met most of my family at the wedding."

"Or at least I shook hands with them in the receiving line. Mostly I was just trying not to throw up on someone, so I don't remember many of the people I met." Kelsey pressed her lips together in a grim expression.

"You made it through the wedding and most of the reception."

Kelsey offered a sad little smile. "Thanks to you."

"I only helped in the end."

"That was enough." She settled back on the couch with a contented sigh. "Tell me about your family."

Jimmy didn't want to admit how pleased her request made him. Should he even hope this was a good sign? "Sure. There's my mom, Mary. I'm the oldest and have two sisters, Janelle and Jenna, and my little brother,

Jeremy. I know you remember him because you danced with him."

"I had no idea he's your brother." Kelsey grinned. "Guess your parents liked names that start with *J*."

Jimmy chuckled. "Yeah, but I'm the only one who got a nickname. I was named after my dad. He was Jim, and I'm Jimmy. I thought maybe once I was grown, people would call me Jim. No, it's still Jimmy."

"You don't like being called Jimmy?"

"I've learned to live with it."

"What about James?"

"Yeah, that's my given name, but no one ever called me or my dad James. That was my grandpa." Jimmy smiled wryly. "My full name is James Madison Cunningham the Third."

Kelsey raised her eyebrows. "Named after a president. That's quite a handle."

"Yeah. I don't go around advertising that name. Guess I should be happy with Jimmy."

Kelsey laughed. "I like your name. Whichever one you choose."

"That's good because you might soon be Mrs. James Madison Cunningham."

"That's a mouthful." Kelsey giggled. "But that remains to be seen."

Jimmy loved the sound of her laughter. Her happiness brightened his mood. Wow! He was already getting too caught up in this woman. He wasn't sure what he was feeling, but he had better get out of here now before he did something he would regret later, like kiss her.

Jimmy jumped up from the couch. "I'd better get going. I've got some accounting to do for my business."

"Okay." With Dolly traipsing along, Kelsey joined him as he headed to the door.

Before he left, he stopped to look at her. His pulse skittered, and he swallowed hard. She was doing crazy things to him. "I'll come by around five and pick you up. My mom has the whole clan over on Sunday evenings, so you'll get to meet the entire crew."

"Okay." Uncertainty clouded her expression. "See you then."

The closing of the door sounded in his ears as he jogged to his car. Despite her obvious hesitation, Kelsey had agreed to meet his family. How would they react if he suddenly married her?

As he drove by his great-aunt Charlotte's house, he thought about her advice and how he'd gone home to pray. He'd prayed that night, but he'd let his busy life push prayer time aside again.

His thoughts about Kelsey should have been a matter of prayer from the beginning, but he'd failed to talk to God about her. Was it because a marriage based on a bargain might not find favor with God? Even if Jimmy made this decision a matter of prayer, how was he supposed to know God's plan?

Jimmy wished prayer had been a regular routine in his life, but it hadn't even though he had renewed his commitment to the Lord. Being more in touch with God would certainly help Jimmy recognize His answer. Jimmy's best shot was to lay it out before God, and if Kelsey agreed to get married at the end of the week, that was what he would do.

CHAPTER FOUR

A delicious aroma greeted Kelsey as she followed Jimmy into his mother's house. Thankfully, today the only nausea she'd experienced had come early this morning. She was thankful she wouldn't have to sit at the table tonight and pick at her food because her stomach was roiling.

This meeting was important to Jimmy, and Kelsey wanted to make a good impression, even if nothing ever came of his suggestion to get married. She could tell he loved his family by the way he talked about them. That should say all kinds of good things about him. But she couldn't figure out why an attractive, kind man would agree to marry a woman in name only when he didn't love her and barely knew her.

Did he want that job so much he was willing to throw away any chance at real love?

Kelsey had to know his reasons before she could give him an answer.

"Kelsey, we're so glad you could join us. I'm Mary Cunningham." Jimmy's mom clasped her hands around Kelsey's. "I'm not sure you remember me from the wedding. I know you met a lot of new people that night."

Kelsey smiled. She already liked Mary, just because she realized that Kelsey probably didn't remember a quarter of the people she'd met at the wedding. "Thanks. You're right. The people at the wedding are pretty much a blur in my mind."

Even though Mary's face showed little signs of age, she sported a head of pure white hair. Her blue eyes sparkled as she escorted Kelsey into the living room decorated with an eclectic collection of furniture. She couldn't begin to guess Mary's age. The hair color said mature, but her face said young.

Mary laughed as she motioned around the room filled with adults and children. "Now I'm going to overwhelm you with people again."

In short order, Kelsey met Jenna, her husband, Travis, and their two toddlers, Grace and Jack. Then came Janelle, her husband, Dan, and their two young boys, Corey and Evan, who looked to be about four and six. They immediately latched on to Jimmy. He picked them up and carried them under his arms as they squealed with delight.

Before Mary could introduce Jeremy, he stepped out from the corner where he'd been standing. "No need to introduce me. We danced at the reception."

"Yes, I do remember that." Kelsey waved as she smiled, but all she was really thinking about was the way Jimmy interacted with his nephews. He obviously liked kids, and they liked him. Was that why he was willing to be a father to her baby?

"Good. I'm glad my big brother has seen fit to bring you by."

Jeremy's statement interrupted her thoughts. His blue eyes twinkling, he put an arm around Kelsey's shoulders. He and Jimmy shared the same dark hair color, but Jeremy got his eye color from his mother. The sisters also had dark hair and blue eyes.

Kelsey caught a glimpse of disapproval in Jimmy's gray eyes as Jeremy proceeded to escort her toward the dining room. She hoped the brothers wouldn't be feuding over her. Here she was in a compromised position, and she had two men vying for her attention. If her situation weren't so distressing, it would be funny. She stifled a nervous laugh.

As if Mary sensed the discord between her sons, she stepped in and pulled out a chair. "Kelsey, come sit by me so I can get to know you a little better."

"Sure. Do you need any help before we eat?" Kelsey put her hand on the back of the chair.

Mary motioned toward the nearby doorway. "No. The girls and I have everything ready in the kitchen. We're doing buffet style. We'll say a prayer, then you can grab your plate and head to the kitchen."

With the family dynamics swirling through the room, Kelsey watched as they gathered around the table and formed a circle as they held hands. Mary reached over and took Kelsey's hand. Jimmy slipped in beside her and took her other hand. Her heart skipped a beat, and she had trouble concentrating on the prayer.

After the prayer, Kelsey picked up her plate from the table as Jimmy slid into line behind her. Was he protecting what he considered his territory from his little brother? She didn't want to be the source of tension between them. Her reaction to holding Jimmy's hand didn't help her decision-making process either. She didn't want an instant attraction to lead her to another heartache.

Jimmy wasn't Brandon. She had to keep that in mind.

Laughter and congenial conversation filled the

evening. Mary's roast beef with vegetables reminded Kelsey of her grandma Fran's roast beef. The evening brought back fond memories of the times she'd spent with her grandmother, especially after Kelsey lost her mother when she was only four.

The women sat at one end of the table while the men sat at the other end, and the kids had their own little table in the corner. The men discussed the latest scoop on college basketball, and the women talked about babies and kids and the highs and lows of raising them. Every now and then Kelsey caught Jimmy looking her way. Had he heard the women's topic of conversation and thought about the child she carried.

After the meal, the men did the cleanup while the women retired to the living room with the kids, who played with the mountain of toys Mary had in one corner. Kelsey sat quietly while she took in the interaction of the sweet children and the love between Mary and her daughters.

Kelsey wondered how things would have worked out if her mom had lived, instead of dying in a car accident. Would she have had a close relationship with her mom, one that would make her feel free to share her troubles?

"It's really sweet of you to pet sit during your spring break."

Kelsey smiled at Janelle's statement. "I don't mind. It's a little warmer here than back in Spokane."

Jenna snickered. "Pineydale isn't exactly a hot spot for young people on spring break."

"I've never done any of the spring-break hot spots anyway." Kelsey lifted one shoulder. "I always went with the group that did some kind of service project, and this year it's babysitting a dog."

Mary reached over and patted Kelsey's shoulder. "That's commendable. I wish more young people would use their spring breaks to do good for others."

Kelsey smiled, but she wasn't feeling commendable. What would Mary say if she knew Kelsey was pregnant and that she was thinking about marrying Jimmy just so she wouldn't have to let anyone know about the stupid mistake she'd made?

The whole thing smacked of deception, but the temptation to seriously consider Jimmy's offer sat there like low-hanging fruit. She could reach out and grab it without a minute's hesitation. She liked his family, and after she finished her classes this semester, she could move here and be close to her sister. They got along a lot better now than when they were kids.

Kelsey just wished there was a clear answer about what she should do. She'd thought about praying. But every time she started to pray, she thought God wouldn't listen. Constant guilt ate at her. She might as well have a huge *A* plastered across her chest, just like Hester Prynne.

"Have you heard from Amanda and Mitch?" Mary asked.

Kelsey nodded. "Amanda sent me a text and said they'd arrived at their hotel. Mitch is pretty excited about this car show."

"Only Mitch would take his bride to a car show for their honeymoon." Jenna laughed.

"I don't think Amanda cared where they went as long as she was with Mitch. My sister is crazy in love with that man." Kelsey wished she could have that same kind of love for a special man. If she married Jimmy, would that mean resigning herself to something less? And what did that mean for Jimmy, too? She had to get to the bottom of his marriage proposal. It had to be more than that job.

"Yeah, I believe you're right. Those two were meant for each other."

Jimmy stepped into the room, a dish towel hanging over his shoulder. Kelsey's heart thudded when she looked at him. Was her reaction due to the secret they shared? That was what she wanted to believe whether it was true or not.

"Is it okay to crash this hen party, or are we men confined to the kitchen?" Jimmy looked directly at Kelsey.

Jenna stood. "Actually, this party is about to break up. Those kids have been good about as long as we can expect. It's close to bedtime for my two."

"Ours, too." Janelle joined her sister. "Thanks once again, Mom, for a great dinner."

"You know I wouldn't miss these Sunday evenings with my family for anything." Mary helped her grandchildren put away their toys.

In a flurry of thanks, jackets, diaper bags, and goodbye kisses and hugs, Jenna and Janelle left with their families. Mary stood in the doorway and waved until the cars carrying her loved ones disappeared down the street.

When they were gone, Mary turned to Jimmy and Jeremy. "You boys up for a few games of Rummikub?"

Jimmy glanced at Kelsey. "You want to play? Mom's the champ."

"I haven't played that game before, but I guess I can learn." Kelsey wanted to talk to Jimmy, not play a game, but she supposed this time with his mom was important to him and probably to Mary as well.

"Great. I'll set up the game at the kitchen table."

Jimmy retrieved a box from a cabinet near the children's toy basket. "Here we are."

Kelsey joined the group at the table. "I can play only one game because I don't want to leave Dolly alone too long. She'll need to go out soon."

"Okay, one game." Jimmy dumped the tiles onto the table.

They all helped turn the tiles facedown as Jimmy explained the rules. While they were turning the tiles, Jimmy's hand brushed against Kelsey's. They immediately withdrew their hands as they looked at each other.

Instant attraction. That was how she'd characterize her reaction to his touch, and it wasn't just one sided either. His look told Kelsey he had felt it, too. Was that a good thing? What did that mean for her insistence that any marriage, if it came about, be in name only? Would she one day want what Jimmy wanted—a real marriage?

Finally they each drew tiles and put them on the racks. Trying not to think about the spark that had danced between them, Kelsey was happy to go last. She had a feeling she wouldn't be much competition for these seasoned players.

"Jeremy, looks like you get to go first." Jimmy's southern accent made Jeremy's name come out sounding like *germy*.

Kelsey couldn't help grinning. She liked the sound of his voice, his family, and his attention to them. Would they welcome this sudden marriage, or would they be suspicious? The doubts tossed her thoughts into chaos. And she hadn't been paying attention to the game.

"You look a little lost." Mary raised her eyebrows as she glanced at Kelsey.

Kelsey tried to smile, hoping no one would guess that her mind had been on something other than the game. "Guess this just isn't my game."

"Too bad you aren't going to be around longer." Jeremy gazed at her. "I could teach you the strategies."

Jimmy's knowing look filled her mind with thoughts of his proposal. She quickly broke eye contact. This game couldn't end soon enough.

When it finally ended, Mary was the winner, as predicted.

"Thanks for playing. It's nice for you young people to hang out with this old lady." Mary grinned as she put the tiles in the box.

Jimmy went over and put an arm around his mom's shoulder. "Don't call yourself old. We love hanging out with you."

Chuckling, Mary patted her head. "This white hair definitely doesn't say young, but I'm glad you kids like to hang out with me."

"You're only as old as you feel. Isn't that what Grandma Cunningham had to say?" Jimmy grinned.

Mary nodded. "And she was a go-getter until the day she went to meet her Maker."

Kelsey took in the exchange. What would it be like to be part of this family? She had a chance to find out, but she wasn't sure she wanted to take that chance. "Thanks for the great food and a lovely evening."

"You're welcome." Mary grabbed Kelsey's hands in the same way she had when Kelsey first arrived. "You can come visit us anytime."

Kelsey smiled, wondering what Mary would say if she knew Kelsey might be her daughter-in-law in a matter of days. "Good night."

After giving his mother a hug, Jimmy escorted Kelsey to the car, with Jeremy loping alongside them. The tension between the brothers had dissipated as the evening went on. That made her feel a whole lot better.

Jeremy stopped beside his car, which was parked in front of Jimmy's. "See you tomorrow. We'll have that talk at lunch."

Jimmy waved. "You got it."

As Kelsey slipped into the car, she wondered what kind of talk Jimmy intended to have with his brother, but she didn't feel free to ask. While Jimmy drove back to Mitch and Amanda's place in the dark, Kelsey gave herself a pep talk so she wouldn't chicken out when it came to asking Jimmy the tough questions.

They rode through town without speaking, the hum of the motor the only sound in the car. Streetlamps cast shadows along the road. Kelsey desperately wanted to say something to fill the silence, but she didn't want to ask her questions until they were sitting face to face in a lighted room. She should say something positive about their evening. That would be a good start.

"I like your family. Your mom's a lot of fun." Kelsey put that fact in the *plus* column in her mental list of pros and cons for marrying Jimmy.

"Thanks. They're pretty special people to me."

When Jimmy brought his car to a stop, Kelsey turned to him. "Do you have time to come in and answer some questions?"

His hands tightened on the steering wheel as he stared at her. "I thought we already covered all the questions."

"Maybe not all of them." Kelsey's voice squeaked.

"Okay." He opened the door, the dome light illuminating the unhappiness on his face.

They walked to the front door in silence. Maybe this was exactly the kind of thing she should be looking for. Was he moody, or were her questions overkill? She unlocked the front door.

When she stepped inside, Dolly greeted them, every ounce of her body wagging.

Kelsey grabbed the leash from the hanger near the entrance to the kitchen. "I'd better get this dog outside. Make yourself comfortable."

Dolly dragged Kelsey out the door.

While Dolly did her business, Kelsey stared back at the house. Was Jimmy upset with her constant questions? She should have questions. This was a crazy scheme, one that brought up lots of doubts. Maybe his reaction was the answer she needed. She should just tell him she appreciated his offer to help but she couldn't accept his proposal.

That would be the end of it. She would watch the dog, go back to school, finish the semester, then face her dad with the bad news. But she didn't want to be a single mother, nor did she want to give her baby away. She looked up at the stars. *God, can you hear me? I need your help.* Dolly's bark interrupted Kelsey's silent prayer.

Kelsey trudged back to the house, doubts swirling through her mind. As soon as she took the leash off Dolly, she bounded over to Jimmy. He leaned over and rubbed her head behind her ears. Her tail thumped on the floor.

The dog liked Jimmy. That was a good sign. She couldn't forget the way he'd played with the kids tonight. They loved their uncle Jimmy, and he obviously loved kids and related to them.

Jimmy finally looked her way as Dolly settled at his feet. "So what's your question?"

Kelsey tried to smile. Had she misinterpreted his earlier expression? The questions circulated through her mind like a giant clog in a drain. Her thoughts came to her in slow motion, and the words stuck in her throat.

"Kelsey, are you all right?" Jimmy frowned.

She nodded, still unable to put her thoughts into a coherent sentence.

Jimmy patted the seat next to him on the couch. "Come here and sit down with me."

Liked a robot under his command, she sat beside him, but the questions still clustered in her brain and found no way out. He surely must think she didn't have any sense.

He took her hands in his. "Tell me what's on your mind."

Kelsey tried not to think about the way his touch not only made her heart beat faster but made her feel cherished somehow. Finally her words came out in a jumbled rush. "Why would you marry me when I don't want a real marriage? How can that be good for either one of us? I know you said you need a wife, but why can't you find someone else—someone you really love?"

"Hey, slow down, and maybe I can give you some answers."

Staring at him, she withdrew her hands as she tried to gain her equilibrium. "Just tell me why."

"Okay." Jimmy took a deep breath and let it out in a loud puff of air. "I thought I could have a fresh start with you."

"What do you mean?"

"I thought you would know this Jimmy Cunningham."

He poked himself in the chest. "Not the one from my past. The one everyone in this town knows had a bad reputation."

Kelsey frowned. "Is your past that bad?"

His stilted laugh sounded in the quiet room. "It's not that good."

"Can't be as bad as the mess I'm in, can it?"

"We just have different kinds of messes, but messes still the same. In the last couple of years, I've learned God is good at cleaning up messes."

Kelsey looked down at her hands. Even though she'd just said a prayer, she wasn't sure it went anywhere but into the air above her head. Why had her faith crumbled? She looked back at Jimmy. "Tell me about your messes."

Jimmy grinned. "I was hoping you wouldn't ask."

Jimmy's grin made Kelsey wish she were in love with this man and they were doing this for the right reasons. "If you want me to marry you, I need to know what I'm getting into."

"Like I said, I'm not what I used to be."

"Me neither, but it sounds like you went from being bad to good, and I went from being good to bad."

"I don't think you're bad. You're fun and thoughtful and considerate. You thought about Brandon's wife and baby instead of yourself. I call that good."

Kelsey studied her hands as she twisted them in her lap. "I just didn't want an innocent party to hurt as much as I was hurting."

"That took a lot of compassion on your part."

"Don't give me too much credit. I was also mortified that I'd been having a relationship with a married man." Kelsey motioned toward him. "That's enough about me. I want to hear about you."

"You would have to get back to that." Jimmy sighed. "You have to know the family history."

"Okay. I'm up for a history lesson."

Jimmy chuckled. "Sometimes it's hard to believe my dad and Uncle Graham were brothers."

"Why?"

"They were so different."

"How?" Kelsey thought about how different she and Amanda were.

"My grandpa James Cunningham ran the variety store that his grandfather started. The store was handed down through the generations. My dad didn't care one bit about that business. He saw it as a dying venture, and it was. But my uncle saw potential, not in that business but in transforming it into something viable for the future."

"You mean Graham Cunningham started with just a variety store and built his businesses around that?"

Jimmy nodded. "My dad worked in construction and then started his own painting company, never caring about getting rich. He just wanted to provide for his family. I loved my dad, but I always envied Mitch because of his family's wealth. Pretty shallow of me, I know."

"So what does this have to do with the bad past you talk about?"

Jimmy gripped the arm of the couch, his knuckles showing white. "I know I'm giving you the long version, but just bear with me."

"Sure." Feeling relaxed for the first time tonight, Kelsey settled back on the couch.

"My uncle got into internet businesses when they were first starting. He took a lot of risk and ridicule when his family was young, but it paid off big time in the end. He bought more businesses, and he wanted his sons to take over and run them. Alec was on board, but, as you know, Mitch had other plans."

"He wanted to run that garage and work on cars."

"I thought he was crazy and still do, just a little." Jimmy grinned.

"But that still doesn't explain your past."

Jimmy laughed out loud. "You are one impatient woman."

"And you're one long-winded man. I thought men were supposed to be quick and to the point."

"Most of the time."

"I think you're avoiding the real reason for this conversation."

Jimmy smiled wryly. "This conversation is helping us get to know each other. If we get married, I'll try to remember that you like me to get right to the point."

"And I'll remember that you like to talk."

Jimmy burst out laughing again. "I do like to talk."

"Then get to talking."

"Okay." An indulgent smile curved Jimmy's mouth. "Mitch and I are the same age, and all through school we were rivals in sports, school offices, and girls. I always thought I had to compete twice as hard because Mitch came from a wealthy family and I didn't."

"So who came out on top in these rivalries?" Kelsey tilted her head.

"It was probably about fifty-fifty. He bested me in baseball and track. I bested him in football and basketball. One year I was class president. The next year he was. But I was voted best looking, and Mitch was voted most likely to succeed."

Kelsey could see why Jimmy was voted best looking. He was definitely a good-looking man with his dark-brown hair and steel-gray eyes, but she wasn't going to say so. "Did this rivalry cause you to do some things you shouldn't have?"

"Not in high school, but later. When we were in high school, I dated Whitney. She was my girl and never looked twice at Mitch. If a high school kid could be in love, I was in love with her. I did everything to impress her. She was the head cheerleader, and I was the star quarterback. We were homecoming king and queen. I got good grades just because of her.

"Maybe if we'd gone to the same college, she would've kept me out of trouble, but her parents insisted that she go to the girls' college in Georgia that her mother graduated from." Regret shone in Jimmy's eyes.

Kelsey took in Jimmy's expression as he talked about Whitney. Did he still care for her? Was that why he'd never gotten married? "What kind of trouble did you get into?"

Jimmy lowered his gaze. "My good high school grades got me a scholarship to ETSU. I lived at home and commuted to Johnson City because the scholarship didn't cover everything. But I got to hanging with a party crowd and started staying out late, drinking, and experimenting with drugs. I was just plain stupid."

"Guess we have that in common."

"Somehow I don't think our mistakes are quite the same." A crooked smile split Jimmy's face. "Anyway, I managed to get through my freshman year and kept my scholarship, but sophomore year I dropped out because my grades were so bad. My dad was furious because I'd frittered away my opportunity for a good education. He told me I'd better get my act together and suggested I join the army. It might give me some discipline."

"Is that what you did?"

"Yeah. I wanted to please my dad, but my mom was worried sick that I wouldn't come back alive. Whitney was disappointed in me. She had ambitions. I didn't live up to them. She started dating Mitch while I was dodging bullets."

Kelsey saw the faraway look in Jimmy's eyes as he stared past her. "So that added to your rivalry?"

"I didn't blame Mitch." Sadness filled Jimmy's eyes. "It was my fault that I had to drop out of college and that Whitney broke up with me. I chose to go into the army to please my dad. Then he dropped dead from a heart attack while I was in Afghanistan. I never got to say goodbye."

Without thinking, Kelsey reached over and put her hand on his arm, then withdrew it just as quickly. "I'm so sorry. That must've been terrible."

Sorrow accompanied Jimmy's nod. "The worst part was knowing I would've been home in a few days because my tour of duty was ending, and I didn't plan to re-up."

"So how was it coming home?"

"I wasn't thinking about Whitney or Mitch. Janelle had just finished her freshman year in college, and Jenna and Jeremy were still in high school. I had to help my mom, who worked part time as a nurse, so I took over Dad's painting business. I made a go of it, and that's one accomplishment I'm proud of."

"You should be." Kelsey knew Jimmy wasn't proud of the way he'd squandered his education, but he had served his country, helped his mom take care of the family, and made a success of his dad's business. She couldn't figure out how that translated into a bad reputation in this town.

"Thanks. I'm going to have Jeremy take over when I start this new job."

"How does he feel about that?"

Jimmy smiled. "He's pretty excited. He's a good worker, and I told him I'd still be around to give him some advice if he needed it."

"Is that why you said you'd be talking to him?"

"Yeah, we've got some things to work out."

"So that means you intend to tell Graham you're taking the job."

"I am." Conviction filled Jimmy's voice. "I plan to make a success of that just like I did the painting business, and that includes finishing my degree and getting married."

Kelsey had to have real answers. Marriage wasn't something to take lightly. She didn't want to think of divorce down the road. Would a marriage of this kind beg for that kind of future? Would his answers satisfy her?

"But you still haven't told me why you're willing to marry me."

"I haven't finished my story."

"Wow! You really are long winded." Kelsey leaned forward. "So tell me what happens next. I'm sitting on pins and needles."

Jimmy laughed out loud. "Are you being a little sarcastic?"

"Just don't keep me waiting."

"Okay." Jimmy got up from the couch and began to pace, Dolly on his heels. "This is the part of the story that doesn't make me proud."

"Now you have my attention."

He shoved his hands into his pockets as he blew out a puff of air. "Did you know Mitch and Whitney eventually got engaged?"

Kelsey shook her head. "That's news to me. Does Amanda know this?"

"If Mitch didn't tell her, someone in town probably did." Jimmy stopped pacing and stared at Kelsey. "It's a moot point now. Mitch and Amanda are madly in love and perfect for each other. Whitney is completely out of the picture. Besides, she was never right for Mitch, and he knows that now."

Kelsey took in Jimmy's assessment of Mitch's past relationship. Did Jimmy believe Whitney had been the right woman for him? Kelsey didn't know how to ask that question without appearing jealous. She didn't want to trade a man who was cheating on his wife for one who was still in love with another woman. Did it matter if the marriage was in name only? Would it stay that way? Jimmy definitely had other ideas. The thought sent a little tingle through her midsection. She shut that feeling down.

Kelsey frowned. "But what does Mitch's relationship with Whitney have to do with your less-than-stellar past?"

"I'm getting to that part." Jimmy started to pace again. "You know how much Mitch loves cars. Our great-uncle Wilbur loved going to car shows, and Mitch always went along. After Wilbur was diagnosed with cancer, Mitch made sure Wilbur got to go to his favorite show down in Florida before he started his chemo treatments."

"Is that the one Mitch and Amanda are at now?"

"Yep."

"So I'm guessing Whitney wasn't much interested in

the car shows."

"You got it, and while Mitch was away, Whitney came looking for me. She said she was lonely and wanted company." Jimmy lowered his gaze. "I'm not proud of what I did, but I realized I still had feelings for her. She came on to me, and I took advantage of the situation."

"So you were trying to steal Mitch's fiancée?"

Nodding, Jimmy pressed his lips together in a grim line as he looked up. "Mitch came back to town unexpectedly because Wilbur was feeling poorly. Mitch caught Whitney and me together."

"What did he do?"

"He punched me and gave me a black eye. I not only had a physical black eye, but my reputation had a black eye."

"So folks in town saw you as the bad guy?"

"Yeah, I'd ruined what everyone considered the perfect match." Jimmy sighed. "Whitney begged for Mitch's forgiveness, but she realized it wasn't coming. I'd not only ruined my reputation but hers as well. She found a job in Atlanta and never came back."

"Never?"

"Yeah. Her parents weren't happy with me. Neither were Mitch's." Jimmy didn't meet her gaze, as if he was afraid to see her reaction. "It was a long time before I was able to get a painting job in Pineydale. In the long run, it turned out to be a blessing in disguise. I had to take my business to the surrounding towns. My work and my reasonable prices garnered me a lot of jobs and recommendations. And eventually people in Pineydale had other things to think about, and my misadventure with Whitney faded in most people's minds."

"If people have forgotten, why do you think you have to start fresh with someone you barely know?"

"Because the single women in town didn't forget. I'm a pariah, and being consumed with my business left me with little time to date." Jimmy rubbed the back of his neck as he broke eye contact again. "And I might as well tell you that when Amanda showed up, I tried to catch her interest because she was new in town."

"You did?"

"Yeah, but she shut me down." Jimmy sat back on the couch. "Are you going to do the same now that you know my past?"

Kelsey wasn't any closer to a decision than she was before he told her all this. "I don't know."

"I understand." Jimmy stood, then headed for the door.

Looking up at him, Kelsey doubted he understood her mixed-up feelings about the whole thing. If the week came to an end and she hadn't made a decision, it would be made for her. She didn't want the time to slip away and leave her undecided. Misery took over her thoughts and made it hard to weigh the outcome of any decision. Marriage or no marriage—that was the question.

Kelsey jumped up from the couch and went after him. "I wish I wasn't so indecisive."

He turned to look at her. "It's okay. It was a crazy idea anyway. Who wants to marry a stranger? I just thought it might help you out."

"And I appreciate the thought." Kelsey tried to smile. "I hope the job goes well."

Jimmy nodded. "Thanks. I hope everything works out for you."

"I've got a lot of thinking to do. I'll probably see you

in church before I leave."

"Sure." Jimmy strode onto the porch.

The sound of the closing door punctuated the end to this conversation. Had she just made a wrong decision to let Jimmy go? No. Marrying someone she barely knew was a crazy idea. What was done was done. She couldn't keep debating with herself. She would spend the rest of this week preparing to face the consequences of her lapse in judgment.

CHAPTER FIVE

The Pineydale Café buzzed with the conversation of the lunchtime crowd as Jimmy walked through the door. The smell of fried food permeated the air. Jimmy's stomach growled. He hadn't realized how hungry he was. He searched the area for Jeremy and spied him sitting in a corner booth with its red faux-leather seats. Jimmy strode that way.

"How was your meeting this morning with Uncle Graham?" Jeremy eyed Jimmy as he approached.

"Good." Jimmy slid into the booth.

"Glad to hear it. Uncle Graham isn't the easiest person to deal with."

Jimmy knew the truth of that statement, but he wasn't going to say so. He picked up the menu, hoping Jeremy wouldn't ask more questions about the meeting. It had gone well, but Jimmy didn't want to mention the big stickler in the deal. Having to find a wife.

Uncle Graham had been adamant about that stipulation, even after Jimmy had argued that trying to find love for the wrong reasons wasn't a good thing. He could still hear his uncle's response. *We don't want a repeat of the Whitney debacle, do we?* Add his uncle's demand to Kelsey's rejection, and that left Jimmy feeling pretty low, despite the new job and a chance to prove himself.

"When do you start?" Jeremy eyed the notebook Jimmy had slapped on the table when he'd sat down "Homework?"

"Yeah." Jimmy sighed. "I start next Monday, so I've got to read through the company policies, financials, and a bunch of other stuff. Got to be up to speed by Monday. I checked in to the summer term at ETSU, and I can get an appointment next month to apply for summer classes."

"Sounds like you're all set." Jeremy opened his menu. "Don't know why I look at this. I always order the same thing."

"Yeah. Me too." Jimmy stuck his menu back into the rack along the wall.

A moment later, the waitress appeared to take their order. After she left, Jeremy leaned forward, his elbows on the table. "Do you have homework for me regarding your business?"

Jimmy nodded. "But you know most of the ins and outs of the daily work schedule. I just need to get you up to speed on the books. When Amanda gets back, she can help you with that. She helped me set up the system last year."

"Okay." Jeremy leaned back and laced his fingers behind his head. "Too bad that pretty sister of hers isn't going to be around long."

"You mean Kelsey?"

"Yeah. Kelsey. I'd like to get to know her."

Jimmy gritted his teeth. Hadn't Jeremy noticed that Jimmy had danced with Kelsey all night at the reception and brought her to supper at their mom's house? Or was Jeremy trying to goad Jimmy into divulging just what was going on between Kelsey and him? "Too bad. She'll be gone in less than a week."

"Counting the days?" Jeremy grinned.

"What are you getting at?"

"Don't play dumb with me. I was just trying to get you riled." Jeremy laughed. "I saw the way you monopolized her time last fall after Amanda's concert and again at the wedding reception. Then you invited her over for the family dinner."

"I was just being polite."

At that moment the waitress arrived with their burgers and fries. The conversation stopped as Jeremy bowed his head. Jimmy did the same, as his little brother's actions reminded Jimmy that he often forgot to pray. That was probably the problem with this Kelsey thing. Or maybe her rejection *was* God's answer.

"You couldn't take your eyes off her the whole evening." Jeremy raised his eyebrows.

Was that true? No doubt Jimmy was attracted to Kelsey. She was pretty, but she was more than pretty. She was fun, compassionate, and despite her mistake, she had a level head when it came to everything else. That was evident when she'd turned down his marriage proposal. Her rejection still stung.

"I won't deny I find her attractive, but as I said, she'll be gone in less than a week."

"What are you afraid of?"

Jimmy frowned. "What kind of question is that?"

"One intended to get some answers. You say you're attracted to her, and I can see she's attracted to you. But I've never seen you so reluctant to go after a woman, even if she lives on the other side of the country." Jeremy's pointed look demanded a response.

Jimmy let out a clipped laugh. "You're suggesting that

I try a long-distance relationship with her?"

Jeremy sent Jimmy a pointed look. "Why not? You like her, and there sure aren't any women around here who haven't forgotten the whole deal with Whitney."

Whitney. This was the second time today someone had brought up her name. Would people never forget that? Sure, the story wasn't the talk of the town anymore, but he was learning that people hadn't forgotten. He'd been honest with Kelsey about his past. Was that why she'd turned him down? Like a dart to his heart, she'd punctured his ego, but had he given up too easily?

Jimmy narrowed his gaze. "Would you try to have a long-distance relationship with her?"

"Yeah, if she looked at me the way she looks at you."

Did Jeremy see something Jimmy had overlooked? "What am I missing here?"

"I don't know, brother. You're the one who's always charming the ladies. Use some of that charm on her."

Had he been so desperate that he'd lost his charisma? She certainly had him doubting himself. "I'll consider your advice."

Through the rest of their lunch, Jimmy talked to Jeremy about business. Jimmy's interest in Kelsey never came up again, and he was thankful for that. He wanted the transition with the painting business to go smoothly. That was his main concern as he started his new job.

When they finished eating, Jeremy stood and shrugged into his jacket. "Better get back to the job site. Are you coming by today?"

Jimmy shook his head. "You're in charge now."

"Thanks, big brother." Jeremy extended his hand.

Jimmy grasped his brother's hand. "Do me proud. And

Daddy. I know it was hard losing him when you were so young, but we can keep his legacy alive."

"We sure can."

Jimmy and Jeremy walked outside together as a cool breeze greeted them, the clouds obscuring the sun. Cloudy day or sunny day, Jimmy knew whatever happened his family would always stand by him. Even when his dad had been unhappy with the decisions Jimmy had made, his dad hadn't turned away. Jimmy wanted to give Jeremy the same kind of support.

"You can give me an update later this week." Jimmy waved as he got into his car.

Jeremy drove away in the company van as Jimmy sat there for a minute. Sadness about giving up what he'd built hit him for the first time, but he drove it from his thoughts. He had to be happy for his brother and for the prospect of a new job and hopefully a new beginning. He wished that new beginning included Kelsey.

As Jimmy drove toward home, he couldn't help thinking about what Jeremy had said. So many confusing thoughts crowded Jimmy's mind. He replayed the events of the other night when he'd explained everything to Kelsey. He was obviously as confused as she was.

He tried to grab on to something that made the most sense, but he couldn't grasp anything. Maybe he should talk to Kelsey again. Maybe she wouldn't see him. Maybe her mind was made up and whatever he said wouldn't change anything, but he had to try one more time. After all, the week wasn't over.

As he drove toward home, Charlotte's house came into view ahead. He had talked with her before about the job offer. He should let her know he'd accepted the position.

Could he also get advice on his crazy marriage idea? Probably not. He couldn't betray Kelsey's confidence. But he should stop and check on Charlotte anyway.

He stopped his car in front of Charlotte's place. The house with its wide front porch filled with rocking chairs and a porch swing always beckoned him to come and stay awhile. He should've spent more time here, just as Mitch had. Maybe things would've turned out differently if he had, but he couldn't undo the past. He had to look ahead, not back.

Jimmy bounded up the front steps and knocked on the door. Within seconds, Charlotte appeared.

"Jimmy, to what do I owe this pleasure?" Charlotte ushered him into the hallway.

"I stopped by to let you know I told Uncle Graham I'd take the job."

"Well, congratulations! We'll have to celebrate." Charlotte motioned toward the living room.

Jimmy stopped short, his stomach sinking when he saw Kelsey sitting in one of the living room chairs. "I didn't know you had company already. I don't want to interrupt."

Kelsey gave him a little wave. "We were just visiting."

"You aren't interrupting. Come on in and sit down." Charlotte motioned toward the empty chair sitting near the one where Kelsey sat.

"Sure." Jimmy took a seat, sure of nothing.

Every nerve zinged. He had no idea why he was so nervous. He'd wanted to talk to Kelsey, but he certainly couldn't talk about his plans with Charlotte here. And Kelsey sat there looking as if she'd eaten something that disagreed with her. Was she going to get sick, like at the reception? Or maybe she looked that way because he was here.

Charlotte sat on the edge of the sofa that faced the chairs where Kelsey and Jimmy sat. "Kelsey, did you hear? Jimmy has a new job."

Kelsey nodded, a forced smile on her lips. "Yes, he told me about it at the wedding reception. I'm glad you decided to accept the job. I'm sure you'll do very well."

The stilted and polite conversation did nothing to calm Jimmy's nerves. Why had he decided to stop? His better nature had prompted him to stop and check on Charlotte. Maybe this stop would make it possible to talk to Kelsey alone. He could hope and pray, though his prayers about this matter continued to be left on the back burner.

"I think we should celebrate Jimmy's good news with some cake and tea." Charlotte popped up from her chair as she glanced at Jimmy. "You don't mind having a tea party with us ladies, do you?"

"I never turn down a piece of your cake even if it's served with tea. Besides, I like the company." Jimmy stood and offered his arm to Charlotte, then turned to look at Kelsey. "I'm game for a tea party as long as Kelsey doesn't mind my crashing your shindig."

"I don't mind." A strained smile curving her lips, Kelsey joined Charlotte and Jimmy as they made their way to the kitchen.

Jimmy cut the chocolate cake and put it on plates while Charlotte set the teakettle on the stove. In minutes the tea was steeping in the white teapot covered in pink flowers. Charlotte carried the teapot to the table nestled in the corner of the kitchen where windows looked out on the yard festooned with daffodils.

While they ate cake and drank tea, Charlotte quizzed

Jimmy about the new job. He informed her about the incredible opportunity and told her how excited Jeremy was to take over the painting business.

"Sounds like everything's falling into place." Charlotte took a sip of tea.

"Yeah." *Everything but the wife part.* Jimmy glanced in Kelsey's direction. Her sad countenance made Jimmy's heart ache. Had he put that expression on her face?

He wanted to see the bubbly woman he'd encountered last fall, but maybe he was making her life more miserable. While he berated himself, Jeremy's comments filtered through Jimmy's mind. Despite what Jeremy had said, Jimmy didn't see that she was looking at him with any favor. She sat there without saying a word, looking crestfallen. Was Jeremy completely wrong?

As they finished their cake, huge raindrops splatted against the nearby window and drew their attention to the outdoors. The earlier breeze had turned into a rush of wind that swayed the bare-branched trees in a frenzied motion against the gray cloudy sky.

"Looks like we're getting quite a storm." Charlotte waved a hand toward the window.

"Yeah. It's been cloudy most of the day, but I didn't think there was rain in the forecast."

"You know the weather forecasts seem to change hourly." Charlotte turned to Kelsey. "Looks like you won't be walking back."

Kelsey sighed. "And I have to get back soon to let that dog out. I certainly don't want her to have an accident. So I can't outwait the rain."

Jimmy jumped on this opportunity. "I can drive you back whenever you need to go."

Kelsey looked at him wide eyed as she tried to smile. "Okay. That's good. I should probably get going."

"Just let me know when." Jimmy collected the plates from the table as he looked at Charlotte. "You want these in the dishwasher?"

"Yes, thank you." Charlotte took another sip of tea. "This has been delightful."

"It has." Kelsey smiled.

Returning to the table, Jimmy took in her smile, his thoughts brighter. "Thanks for celebrating with me."

Charlotte motioned for him to come closer. "Give your old aunt a hug."

"There's nothing old about you, Aunt Charlotte." Jimmy put his arms around her shoulders.

Charlotte patted her cheeks. "These wrinkles say I'm old."

"Not in my book." Jimmy shook his head.

"Your visits keep me young." Charlotte turned to Kelsey. "I've enjoyed getting to know you better. I so loved having Amanda here with me. It's a shame you have to go back to Washington."

Kelsey sighed. "I have to finish school. Otherwise I might be tempted to stay. It would be fun to be close to Amanda now that we're older and aren't bickering with each other all the time."

Jimmy laughed. "That's sisters. I should know. Janelle and Jenna fought like cats and dogs the whole time they were growing up. Now they're best friends."

Kelsey took the last sip of her tea, then glanced at Charlotte. "Would you like me to wash out the teacups and pot? I'm sure you don't put those in the dishwasher."

Charlotte waved a hand at Kelsey. "Just set them in the

sink. I'm going to sit here and have a little more tea. You two can run along and take care of that dog."

Jimmy jumped up from his chair and reached for the teacups as he looked over at Kelsey. "I'll take those to the sink while you get your jacket. Then we'll be on our way."

Kelsey went over and hugged Charlotte. "You enjoy your tea. I'll stop over another day before I leave."

"I'd like that."

Smiling, Kelsey picked up her jacket from the barstool. "See you later."

Jimmy waved as he escorted Kelsey out of the kitchen and toward the front door. "Would you like me to get the umbrella I keep in the car?"

"I can run for it." Kelsey held her jacket over her head.

"Okay. One, two, three. Go."

Jimmy dashed through the rain and opened the car door for Kelsey, then raced to the driver's side and hopped in. He ran a hand through his hair and down his face to wipe away the rain. He glanced over at Kelsey. Her pretty face glowed with the dampness from the rain. She pushed a strand of her dark hair away from her cheek. He swallowed hard. His heart beat faster than the raindrops pinging on the hood of his car.

He wanted her for his wife, but could he withstand having this attraction to her and not being able to do a thing about it? He didn't have to worry about that. She was ready to go back to Washington and had no interest in a marriage of any kind, real or in name only. So why was he still thinking about it? Because he couldn't get it off his mind, especially in her presence.

The car engine's hum accompanied the sound of the rain as Jimmy drove toward Mitch and Amanda's house.

The windshield wipers sloshed back and forth, pushing away the rain. He wished he could push away his doubts and crazy thoughts as easily.

Kelsey didn't say anything as she sat there looking straight ahead. Was she just counting the minutes until she could be rid of him? What would she say if he asked to come in and talk with her? He couldn't be a coward. He would give this one last shot.

Jimmy turned into the driveway and shut off the engine. "You want to wait a minute and see if the rain lets up?"

Kelsey shook her head. "I'd better get inside and take care of Dolly."

"You're going to get wet taking her out."

"I won't melt, as my grandma used to say."

Jimmy chuckled. "I know, but you're a mother-to-be, so maybe you shouldn't be getting wet. Let me take the dog out."

"Why are you being so nice?" She stared at him in the dull light of a rainy afternoon.

"Haven't you figured out yet that I'm a good guy?" He hoped she would take his statement in the jovial way it was intended.

"You are. If you want to take the dog out, you can." Nodding her head, she lowered her gaze. "Besides, I have something I want to tell you afterwards."

"Sure. Let me come around to your side with the umbrella so we don't get wetter than we already are." Grabbing the umbrella from the backseat, Jimmy took in her agreement to his statement with optimism. But her request to talk tempered that. He might not like what she had to say.

Jimmy held the umbrella as they huddled together under it. Kelsey opened the front door, and Dolly greeted them with a bark and wagging tail. Kelsey immediately found Dolly's leash, and Jimmy took the dog out the back door.

Kelsey stood in the kitchen as Jimmy came inside through the laundry room. "That was quick."

"Dolly doesn't like to be out in the rain any more than we do." Jimmy kept a tight rein on the leash while Dolly shook from one end to the other. "There's been a shower in here. I need an old towel to mop it up."

Kelsey motioned to the cupboard above the washing machine. "Check in there."

Jimmy opened the cupboard. "Success. I'll have this cleaned up in a minute."

Kelsey leaned down and took the leash off Dolly. "Thanks. I'll take care of her."

The dog trotted after Kelsey as Jimmy swiped the towel across the floor. He saw himself in the dog, following Kelsey around hoping for a pat on the head, a smile, or a treat of some kind. He had to admit the situation was pathetic, but he couldn't chase away these feelings.

After he finished the task, he dumped the towel in the nearby laundry basket. He made his way into the living room, where Kelsey sat on the couch with Dolly curled up at her feet. The scene created a warm sensation in his chest. He wasn't sure what these crazy feelings were, but they scared him.

She looked up at him with an uncertain smile. "I have something to say to you."

"Okay. Go right ahead. I'm listening

"Do you have to stand there staring at me?"

Jimmy held out his hands in front of him. "What would you like me to do?"

"Sit somewhere so it doesn't feel like you're staring down at me."

"Sure." Jimmy plopped onto the other end of the couch. Dolly looked up at him with sad eyes, as if she knew Kelsey was planning to give him bad news.

Kelsey twisted her hands in her lap. "I've made up my mind about getting married."

Jimmy frowned. "I thought your mind was already made up."

"No." She stared at him, worry in her eyes. "I just couldn't decide. Then you left."

"I left because you couldn't make up your mind. That told me you weren't interested in marrying me. So I didn't see any point in hanging around."

Her lips parted slightly. She looked as though she wanted to say something, but the words wouldn't come. She said she'd made up her mind. So why didn't she just say it?

"So what's your decision?"

CHAPTER SIX

The expectation on Jimmy's face curdled Kelsey's stomach. Her previous indecision had led him to conclude she wasn't interested in the marriage. She could understand that. What guy was going to stick around when a woman refused his proposal?

Now she couldn't get the words out of her mouth. They sat on the tip of her tongue. Her pulse pounded in her head, and she stared at him as if she had no brain. She had to say something, anything.

"I want to get married." The words tumbled from her mouth. She swallowed hard.

Jimmy blinked as disbelief spread across his face. "You want to get married?"

Kelsey nodded as another lump formed in her throat. She knit her brow and stared at him, her heart thundering. "Are you still good with that? A marriage in name only?"

Jimmy closed the gap between them on the couch. "Not exactly what I was counting on, but let's talk about it. What brought you to this decision?"

Kelsey took a deep breath, hoping Jimmy would understand her doubts and fears. "My dad called to see how I was doing. During the conversation, he mentioned that Brandon was there for a delivery and asked about me."

"Wow! What did your dad say?"

"Told him I was in Tennessee for my spring break."

Jimmy narrowed his gaze. "Why would that snake be asking about you?"

"He's probably still worried that I'll somehow tell his wife. That's my guess."

"That figures." Contempt showed on Jimmy's face. "How well does your dad know this guy?"

"Not that well, but he knows we were dating off and on. Dad will remember Brandon was with me the night Noah went to the hospital. And if I go home and tell my dad I'm pregnant, he'll put two and two together and know Brandon's the father." Kelsey pressed her lips together.

"Bad news for Brandon."

"Bad news for both of us. My dad will have a double fit when he learns Brandon's married."

"But you didn't know that."

"I'm afraid my dad won't look at it that way. He'll say I shouldn't have…" Threatening tears kept Kelsey from finishing the sentence. She closed her eyes to keep the tears from coming. She could just see her dad confronting Brandon. She couldn't let that happen.

"Hasn't your dad ever made a mistake?"

"Of course. We all make mistakes, but he'll be so disappointed in me. And he won't stand by and let Brandon get away with not supporting this child." Kelsey wrinkled her brow. "But I don't want to ruin a whole bunch of lives. What about his wife and daughter? How terrible for them."

"I've said so before. You're too kind." Jimmy reached over and took her hands in his. "You're a better person than I am. You imagine your dad threatening Brandon. I'd be right there with your dad. I'd like to confront the…I can't say the word I'd like to say."

"What good would it do to make more people miserable?" Kelsey raised her eyebrows as she gazed at Jimmy. He made her feel safe. Was she misplacing her trust, as she had done with Brandon? She wished she knew for sure, but she couldn't know anything for sure. "Marrying you seems like the best thing to do."

"So I'm the lesser of two evils?"

Kelsey shook her head. "It's not like that at all. You're the best option."

Jimmy smiled. "So you actually want to get married?"

Jimmy's smile made her heart skip a beat, but she couldn't let that change her mind about the type of marriage this would be. He had to understand that. The mess with Brandon tainted everything. She just couldn't bring herself to have sexual relations with a man she barely knew and didn't love. Someday, but not now. "As long as we agree to the terms of the marriage."

"In name only?" A look of resignation replaced Jimmy's smile.

Kelsey nodded, afraid to say anything else. Was it right to make this stipulation?

"I hope that can be renegotiated somewhere down the line."

A sick feeling hit Kelsey in the gut, and it had nothing to do with her pregnancy. *Marriage was forever. Till death do us part.* What if she never fell in love with Jimmy? She definitely liked him, but that wasn't the same as loving someone.

"We won't be together in the beginning anyway, since I'll be going back to school. Can we revisit this after the baby is born?" Kelsey bit her lower lip. Was that fair?

Lowering his gaze, Jimmy rubbed the back of his neck.

"I suppose that'll have to do."

"Jimmy?"

"Yeah?" He looked up at her.

"Don't go through with this on my account if this arrangement isn't going to suit you. I'll deal with my dad and Brandon and this baby however I have to." Her stomach somersaulted while she waited for his response.

Jimmy raised his eyebrows. "Remember—I asked you to marry me to help with my job, and besides, I like you. You're fun to be with. So let's do this."

"And I like you." But was that enough? The question she was afraid to voice made her heart sink. Her dad's phone call had precipitated her decision to accept Jimmy's offer. She couldn't waver now. "So when should we get married?"

"As soon as we get the license. We have to do that at the county clerk's office."

"Who's going to marry us?"

"Good question." Jimmy leaned forward. "What do you think?"

"Can we get married at the courthouse?"

"So you don't want a church wedding?"

She shook her head. "No fanfare. Just you and me and whoever marries us. I already read that you don't have to have witnesses in Tennessee."

"When did you do this?"

"Last night when I was trying to figure out what to do."

Jimmy stood and retrieved his phone from his pocket. "My grandpa's cousin is a retired judge. He could marry us."

Kelsey nodded. "That would be fine with me."

Jimmy tapped the screen on his phone, then scrolled. He tapped again, then looked at her as he put the phone to his ear. "I'm calling Grandpa's cousin Davis Cunningham."

Kelsey waited while Jimmy talked, her heart doing a tap dance. When he finished the call, he looked her way. The reality of what they were intending to do hit her with full force. She couldn't keep waffling. She had made the decision.

"What did he say?"

Jimmy grinned. "He'll marry us tomorrow at his house. All we have to do is show up with the marriage license. He just asked me to call and let him know when we're coming."

Tomorrow. The word rattled around in Kelsey's brain. Was she ready for that? She shut down the question. The decision was made, and she would stick with it. "Okay."

Jimmy narrowed his gaze. "You don't sound so sure."

"I'm sure. It's just a big step. That's all." Every little girl dreamed of her future wedding. This was not Kelsey's dream. It was reality. Her reality.

"Do you want to exchange rings?" Jimmy's gray eyes held a hint of uncertainty.

Kelsey hadn't even thought about that. She'd thought about the vows. How could she promise to love? How could she stand before God and say things she didn't feel? She'd already messed up with God. The vows were like a noose tightening around her neck. She had to say something. "Yeah. I want to exchange rings."

"Then we'd better go shopping."

Standing, Kelsey held out her hands and looked down at her clothing. "What am I going to wear? I certainly didn't bring anything to get married in. What are you planning to wear?"

He looked at her with a curious smile. "You want to get dressed up? You want me to wear a suit?"

"I'd like to have a simple dress. You can wear what you're comfortable with." Was she being silly? They would stand before a judge, no witnesses. Even so, she didn't want to get married in blue jeans or even the slacks and jacket she'd worn to the rehearsal dinner. That was all she had with her besides the bridesmaid dress from Amanda's wedding, and she certainly didn't want to wear that.

"Whatever you want." Jimmy motioned to the door. "Let's go to the mall over in Johnson City. I'm sure we can find everything we need there."

"Okay. You know where to go."

Jimmy looked out the window. "Looks like it stopped raining. I'll take Dolly out."

"Thanks." Kelsey grabbed her jacket. "I'm going to take a pit stop, too."

As Jimmy headed out the back door, Kelsey made her way to the bathroom off the hall. After closing the door, she looked at herself in the mirror. A pink flush colored her cheeks. At least she wasn't pale like the day of Amanda's wedding. Tomorrow would be her own wedding. The prospect seemed unreal. The sound of the back door and Dolly's bark prompted Kelsey to quickly finish up in the bathroom.

Jimmy smiled when she reappeared. "Ready to go?"

Her heart tripping over his smile, Kelsey nodded and followed him to the car. During most of the trip to Johnson City, he didn't say much. She agonized that he was having second thoughts.

"Could I ask you a question?"

"Sure. Ask away." Jimmy glanced her way before turning his attention back to the road.

"What kind of vows are we going to say?"

He glanced at her again as they drove along a street lined with businesses. "Do you have something in mind?"

"I don't want to make promises I know aren't true." Kelsey puffed out her cheeks as she expelled a loud sigh. "How can we promise to love each other when we don't?"

"Lots of people get married and make those promises and intend to keep them, but they don't."

"That doesn't mean we should make promises we don't intend to or can't keep."

Jimmy let out a low whistle. "Does that mean you don't think you'll ever love me? Are you already having second thoughts about this?"

"Are you?"

"I asked first." Jimmy stopped at a traffic light.

"They aren't second thoughts. Maybe third, fourth, and fifth thoughts."

Jimmy glanced her way. "That's a lot of thinking. Maybe overthinking?"

"Yeah. I'm overthinking this. Maybe it's pregnancy hormones." Kelsey sighed.

"Maybe those will be evened out by the time you finish school and come back."

Kelsey frowned and waved a hand at him. "Are you making fun of me?"

"I was trying to move the conversation into less serious territory."

"So you don't want to discuss the vows?"

"There's the mall." Jimmy turned the corner and stopped at the traffic light at the mall entrance.

Kelsey twisted her hands in her lap as Jimmy found a parking spot. He didn't want to talk about the vows. Did he believe they would ultimately fall in love? Is that why he was willing to go along with this charade of a marriage? She liked Jimmy. He was easy to like, easy on the eyes, and easy to have fun with, but would that eventually translate into love?

Why did she keep second-guessing herself?

Jimmy shut off the car, then turned to her. "Okay. Let's get those vows hammered out."

"We're going to write our own?"

Jimmy nodded. "That's the best solution."

"Will the judge go for that?"

"I'm not a wedding expert, but I'm sure most officiants let the bride and groom recite their own vows."

"You mean I have to memorize them? I'll be too nervous to remember."

"We'll make them simple, and you can have them written on a note card."

Kelsey took a deep breath and let it out slowly. "So when do we write them?"

"Now." Jimmy pointed toward her side of the car. "There's a pen and a pad in the glove box."

Kelsey opened the compartment and found the pen and pad. She held them out to Jimmy. "Here."

He gently pushed her hand back. "You do the writing."

"Okay." Kelsey looked down at the pad, wondering what she wanted the vows to say. When she looked back at Jimmy, he was gazing at his phone. "What are you looking at?"

"Vows." He didn't look up.

"What are you finding?"

"Stuff." He held the phone out to her. "What do you think of this?"

Kelsey took the phone and read through the nontraditional vows. After she finished, she looked up, her heart lighter. "I think we can work something out with these."

"You write down what you'd like to say. Then you can read it to me."

"Okay." Kelsey scribbled on the pad, the scratching of the pen against the paper the only sound in the car. She wrote, then crossed out several lines, then wrote some more.

When she was finished, she looked up. Jimmy smiled, and the things she'd just written made a lot of sense. She could be a friend to this man and stand by him. Maybe she would even fall in love.

"I want to hear what you've got." Jimmy held his hand out for the phone.

Kelsey swallowed the lump in her throat as she handed the phone back, then gazed down at the paper. "Here's what I have.

"'I, Kelsey, accept you, Jimmy, as you are. You are my friend. I will respect you as a person, a partner, and an equal. I will listen to you with kindness and empathy, and give encouragement. I promise to rejoice with you in good times and struggle alongside you in bad times. I promise to laugh with you, cry with you, and grow with you, even as time and life change us both. I promise to learn with you, to support your dreams, and to understand our differences. I take you to be my husband, my companion, and the friend of my life. With these words and this ring, I marry you and bind my life to yours.'"

Afraid to look up and see Jimmy's reaction, Kelsey kept her eyes trained on the paper. He touched her hand, then lifted her chin with the tips of his fingers until she was looking into his eyes.

"Perfect."

Her fears ebbed away like water on the outgoing tide. "Will you say the same vows?"

Jimmy shook his head. "No, I think I'll say I, Jimmy, accept you, Kelsey. And I'll take you as my wife, not my husband."

Happiness bubbled up inside her until it spilled out in laughter. "That part about the laughter won't be hard to accomplish."

"Not many brides and grooms write their wedding vows in a mall parking lot. Safeguard that paper." Jimmy opened the car door. "Ready to shop for rings and a dress?"

They walked to the entrance without saying a word. Even though he'd said the vows were perfect, in her mind, there was nothing perfect about this arrangement.

Once inside the mall, Jimmy headed straight for the directory of stores, then turned back to her. "Rings or dress first?"

"Rings."

He turned back to the directory and placed a finger on the name of the jewelry store. "We can start here."

"Okay." Kelsey hurried to keep up with Jimmy's long strides. "I just want plain gold bands. I hope that's okay with you."

"It is."

When they reached the jewelry store, Jimmy ushered

her inside. With every step they took, the actuality of what they were about to do became more real. In minutes they picked out rings with little fanfare, and Jimmy insisted on paying for them.

As they left the store, Kelsey frowned. "Shouldn't I have bought yours?"

"There's nothing traditional about what we're doing. So let's break tradition all the way." Jimmy motioned down the cavernous hallway lined with stores. "There's a big department store where you can look for a dress. If you don't find something there, we can try some smaller stores."

After they reached the department store, Kelsey pointed down one aisle. "I see dresses over there. Do you want to do something else while I look?"

"No, I want to see what you pick out."

"Isn't it bad luck to see the bride in her dress before the wedding?"

Jimmy shook his head. "We said we weren't following tradition. Besides, I don't know that there's any luck involved here. Just the decision to make this work."

Make this work. The words circled through her mind as if they were on a merry-go-round. The decision to get married also carried with it the decision to make the marriage work. Was that possible when they didn't love each other? Maybe it would work because there were no expectations.

Kelsey strode to a rack containing dresses suited for special occasions. Her wedding should be a special occasion, but she doubted there would be anything special about it. She rifled through the dresses until she came to an ivory dress made of a crinkly cotton material decorated with a touch of lace. She held it up in front of her.

"Is that what you want?" Jimmy gazed at her.

"I have to try it on."

"Are you going to model it for me?"

"I guess since there's no bad luck involved here."

"Only good." Jimmy grinned.

Kelsey went into the fitting room and hung the dress on the hook, then took off her jeans and top. She gazed at herself in the mirror and ran a hand over her stomach. How long before it would be obvious she was pregnant? With all the nausea, she had actually lost weight. How long before she would have to buy maternity clothes? She had several tops that were full and blousy. They would surely do until she finished school.

Kelsey shimmied into the dress and pulled up the side zipper. It was a perfect fit. She ran her hand over the lacy material. *Make this work.* The words wouldn't leave her alone, like a song that kept floating through her mind for a whole day. She didn't want to compound the problems in her life by letting this marriage become part of the divorce statistics that Jimmy had mentioned. These words weren't just for a day. They were for a lifetime.

"Are you hiding out in there?" Jimmy's voice floated back to the stall where Kelsey stood.

Casting one more glance in the mirror, Kelsey pulled her hair up on top of her head, then let it fall to her shoulders. How should she wear her hair? Up or down? Why did she care? She'd said she didn't want any fanfare, but deep down she had always dreamed of fanfare like at Amanda's wedding. Maybe she should have opted for the blue jeans anyway.

She walked to the doorway and peeked out. She didn't

see anyone.

"Looking for someone?"

Kelsey jumped and placed a hand over her heart. "Jimmy, you scared me. You sounded like you were right outside the door when you called to me."

"I was until this elderly lady gave me the evil eye when she came out of there. I decided to hide out until you showed."

Kelsey laughed inwardly at the thought of Jimmy being intimidated by an elderly woman. "She was just putting you in your place. You really should learn to be more patient."

"Yes, I should." He looked her over from head to toe. "You in that dress is definitely worth waiting for. It's perfect, except those shoes."

"You mean I shouldn't wear these?" She glanced down at the canvas tennis shoes.

"The hot pink just doesn't go."

"Are you sure?"

Jimmy held up his hands in surrender. "If that's what you want, I'm not going to argue."

Kelsey laughed. "Just kidding. The shoes I wore for Amanda's wedding will go with this dress. I won't be wearing these."

Jimmy made a mock gesture of wiping his brow. "Whew! One thing I don't have to worry about."

"Are you worried?" She wished she wasn't, and she wished she hadn't asked. She didn't want to know that he was worried. She was worried enough for both of them.

Jimmy took her hands. "I'd be lying if I said I wasn't. This is a big step, and I know we're doing this for nontraditional reasons. You have my word I'll do my best to make you happy."

"But will I make you happy?"

Jimmy squeezed her hands. "That's one thing I'm definitely not worried about."

Kelsey stared up at him. How could that be when she didn't plan to be a real wife, or was he counting on a change in her attitude? She didn't want to think too far into the future. That was what really scared her. The uncertainty of the coming days loomed ahead of her like a monster waiting to devour whatever happiness she might find in this marriage. She had to put those thoughts away and just concentrate on today. Just like an addict, she had to take one day at a time.

Jimmy let go of her hands. "Your silence tells me you're worried."

Kelsey mustered a smile, even while she noticed how Jimmy's cocky confidence faded from his eyes. "Only when I think about telling my dad I've eloped."

Jimmy wrinkled his brow. "Should I be concerned about your dad?"

Kelsey wished the specter of her father's disapproval didn't loom over her thoughts at every turn. If she did get married or didn't get married, he would be a problem. "I know you'll win him over."

"With that happy thought, let's buy this dress and head back to Pineydale. I'm going to show the future Mrs. James Madison Cunningham where she's going to live."

"Okay." Kelsey hadn't thought about living with Jimmy. She'd been so focused on whether to marry him or not, she had completely failed to think about what happened after she finished school. She would return and move in with him. She had never even seen the outside of his house, much less the inside.

As they stood in line to pay for the dress, thoughts wound through Kelsey's mind like a swirling kaleidoscope, changing and scattering before she could settle on one and make sense of it. She insisted on paying for the dress, even though Jimmy had offered. Despite her spinning thoughts, she was certain her dad would cut off her credit card as soon as he learned of her marriage. She would be on her own.

***

Surrounded by bare-branched trees, the gray-sided house with the white trim and black shutters stood in the center of the block. A white balustrade surrounded a front porch running across the entire front. Similar modest houses with good-sized lots lined both sides of the street. Jimmy pulled his car into the driveway and hit the button that opened the garage door. What would Kelsey think of his fixer-upper? He'd finished the renovations in the kitchen, dining room, and main living area. Hopefully, he could squeeze in the time to get the rest done before she moved in permanently.

"Well, we're here." He turned off the ignition. "I hope you can overlook the mess. I'm still renovating this place."

She smiled at him. "You're a man of many talents."

Her smile and her comment touched him deep inside. He'd gotten used to people seeing him as the black sheep of his family, the one who messed everything up. Her praise gave him hope that this crazy, impetuous marriage thing could work.

He just needed to live up to her expectations. He hadn't

lived up to Whitney's. He hadn't lived up to his dad's. Could he do it right this time? For years he'd perfected his swagger and nothing-bothers-me attitude, but it was all for show. He buried his feelings of inferiority deep inside, but they threatened to surface whenever things didn't go as planned.

"Let's go inside." He hopped out of the car.

"Don't forget Dolly. You know where you want to take her."

Jimmy looked at the dog that had smeared her wet nose all over the window in the backseat. He hoped their plans wouldn't make a smeary mess of their lives.

Yeah, he knew where he wanted to take the window smearer. Right back to Mitch's place. But Kelsey had insisted they stop and take the dog out, then begged him to bring the big ball of fur with them. Before long, she would suggest that the dog be part of their wedding because they would be away a good part of the day tomorrow.

Jimmy opened the back door and grabbed the dog's collar. "Come on, Dolly. Let's get this leash on you."

Kelsey leaned over and snapped the leash on the collar as she patted the dog on the head. "Dolly, you be a good girl. No messing up Jimmy's place."

Jimmy wanted to correct Kelsey and say it was their place, but she certainly didn't see it that way. Would she take ownership once she moved here, or would this always be a place to camp and not a home for her? He purged the negative thought.

With the dog hooked on her leash, Jimmy traipsed through the garage to the back door and opened it. "You don't have to worry about Dolly. There's not much she can mess up. Go on in."

Kelsey stopped short as she stepped into the kitchen. She turned to Jimmy. "You did all this work?"

Jimmy nodded. "In my spare time."

"Is it okay if I unhook Dolly's leash?"

"Sure." Jimmy waved a hand toward the pup. "She'll be fine."

After unleashing the dog, Kelsey ran her free hand over the nearby granite countertop, then the mahogany cabinet above. "These are beautiful. You *are* talented."

"Thanks. It's too bad I don't cook."

Kelsey laughed.

"What's so funny?"

"We're going to be quite a pair. Here's this beautiful kitchen, and neither one of us knows how to cook?"

"Then we'll have to learn together." Jimmy liked the sound of that. He could just imagine evenings spent with Kelsey in this kitchen. He would have to get his mom to give him some of her recipes. They could start there, but he wouldn't spring that idea on Kelsey now. He had a feeling he would have to ease into their new life. "I can make toast."

Kelsey laughed again. "Good, because I usually burn mine."

"Thanks for letting me know. I'll be sure to make the toast."

"This is a beautiful table. Is this real mahogany?" Kelsey placed her hands on the back of one of the ladder-back chairs.

Jimmy joined her beside the table. "Thanks. It is. It belonged to my maternal grandparents. I just refinished it and moved it in here last week."

Kelsey raised her eyebrows. "You refinished this? You

are amazing."

Drinking in her praise, Jimmy motioned for her to go ahead into the adjoining great room. "Let me show you the rest of the house."

Kelsey walked beside him as Dolly sniffed her way through the room. "This room's cozy. I love the floor-to-ceiling brick and the mantel on the fireplace."

"This was an old timber from my grandpa's fishing cabin up in the mountains where my dad used to fish."

"Do you like to fish?"

Shaking his head, Jimmy frowned. "Too boring, but my dad and grandpa loved it. So I used to go, just because I liked hanging out with them."

Kelsey remained silent as she went around the room inspecting everything. Jimmy wanted her to like what he'd done, and her silence made him nervous. She opened and closed the drawers and cabinets of the built-ins on either side of the fireplace.

As he watched her, realization hit him. His desire for her approval had him trapped in a web of uncertainty. He'd done the same thing with Whitney—always trying to win her approval with his accomplishments. He'd failed. Fear of failing again grabbed hold of his mind. He couldn't...he wouldn't fail this time.

"Does it meet your approval?"

She turned to him with a look on her face that made him think she was lost in her own little world. "Did you make these and the cabinets in the kitchen?"

"Yeah." Jimmy hated the self-doubt her question triggered. "Why are you asking?"

She opened one of the drawers and pointed to the dovetailing. "This shows real craftsmanship. You keep impressing me with your work."

Jimmy's insecurities dissipated like the storm clouds breaking for the sun now shining through the windows at the back of the house. "Thanks. Would you like to see my workshop?"

"Where is it?"

"Out back." Jimmy pointed out the nearby window. "You see the roof of that building just beyond those red cedars?"

"Yeah, but let's finish in here first."

"Sure." Jimmy held a hand out toward the hallway. "Through that door. That's where the mess is."

"Do I need a hard hat?" Kelsey raised her eyebrows.

"It's not that bad." Jimmy laughed. "But you do have to watch your step in a couple of rooms, and there's only a bare subfloor in the hallway, bathroom, and two of the bedrooms."

Kelsey walked behind him until they came to the first door. "As you can see, I'm completely renovating this bath. Not much to see in here except the toilet. I'm waiting for the new countertops, sink, and tile."

"Again, it looks like you've got your work cut out for you here."

"That's pretty much what the rest of the place looks like. A lot of work ahead of me." Jimmy hoped she would like the completed renovation. "Two bedrooms are across the hall. There's not much to see there. Just two empty rooms that need paint, new flooring, and furniture."

"How many bedrooms do you have?"

"Three on the main floor, and I plan to eventually finish the basement."

Kelsey eyed him. "So if these two bedrooms aren't

finished, where do you expect me to sleep?"

With me. The words popped into his mind. He was thankful he hadn't said them out loud. "I can sleep on the couch, and you can have my bed. I'll show you my room."

"Okay." Uncertainty colored her voice as she followed him.

He stepped aside as he motioned for her to go in. He'd furnished this room before he'd been thinking about a wife. The furnishings made of heavy oak were on the masculine side. "The master suite has a bathroom and walk-in closet."

Kelsey poked her head into the bathroom and the closet, then turned to him. "I love the rain shower and the big soaker tub. Did you do the cabinets and built-ins in the bathroom and closet?"

Jimmy drank in her enthusiasm for his work. "I made all the cabinetry."

"You have a real talent for woodworking. It's amazing."

"Thanks. It's something I enjoy doing." Her statements didn't sound like flattery. He hoped she wasn't just being polite.

Kelsey motioned around the room. "I can't take your room from you and expect you to sleep on the couch. Besides, I still have to take care of Dolly. You could stay with me at Mitch's place."

"That might work. Let's see the workshop, and I'll think about it." Jimmy looked at Dolly. "Put the leash on the dog, and we can check it out."

Kelsey clipped the leash on Dolly's collar. "All set."

"We'll go out the back through the laundry room off the kitchen." Jimmy led the way and opened the door for Kelsey, the whole time thinking about her question. He had to prepare himself for sharing the same house with her but not sharing her bed. He had to be good with that.

As they stepped into the yard, Dolly strained at the tether. Kelsey pulled hard to keep the dog from jerking it from her hand.

"Let me take her. She must smell a rabbit or something." Jimmy reached over and took the leash.

"Thanks. I was afraid she was going to take me for a run through the yard." Kelsey relinquished the lead, a smile curving her mouth. "You've got a peaceful backyard, with all the trees. Is that a garden plot over there?"

Jimmy nodded. "The previous owners had a garden there, but I've never planted one. I didn't have the time to tend it."

"Do you care if I plant one when I come back in May?"

Kelsey's request lifted Jimmy's heart. "Sure. You can do what you want. It's your place, too."

"Thanks." She walked over to the area and dug into the dirt with the toe of her tennis shoe. The hot-pink shoes showed as a bright contrast against the rich brown earth. "It looks like pretty good soil for a garden."

Jimmy couldn't help thinking that Kelsey's presence was like those pink shoes. She brought optimism and light to his life. "Are you an experienced gardener?"

A smile tugged at the corners of her mouth. "Hardly. But my stepmom, Maria, planted a garden every year when I was a kid. She would let me have my own little space. She even let me pick out what I wanted to plant. Then I took care of it."

"What did you plant?" Jimmy loved the thought of Kelsey as a little girl tending her garden. Was her baby a little girl who would love to garden alongside her mother?

"Beans and peas, a few carrots and radishes."

"What kind of a kid plants radishes?"

"Don't make fun of me." Kelsey let her lower lip protrude.

Still holding Dolly's leash, Jimmy joined Kelsey near the garden and put an arm around her shoulders. "That's okay. I like radishes."

Kelsey laughed. "Me, too. I love them in salads. I can make salads."

Jimmy squeezed her shoulders, realizing he liked being close to her. How would he handle that when she didn't want a real marriage? Could he change her mind? After all, she'd said they could revisit the issue after the baby was born. Could he hope they'd eventually fall in love? Yeah, that was his hope—for love and a real marriage. For now he'd think about cooking, not what he couldn't have. "You can make salad, and I can make toast. That's a good start on our cooking."

"It is." Kelsey extracted herself from his embrace. "Let's see your workshop."

"Sure." Jimmy let the dog lead the way as he followed Kelsey down the rock-lined path. Her obvious desire to get away from him punched a hole in his ego. Here he was wishing to be close to her, and she wanted just the opposite.

Trying to escape his troubling thoughts, Jimmy jogged ahead and unlocked the door. He motioned for Kelsey to go in. He stood back and waited for her reaction to his multiple projects as he unleased Dolly.

Dolly quickly joined Kelsey as she studied each piece, running one hand along the wood. She finally looked at him. He lounged against the wall at the door while he tried to look nonchalant. Once again he found himself hoping for a woman's approval. Was he falling into the same trap again? No. This was completely different from everything that happened with Whitney. Kelsey would be his wife, but not actually.

Kelsey whirled around, a smile lighting her features. "Jimmy."

Her expression and the awe in her voice made him think she was pleased with what she saw, but he still waited with trepidation to hear her reaction. "Yes?"

"These pieces are amazing. You made them?"

His spirit soaring, Jimmy pushed away from the wall and joined her next to the curio cabinet he'd been working on for nearly a year. "I just finished this. I made it from the big oak tree my mom had to have cut down because the roots were starting to go into the foundation of her house. I'm going to give her the cabinet for Mother's Day."

"How wonderful!" Kelsey turned and touched the cabinet again. "She will love this. It's beautiful."

"Thanks."

"When do you have time to work on these things?" Kelsey motioned around the room.

"Evenings. Weekends."

"But aren't you tired after a long day of painting houses?"

"I love doing this so much that it doesn't seem like work."

"And all of this equipment and tools." Admiration showed in Kelsey's eyes.

"I got a bargain on this stuff when an old craftsman passed away and they had an estate sale." Jimmy ate up her praise. Could he keep her respect—something he had failed to do with Whitney? "Now that you've seen my projects, would you like to get something to eat? We'll have our own version of the rehearsal dinner."

Kelsey laughed. "You make me smile. And I would love to have dinner with you, but we have to take Dolly home first."

"Will do." Jimmy put the leash back on the dog and headed for the door.

With Kelsey falling into step beside him, Jimmy let a feeling of accomplishment wash over him. This day left him with hope, despite her question about the sleeping arrangements. Tomorrow he would make Kelsey his wife. He said a silent prayer that this marriage would work out for both of them.

CHAPTER SEVEN

The sun glinting off the hood of Jimmy's car reminded Kelsey that she should have sunny thoughts about this occasion. Even though it wasn't the life she'd imagined, she'd make the best of these circumstances on this warmer-than-normal beautiful day. A perfect day for a wedding.

Her dress hung in the backseat next to Jimmy's suit. The two items next to each other projected an image of togetherness and belied the truth of this marriage. Hoping for the best, she clutched the bag containing her shoes, hairbrush, and other toiletries she needed to get ready to take this important step.

Jimmy's silence while he drove along the blacktop made her worry. What were his thoughts this morning? He'd been all smiles while they'd gotten their marriage license, but now his somber demeanor told a different story.

Kelsey wanted to break the silence, but she didn't know what to say. Would they sit around with nothing to talk about while they shared a house? Jimmy had agreed to stay at Mitch and Amanda's place, but Kelsey fretted that her request didn't make him happy. And what would their parents say? When did he plan to tell them?

Jimmy turned the car onto a winding lane lined with a mix of deciduous and evergreen trees along a fence.

"We're here. Are you ready to get married?"

"Yes." She wanted to ask the same of him, but she held the question in check. It would serve no purpose. She had made the decision, and she was going through with it. "You're sure it's okay for us to change here, right?"

He looked at her with a smile. "Absolutely. When I talked to Shirley, she was excited that we planned to do that. From what she said, they have occasional weddings at their house, and she loves to help the bride get ready. I hope you don't mind."

"I don't." Kelsey couldn't help thinking about Amanda's wedding and the people who had come to share her day.

A little ache crept into Kelsey's heart. She would have no family and friends to share this day. That was what she thought she'd wanted, but now loneliness inundated her. But she'd made this choice, and she would stick to it. Why was her every other thought a promise to follow through with her decision?

"I also told Davis about the vows we've written, and he said whatever we want is fine."

"Good." Kelsey stared straight ahead as the Queen Anne Victorian house came into view. The redbrick structure had a wraparound porch and high gables decorated with colorful spandrels and wooden shingles. "Oh wow! This is like a fairy-tale house with those gables and dormers."

"I thought you might like it, and wait until you see the inside." Jimmy slowed the car as they drew closer. "I haven't visited in years, but it looks the same as I remember. We used to have Cunningham reunions here in the summer."

The flower beds on either side of the walk overflowed with daffodils, lilies of the valley, hyacinths, and crocuses. Two tiered fountains in the middle of the flower beds gurgled and bubbled as the water cascaded from tier to tier. The sight filled her with delight as she retrieved her dress from the backseat "This place is huge, and the flowers are amazing."

With his suit slung over his shoulder, Jimmy pointed ahead. "Check out the leaded and stained glass surrounding the front door. When I was a little boy, it always reminded me of a church. I thought Cousin Davis must be a preacher."

Kelsey smiled at Jimmy's memories. With a feeling that her wedding wouldn't be totally void of ambience, Kelsey glanced at Jimmy as they went up the front walk. She wondered what he'd been like as a little boy. Even though he'd told her about his rivalry with Mitch, she still had a lot to learn about the man who was about to become her husband.

"You should've told me we were getting married in a fairy-tale house." Kelsey motioned toward the porch.

Jimmy raised his eyebrows. "I thought you didn't care."

Kelsey couldn't keep the impish smile from escaping. "I didn't think so either, until you mentioned Shirley helping me. I realized I'll miss having my family here."

Jimmy reached over and took her hand. "I wish this could be everything you want it to be."

Kelsey swallowed the lump in her throat as his touch made her heart beat faster. "It's okay. I made this choice, and you've been so willing to help me. I shouldn't complain."

"I don't consider it complaining." He squeezed her hand. "I just wanted you to know I understand."

"Are you sad that none of your family will be here?"

"Technically Davis and Shirley are family."

Kelsey frowned through her smile. "You know I meant your immediate family."

"Yeah. I know." Jimmy made a face. "I'm afraid my mom isn't going to be happy she's not here."

"I thought about that. I'm sorry." Kelsey hung her head. "I hope your mom won't be too upset. I want her to like me."

Jimmy put a finger under her chin and lifted her face until she was looking into his silver-gray eyes. "She likes you. You don't have to worry about that."

"I hope you're right." Kelsey sighed.

"I am. Now let's get ready to say 'I do.'"

Before they reached the steps, the front door opened, and a plump older woman with graying hair and a ready smile stepped onto the porch. "Jimmy, it's so good to see you and your lovely bride-to-be."

"Thanks, Ms. Shirley." Jimmy escorted Kelsey up the steps. "I'd like you to meet Kelsey."

Shirley grasped Kelsey's free hand in the same way Jimmy's mother had done. "Welcome. I hope we can make this a special day for you and Jimmy."

"Thanks." Kelsey hoped that, too. She wanted to look back on her wedding with happiness, not regret.

"I've put on my Sunday best." Shirley smoothed her pale-green chiffon dress with the embroidered matching jacket.

"Your dress is lovely," Kelsey said.

"You always look great." Jimmy gave Shirley a peck

on the cheek, then glanced around. "Where's the judge?"

Shirley motioned toward the house. "He's doing something in his study and will be out shortly. Let's go inside."

Shirley led the way as Kelsey and Jimmy followed her into a grand entrance hall, where a round Oriental rug with a pattern of navy, coral, and off-white colors lay on the dark-oak flooring. A small oval table with a marble top sat under a multitiered chandelier that sported creamy-white globes. Flowers from the yard made up an arrangement adorning the table.

"Your house is amazing." Kelsey took in the ornate columns that decorated the entrance to the living room on the left and a dining room to the right.

"Thanks." Shirley's face beamed. "It's been a pleasure to live in the house Davis grew up in. It was built in 1905."

"It must be awesome to have a family home like this."

As Kelsey looked toward the far end of the hall, a tall, broad-shouldered man with thinning white hair came into view. He slipped into a dark-gray suitcoat as his shiny black brogues clicked on the floor.

The man smiled broadly. "I see our bride and groom have arrived."

Jimmy stepped forward and extended his hand. "Good to see you, Judge."

"Good to see you, too, Jimmy. You can call me Davis." The older man smiled. "I know when you were a kid, your mama always made you call me Judge."

Laughing, Jimmy nodded. "She sure did, and old habits die hard."

"And who is this lovely lady?" Davis turned his attention to Kelsey.

Jimmy put a hand to Kelsey's back and guided her forward. "This is Kelsey Reynolds."

"Soon to be a Cunningham." Davis smiled as he took Kelsey's hand. "Jimmy's a lucky man to have such a lovely lady accept his proposal."

"I sure am." Jimmy put an arm around Kelsey's waist and pulled her close.

She looked up at him, her breath catching in her throat. He was pretending for Shirley and Davis. She had to prepare herself for the pretending in her future. But what would she do about the physical attraction to Jimmy that jumped out and grabbed her every time he touched her? She could give Jimmy the kind of marriage he wanted. No. She wanted real love, not just something physical. She thought she'd had love with Brandon, but she'd learned the hard way it was all a lie.

She should be thankful she and Jimmy would spend seven weeks apart.

"We'll have the ceremony right here in the front hall." Davis patted the marble top of the small table. "That way you'll have these lovely flowers as a backdrop."

"That'll be nice." Kelsey hadn't even thought about flowers. She had only thought of a no-frills way to say "I do." These simple touches made her wish for the real thing—a marriage built on love, not pretense.

"Kelsey, follow me, and I'll show you where you can change." Shirley's voice interrupted Kelsey's troubling thoughts. "Davis, I'll let you take care of Jimmy."

"Yes, dear." Davis kissed his wife on the cheek, then turned to Jimmy. "I want you to remember one thing. My daddy always told me, 'Happy wife, happy life.'"

Jimmy chuckled as he gazed at Kelsey. "I'll try to keep

that in mind."

Kelsey wasn't sure what to make of Jimmy's expression. Despite his jovial response to the advice, his eyes held a hint of sadness. A groom shouldn't be sad on his wedding day.

Trying to block the image of his sad eyes from her mind, Kelsey followed Shirley up the stairs on the left. A stained-glass window with colors the same as the Oriental rug looked down on the landing where the stairs turned in the opposite direction.

When Shirley reached the top of the stairs, she gestured to the right. "You can use the bedroom over here. It has its own bathroom. I'll be in the room across the hall. When you're finished getting ready, come knock on my door."

"Okay. Thanks." Kelsey scurried into the bedroom and hung her dress on the hook on the bathroom door.

Taking a moment, she surveyed the bedroom with pale-green walls. A cherry four-poster bed sported a lacy canopy that matched the floral bedspread of pinks and greens. A high chest sat along one wall, while a dresser occupied the opposite wall.

She closed the door and leaned against it while a cascade of emotions rushed through her mind like the water spilling over the fountains outside. She went to the window and looked out. The water sparkled in the sunlight. As far as she could see, tree-covered rolling hills surrounded the house. The scene painted a picture of peace, but peace escaped her. Her secret sin weighed her down.

But it wasn't a complete secret. God knew. Jimmy knew. And she knew. Despite her doubts, marrying Jimmy was the right thing to do. She would give her child a father and save another woman from heartache.

With those thoughts stamped on her mind, she went into the bathroom with its black-and-white tile and washed her face. She put on a little blusher and a hint of lipstick. She rarely used makeup, so her supply was limited. After applying mascara, she brushed her hair. Her dark tresses shone in the lighting around the mirror. She wished she knew how to wear her hair. Maybe Shirley could give her advice.

Finally Kelsey took her dress off the hanger and slipped it over her head. She stared at herself in the full-length mirror. The simplicity of the dress made her smile. She twirled around, her arms over her head like a ballet dancer. The skirt fluttered and came to rest around her calves. Hoping to make this a great day, she slipped on her peep-toe pumps and ventured across the hall.

Kelsey knocked on the door. "Shirley, I'm ready."

The door popped open, and Shirley stuck her head out. "Come in. Come in."

Kelsey ventured into the spacious bedroom with crown molding and hard-wood flooring. A king-sized bed with a brown-and-tan comforter and decorator pillows sat against one of the walls. "This is another beautiful room. Your house is amazing."

Shirley smiled as she patted Kelsey's shoulder. "I'm happy to share it with you on your special day."

"I really appreciate that." Kelsey wondered whether Shirley and Davis speculated about this wedding that included no family.

Shirley looked Kelsey over from head to toe. "You look lovely. Jimmy won't be able to take his eyes off you."

"Thanks, but I'm not sure what to do with my hair."

Kelsey pulled it up with one hand, then let it fall back to her shoulders.

"I think I have just what you need." Shirley waved Kelsey over to a small chest in the corner. "What do you think about putting this in your hair?"

Kelsey looked at the delicate headband made of little white flowers and pearls. "It's beautiful."

Shirley motioned to a small dressing table with a chair. "You can sit right there, and I'll work this into your hair."

"Okay." Kelsey sat on the padded chair and looked into the mirror.

Shirley stood behind Kelsey. "I can braid your hair and incorporate the headband into the braid. What do you think?"

"That sounds nice."

"Now you let me know if it's not to your liking. I won't be offended."

"I'm sure whatever you do will be just right."

Kelsey watched in amazement as Shirley expertly wove the headband into Kelsey's hair. The delicate flowers and pearls lay across the crown of her head, then trailed down the side, interwoven in the braids.

After Shirley finished, she stepped back and gazed at Kelsey. "So what do you think?"

Kelsey ran a hand along one of the braids as she surveyed her reflection. "I love it. Thanks so much."

"Jimmy won't know what hit him when he sees you." Shirley winked.

Laughing, Kelsey stood and hugged Shirley. "Thanks again."

A knock sounded on the door, and Shirley opened it a few inches. "Yes, dear. We're ready."

"Who was that?" Kelsey asked.

"Davis. He wanted to know when we're coming down. You're groom is getting anxious." Shirley went over to the armoire in the corner. "I've got one more thing for you."

Kelsey stood behind Shirley as she opened the armoire and reached inside. In a second she turned. "I made a small bouquet of lily of the valley and hyacinths from my flower beds, and I wove in a little ivy for greenery."

Kelsey took the bouquet, her heart bursting with joy. "You are so kind to do this."

"Oh, it's my pleasure. I love doing it." Shirley placed a hand over her heart. "I used to do interior design before I retired. This kind of thing is something I enjoy."

"You're making this day better than I had ever hoped for." Kelsey gave Shirley another hug. "Shall we go?"

Shirley went into the hall, opened a little cupboard recessed in the wall, then turned to Kelsey. "One of my grandsons set this up for me, so I can play music while you walk down the stairs. It lets Davis know you're coming. Is that okay?"

Kelsey nodded, then remembered the ring and note card on which she'd written her vows. She had left them in the bag with her toiletries. "I forgot something in the other room."

"Go get what you need. I'll wait to start the music until you're ready."

Kelsey hurriedly found the note card and the ring at the bottom of the bag, then folded it against the handle of her bouquet. She stepped back into the hallway, clutching the flowers and the ring in her hand.

This was almost like a real wedding. Almost.

"Ms. Shirley, will you hold the ring for me? I don't

have any place to put it."

"Certainly, my dear, and I'll hold your bouquet whenever you need me to."

"Thanks." Kelsey gave Shirley the ring.

The only thing missing was family, but she couldn't think about that now. She had to walk down the stairs so she could exchange vows with Jimmy—the vows that said nothing about love. Would Davis and Shirley notice?

"Go ahead." Shirley started the music.

Kelsey swallowed the lump in her throat and somehow made herself put one foot in front of the other as she walked toward the stairway. When she reached the first step, she clutched her bouquet tighter and stepped down. She couldn't see Jimmy or Davis until she came to the landing.

Jimmy stood there in his black suit, a boutonniere on his left lapel. As their gazes met, he smiled. Kelsey's heart beat a little faster with each step until she thought it might beat right out from under her rib cage. She gripped the bouquet as if it might save her from whatever she was feeling. Fear. Gratitude. Hopefulness.

When she reached Jimmy's side, he took her free hand. Warm and strong, his fingers enveloped her hand. She took a ragged breath and gave him a tentative smile.

Davis cleared his throat. "Jimmy and Kelsey, you have come here today to bind your lives together in marriage. Although I'm not a preacher, I'd like to read a couple of Scriptures. This first one is from Ecclesiastes 4:9–12. 'Two are better than one, because they have a good return for their labor: If either of them falls down, one can help the other up. But pity anyone who falls and has no one to help them up. Also, if two lie down together, they will keep warm. But how can one keep warm alone? Though one may be overpowered, two can defend themselves. A cord of three strands is not quickly broken.' Let these words be a reminder of how you will help each other in your marriage.

"The next Scripture is from Proverbs 18:22. 'He who finds a wife finds what is good and receives favor from the Lord.'

"Do you both come here today of your own free will?"

"Yes." Kelsey couldn't help thinking how the Scriptures fit their circumstances almost as if Davis knew the reason for their marriage.

"Yes." Jimmy squeezed her hand.

With a smile, Davis looked first at Jimmy, then Kelsey. "In marriage you make a commitment to each other. A strong marriage nurtures each of you as separate individuals and allows you to maintain your unique identity and grow in your own way through the years. Marriage allows each of you to become your best self while together you both become better than you ever could be alone.

"I understand that you have written your own vows and will exchange rings."

"Yes," Kelsey and Jimmy replied in chorus.

"Good. You may face each other." Davis's eyes twinkled as his smile broadened. "Jimmy, you may go first."

Shirley held out a hand to Kelsey. "Would you like me to take your bouquet?"

Kelsey nodded as she handed it to Shirley, then faced Jimmy.

Jimmy smiled down at her. His Adam's apple bobbed as he withdrew a familiar-looking note card from a pocket in his pants. His voice strong, he read the vows they had created in the mall parking lot. He paused for a moment and reached into his pocket again and brought out her ring. He set the note card on the marble-topped table.

"With these words, and this ring, I marry you and bind my life to yours." Jimmy took her left hand and placed the ring on her finger.

Warm from his touch, the ring encircled her finger, while his words, the words they had chosen, warmed her heart. Kindness radiated from his eyes.

Davis looked at Kelsey. "It's your turn now."

As Kelsey unfolded her note card, she hoped she could speak past the lump in her throat. She looked up at Jimmy, his eyes full of tenderness. Finally finding her voice, she read the familiar vows, which promised friendship, companionship, and support for each other. As she reached the last sentence, she looked over at Shirley, who handed Kelsey the ring. She took Jimmy's left hand and placed the ring on his finger, and he grasped both of her hands in his.

"By the power given to me by the state of Tennessee, I pronounce you husband and wife. You may now share your first kiss as husband and wife," Davis proclaimed.

First kiss. The words fluttered through Kelsey's brain. This was not only their first kiss as husband and wife. It was their first kiss ever. Her heart thundered. Wide eyed, she looked up at Jimmy and read the question in his eyes. She couldn't hesitate. They had to keep up the appearance of a couple in love.

Kelsey stood on her tiptoes as she put her arms around his neck and pulled him closer. He took the clue, and their lips met. He held her tight, and she melted into his embrace. The tenderness in his kiss matched the tenderness she'd seen in his eyes as she'd read her vows. The kiss had all the promise of a real marriage, but Kelsey couldn't let that happen. She didn't want him to hope too much that she would change her mind about the reality of this marriage.

When the kiss ended, Kelsey didn't meet Jimmy's gaze. She was afraid her eyes would convey how much the kiss affected her. The kiss left her feeling cherished, almost loved, but then she'd been fooled by kisses before—kisses that were all lies. She didn't want to be taken for a fool again.

Davis shook Jimmy's hand and hugged Kelsey. Shirley hugged Jimmy and Kelsey, her face beaming.

Shirley patted her chest. "That was a lovely ceremony, and now I'd like to take some photos, if that's okay with you. I already snapped a few during the ceremony."

Jimmy glanced over at Kelsey. "Okay?"

Kelsey nodded, still remembering that kiss.

"Wonderful! Let's go into the living room. I'll take a couple of pictures of you standing together in front of the window." Shirley ushered them into the room.

Jimmy held out his hand for Kelsey. She took his hand as he led her to stand in front of the drapery-covered window that looked out on the porch and yard beyond. They stood arm in arm for a couple of photos.

"Now let's have another kiss." Shirley waved her phone at them. "Never too many of those."

Kelsey's heart hammered at the thought of kissing Jimmy again, but it had to be done to keep up the pretense. She thought she would be better prepared this time, but his second kiss made her heart beat faster than the first. Everything was better the second time around. When the kiss ended, he smiled down at her, as if he knew what she was thinking. His kisses could only be described as sweet, intoxicating, and dangerous. Oh my! Was she in trouble!

Then Shirley proceeded to drag them from room to room, taking photos and insisting on more kisses. Kelsey breathed a sigh of relief when Davis asked them to sign the marriage license, rescuing them from Shirley's photo taking.

After they signed the license, Shirley stepped their way. "I've prepared a little lunch. I hope you will join us."

Jimmy glanced Kelsey's way. "What do you think? Will Dolly be okay?"

"Who's Dolly?" Shirley asked.

"A dog. I've been taking care of the dog that belongs to my sister and brother-in-law." Kelsey wasn't going to mention that they were on their honeymoon. There would be no honeymoon for her and Jimmy. "I think she'll be okay since we left her in the kennel with water."

"Good news then!" Shirley turned to Davis. "Take our bride and groom to the dining room, and I'll get the food."

"Do you need help?" Kelsey asked.

"Oh, no. I've got everything ready." Shirley scurried off.

Davis smiled after his wife. "I'm so glad you could stay. She loves doing this and would've been disappointed if you couldn't have joined us. I keep telling her she shouldn't spring surprises on our newlyweds, but she never listens."

Kelsey and Jimmy sat where Davis indicated. Then he held open the swinging door as Shirley wheeled a serving cart into the room. The cart held plates with little sandwiches and a salad. A small cake sat to one side.

When everyone was seated, Davis held out his hands.

"I'll say a blessing for the food and your marriage. Dear Lord, we ask your blessing on this food. Be with Jimmy and Kelsey as they start their lives together. Bless their marriage. Amen."

Kelsey raised her head and produced an uncertain smile. Jimmy was her husband. That fact hardly seemed real, and she wondered how God could bless a marriage built on a false pretense. But she wouldn't fret over that while they ate their lunch. Kelsey grinned at Jimmy when she stabbed a radish in her salad and paused a second before putting it into her mouth. He grinned back. Was this what marriage involved—shared secrets?

They shared a big one. Would it be their undoing? Kelsey hoped not. She truly hoped they would fall in love—that this marriage could be real in every sense, but that would depend on love. Love was the key.

After they finished eating, Shirley brought out a silver knife tied with a white ribbon and insisted they cut the cake and feed each other, just as any bride and groom would do at their wedding reception.

When they were done, Shirley wrapped the leftover cake and handed it to Kelsey. "Put it in the freezer, and eat it on your first anniversary. I'll also email the photos to you."

"Thank you for everything. This was so much more than I had expected." Kelsey hugged both Shirley and Davis.

Jimmy shook Davis's hand and hugged Shirley. "We'd better get going to take care of that dog."

"I brought your things down from upstairs. They're sitting by the door." Shirley grinned from ear to ear. "Thanks for letting us make your day special. It's always so much fun for me. It does these old bones good to share in a wedding."

Davis and Shirley walked with Kelsey and Jimmy out to the car, and Shirley threw a little birdseed into the air as Kelsey and Jimmy got into the car. The older couple stood in the drive and waved as Jimmy drove away.

Kelsey waved back, while her emotions wavered between happiness and worry. This marriage meant she wouldn't have to be a single mother. She wouldn't have to explain to her father why she was pregnant and unmarried. But they had to explain to a host of family and friends why they had eloped.

That challenge loomed in their future—a future that held pitfalls at every turn.

CHAPTER EIGHT

While Jimmy drove back to Pineydale, the wedding ring on his left hand sparkled in the sunlight beaming through the car window. He glanced over at Kelsey. A shy smile curved her mouth.

"How does it feel to be Mrs. James Madison Cunningham the Third?"

She shrugged "About the same as being Kelsey Reynolds."

"Are you ready to make it more real by telling my family?" Jimmy wished it were real in every sense, but he had made a bargain with Kelsey. He intended to keep that bargain, even though her sweet kisses made it difficult not to wish things were different.

Kelsey sighed. "I suppose we have to do that, but not until we take Dolly for a walk."

"Maybe we should walk over to my mom's house with Dolly. It's not that far."

"You think that'll give us time to figure out what we're going to say?" Kelsey's nervous laughter punctuated her worry.

"We'll just tell her we got married."

Kelsey frowned at him. "And you think she won't have questions? We need to be on the same page with our answers."

Jimmy gripped the steering wheel tighter. Would he have to field a lot of questions from his mom? He was hoping she would just accept the marriage and be happy for him. "How about if I answer my mom's questions and you take a clue from that. Then you deal with your dad's questions, and I'll take a clue from your answers to him."

"Trying to avoid dealing with my dad?"

Jimmy raised his eyebrows. "You figured that out, huh?"

"Well, I have kind of painted him as a bit of an ogre." Kelsey wrinkled her nose.

Jimmy's heart thudded as he took in her expression. Still in her wedding attire, she was a picture of loveliness. He could see himself falling in love with Kelsey. Would she follow suit?

He couldn't deny the physical attraction, and he was sure she felt it too. But that wasn't love. How did a person know when they were in love? He thought he'd been in love with Whitney, but he wasn't sure about that either now. Would he figure it out in time? Would Kelsey? He had to pray they would.

"What do you think your dad will say?"

A little pucker appeared between Kelsey's eyebrows. "He might yell, but if we do a video call, he might temper his reaction."

"Or he might wish he could reach through the screen and wring my neck."

"But he can't do that, can he?" Kelsey laughed as she reached over and touched his arm.

Jimmy's heart stuttered. Would he have to ask her not to touch him, or would he just deal with his reaction to her touch?

"How have you been feeling?"

"You mean the nausea?"

Jimmy nodded, hoping he wasn't asking something he shouldn't. How was he supposed to navigate through a marriage built on a bargain? "You seemed okay today."

"I was sick this morning before you came to pick me up." Her face brightened as she gazed at him. "But I've been okay since then. It's better than feeling nauseous all day long like I was the day of Amanda's wedding."

He guessed she was about a month along, but he could be wrong. "I asked whether you've seen a doctor, but you never told me. You didn't want to talk about it the night of the reception."

Kelsey hung her head as she twisted her hands in her lap. "I haven't seen a doctor. I just kept hoping the pregnancy test was wrong. But when the nausea started the day of Amanda's wedding, I could see the handwriting on the wall."

"Do you want to see someone here?"

Kelsey shook her head. "I'll see a doctor in Pullman when I get back to school. I can find a doctor here when I return."

"Guess that sounds like the best thing to do."

"Yeah."

Pulling into the drive at Mitch's house, Jimmy wished this could be a happy time for Kelsey. He remembered how excited his sisters had been when they found out they were pregnant. Maybe once the baby arrived, Kelsey would feel differently.

Kelsey took out the keys and unbuckled her seat belt almost before he stopped the car. "Gotta take care of Dolly."

Jimmy strode up the walk behind her. She had the door open in seconds and raced to the basement, where Dolly lay in the kennel. He stood halfway down the stairs as Kelsey opened the kennel, and the dog bounded out wiggling from head to tail and licking Kelsey's face.

Kelsey laughed as she grabbed the leash. "Hold still, girl, so I can get this on you. Then we can go out."

"Need some help?"

Kelsey looked up at him almost as if surprised to see him. "I've got it."

In a second she joined him on the stairs, and they walked outside together. Dolly did her business as soon as she hit the yard.

"Good dog, Dolly." Kelsey leaned over and patted the pup's head. "You're a super dog, and for a reward you get to go visiting. How about that?"

Dolly barked as if she knew exactly what Kelsey had said. She laughed, and Jimmy's stomach churned. He tried to tell himself that the thought of telling his mom about their marriage had his insides churning, but he couldn't deny that a cute little woman still in her wedding clothes had him tied in knots.

Kelsey looked at him, and his pulse skyrocketed. Living with this woman wouldn't be easy, but he had seven weeks to work on a shield against her charms. He wasn't going to let a woman rule his life like he'd done with Whitney. Or was he? Kelsey's warm heart, sweet kisses, and vulnerability already had him ready to follow her around just like Dolly did. Truth be told, Kelsey already had a leash around his heart. He wanted to be her hero. Now and forever.

"I'd better call my mom to let her know we're coming

over." Jimmy pulled his phone from his pocket.

"Yeah, that would be good. It would be a double whammy to show up unannounced and spring this marriage on her, too."

Jimmy punched the screen on his phone. A bubble popped up announcing an email from Shirley. He looked over at Kelsey. "We've got mail."

"We do?" Kelsey walked Dolly over to him and leaned in as she looked at his phone. "Our photos?"

"Let's see." Jimmy tapped the screen, and several emails with attachments appeared.

Kelsey moved even closer. "Let me see."

Trying not to let her nearness affect him, he opened an attachment. A photo of Kelsey putting the ring on his finger showed on the phone. "Maybe we should look through these before we go see my mom."

"We can look at them on my tablet." Kelsey tugged on Dolly's leash. "Come on, Dolly. We've got pictures to look at."

After they were inside, Kelsey retrieved her tablet from the bedroom.

Jimmy joined Kelsey on the couch, thinking about the few days they would share this house before she left for school. He didn't look forward to treating her like one of his sisters, but maybe that was his only choice.

"Here's the tablet." Kelsey handed it to him.

In seconds he brought up the email attachments. "Do you want me to download these onto your tablet?"

She smiled. "That would be great. It's something I can show Amanda after she gets back."

Jimmy stopped and looked at her. He'd been so worried about parent reactions that he hadn't even thought about what Amanda and Mitch would say or his own brother and sisters. "How do you think she'll react?"

"I hope she'll be happy." A little pucker appeared between Kelsey's eyebrows. "I always got the impression she liked you."

Jimmy laughed. "I'm not so sure about that. I did tell you she blew off my attempts to date her when she first came to town."

"Yeah, but just because she didn't want to date you doesn't mean she doesn't like you."

"Just because she likes me doesn't mean she'll like the idea of her little sister marrying me, especially since you've only known me four days."

"We met last October. So technically we've known each other for five months."

Jimmy grinned. "Does that mean we've been having a secret relationship for all this time?"

Kelsey's eyes widened. "We don't have to say that. Just remind them that we've known each other that long. Maybe that will lessen their surprise."

Jimmy sighed. "Somehow I think not, but I'll let you handle your sister."

"And my dad."

"Remember, I have two sisters and a brother, too."

Kelsey gazed at him. "Maybe you should have a family meeting rather than just talking to your mom. What do you think?"

"Good idea. That would make it easier than telling everyone individually." Jimmy leaned back on the couch and rubbed a hand down his face. "Too bad you won't be here Sunday night when mom has her weekly dinner."

"I don't think we should wait that long."

"Yeah. You're right."

"What about inviting your family over to your place for supper tonight? Do you think they could make it on short notice?"

"Probably, but remember, I don't cook, and neither do you." Jimmy grinned.

"We can order pizza or something. I do know how to make a salad." Kelsey's brow wrinkled in a question.

"Okay." Jimmy wanted to hug Kelsey in the worst way, but he stood up and walked to the other side of the room to keep from acting on the thought. "I'll give them a call and see what happens."

Jimmy punched his mom's name on his phone. When she answered, his stomach had that sinking sensation, but it soon subsided when she accepted his invitation without question. His sisters weren't quite so eager, but he convinced them by saying he had an important announcement he wanted to share with the family. Jeremy was an immediate yes. He was always on the lookout for free food.

Jimmy looked up at Kelsey as he pocketed his phone. "Okay. They're all coming."

"That's good, and it's a good thing you're done talking on the phone."

Jimmy frowned at her. "Why?"

"Because you were about to wear a path in the carpet with your pacing." Kelsey waved a finger back and forth.

Jimmy imitated her as he smiled. "We have to go shopping because there's nothing in my fridge except some expired milk and a few soft drinks. Maybe some moldy cheese."

"That sounds really bad." Kelsey hopped up from the

couch. "Is the store close enough for us to walk?"

Jimmy gave her an indulgent look. "I suppose that means we're taking Dolly for a walk?"

"You're a pretty good mind reader."

"I just know your mind when it comes to that dog." Jimmy wished he could read her mind, but maybe not. He might not like what he learned. "I've got a better idea."

"What's that?"

Jimmy held out his hands as he glanced down at himself. "I don't want to traipse all over town in my suit. You change, then we'll walk the dog to my house, where I can change, then walk back here to drop off the dog. Then I drive to the store."

"That's an excellent plan. You're a very smart man, Jimmy Cunningham."

"Thanks." *Aren't you glad you married me?* Jimmy pressed his lips together to keep the words from popping out of his mouth. He didn't want to witness any hesitation in her answer. He would just glory in her praise. Right at this moment she made him feel important, needed, and gallant. He didn't want to ruin those feelings by asking that question.

"I'll go change, but do you think it'll be okay to keep the headband? I hate to ruin Shirley's braids." Kelsey raised her eyebrows.

"Do whatever makes you happy."

When she returned wearing an off-white sweater, a pair of jeans, and those hot-pink tennis shoes, he couldn't take his eyes off her. She was his wife, and he wanted to make her happy and be her hero. He might not know much else, but he knew that one thing.

***

"My mother will be impressed with your decorating skills."

Kelsey turned at the sound of Jimmy's voice. Her heart did a little flip-flop as he came closer to where she stood in the kitchen eating area. "All I did was set the table and put a vase of flowers on it. What everyone should really love is this table. Have you shown it to your family yet?"

Jimmy shook his head. "Because I'm still renovating, I never invite people over. So this is a first. I think that's why everyone accepted the invite."

Kelsey fingered one of the placemats on the table. Her heart thudded at the prospect of facing Jimmy's family and announcing their marriage. She prayed they wouldn't hate her for the hasty nuptial.

"You don't have to look so tortured. Everything will be fine. The lasagna and garlic bread are in the oven. The salad's in the fridge, complete with radishes."

Kelsey laughed. "The radishes definitely make it complete."

"For sure. We're ready to entertain." Jimmy put an arm around her shoulders. "Good call on getting the garlic bread and lasagna out of the freezer section at the grocery. Better than pizza. It'll seem more like a home-cooked meal."

"Thanks. I'm glad you agreed with my idea." Kelsey tried to smile, but her nerves still stood on edge.

A pretend home-cooked meal. Just like their marriage. This marriage was right for her, but she fretted that it wasn't right for Jimmy, even though he was the one who'd suggested it. The way he touched her and the kisses they'd shared for Davis and Shirley's benefit told Kelsey that Jimmy would gladly make this a real marriage. And his kisses scored at the top, if there was such a thing as a kiss meter.

Kelsey wanted to think about something else, anything else. She would get through these remaining days until she went back to school. Then she'd have seven weeks to figure out how she would deal with the bargain they'd made.

Kelsey glanced at the clock on the microwave. Less than an hour before everyone would arrive. "Do you want to announce our marriage first thing or get everyone eating and then tell them?"

"What do you think?"

Kelsey shrugged. "You know your family better than I do. You decide."

"I wish I could say I knew how they'd react."

"I wish I knew how they'd react, too." Kelsey eyed Jimmy. "Getting nervous? I know I am."

"Yeah. I'm nervous." Jimmy grinned at her. "I don't know why."

"Because I don't know what they'll say. I don't want your family to be angry with me."

"My family won't be angry. Surprised. Shocked. Speechless." Jimmy wrinkled his brow. "Probably one of those."

"I have an idea." Kelsey raced into the great room and retrieved her tablet. "Let's call my dad and practice on him."

An incredulous expression spread across Jimmy's face. "You want to practice on your dad?"

"Yeah." Kelsey punched at the tablet screen. "We can

do a video call with him. He'll be at work, and he won't be able to yell."

"I'm not believing you." Jimmy narrowed his gaze.

"It'll be better this way. We do it, and then I don't have to think about it anymore. Like ripping off a bandage. Get it over quickly."

Jimmy gripped the back of the nearby chair. "Okay. If that's what you want to do."

"I do." She punched the screen again, and a ringtone sounded through the kitchen.

"Kelsey." Grady's voice came over the speaker. "This is a surprise. Is everything all right?"

"Yeah, Dad." Her heart racing, Kelsey looked at Jimmy over the top of the screen. "I've got something I need to tell you."

"What's that?" The video conveyed the concern on her dad's face. "You didn't have a car wreck, did you?"

"No, nothing like that." Kelsey motioned for Jimmy to join her. "It's good news."

Jimmy looked apprehensive as he put a hand on one side of the tablet, his face coming into the picture in the corner of the video. "Hi, Mr. Reynolds. It's Jimmy Cunningham."

"Well, hello, Jimmy." A question sounded in Grady's voice. "Mitch's cousin, right?"

Jimmy nodded. "Good memory."

"As I recall, you spent a good portion of the wedding reception dancing with Kelsey."

"That's correct, sir." Jimmy put an arm around Kelsey's waist and pulled her closer.

"I'm glad you noticed that, Dad, because Jimmy and I got married today." Leaning on Jimmy for support, Kelsey held her breath.

The blank expression on her dad's face did nothing to quiet Kelsey's nerves. Silence. Dead air. Nothing. His non-response made everything worse.

"Dad?" Kelsey almost wished he'd yell. At least she'd know what he thought.

"Married, not engaged, but married?" The words came out of Grady's mouth in a slow, measured way, as if he was trying to contain his agitation.

"Yeah, married."

"Why couldn't you have waited until the end of the semester?" Grady's voice didn't have a hint of anger, despite his facial expression, which told a different story.

"We discussed it, and we didn't want to wait." Kelsey swallowed hard. "I'm coming home just as planned. I'll finish school. As soon as the semester's over, I'll be moving here to be with Jimmy. I've already checked into finishing my degree at East Tennessee State."

"At least you thought of that much." Grady paused. "Jimmy, since Kelsey's your wife, the rest of her schooling is on you. She's off my payroll."

"Yes, sir. Kelsey told me you'd say that. We've got that worked out, too. I'm starting a new job, and it has good benefits. Kelsey and I plan to pay for the rest of her college."

Kelsey detected a little surprise in her father's expression. "Dad, I hope you'll be happy for us."

Again, silence.

Grady sighed. "I'd be happier if you'd waited and let me walk you down the aisle, but what's done is done. So I'll see you when you get home."

"Okay, Dad." Kelsey felt like telling him how much

money she'd saved him by eloping, but she figured he wasn't in the mood to hear that. "See you Sunday."

"Jimmy, you'd better be good to my little girl."

"You can count on that, sir. Goodbye." Jimmy moved away, letting go of the tablet.

"Bye, Dad. I love you."

"Love you, too, Kelsey." The call ended.

With a heavy sigh, Kelsey sank down on the nearby chair. "That went better than I thought it would."

"I think you had a good idea about calling him at work." Jimmy released a low whistle. "I believe the anger was just below the surface."

Kelsey grimaced. "I hope that's gone by the time I get home."

Jimmy put a hand on her shoulder. "He's not going to be angry with his little girl. It's her big, bad husband your dad isn't happy with."

"It'll work out." Kelsey made the statement, wishing she knew that as a fact. "Your family's next. What's your plan?"

"I'm going to wing it."

Kelsey frowned. "Do you think that's a good idea?"

"I do." Jimmy grabbed the hot pads from the counter. "I'm going to check the stuff in the oven."

"Do you have any idea what you're checking for?" Kelsey wished he'd figure a plan for his family, but he obviously didn't want to discuss it.

Jimmy laughed. "I think if it's bubbling, that's good."

They gazed into the oven, where the big pan of lasagna indeed bubbled away at the edges.

Kelsey stared at the open oven. "So would you say it's done?"

"Let's turn off the oven but leave the lasagna in there until everyone gets here. What do you think?" Jimmy laid the oven mitts on the counter.

"Sounds okay to me." Kelsey shut the oven door. "When do you think they'll get here?"

Jimmy pointed to the clock on the stove. "Five minutes? Give or take."

"Waiting is making me nervous."

Jimmy stepped closer and took her hands in his. "It went pretty well with your dad. Isn't that a good sign things will go okay with my family?"

"Yeah, but my dad wasn't in the same room with us."

Before Jimmy could respond, the doorbell rang.

"Sounds like your wait is over."

Kelsey blew out a harsh breath. "Ready if you are."

"I'll get the door." Jimmy strode across the room and glanced out the sidelight. "Looks like they're all here at once."

Kelsey didn't know if that was good or bad. Her stomach roiled, and a lightheaded sensation hit her. Those feelings had nothing to do with her pregnancy and everything to do with facing her in-laws. She had in-laws. Sisters-in-law. Brother-in-law. Mother-in-law. Her knees wobbly, Kelsey grabbed the back of the nearby chair.

When Jimmy opened the door, his family flooded into the room like a wave of human happiness. Kelsey prayed they'd still be happy when they learned of Jimmy's marriage. The little boys grabbed on to Jimmy, and he dragged them around the room while they clung to his legs, their squeals of delight filling the air.

Kelsey hung back in the eating area at the far end of the kitchen as coats, toys, and a pile of paraphernalia collected on the couch in the great room. Everyone seemed to talk at once, exclaiming over the work Jimmy had done on his house.

Finally, Jimmy produced a shrill whistle. The room grew quiet, and Janelle looked in Kelsey's direction.

Janelle smiled. "Kelsey, I didn't know you were here."

Everyone turned and looked at Kelsey. Warmth radiated across her face. She was sure a blush colored her cheeks. She gave a little wave as Jimmy hurried to her side.

Before Jimmy could open his mouth, Janelle squealed as she raced toward them. "I don't believe it. You guys got married."

A cacophony of voices filled the room as Janelle pointed to their ring-clad hands. Her heart racing, Kelsey stared at Jimmy's family, who stared back at her.

"I knew something big was up when Jimmy invited us over for supper." Jeremy clapped Jimmy on the back. "Congratulations, big brother."

Kelsey took in the exchange between the brothers. At least one member of the family seemed happy about the marriage. Although Janelle was excited to point out that they were married, Kelsey couldn't tell whether her new sister-in-law approved. Then there was Mary. Kelsey was afraid to look in Mary's direction.

Jeremy enveloped Kelsey in a big hug. "Welcome to the family."

"Thanks." Kelsey stepped back, still afraid to look at anyone else.

"Jimmy." Mary's voice sounded strained.

Kelsey looked over at her husband as Mary looped her arm through his. She didn't look happy.

"Yes, ma'am?" Jimmy's expression held concern.

"Why didn't you include your family when you got married?" Mary raised her eyebrows.

Jimmy's Adam's apple bobbed as he looked down at his mother. "Because I thought you'd think we were too impulsive and try to talk us out of it."

Mary eyed him. "True. I might have, but in the end I would like to have been there for my son's wedding."

Jimmy hugged Mary. "I wish you could've been there, too, but I want you to be happy for us."

Kelsey wanted to shrink away somewhere. Had she made a big, big mistake? Mary didn't seem happy about anything. Would Jimmy's family begin to suspect that this marriage was even crazier than they first thought once they realized there was no declaration of love? Kelsey had thought dealing with her dad would be hard, but this was much harder.

Mary stepped out of Jimmy's embrace and looked over at Kelsey. She swallowed hard as Mary drew nearer. *Please, Lord, don't let her hate me.* Kelsey tried to smile. What could she say to this woman who was now her mother-in-law?

Before Mary could say anything to Kelsey, Jimmy stepped closer and put an arm around her waist, pulling her close. "We've got some photos for you to see."

"That's not the same as being there." Mary focused her attention on Kelsey.

Despite Jimmy's support, Kelsey couldn't rid herself of the crushing sensation in her chest. Mary wasn't happy. Kelsey didn't want to cry, but tears threatened. Those stupid pregnancy hormones worked overtime on her emotions. Blinking rapidly, she tried to keep the tears from coming. She couldn't let these people know she was upset.

Jimmy stepped away from Kelsey and inserted himself between her and his mother as he confronted her. "Mom, I take the blame entirely. It was my idea to call Grandpa's cousin Davis to marry us."

Mary's sigh revealed her displeasure. "I'm not trying to blame anyone, but this is very disappointing."

"Please just be happy for us." Jimmy's voice projected frustration.

"How can I be happy when you've run off and gotten married without telling anyone?" Mary's frown spelled out her disapproval more than anything she said.

Slowly backing up, Kelsey wished she could make everyone except Jimmy disappear. Everything had seemed wonderful when it was just the two of them. Or maybe she should just disappear. She wanted to run away, far away. Thankfully, she would be back in school in a few days and wouldn't have to deal with any of this.

While Jimmy tried to soothe his mother's displeasure, Kelsey shuffled back toward the corner. If she could escape, she would. She spied the back door. With one swift move, she raced out the door, across the yard as tears dampened her cheeks. She was tired of making the wrong decisions. Hoping against hope that Jimmy's family would welcome her and this sudden marriage with open arms was another big blunder.

CHAPTER NINE

The door slammed, and Jimmy turned around. His stomach sank. Kelsey had left. He whirled back toward his mother. "I hope you're happy now."

Jimmy didn't wait for his mother's response. He sped out the door. He had to find Kelsey. She didn't have her jacket, and it had cooled off considerably since this afternoon. It was still daylight, so he should be able to find her and apologize. He couldn't believe he'd been wrong about his mother's reaction.

He just didn't understand why his mom, who was usually so kind, had made Kelsey feel so bad that she'd left. Standing in the driveway, he looked up and down the street. No sign of her. How could she have gotten so far in so little time? He debated about looking for her on foot versus driving his car.

Then he realized he couldn't get his car out of the garage anyway, because everyone else's car blocked him in. Just as he was about to go back into the house to ask Jeremy for his car keys, he came out the front door.

"Jimmy, let's take my car to find her." Jeremy held up his keys.

"Little brother, you read my mind." Jimmy hopped into the passenger side as the engine of Jeremy's car roared to life.

Jeremy backed out of the driveway, then glanced at Jimmy. "Which way do you think we should go?"

"Toward Mitch's place." Jimmy wondered what Jeremy was thinking. His brother was the only one who'd congratulated him on the marriage. "What's going on with Mom? I couldn't believe how negative she was."

Jeremy frowned as he turned at the end of the block. "Got me. I'm just glad you decided to go after what you wanted. I was a little shocked that you guys got married so soon, but I'm happy for you."

"Thanks." Jimmy rubbed the back of his neck. "I knew everyone would be shocked, but I thought their reaction would be like yours. Stunned, but happy for us."

They fell silent as Jeremy drove all the way to Mitch's place without seeing Kelsey. Jimmy could only think that this marriage was going to be hard enough without having some in his family reluctant to accept it. He hadn't counted on that. He'd expected it from Kelsey's family, not his own.

Jeremy stopped the car in front of the house. With an arm slung over the steering wheel, he looked at Jimmy. "I don't think she could've gotten this far on foot without us seeing her. Could she have stopped somewhere between your place and here?"

"I don't know, but I'm going to check the house just to be sure." Jimmy slid out of the car.

"Check the garage to see if she by some chance got here and took one of the cars," Jeremy called out.

"I will." Jimmy strode up the front walk. He rang the doorbell and knocked on the door. "Kelsey, are you in there?"

No answer, but Dolly's bark sounded from inside.

Reasonably sure Kelsey wasn't in the house, Jimmy peeked into the garage through the small windows near the top of the garage door. Both vehicles were still parked inside. So Kelsey was on foot wherever she was. That conclusion didn't make him any happier.

Jimmy jogged back to Jeremy's car and got in. "Charlotte's. Maybe she headed over there. That's in the opposite direction and would explain why we haven't seen her."

"I'm headed that way." Jeremy maneuvered the car away from the curb.

The musical tones of Jimmy's phone filled the car. He pulled the phone from his pocket and looked at the screen. Janelle. "Hey."

"Have you found her?" Janelle asked.

"No."

"Mom's sorry."

"I'm sure she is, but that's not going to help us right now. I'll call you when we find Kelsey. In the meantime, you guys can go ahead and eat. There's stuff in the oven and a salad in the fridge."

"Are you sure?"

"Yeah, otherwise everything will be cold."

"But you won't get to eat."

"I'm not thinking about eating right now. This is not the way I expected the evening to go. Talk to you later." Jimmy ended the call.

"Janelle?" Jeremy glanced Jimmy's way.

"Yeah. Trying to smooth feathers." Jimmy pocketed his phone.

Jimmy fretted the whole way to Charlotte's house. Even when he found Kelsey, could he persuade her to come back to his place? He despaired she wouldn't want to face his family. Could he blame her?

After getting out of the car, Jimmy raced to Charlotte's front door. He rang the bell and waited. She couldn't have gotten this far on foot, but maybe she would show up while he talked to Charlotte.

"Jimmy and Jeremy. Come in. Come in. What a nice surprise." Charlotte stepped aside as she motioned toward the back of the house. "Would you like to join me? I was just sitting down to eat."

Jimmy shook his head. "Thanks, Aunt Charlotte, but we're looking for Kelsey. Have you seen her?"

"No. I thought she might come over today for tea, but she didn't come." Charlotte frowned. "Is something wrong?"

Jimmy held out his left hand. "Kelsey and I got married today. That's why she didn't come over for tea."

"Oh my! Even though I've been thinking you two would make a good pair, it's still a surprise." Charlotte placed a hand over her heart as a little frown formed on her face. "If you just got married, why are you searching for her?"

Feeling as though a large hand was squeezing his heart, Jimmy recounted the scene at his house. "So she took off, and we can't find her. I don't understand my mother."

"Come sit down. I might have an explanation." Charlotte gestured toward the living room.

Jimmy didn't move. "Aren't we keeping you from your supper?"

"It's warming in the oven."

Jimmy followed behind Jeremy as he sat on the couch with Charlotte. Jimmy tried to tell himself he'd find Kelsey one way or another. She would eventually go back to Mitch and Amanda's place because she wouldn't neglect Dolly. He was probably wasting time here rather than waiting at Mitch's, but he would hear what Charlotte had to say. "So what's your theory about Mom?"

Charlotte sat next to him and patted his hand. "Your sweet mother is probably remembering your dad today more than usual, and your marriage brought this to mind."

"But why today?" Jimmy knit his brow.

"You obviously don't know this story. Probably for good reason, your parents never mentioned it."

"Mentioned what?"

"Thirty-four years ago today, when your mom was eighteen and still in high school, she ran off with your dad and planned to get married."

Jimmy raised his eyebrows. "But they had an August anniversary."

"You're right. They never got married that day because your mother's parents caught wind of what Mary and Jim were planning and stopped the whole thing."

"Wow!" Jimmy ran a hand through his hair. "I can't believe none of us kids ever knew about this."

Charlotte rubbed her chin. "I suspect it's something they didn't want to talk about, especially since they eventually got married in a beautiful ceremony in the church the Cunninghams have been part of for decades. They had a wonderful, happy marriage and four great kids, and there was never a need to talk about that failed elopement."

Jimmy frowned. "But you'd think Mom would understand better about our marriage, having gone through that experience."

"What I'm thinking is she was eventually glad her parents stopped her. As I said, they had a wonderful wedding, and they started their marriage with the full support of their families, rather than running off and getting married." Charlotte bobbed her head. "And I think your surprise marriage brought back those memories and made her miss your daddy even more. It's hard to lose a spouse. I miss my Wilbur so much."

"I know you do." Jimmy didn't miss the tears that sparkled in Charlotte's eyes. He scooted over on the couch until he was sitting next to her. He hugged her. "Thanks for sharing that story."

"I hope your mom won't be upset that I did."

"The only person she's upset with now is me." Jimmy closed his eyes and sighed, then opened them again. "Do you have any ideas about where I might find Kelsey?"

"I wish I did." Sympathy radiated from Charlotte's eyes. "If I were you, I'd go back to Mitch's place and wait for her to show up. What do you think, Jeremy?"

"Yes, ma'am. I agree." Jeremy stood. "Big brother, we should be on our way and let Charlotte have her supper. We've got a stakeout to attend."

Charlotte walked Jimmy and Jeremy to the door. They each hugged her.

Jimmy opened the door. "Thanks again, Aunt Charlotte. Everything makes a little more sense now that we've talked to you."

Charlotte patted his shoulder. "Glad I could help. Let me know that you've found Kelsey. If she happens to show up here, I'll be sure to let you know. And I'll be praying for ya'll."

"Okay, thanks." Jimmy held open the door for Jeremy.

Back in the car, Jimmy wished he knew how to handle this situation. When he did find Kelsey, what could he say to her? He was sure he'd find her. He just didn't know how she would react. As Jeremy drove back to Mitch's, Jimmy closed his eyes and prayed. Or at least, he tried to pray. He wasn't sure what to pray for. He thought Kelsey's agreement to get married was an answer to his prayers. Now helplessness inundated his thoughts.

"We're here." Jeremy brought the car to a stop in Mitch's driveway.

Jimmy opened his eyes and looked at the house in the waning light, an ache filling his chest. "I'll go check again."

"Before you go, do you think Mitch has a spare key hidden somewhere? Then you could check inside for sure."

Jimmy hated the thought that Kelsey wouldn't answer the door if she was there, but he couldn't dismiss that possibility. "I don't know, but I could check around if there's no answer."

Once again, Jimmy knocked, rang the bell, and called out to Kelsey. Still no answer, only Dolly's bark. He looked in the obvious places for a spare key. Under the mat. In the flowerpot. Under the bricks lining the flower bed. No key.

Jimmy trudged back to the car and got inside. "I say we wait for fifteen minutes. If she doesn't show up by then, we should go back to my house."

Jeremy nodded. "Sounds good to me."

Jimmy's mind whirled with what-ifs. Could something have happened to Kelsey? They lived in a safe little town, but it was as if she'd completely vanished. Could she have hitched a ride with someone she knew or, at worst, someone she didn't know? She didn't have anything with her. She'd left without her purse, her tablet, and her jacket.

Jimmy hit the heel of his hand on his forehead. "I know where she is."

"Where?"

"She didn't take a thing with her. She couldn't get into Mitch's house because her purse is still at my house, and her keys are in her purse."

"So where is she?"

Relief washed over Jimmy as he smiled at his brother. "I'm sure she's back in my workshop. That's the only explanation as to why we didn't see her anywhere. Drive back to my house."

"I hope you're right." Jeremy headed the car toward Jimmy's place.

"Me, too."

Almost before Jeremy had the car stopped at the curb, Jimmy jumped out and ran through the backyard to the workshop. He was ninety-nine percent sure she was here, but that one percent made him hesitate before he went inside. "Lord, please let her be here."

With that prayer on his lips, he turned the knob and slowly opened the door. It creaked on its hinges. A little sob sounded from a far corner.

Jimmy's heart went into his throat. "Kelsey?"

"Jimmy?"

Jimmy found the light switch near the door and flipped it. The florescent lights flickered to life, and he spied her huddled in a chair. He sprinted to her side. "Are you okay?"

She looked at him, her cheeks stained with tears. "I'm sorry I ran out. I just had to get out of there. I felt like I'd ruined everything for your mom."

"You can't take all the blame. There are two of us in this marriage." Hunkering down next to the chair, he put his arms around her and pulled her close as relief calmed his nerves. "You don't need to be sorry. I was concerned about you."

Kelsey pushed herself out of his embrace. "Your family isn't happy. Are you sorry you married me?"

Jimmy wiped the tears from her cheeks with his thumb. "No, I'm not sorry. Are you?"

She stared at him for what seemed like the longest time without answering.

Jimmy stood, bringing her with him. "You must be if you can't answer."

"I don't know what to think." Misery painted every inch of her face. "We can get the marriage annulled. I don't think I can be part of a marriage that makes your mother unhappy. How can that be good?"

"But I still need a wife." Jimmy wasn't sure why, but he didn't want to lose Kelsey. Maybe he was already falling in love. She definitely checked off most of the boxes on his list for a wife. He'd made this commitment, and he intended to carry it through. "Besides, my mom's sorry about her reaction."

"She said that?"

Jimmy nodded. "Janelle called and told me when I was looking for you. You scared me when you took off."

Kelsey expelled a shaky breath. "I'm sorry about that, too."

Jimmy sat on the chair and brought Kelsey down onto his lap. Thankfulness flooded his mind when she didn't resist. "I went to Charlotte's tonight because I thought you might be there, and she gave me some insight into my mom's reaction."

"What did she say?"

Jimmy related what Charlotte had told him. "Please don't say anything to my mom. She doesn't need to know that we know."

"I won't."

"Does that mean you're going to stick with me?"

Kelsey nodded ever so slightly. "I guess this is the first test of those promises I made today. I promised to rejoice with you in good times and struggle alongside you in bad times."

"We can walk back into the house together with our heads held high." Jimmy helped Kelsey to her feet. "We should get something to eat. I'm hungry."

Still holding his hand, Kelsey looked up at him. "I'm not sure I'm hungry. I've been too upset to think about eating."

"You need to eat. You know you're eating for two. Your little one needs some nourishment."

A shy smile crept across her face. "Jimmy Cunningham, you are the kindest man I know. You're one of the good guys."

"Thanks." Jimmy wasn't sure he deserved such praise. He hadn't always been a good guy, especially where Whitney was concerned. Was it true that good guys finished last? He definitely didn't want to finish last with Kelsey.

"Jimmy, Kelsey, are you guys coming back inside?" Jeremy's voice floated in from the doorway.

"Yeah, we're coming." Jimmy held Kelsey's hand as they walked together toward the door.

"Good, because I've got everyone on the same page." Jeremy squeezed Kelsey's shoulders. "They're ready to welcome you to the family. And good news, they've fed the kids, and the adults waited for us to eat with them."

Jimmy laughed. "Glad to hear it. I was just saying how hungry I am."

The three of them made their way back to the house. "Be easy on Mom. She's feeling terrible about her negative response."

Stopping at the back door to his house, Jimmy took Kelsey by the shoulders. "Are you going to be okay? I'll be standing right here with you."

Kelsey stared into his eyes. "Jeremy says your family's ready to accept our marriage. If that's the case, then I should be good."

As Jimmy opened the door and let Jeremy go in first, he was thankful for his brother. Jeremy had stood with Jimmy when everyone else in the family had not. No matter how this marriage started, Jimmy prayed it would be everything it should be. Holding Kelsey's hand, he stepped into the kitchen, his shoulders squared as he looked at his mother.

***

Gripping Jimmy's hand like a lifeline, Kelsey surveyed the group, who looked as if they might like to run the other way. She swallowed hard as her stomach sank. The children's quiet play filled the uncomfortable few seconds. Was this going to be no better than when she'd left?

As Kelsey was wishing someone would say something, anything, Mary rushed forward. "Kelsey, can you forgive me? I didn't mean to make you feel unwelcome. Your marriage just took me by surprise, and I acted without thinking."

Nodding, Kelsey tried to hold back the tears of relief. "And I'm sorry I ran away. That wasn't good either."

Mary took Kelsey's hands much the same as she'd done the night Jimmy had brought her to supper. "But who could blame you when you were faced with an unfriendly greeting. We want to make it up to you."

"Thanks, Mom." Jimmy hugged his mother. "That makes me feel so much better."

"It makes us all feel better, too." Mary motioned to the table. "We waited for you. So let's eat."

Kelsey glanced at the table, still set the way she'd left it with place settings for eight adults. She swallowed another lump in her throat as she grabbed the back of the nearest chair. Jimmy put a hand over hers as he came to stand beside her. She couldn't ask him to be more supportive.

He was a gem among men, but that still didn't change the fact that she'd entered into this marriage as a bargain. He needed a wife, and she needed a father for her baby. Would they fall in love in time? She couldn't answer that question, but it sat in the middle of her thoughts. What if she fell in love with him, and he didn't fall in love with her? Would his kindness be enough?

While Mary retrieved the lasagna and garlic bread from the oven, Janelle got out the salad and a couple of bottles of dressing from the refrigerator. As everyone sat at the table, Kelsey marshaled the troubling questions into a corner of her mind and shut the door. She had to deal with here and now, not worries from the future.

Mary stood at the end of the table as her gaze roamed over her family. "Jeremy, would you say a prayer for this occasion?"

"Yes, ma'am." Jeremy held out his hands to Mary on his right and Jenna on his left.

As the family joined hands around the table, Jimmy's strong fingers encased Kelsey's hand. He made her feel treasured, but was it all for show? While Jeremy prayed, she squashed that question. No questions. No answers. She'd just take everything as it came and be glad for Jimmy, the man willing to step up and claim another man's child as his own.

"And, Lord, bless Jimmy and Kelsey's marriage. Amen." The last line of Jeremy's prayer penetrated through the fog of Kelsey's troubling thoughts.

"Thanks, brother." Jimmy pulled out the chair for Kelsey.

She smiled up at him as she took her spot at the table. As Jimmy's family passed the food, some of Kelsey's earlier awkward feelings melted away. But she still had an inkling they were passing judgment and wondering why Jimmy married her without telling them.

The group ate in silence for a moment. Then Mary cleared her throat as she tapped a knife against her glass. "If I could have everyone's attention, I'd like to say a few things."

Everyone looked Mary's way, and Kelsey's nerves stood on end, emotions of every stripe running rampant through her mind. She felt as if she might explode from emotional overload.

When the murmurs of consensus ended, Mary looked over the group from her place at the head of the table. "I know we were surprised to learn that Jimmy and Kelsey got married, but it shouldn't have come as a complete surprise. I remember the way you two hit it off last fall. Then I saw you together again at Mitch and Amanda's wedding. It was as though you were meant to be together."

Another murmur of agreement rose from Jimmy's family. Kelsey tried to smile at her new in-laws.

Mary held up a hand. "Let me finish. I have a confession to make. I want you to know why I let the shock of their marriage lead me to say some things that I regret."

As Mary wiped a few tears from her eyes, she told her family about the near-elopement. A crescendo of voices filled the room as Jimmy's family exclaimed over Mary's story.

Mary held up a hand again to quiet her clan. "So you see, when I realized these two had gotten married, it brought back those feelings, regrets, *and* the lifetime of wonderful memories I shared with your father. I miss him terribly, and I let my hurt bubble over into something that hurt Jimmy and Kelsey. I want to say again I'm sorry. But I still have to be honest and say I'm disappointed we weren't there to share in your wedding."

Jimmy reached over and placed a hand on his mother's arm. "Mom, you don't have to apologize again. We understand, and we'd like to share the photos Shirley took."

"Before we look at photos, I have a little surprise for you." Mary jumped up from the table and went to the nearest cupboard. "While you were out looking for Kelsey, Jenna ran to the store and picked up a cake. And Karen Melson, my neighbor who makes special-occasion cakes and always has a ready supply of decorator's frosting, added her little touches to make it a wedding cake."

"Thanks, everyone, but that was completely unnecessary," Jimmy said.

"It's a peace offering." Mary set the cake on the table, then handed Jimmy a knife. "I'll let you two cut the cake."

As the kids gathered around Jimmy and Kelsey, they cut the cake much the same as they had done at Davis and Shirley's. Jimmy helped Corey and Evan sit on the barstools at the counter in the kitchen, then placed a piece of cake in front of each of them.

With a serious expression, Corey looked up at Jimmy. "Thank you. Is it true that we can call your wife Aunt Kelsey?"

"You sure can. She's part of our family now." Jimmy grinned as he turned and winked at Kelsey.

Her stomach did a little flip-flop. She liked the thought of being part of this family, but it wasn't real. Mary's confession created guilt in Kelsey's mind. Her mother-in-law had shared her secret with her family, while Jimmy and Kelsey held on to theirs. Would they eventually have to make a confession of their own?

While everyone ate cake and watched the photos that Jimmy projected onto his TV, Kelsey couldn't help thinking about the future. No one really knew their plans.

"Now that's a kiss." Jenna grinned at Jimmy and Kelsey.

"Eew, kissing." Corey scrunched up his face as he closed his eyes.

Evan imitated his big brother's antics, and the adults laughed.

Jeremy went over and put his arms around the boys. "It won't be too many years before you'll think that's something you want to do."

"No way!" Corey shook his head, his floppy hair sticking out in all directions.

While the group joked about the little boys' reaction to the succession of photographed kisses, Kelsey wondered whether they really looked like a couple in love. She couldn't deny the excitement of Jimmy's kiss, but she wanted love, not a physical attraction. If she held out for love, would that ruin everything? Why did these disconcerting questions pound at her brain like a never-ending hammer?

As Jimmy unplugged the tablet from the TV, Janelle came over to Kelsey. "Kelsey, I loved your dress and your hair. I'm glad you didn't take your hair down after you changed out of your dress."

Kelsey smiled. "Shirley did my hair. She was so sweet. They fed us lunch, too. And this is our second cake today. Shirley also had one."

Janelle hugged Kelsey. "I'm glad she made your day so nice. And it'll be fun having a new sister."

"Thanks." Kelsey glanced over at Jimmy. "We need to tell them our plans."

"Yeah." Jimmy set the tablet on the table and put an arm around Kelsey's waist. "We're spending the night at Mitch and Amanda's because we have to take care of the dog. Also, Kelsey has to go back to school. She's leaving on Sunday and won't be back until after she takes her finals at the end of the semester."

"Oh wow! I didn't realize that. Why—"

"Don't ask. We didn't want to wait to get married." Jimmy jumped in before Janelle could ask her question. "So we're not trying to rush anyone off, but this is our wedding night."

"On that note, we also got you a little wedding gift." Laughter rolled through the room as Mary retrieved an envelope from the kitchen counter and handed it to Jimmy.

"What's this?" Jimmy gazed at the envelope.

"Open it and find out." Mary grinned.

Jimmy tore into the envelope and pulled out a card. He opened it and held it so Kelsey could see it. The card had a sentimental greeting about love and marriage. Everyone in the family had signed it, even the kids with the help of their parents. As Jimmy and Kelsey looked over the card, a piece of paper fluttered to the floor.

Kelsey retrieved it. When she read it, her mouth grew dry, but she managed to speak. "How nice! A night at a bed-and-breakfast."

Jimmy reached for the paper, then looked up at his family. "You guys shouldn't have. We can't use this because we have to take care of Dolly."

Mary wagged a finger in the air. "Don't worry about that dog. You two go on your way. We'll clean up here, and we'll be responsible for the dog until you get back. Enjoy your wedding night."

"I don't think you have to tell them to do that." Jeremy chortled as he waggled his eyebrows.

Jimmy didn't say anything, and a blush warmed Kelsey's cheeks.

"I have to get my things. Then we'll have to stop and get Kelsey's stuff, so we'll put the dog in her kennel. I don't know how she'll like being there all alone."

"I can always take her home with me," Jeremy said. "You guys don't worry about Dolly. We'll take good care of her."

Jimmy hurried off to his bedroom, while Kelsey stood there feeling awkward again. She needed to say something. "Thanks."

"It's the least we could do on short notice." Mary grasped Kelsey's hands. "Thanks for not holding my outburst against me."

"It's forgotten." Kelsey wished they hadn't been so generous. How would she and Jimmy deal with a wedding night that most definitely wouldn't give them separate bedrooms?

"Thanks." Mary hugged Kelsey. "Have you told Mitch and Amanda about your marriage?"

Kelsey shook her head. "We've only talked to my dad. He took it pretty well, especially after he found out I was coming back to finish my semester at college."

"That's good," Mary replied.

Before Kelsey could respond, Jimmy appeared with a gym bag slung over his shoulder and rescued her from any more inquiries. "Ready?"

Kelsey nodded, then turned to these people who would be her family going forward and waved. "Good night, everyone."

A chorus of good nights followed them outside. Jimmy didn't say anything as he opened the car door for her and tossed his bag onto the backseat. Maybe he didn't know what to say after his family had sprung the surprise bed-and-breakfast gift on them. Maybe one good surprise deserved another. Or maybe he was thinking about the real marriage he wanted but wouldn't have.

Kelsey had to trust that Jimmy wasn't like Brandon. But did she really know Jimmy? For one instant, doubts flooded her mind. She swallowed hard as she looked over at him. He glanced at her with a smile. Jimmy was an honorable man. She had to believe that, or this whole marriage bargain had been a big mistake.

CHAPTER TEN

L ights shone from the windows of the historic bed-and-breakfast as Jimmy stopped his car in the drive. The streetlamps illuminated the old brick facade and dark-green shutters on the windows.

Kelsey had been unusually quiet on the forty-minute drive. He hadn't said much himself. He didn't know whether to discuss their situation or wait until they arrived and then figure it out. He didn't want to think of a real wedding night, but his mind kept wandering into that territory. The memory of Kelsey's sweet kisses didn't help.

"Looks like we're here." He looked her way. "You want to stay here while I check in, or do you want to come with me?"

"I can stay here." Shadows obscured her expression.

"Okay. I shouldn't be long."

Jimmy strode to the front door of the inn, his thoughts filled with Kelsey. From the moment he'd seen her at the Ryman last fall, she'd captured his interest. Seeing her again at Amanda's wedding had only heightened that interest. Now she was his wife, and there was no denying he wanted her to be a wife in every aspect, not in name only. But he'd agreed to this kind of marriage. He had to reckon with that reality.

His feelings for her had skyrocketed way beyond

where he had anticipated. He didn't know whether to call it love, but an emptiness had filled him when she'd run away. In such a short time, he couldn't imagine his life without her. How had that happened? Was he confusing physical attraction for something else? He didn't know. His uncertainty only complicated the matter.

Once inside, he rang the little bell on the desk near the door, his mind still whirling with questions. Where did the physical attraction end and love begin? Was he counting on her to fall in love with him? What if that never happened?

The appearance of a tall, slender man with salt-and-pepper hair combed back from his forehead brought Jimmy's thoughts to a sudden halt. "Hi, I'm Jimmy Cunningham, and I believe you have a reservation for my wife and me."

My wife and me. Jimmy liked the sound of that phrase.

"Hello, I'm Forrest Sparks. My wife and I are the proprietors here." The man tapped on the keyboard sitting on the desk as he looked at a monitor. Then he looked up with a smile. "Yes, we have a reservation for you. The note here says you're newlyweds. Congratulations!"

Jimmy smiled. "Yes, sir. Thanks."

"We've got a wonderful room reserved for you." The man stepped from behind the counter. "Do you need help with your bags?"

Jimmy shook his head. "I'll get my wife and be back in a minute."

"Sure. Then I'll show you to your room."

Jimmy stepped outside. Kelsey sat with her head down, as if studying something. Her flowered headband almost glowed in the light shining into the car. It made her look as though she had a halo. Maybe she was praying. That was what he should do. Pray that he could be a good husband, a man worthy of her trust.

With those mixed-up emotions crowding his thoughts, he approached his wife. She looked up just as he touched the door handle. "Ready to go in?"

Nodding, she opened the door and stepped out, a timid smile on her face. "Have you seen our room?"

"No, but I'm sure it'll be nice." Jimmy hoped with all his whole being that this would work out. "I'll take care of the bags."

"Thanks."

Jimmy slung his bag over his shoulder and wheeled Kelsey's bag in front of him as they traipsed silently up the walk to the door. He glanced at her. A somber expression marked her features.

Was she anxious about what they would find? Like a bed they would have to share? He could always offer to sleep on the floor. He wasn't a stranger to sleeping there. He'd spent plenty of nights on floors after partying too hard his freshman year in college. He didn't want his wedding night to remind him of that misspent year, but he'd sleep on the floor for Kelsey.

As soon as they entered the door, Forrest greeted them and immediately led them down a hallway and showed them where they would find breakfast in the morning. Finally he stopped in front of a door halfway down the hall. He motioned for them to enter as he showed them the amenities in the room, everything from the basket of treats to the private bathroom.

"If you have any questions, just let me know."

"Thanks. Everything sounds wonderful." Jimmy set his bag on the floor next to Kelsey's suitcase.

"Have a good evening." Forrest smiled as he left, closing the door behind him.

Jimmy looked over the room with its canopied queen bed covered with a floral print comforter. Two overstuffed chairs covered in a blue fabric that matched the flowers on the comforter occupied the space near the window with curtains made from the same fabric as the comforter. A small doily-covered table sat in between the chairs. He didn't relish the idea of sleeping in either one, but it was either that or the floor.

"Do you want to hang up your clothes?" Jimmy pointed to the armoire in the corner.

Kelsey shrugged, an uncomfortable look on her face. "I don't have that much."

"Me neither." Jimmy unzipped his bag and pulled out his business binder. "I hope you don't mind that I plan to study. I need to know this stuff by Monday."

Her expression turned from uneasy to surprised. "Oh, okay. I've got books on my phone I can read."

"These chairs are perfect." Jimmy sat in one and opened his binder, hoping he wouldn't have to sleep here, too.

Kelsey walked toward the chairs, her eyes focused on her phone. She stopped and stared at him, but didn't say anything.

"Yes?" He raised his eyebrows.

She blew out a big puff of air as she continued to stare at him. "We…we can't continue to ignore the fact that we have one bed in here."

"I'll sleep on the floor."

"I don't want you to sleep on the floor."

Jimmy heart skipped a beat. Had she changed her mind

about marriage in name only? Did he dare hope? "Then where do you suggest I sleep?"

"We can share the bed."

"Does this mean—"

"No." She motioned toward the bed. "There are plenty of extra pillows there. We can put them down the center."

"And you trust me to stay on my side?" He didn't trust himself.

"I do."

"I'm a restless sleeper."

"Does that mean you might take more than your share of the bed?"

"Possibly." He couldn't believe he was having this conversation.

"So you're a bed hog."

He tried not to laugh, but a chuckle escaped as he gazed at her. "If that's what you want to call it. I'm not used to sharing a bed."

"Neither am I."

"If you trust me to stay on my side, I'll be glad not to sleep on the floor."

She narrowed her gaze. "Do you snore?"

Jimmy laughed out loud. "Do you?"

"I asked first."

"I can't honestly tell you."

Kelsey lowered her head. "I might snore sometimes."

Jimmy laughed again. "Are you worried you'll keep me awake?"

She shrugged. "I thought you ought to know."

"Thanks for the warning." Jimmy doubted her snoring would keep him awake. Her close proximity had more chance of giving him a sleepless night. Maybe the floor was a better option.

"Okay. Now that we've settled that, I'll let you get to your work." She sat in the chair and tapped her phone.

Jimmy tried to concentrate on the business plans and figures in the notebook, but his mind wandered to the thought of sharing that bed with Kelsey. He had to quit thinking about what he couldn't have and start learning this stuff. He forced himself to focus on the information on the pages of the notebook and not on Kelsey.

For the next hour he managed to cram this material into his brain. Once he started school again, he'd be doing a lot of studying. Hopefully, that would keep him occupied so he wouldn't think about what he couldn't have when it came to Kelsey.

"Jimmy?"

He looked up, realizing he'd actually forgotten her presence for a few minutes. "Yeah?"

"Are you all right?"

"Sure." He wrinkled his brow. "Why?"

"Your face is scrunched up."

"Trying to remember all this stuff. It's been a long time since I've done this much studying."

"Would you like me to help?"

"How can you do that?"

She set her phone on the table and held out a hand. "I can quiz you on the stuff you've studied so far."

"That might help, but it also might show that I can't keep a thing in my brain anymore."

"Let's give it a try."

Jimmy handed her the notebook. "Okay. You can start at the beginning."

For a few moments, Kelsey studied the pages, while

Jimmy studied her. His pulse raced. She was kind and thoughtful besides being pretty. He couldn't let her break his heart, but maybe that was already happening because he'd let himself care too much.

When she looked up at him, she smiled. "Okay. Let's see how much you remember."

"Fire away." He hoped he wouldn't come across as a complete dunderhead.

As Kelsey asked him about different aspects of Graham Cunningham's business dealings, he surprised even himself at how much he recalled. After about thirty minutes of quizzing, Kelsey closed the notebook.

"Are we done?"

She smiled. "Jimmy Cunningham, you are brilliant."

"Really?"

"Yeah. You know this stuff. How do you remember all that after one reading?"

He ate up her praise like a starving man, but he couldn't deceive her. "I could make you think I'm brilliant, but I have to admit I've been studying this every possible minute since Graham gave it to me on Monday."

"But this is only Tuesday night, and you've been occupied with a few other things."

"Okay. I'll let you call me brilliant." He laced his hands behind his head and stretched his legs out in front of him.

Kelsey's laughter filled the room. "On second thought, I don't want to give you a big head."

"I don't mind in the least." Jimmy savored her praise. She made him want to fulfill all her expectations. From the very moment they'd met, she had made him feel like someone important. He wouldn't let her down. He would be whatever she needed him to be.

"I'm sure you don't." She got up and stretched her arms over her head. "I'm going to get ready for bed. Is that okay with you?"

"Sure. Do you usually go to bed early?"

She picked up her phone from the little table and glanced at it. "It's not that early." She held the phone out where he could see the time.

"Okay. It's almost ten."

"Pregnancy has made me sleepy all the time." She yawned. "I hope I can stay awake in classes when I go back."

The thought of her leaving made him sad, but he wasn't going to say so. "You can use the bathroom first."

"Thanks. I'll try not to take too long."

"Take your time. I'm in no hurry."

She put her hand on the doorknob of the bathroom door, then turned back to him. "You don't sleep in the nude, do you?"

He grinned. "Would it be a problem if I do?"

Her eyes opened wide. "Guess there's a lot we don't know about each other. Could you wait until the lights are out to undress?"

Jimmy laughed. "I'm only teasing you. I sleep in a T-shirt and gym shorts. I'll change while you're in the bathroom."

She shot him an annoyed look. "Do you have fun teasing me?"

"Just a little."

"Well, stop."

Jimmy saluted. "Yes, ma'am. No more teasing."

"Thank you." She turned and flounced into the

restroom.

Jimmy stood there and stared at the bed. How would this ever work? The sound of running water filtered out from the bathroom, then the buzz of an electric toothbrush. So Kelsey used an electric toothbrush. She'd been right. They had a lot to learn about each other. With those thoughts filling his mind, he quickly changed.

Moments later, Kelsey opened the door a crack. "Are you decent?"

"Yeah." He should've asked what she slept in, or maybe not.

Without looking his way, she stepped into the room, a robe covering her from head to foot and her fancy headband gone. "The bathroom's yours."

"Thanks." He grabbed his bag.

While he brushed his teeth, he wondered if they'd be tiptoeing around each other once they started living together, even though they wouldn't have to share a bedroom. He didn't want her to feel uncomfortable in her own home. Could he talk to her about it? Maybe it was just better left until she actually moved in with him in seven weeks. That was where he'd leave it for now.

After he finished getting ready for bed, he opened the bathroom door. The room was dark except for the tiny lamp sitting on the bedside stand. Kelsey had built her divide of pillows down the middle of the bed, and she lay on the other side with her back to him, her dark hair splayed against the pillow.

He turned off the light and sat on the edge of the bed. Trying not to think of this as his wedding night, he slipped under the covers, his feet coming into contact with the mountain of pillows in the middle of the bed. Was Kelsey already asleep?

"Good night, Kelsey," he whispered into the darkness.

"Good night, Jimmy."

Jimmy drank in the sound of her sweet voice and prayed he wouldn't make a complete mess of this whole marriage thing. Somehow this had to work out for both of them.

Hours later, a warm presence clinging to Jimmy woke him. The dim light of early morning filled the room. He found Kelsey lying snuggled against him. His insides a jumble of emotions, he swallowed hard. She slept soundly with her arm draped over him.

Did he dare wake her? He'd better, or he might be sorry.

"Good morning, Mrs. Cunningham."

Kelsey's eyes fluttered open, and she stared at him, her lips parted slightly. He used all his willpower to keep from leaning closer and kissing her.

He grinned at her. "Seems that you're the one who's a bed hog. I know I said I wouldn't tease you again, but I can't help it."

"I…I'm so sorry." She scrambled out of the bed. Even though her pajamas with a large cartoon cat face on the shirt and little cats all over the bottoms covered every inch of her, she still looked enticing.

"Don't be sorry. I didn't mind at all." Jimmy forced himself to look only at her face.

"Jimmy, please don't tease." She held a pillow in front of her, almost like a shield. "I don't want you to get the wrong idea."

"I understand just where things stand between us. You don't have to worry. We have a bargain, and I intend to keep it."

Kelsey's face turned pale, and she ran into the bathroom, slamming the door closed as she went. The sound of retching came from the other side of the door. Morning sickness. Would that happen every morning?

Jimmy settled in one of the chairs. When Kelsey remained in the bathroom for more than ten minutes, he went to the door and listened. No sound.

"Kelsey, are you okay in there?"

"As okay as I can be. I'm just waiting to make sure the nausea has passed for good."

"Would you like your suitcase so you can get dressed?"

She opened the door just enough to poke her head out. "That would be good. I hope you don't need to get in here anytime soon."

"I'm good." Jimmy grabbed her suitcase, which sat nearby, and pushed it through the opening.

"Thanks."

Jimmy went back and settled in the chair. While he looked at email and news on his phone, running water sounded from the bathroom. He contemplated how Kelsey's presence in his life would bring about changes, especially in him. He had someone else to think about instead of just himself. Eventually there would be a child who would call him Daddy. He needed God's help to do this right. Jimmy couldn't let himself forget that important thing.

***

The following Saturday evening, Kelsey glanced over

at Jimmy as he leaned against the kitchen counter in Mitch and Amanda's house. "Are you ready?"

Nodding, Jimmy released a harsh breath. "As ready as I'll ever be. These marriage announcements are getting to be a regular thing. First your dad, then my family, Charlotte, now Mitch and Amanda. This should be a piece of cake."

"Don't count on it. You thought your mom wouldn't be a problem. Look how that turned out."

"Yeah, well, I misjudged that one." Jimmy produced a silly grin. "But it turned out okay in the end. Even the B and B."

Kelsey forced herself to smile. He might have thought the night they'd slept in the same bed turned out okay, but she couldn't forget how it felt to wake up in his arms. She'd almost kissed him. She couldn't let her emotions and pregnancy hormones lead her into doing something she'd regret.

She wanted love, but Jimmy wasn't offering love. He was offering her a home and giving her baby a father. That was the bargain. He needed a Mrs. Cunningham to stand by his side. He'd said he knew where they stood with each other—a marriage in name only. He wanted more, but he was willing to abide by her wishes.

If she didn't stifle her runaway thoughts, they would surely get her in trouble.

Every morning when she'd had an episode of morning sickness, he'd been kind beyond anything she'd expected, just like that night at the reception. Even with what happened with Mitch's fiancée, why had anyone in this town thought Jimmy Cunningham wasn't an upstanding man?

"You're awfully quiet. Are you worried?" Jimmy gave her a quizzical look.

"I have no idea what Amanda will think." Kelsey sighed. "I wish they'd get here so we can get it over with."

"You're not giving me much confidence that this will go well." Jimmy rubbed the back of his neck. "Do you realize you and Amanda will be sisters-in-law as well as sisters?"

Kelsey let out a halfhearted laugh, then motioned toward the window. "I just saw the lights of a car in the driveway. The garage door is going up."

Jimmy pushed away from the counter and stood beside her as he put an arm around her shoulders. "United we stand."

Dolly whined at the door, and Kelsey stepped forward to move the dog out of the way in preparation for the door to open. "Come on, Dolly. Mitch and Amanda will be here soon."

"I believe our charge knows Mommy and Daddy are home."

Kelsey giggled as she held Dolly's collar. "I'm not sure Amanda and Mitch want to be considered Dolly's parents."

"It's just an expression." Jimmy hung back.

Before Kelsey could make another comment, Mitch opened the door and Amanda scooted into the kitchen. She hugged Kelsey, then bent over to rub Dolly behind the ears. "It's good to be home. Did you and Dolly get along?"

"Everything went fine with Dolly. Did you guys have a good time?" Kelsey asked as Amanda continued to pet the dog.

"We had a fabulous time." Amanda looked up and

stopped short. "Jimmy, what are you doing here?"

Just at that moment, Mitch wheeled the suitcases into the kitchen. "Jimmy, what are you doing here?"

Jimmy gathered all his resolve and stared at Mitch. "Guess I'd better explain."

Kelsey returned to Jimmy's side. "We've got something to tell you."

"Yeah. What?" Amanda's gaze went from Kelsey to Jimmy and back again.

"We got married while you were gone." Kelsey pressed her lips together.

Her mouth hanging open, Amanda stared at Kelsey. "You got married? You're kidding, right?"

"No, we got married on Tuesday." Kelsey swallowed hard as she took in Amanda's incredulous expression.

"Why would you do that? You barely know each other." Amanda stood there wide eyed, her mouth still hanging open.

"Because we wanted to, and for the record, we've known each other since last October."

"So you're saying you've been carrying on a long-distance romance all this time without telling me?"

Kelsey's stomach sank. This was not going well. Why couldn't her sister, of all people, be on her side? "No, but it's not like we're strangers."

"I just don't believe this. I thought you were supposed to be the sensible one." Amanda frowned. "Does Dad know? What about school?"

"You sound just like Dad." Kelsey laughed nervously. "I'm going back to school on Sunday, just like I always planned."

"Then why on earth wouldn't you wait until you

finished the semester before you got married?" Amanda's frown didn't fade.

"We didn't want to." Kelsey hoped Amanda didn't keep demanding answers.

"It sure would've made more sense." Mitch stepped past Amanda and eyed Jimmy and motioned toward the other room with a slight turn of his head. "We need to talk."

Kelsey moved forward until she was standing right in front of Mitch. "Whatever you've got to say to Jimmy, you can say to me. We're together in this."

"All right." Mitch's gaze narrowed as he looked at Jimmy. "Does she know about your job offer and its requirements?"

"What job offer?" Amanda asked.

"I know all about that." Kelsey lifted her chin as she stared up at Mitch. "Jimmy proposed, and I said yes. Can't you just be happy for us?"

A bewildered look marking her features, Amanda glanced from Mitch to Kelsey. "Can someone please fill me in on this job-offer thing and what it has to do with you guys getting married?"

Jimmy and Mitch both started talking at once, their voices raised.

"Stop!" Kelsey held her arms up in the air. Tears threatened as her crazy hormones kicked in again. She let her anger push away the tears as she turned to face Amanda. "Here's the deal. Mitch's dad offered Jimmy a job with two requirements. He has to finish his college degree and find a wife."

Amanda looked over at Mitch. "Really? Your dad would require someone to get married in order to have a job?"

A muscle worked in Mitch's jaw. "He didn't say Jimmy had to be married on day one, just that he should get married. He believes married people have a more stable home life and it contributes to good work habits."

"So if you'd decided to work for your dad, he would've said you should get married?"

Mitch nodded. "He would've told me the same thing."

"Don't you think that's a bit much?"

"Yeah," Jimmy and Mitch chorused, then burst into laughter.

The tension in the room dissipated, and Kelsey breathed a sigh of relief.

Mitch offered Jimmy his hand. "Sorry, man. I didn't mean to get testy. Congratulations on the marriage."

"Thanks." Jimmy shook Mitch's hand. "I don't want to be at odds with my new brother-in-law."

Mitch stared at Jimmy. "We'll be good as long as you treat Kelsey right."

"That's what I intend to do."

Kelsey gazed at Amanda. "What about you? Are you going to join in the truce?"

Amanda's shoulders sagged, and she pulled Kelsey into an embrace. "I'm sorry I reacted in that way. It was just such a shock to find out you got married. I hate that I missed your wedding."

With a little laugh, Kelsey hugged Amanda back. "You sound just like Jimmy's mom. She felt the same way."

Amanda raised her eyebrows. "First I sound like Dad, then like Jimmy's mom. Anyone else you want to compare me to?"

"No." Kelsey looped her arm through Jimmy's. "This

marriage is what we want, so please wish us the best."

"I do." Amanda pressed her cheek to Kelsey's. "I just wish I could've been here to share the day with you."

Kelsey prayed Amanda wouldn't make this difficult. "Like we told Jimmy's family, we eloped because we didn't want anyone to try to talk us out of it. And I know from your reaction tonight, you would've tried."

"I suppose." Amanda grimaced.

"Would you like to see the photos?" Kelsey reached for her tablet.

"What? Did you go to Nashville and have an Elvis impersonator marry you?" Amanda asked.

Kelsey laughed. "No, Jimmy's distant cousin who's a judge married us, and his wife took photos."

Mitch looked at Jimmy. "You mean the Judge?"

Jimmy smiled. "Yeah. Davis Cunningham. I called him up, and he was glad to marry us. Kelsey has the photos on her tablet."

Amanda clapped her hands. "Let's see them."

For the next few minutes the foursome gathered around while Kelsey laid her tablet on the kitchen table and scrolled through the photos. She glanced at Amanda to gauge her reaction, but her expression didn't change. While they looked at the photos, guilt stalked Kelsey. Would someone see right through the facade of this marriage?

"So that's it." Kelsey stopped on the last photo, then looked up from the table as she waited for Amanda to say something.

With one arm, Amanda squeezed Kelsey's shoulders. "Those are wonderful photos. Did you guys plan all that?"

Kelsey shook her head. "The only thing I did was buy the dress because I didn't want to get married in jeans."

"And I wore the suit I bought for my dad's funeral. I wore it to my sisters' weddings and your wedding, too." Jimmy's laughter conveyed his discomfort. "Guess you could call it my funeral and wedding suit."

"Did you do your own hair? I love how that headband was incorporated into the braid." Amanda scrolled back to one of the photos.

"Shirley did that." Kelsey remembered how the older woman took charge of the day. "She told me she loves to help the brides when Davis performs a marriage ceremony. She did the lunch, cake, and photos all on her own."

"How sweet." Amanda smiled. "Even though you eloped, it was lovely."

"Thanks." Kelsey stood. "Now I think it's time we headed home and let you two have some privacy."

"If the photos of those kisses are any indication, seems like you two are eager to be alone yourselves." Amanda gave Kelsey a knowing look. "You guys will have to take a belated honeymoon when Kelsey returns."

"You mean you don't think babysitting a dog is much of a honeymoon?" Jimmy laughed. "My mom did give us a night at a nearby B and B for our wedding night, and Jeremy watched Dolly."

"That was nice. At least you had that much." Amanda looped her arm through Mitch's and gazed up at him. "I don't know how you guys are going to stand being away from each other for seven weeks. I know how much I missed Mitch when I was on tour. It made me finally realize he was more important than anything else."

"You know what they say. Absence makes the heart grow fonder." Mitch looked at his wife, then at Jimmy. "But they also say, out of sight out of mind, don't they?"

Taking a step closer, Jimmy eyed his cousin. "And just what's that supposed to mean?"

Kelsey stepped between the two men. "Mitch, I'm glad you married my sister, but you're out of line if you're thinking bad things about Jimmy. I won't let you define him because of one bad incident. You need to get over the past."

"So he told you about Whitney?" Mitch looked between Kelsey and Jimmy.

Kelsey eyed Mitch. "Jimmy told me the good and the bad about his past, and he knows about mine. So let's get over the past and start fresh today."

Rubbing the back of his neck, Mitch sighed. "I'd like to do that. I'd thought I'd put away the bad blood between Jimmy and me, but I haven't forgotten what he did. I don't want him to do to you what he did to Whitney."

Kelsey forced herself not to shout. She didn't want to start out ruining her relationship with her sister and her husband, but Mitch wasn't being fair to Jimmy. She took a calming breath as she put an arm around Jimmy's waist.

"When you look at Jimmy, you only see that one event. When I look at him, I see a man who loves his family, served his country, helped his mom after the sudden death of her husband, and continued his dad's legacy by growing the painting company. Now he wants to prove himself in another venue, and I'm a part of that venture. I hope you can see what I see in this wonderful man."

Jimmy tightened his arm around her waist in an unspoken thank-you. She was thankful for what he'd done for her, and she couldn't stand by and let Mitch imply bad things about Jimmy. He'd rescued her from an embarrassing situation, and he deserved everyone's respect. Not reminders of his past.

"Okay then. My new sister-in-law has put me in my place, and deservedly so." Mitch turned to Jimmy. "Will you forgive me for being out of line?"

Jimmy hesitated but finally held out his hand. "Okay. Seems like we did this already tonight. Can we make the truce stick this time?"

"I hope so." Mitch grimaced as he shook Jimmy's hand. "Every time I think I have the bad feelings between us put behind me, I let something resurrect them. Maybe you need to pray for me."

A serious look came over Jimmy's face. "Let's pray for each other."

"We can do that right now." Amanda held out her hands.

Kelsey grabbed on to Jimmy's hand, and Amanda took hold of Mitch's as they made a circle next to the kitchen table. Kelsey hoped they wouldn't be praying out loud. The guilt of her secret sin weighed heavily on her. Sometimes she thought she might feel better if she just confessed the whole thing, but she didn't want to face the consequences. Now that she and Jimmy were married, what would be the point in a confession? She settled on that rationalization.

"I'll go first." Jimmy bowed his head. "Lord, forgive me for the things I've done to hurt other people. Please help Mitch and me bury the old hurts and move forward in a way that would please You. Amen."

Kelsey swallowed hard as Jimmy squeezed her hand. She didn't want to go next. She didn't say anything, and finally Amanda prayed for the two new marriages and peace between Mitch and Jimmy. Then Mitch said a prayer that echoed much of what Jimmy had said.

As Mitch said amen, Kelsey's mouth felt as though it was stuffed with cotton. Her pulse pounded in her head. Her turn had come. Would her prayer be in vain? How could she ask anything when she was living a lie? She took a shaky breath. "Dear God, thank you for Jimmy, Amanda, and Mitch. Help us live in peace in a way that's pleasing to You. Amen."

"Amen," the others chorused.

Jimmy and Mitch shook hands again, while Kelsey and Amanda hugged each other.

"We'd better get going. Our stuff is already in my car." Jimmy bent over and patted Dolly's head. "Dolly, you take care of these two."

Dolly barked and wagged her tail.

"Thanks for watching her." Amanda walked to the door with Kelsey. "I still want to take you to the airport tomorrow, like we originally planned, so we can spend a little more time together."

"After church we can drive into Johnson City, have lunch, then take you to the airport." Mitch looked at Jimmy for confirmation.

"Does that work for you?" Jimmy looked over at Kelsey.

Nodding, Kelsey manufactured a smile. This scenario would require more pretending—hugs, kisses, and tearful goodbyes. "That works for me. We'll see you in the morning. Good night."

Mitch and Amanda stood on the front porch and waved as Kelsey followed Jimmy to his car. She waved as she opened the door and got inside. Now that she had passed the Mitch-and-Amanda test, she had to face a night in Jimmy's house, where there was only one available bed.

She didn't want a repeat of the night at the B and B.

As Jimmy started his car, he immediately turned on the radio. Country music filled the interior. Kelsey took it as a signal that he didn't want to talk. She shouldn't read anything into it. He might just enjoy the music. It had nothing to do with not wanting to talk to her. She had to quit being paranoid.

Jimmy pulled his car into the garage and turned off the engine. "Well, Mrs. Cunningham, here we are. Home sweet home."

"Yeah." Kelsey wished she could control her racing heart. "What do we do about the sleeping arrangements?"

Even in the dim light of the garage, Jimmy's eyes twinkled. "I've got plenty of pillows."

Was he serious or joking? "I can sleep on your couch."

The twinkle faded from Jimmy's eyes. "I should sleep on the couch. You can have the bed."

"No. You shouldn't have to give up your bed. I'm perfectly happy to sleep on the couch."

"But I won't be able to sleep knowing you're not in a comfortable bed. Besides, it's the least I can do to thank you for sticking up for me tonight." He smiled. "You don't know how much that meant to me."

Kelsey returned his smile. "And I meant every word."

"Let me sleep on the couch so you'll have access to the one working bathroom when you get up in the morning."

"Are you saying you think I'll need one close by?"

"If the past week is any indication, yes." Jimmy snorted.

Kelsey nodded. "You certainly don't want me barfing in your living room. So you win. I'll take the bedroom."

"Good. Now that we have that settled, let's get our

suitcases inside."

After Jimmy delivered Kelsey's suitcase to the master bedroom, he stood in the doorway. "Can I get you anything?"

Kelsey shook her head. "No thanks. I'm going to get ready for bed and read for a little while. If that's okay, I'll see you in the morning."

"Sure. Sweet dreams." Jimmy turned to go, then turned back. "If you need anything, just holler."

Dreams for sure, but whether they would be sweet was another matter. "Okay, but I'm sure I'll be fine. Good night."

Jimmy closed the door as he left. Kelsey plopped onto the bed and sat there for a minute. In seven weeks, this would be her home. Would Jimmy have the other rooms ready by the time she returned? She hated the thought of him sleeping on the couch, but she wasn't ready to be a real wife. He knew that, so why did she feel so guilty about it? Guilt inundated her from all sides. She had messed up her life. She didn't want to mess up his, but maybe she already had.

CHAPTER ELEVEN

The airport buzzed with passengers checking in luggage and waiting for their flights as Jimmy helped Kelsey check in her bag. He hated to see her leave. They'd been married for nearly six days, and even though it wasn't a real marriage, he felt connected to her in a way he hadn't expected. Was she glad to be going back to school where she wouldn't have to deal with him?

After he put the suitcase on the scale and the agent behind the counter tagged the bag and whisked it away, he turned to Kelsey. "Looks like you're set."

"Yeah." She didn't look at him but fiddled with her purse.

"You okay?" He leaned closer so Mitch and Amanda wouldn't overhear their conversation. "You're not getting sick, are you?"

Shaking her head, she looked up at him, a little smile curving her mouth. "No, but I sure hope that doesn't suddenly hit me on the plane. I would feel sorry for the people sitting next to me if I have to use the airsick bag."

Jimmy put his arm around her shoulders. "I'll pray that doesn't happen, for your sake and for theirs."

Kelsey laughed, and a gratifying sensation filled his chest. He loved it when he could make her laugh, but he couldn't let himself get too caught up in this marriage. If he was honest with himself though, he'd have to admit he already had, so her leaving was a good thing. While she was gone, he could get his thoughts in order and prepare to share the same house with her but not her bed. He couldn't forget that night at the B and B and how he'd awakened the next morning with her in his arms. For the rest of the week, he'd lain there at night thinking how right that had felt.

"You two doing okay?" Amanda asked as Kelsey and Jimmy approached.

"Yeah. Why?" Jimmy raised his eyebrows as he looked between Mitch and Amanda.

"I can see you're sad about this parting." Amanda gave Kelsey a pat on the arm.

Kelsey looked up at him with a little smile. A knowing look in her eyes said, *We're doing a good job with this make-believe marriage thing.* He was thinking it was all too real—his feelings for her. In the beginning, he'd thought it was only a physical attraction. Now that he faced the prospect of being without her, it was completely clear that he already loved her. How had he let that happen in such a short time?

Trying to think about something else, Jimmy checked his phone for the time, then looked at Kelsey. "You're here in plenty of time to catch your flight. Do you want to sit in the restaurant until you have to go through security?"

Kelsey glanced toward the nearby security checkpoint. "Sure. They aren't very busy. It won't take me long to get through."

Jimmy led the way to a table and pulled out a chair for Kelsey. After everyone was seated, he glanced around the table. "I know we just ate, but we could order a soda."

"I think I'll order something to take on the plane. The

stuff they sell during the flight usually isn't very good, and I'm never sure I'll have time to grab a bite during a layover."

"Great idea." Jimmy handed Kelsey a menu.

While she looked at it, Jimmy couldn't stop watching her. What would it take to win her love? He couldn't push too hard. He would have to be the best husband he could be. She'd said some nice things about him last night. That was a good start, but he didn't want to overplay his hand. He should pray for wisdom, but he had his doubts about getting a positive answer when they were perpetuating a falsehood.

"Don't look so down, Jimmy." Amanda patted his arm. "You and Kelsey can do a video call every day. I know it's not the same as being together, but it's the next best thing."

Smiling, Jimmy looked over at Kelsey. "Amanda's right. We'll have to work out the best time since there's a three-hour time difference."

"I'll send you my class schedule, and you can let me know how that works with your job. I suspect evenings will work the best." Kelsey laid the menu aside.

"Me, too." Jimmy wondered whether the video calls might make missing her worse. He would deal with it.

"I know you two will miss each other, but it might be to your advantage. Kelsey will concentrate on her classes, and Jimmy can concentrate on his new job." Mitch snorted. "No distractions will be a plus when working for my dad."

"I plan to finish the work on my house in the evenings." Jimmy hoped his new job wouldn't keep him from doing that, but he had to remember that Graham Cunningham was a boss who expected a lot from his employees.

Mitch quirked an eyebrow. "Good luck with that."

Would his new job require so many hours that he wouldn't have time to work on his house? That would be a disaster. If nothing else, he had to finish that bathroom and one bedroom. He might be burning the midnight oil.

While Jimmy stewed, a waitress appeared and took the order for their drinks and Kelsey's sandwich to go and reappeared moments later with their drinks.

"Your sandwich will be ready in a few minutes." The waitress laid straws on the table as she looked at Kelsey.

"Thanks. My plane takes off in about forty minutes." Kelsey removed the paper from her straw and stuck it in her soda.

Jimmy took a big gulp of his drink and wished he was alone with Kelsey, but she wanted to spend time with her sister, probably more than she wanted to spend time with him. He banished that thought. A negative attitude would do him no good.

"Are you excited about starting your new job?" Amanda asked.

Jimmy nodded. "Excited, nervous, energized. I'm looking forward to this opportunity."

"And I'm sure you'll do well." Mitch gave Jimmy a thumbs-up. "Just remember, my dad can drive a hard bargain, but he's fair."

"Jimmy knows those companies inside and out." Kelsey smiled. "I helped him study."

Jimmy basked in Kelsey's praise. Could he turn her praise into love? Or was he asking for trouble to look at it in those terms? How could he get this right when he had outdistanced her on the road to love?

The waitress appeared with Kelsey's sandwich in a togo box. She tucked it into her carry-on bag.

Jimmy paid the bill, then glanced at his phone with a sigh. "I hate to say it, but it's probably time for you to get through security."

"We'll walk over with you." Amanda stood and looped her arm through Mitch's.

The foursome walked together until they reached the point of no return for passengers. Kelsey hugged Mitch, then Amanda. Jimmy wasn't sure what his next move should be. He wanted to kiss Kelsey in the worst way. If they wanted to keep up the pretense of a newlywed couple, he should definitely kiss her.

His pulse pounding, he put his arms around her waist and gazed into her eyes. "Well, this is goodbye."

She smiled up at him. "Let's not say goodbye. Let's say see you in seven weeks."

"Yeah." Jimmy pulled her closer.

She stood on her tiptoes and whispered in his ear. "You should kiss me."

"I thought you'd never ask," he whispered back.

Kelsey giggled as she wrapped her arms around his neck, and he leaned in for a kiss. She was sweetness, gentleness, and everything he wanted. She smelled like fresh flowers and sunshine. He had to make this work for both of them.

"Aren't you taking advantage of the situation?" Kelsey whispered.

"Yeah, but I enjoy kissing my wife." Jimmy wished she felt the same way about kissing him. She didn't hold anything back when she kissed him, but she was playing to their audience, while he was wishing it were real.

Would absence make her heart grow fonder for him?

He had no doubt that his feelings for her had outpaced her feelings for him. He had fallen in love.

When she stepped out of his embrace, it was like losing part of himself. He wanted to snatch her back into his arms, but he didn't want to mess up the good thing they had going. He couldn't forget that the hugs and kisses wouldn't have happened if Mitch and Amanda weren't here.

Kelsey motioned toward security. "I just heard the first boarding call for my flight. Guess I'd better get going. Don't want to miss my plane."

"Promise me you'll call when you land. I want to know you got home safely."

"Promise." Kelsey held up a hand as if giving a pledge. "I'll call you when I land *and* when I get back to Pullman."

Jimmy took her promise to call twice as a good sign. "I'll be waiting to hear from you."

Kelsey stepped closer and hugged him again. Jimmy held her tight. As they stood in each other's arms, he prayed for her safety and his sanity. It would be a long separation, for him at least.

She moved out of his embrace and gave him a peck on the cheek. "This is a long goodbye."

"Yeah." *Because I love you.* The words threatened to tumble from his mouth, but he pressed his lips together to keep from saying them. She wasn't ready to hear that from him. Maybe someday she would welcome his declaration of love.

Kelsey waved to Mitch and Amanda as she handed her ID and ticket to the TSA agent. Jimmy stood and watched. What was he going to do with these emotions that bubbled up inside him? He should be grateful he had seven weeks to get them under control.

"Hey, man." Mitch clamped a hand on Jimmy's shoulder. "A tough goodbye."

Jimmy let out a harsh breath. "I have a long seven weeks ahead of me, but I'll be busy. Hopefully, that'll make the time go fast."

"Yeah, my dad will have you working overtime."

Jimmy hoped there wouldn't be that much overtime. "I hope you guys don't mind if we wait until Kelsey's plane takes off. I'd like to know she got off safely."

Amanda gazed at him, a tiny smile curving her mouth. "You really do love her, don't you?"

Did he admit his feelings for Kelsey and have that admission get back to her? Was there any reason the sisters would discuss it? Probably not. Kelsey wasn't going to open that can of worms with Amanda. Of course he had to admit it. "Is there any doubt?"

Amanda shook her head. "It just happened so suddenly. I had my doubts at first, but seeing you together has changed my mind."

"Good. With that settled, there should be no more questions about my feelings for Kelsey."

Even though Jimmy said things were settled, he worried that the truth would eventually come out. He wanted to protect Kelsey. Be her hero. Could he do that when it was based on a lie? That question haunted him over and over.

Jimmy headed for the observation deck and hoped that would be the last of Amanda's questions. He couldn't blame her for being concerned about her sister. As he found the best spot to observe the takeoff, his phone dinged. He pulled it from his pocket and looked at it. A message from Kelsey. *I'm buckled in and ready for takeoff.*

Call you when I get to the other end. Be good while I'm gone. ☺

"A love note from Kelsey?" Amanda raised her eyebrows.

Jimmy typed a message back. *You can count on me.* "That's between Kelsey and me."

Did Kelsey think he wouldn't behave himself while she was away? She'd put a smiley face at the end of her comment, so he shouldn't take it too seriously. But he still couldn't shake the specter of his bad reputation. It popped up to remind him of his faults. He shouldn't worry. She had stuck up for him when Mitch had painted Jimmy in a bad light. He tried to convince himself that she had faith in him, even if she didn't love him.

While Jimmy stood there looking toward the runway, Mitch joined him. "I'm glad we've been able to talk things out."

"Me, too." Jimmy stuffed his hands into the pockets of his pants. "It'll make life easier if we're friends as well as brothers-in-law."

"Yeah." Mitch grinned. "Kelsey was a little tiger when she was defending you. She made me recognize the good things you've done."

"Thanks for letting me know."

"You're welcome." Mitch smiled. "If you need some help with your house, give me a call. I can come over any evening. I'm sure Amanda will be happy to help, too."

Jimmy nodded. "Thanks. I appreciate that. Let me see how things are with this new job."

"Is that Kelsey's plane? Mitch gestured toward the jetliner ready to take off.

"Yeah." Jimmy's gut twisted in a knot. He had no love

for flying. The flights he'd taken in the army had made him hate flying. He was a white-knuckle flyer and couldn't rest easy until he knew Kelsey was safely home.

"There she goes." Amanda glanced at her phone. "Right on time. She'll gain three hours on the flight, but she has to change planes twice."

Jimmy's stomach curdled at the thought of having to land and take off two more times as he watched Kelsey's plane rise into the clear blue sky—the color of her eyes. "I had no idea that she had to change planes that many times."

"One advantage. She can call or text you each time she lands." Mitch grinned.

"True."

While they walked back to the car, Jimmy hoped she would contact him, but he doubted she would. After all, this wasn't a real marriage, and she had no one to pretend for now that she was gone. He still had a whole audience to put on an act for. His family. Mitch and Amanda. Aunt Charlotte. Graham Cunningham. Jimmy might as well say the whole town of Pineydale. But for him it wasn't an act. He really loved his wife.

***

The door to Graham Cunningham's office stood open as Jimmy approached. He'd been on the job for a little over two weeks, and things were going well. At least, he believed they were good. But every time Uncle Graham called Jimmy into the office, he worried that he'd done something wrong.

With nervous energy pulsing through his body, Jimmy knocked on the open door and waited.

"Jimmy, come in." Graham, who was already seated, motioned for Jimmy to sit on the chair in front of the desk. "I've got a special project for you."

"What's that?"

"I want you to meet face to face with one of our suppliers."

"Sure. Which one?"

"That group in Spokane, Washington." Graham waved a finger in the air. "I thought you might like the opportunity to visit that pretty little wife of yours."

"Great. That would be fantastic." Jimmy hoped he sounded convincing. Yeah, he wanted to see Kelsey, but that meant flying clear across the country. He'd never admitted to anyone how much he hated to fly. "When do you want me to go?"

"Got your boarding pass for tomorrow right here." Graham slid a paper across the desk.

Jimmy picked it up and looked at it. "Wow! That's quick."

"Yes, I booked your ticket so you could spend a day with the suppliers and a long weekend with your wife and her family. It's Easter weekend, and I've given you Good Friday and Easter Monday off, so enjoy your little mini-vacation."

"Thank you, sir."

"One more thing before you head home." Graham tapped his desk. "This came about because I had a call from your father-in-law. He is eager to get to know you better and asked if I could see fit to give you a little time off to visit. So the whole thing worked out. And he'd like to make this a surprise for your wife. So don't tell her you're coming."

"Yes, sir. I've got it." Jimmy picked up the ticket information as he stood, a mix of joy and trepidation filling his mind. "Do you have any special instructions for me concerning this meeting?"

"I do." Graham pulled a folder out of a desk drawer and handed it to Jimmy. "The information you need is right here. I expect to hear a good report when you get back."

Jimmy nodded. "You will. Thanks again."

"I know I don't have to tell you to have a good time while you're gone. Say hello to your in-laws for me."

"Yes, sir." Jimmy shook Graham's hand, then hurried to his own office.

Jimmy sat at his desk and flipped through the folder. He could study this on the plane. Maybe it would distract him from the fact that he was thirty-five to forty thousand feet in the air in a slender steel tube traveling close to six hundred miles per hour. And maybe it could take his mind off the looming command performance for his in-laws.

He would have to tell his mom that he wouldn't be here for Easter dinner. She would be happy for him, yet sad that he wouldn't be with the family. His sisters had married local boys, so they traded hosting holiday dinners. This was the first time he'd thought about what it meant to be married to someone whose family lived far away. Would the sisters want to go home for holidays? That was something Jimmy needed to consider once Kelsey moved to Pineydale.

Straightening his desk, he gathered everything he needed for the trip to Spokane. He wanted to make sure he did this right. Besides a little vacation, this was certainly a test of his negotiating skills, and he wanted to make it a success in Graham's eyes. At least his uncle was happy with Jimmy's marriage.

The smell of fresh paint greeted Jimmy as he walked into his house. One of the bedrooms was nearly done, thanks to Mitch and Amanda. They had spent evenings last week painting. This past weekend they had helped him shop for furniture, bedding, and window treatments with Kelsey on video. He liked having her opinion. She made him smile.

Even though they'd been together for less than a week before she'd left, he missed her presence when he came home at night. The house was lonely. He'd been coming home to an empty house for years. Now he hated the solitude. He hadn't realized how solitary his life had been, even with family nearby, until Kelsey came along.

He plopped onto the couch and picked up his tablet from the coffee table. He sat there for a few minutes with it on his lap. Tonight he had to be careful not to let anything slip out about his upcoming trip. That would be hard because he was so eager to see her. Would she be able to tell something was up?

A video call with Kelsey made his day. He looked forward to it every night. He punched the screen and listened to the ring. In a few seconds her face appeared on the screen.

"Hey, how's everything back in Pineydale?" Her smile sent a whirling sensation through his gut.

"Good. How are things in Pullman?"

She wrinkled her nose. "The weather's nasty and cold. I wish I were in Pineydale."

"Because you miss me?"

She laughed. "You know it."

Kelsey's response let him know that her roommate,

Brianna, was within hearing distance. Jimmy's suspicions were confirmed as Brianna peered over Kelsey's shoulder. During their very first video call the night Kelsey had gotten back, Brianna was there and squealing with delight over Kelsey's marriage, but not understanding how Kelsey could leave Jimmy behind. Brianna had given him a nickname that she never failed to use.

"Hi, Mr. Eye Candy. I'm keeping your wife out of trouble."

"Thanks, Brianna. I'm sure it's the other way around. She's keeping you out of trouble." Jimmy chuckled.

"Can't talk long. Got lots of schoolwork. See you later MEC." She waved before disappearing from the camera view.

Jimmy wished Kelsey actually missed him. Maybe she did just a little, because she was happy to talk to him each night.

"Do you have lots of classwork?" Jimmy asked.

"Always. I've got a couple of tests to study for." She sighed. "I'll be glad when this week is over. I'm going home for Easter. Do you have plans?"

Jimmy didn't want his expression to give anything away. "My mom's having a big family get-together at her house after church. The kids will hunt Easter eggs. It's always a good time."

"I'm sorry I'll miss it." Kelsey actually looked sad.

"Me, too." He shouldn't read anything into her expression. His heart was obviously ruling his thoughts. He had to be realistic. She was keeping up the pretense in case Brianna happened into the room again.

"How are things proceeding on the house?"

"That bedroom is almost done except the flooring.

That's going to be an all-weekend project. Probably in two weeks. Mitch, Jeremy, Travis, and Dan are going to help."

"That'll be great." She smiled. "I've got to go so I can study. Talk to you tomorrow."

"I might not be able to talk tomorrow. Graham has me working on a special project, so I might be tied up. If you don't hear from me, you'll know why."

"Sure." Her smile faded just a little. "You can text me when you're free."

"Okay. I'll do that. Goodbye, Kelsey."

"Bye."

The screen went blank. Every time he said goodbye, he had to stop himself from telling her he loved her. One of these times, he was afraid it would pop out. He didn't want to put too much hope in the fact that she took pleasure in their daily conversations. Maybe she was doing it to keep up the pretense with Brianna, but even if that was the case, Kelsey appeared to enjoy talking to him.

How would she react when he showed up unannounced? They would have to share a bed at her parents' house. Did she have enough pillows to erect her barricade? Would she find her way across it into his arms again? He could only hope.

***

"I've got a surprise for you, Kels."

"What's that, Dad?" Kelsey couldn't imagine what kind of surprise her dad had for her. He wasn't usually a surprise kind of guy.

"Maria and I have dinner reservations at that steak house in downtown Spokane. You know the one we always go to?"

"Yeah. So how is that a surprise for me?"

"We want you to meet us there, and you'll see your surprise."

"Okay. I'm leaving here in about twenty minutes. What time is our reservation?"

"Six."

"I should be there in plenty of time."

"Good. Drive safely."

"I will, Dad. See you soon." Kelsey ended the call, then headed for her bedroom to get her things.

Before she put on her jacket, she stared at her reflection in the full-length mirror. Thankfully, her pregnancy still didn't show. Her pants weren't even tighter, probably because she had lost weight with all the morning sickness. It had subsided, but there were still mornings when she woke up feeling nauseous. She hoped it wasn't something that would last the entire pregnancy. If it did, maybe that was her punishment.

Sometimes she thought this was all a bad dream. She would wake up and find out she wasn't pregnant, she hadn't married a man she barely knew, and she wasn't moving to the opposite corner of the country in four weeks. But it wasn't a bad dream. It was her reality, and she had to deal with it.

As she drove along highway 195 through the Palouse country with its barren rolling hills and tiny towns, Kelsey tried to figure out what possible surprise her father had for her. He hadn't said much about her marriage. He seemed to begrudgingly accept it.

Pine trees lined the road as she drew closer to Spokane. She looked forward to being with her dad, Maria, and Noah for the Easter weekend. Uncle Clay and Aunt Beth and their kids would probably join them for Easter dinner. Unlike Amanda, Kelsey had always loved living in Pinecrest. It was more home than anyplace else. In a few weeks she would make Pineydale her home. Amanda had called Pineydale a "Pinecrest with a southern accent" when she'd been stuck there with her broken-down car. She hated the place until Mitch showed her how wonderful a small town could be.

Kelsey thought about Jimmy. Brianna teased him about being eye candy, and Kelsey couldn't dispute the fact that her husband was a very attractive man. His nightly calls buoyed her spirit. He was funny and kind. He shared her secret. But could she learn to love him? Would he ever love her? Those questions haunted her. She didn't see how the marriage could survive without love. Being apart certainly did nothing to kindle any love between them.

The sun sat low in the sky above the tree line as Kelsey drove into Spokane. She found a parking spot on the street not far from the restaurant. After she turned off the car and put the keys in her purse, she got out her cell phone. She punched in her dad's number and listened to the ring, her stomach in a knot of anticipation over this surprise.

"Kelsey, where are you?" Her dad's voice sounded over the phone.

"I'm parked a couple of blocks from the restaurant. Where are you?"

"I found a spot almost directly in front. We'll wait outside until you get here."

"Okay. See you in a few." Kelsey dumped her phone into her purse and got out of the car.

Walking toward the restaurant, she squinted as she

gazed ahead. She didn't see anyone. Maybe they were still sitting in the car. She continued to scan the area and finally spied her dad's car. In the next second, her dad and Maria got out and stood on the sidewalk.

"Dad, Maria." Kelsey quickened her pace and waved a hand above her head.

They turned and walked in her direction. When she reached them, her dad enveloped her in a big hug.

Maria hugged her, then stepped back and patted Kelsey's cheek. "You look so much more rested than after I saw you the last time. You've got a little color in those cheeks."

Kelsey smiled. "I'm just feeling good because I aced my exams."

"Good for you." Her dad squeezed her shoulders.

"So what's my surprise?" Kelsey gazed up at her dad.

Her dad grinned. "Your surprise is in the car. Go over and see what it is."

Cautiously, Kelsey approached the car. What if she didn't like the surprise? She didn't want to disappoint her dad if he went to a lot of trouble to get whatever she would find. She prepared herself to pretend she liked it. She should be good at pretending. She'd been doing a lot of that lately.

Before she got to the car, the door opened, and Jimmy stepped out, a grin showing off his perfect white teeth. Stunned, she blinked, then blinked again. She should be happy. Or should she? She should run to greet him, but her legs wouldn't move. Her mind whirled. Her heart pounded. She couldn't catch her breath. She grew lightheaded and thought she might faint right there on the street.

"Kelsey." Jimmy rushed to her side and gathered her

into his arms. "Are you okay?"

Even in her confusion, she knew one thing. Jimmy Cunningham was a man she could count on no matter what. "I'm okay. Just in shock."

"I thought you were going to faint."

"Me, too." She held him tight and whispered, "You need to kiss me."

He smiled wryly, then whispered back, "I thought you'd never ask. I know the drill."

Kelsey's heart sank. He knew the drill. Play it up for their audience, her dad and Maria. Kelsey wondered how long she could keep up the charade before she succumbed to his kisses and did something she would regret. How could she hold the line and still make people believe this was a real marriage? It was like negotiating the rapids of a fast-moving river. Dangerous. Crazy. Impractical.

All thought fled as Jimmy kissed her. His kisses made her feel as though she had come home to a place where she was cherished and loved. Even when she fretted about marrying someone she'd known for such a little time, he made her feel this way. But she couldn't let herself believe that. It was all for show. Pretend. Make-believe.

"Okay, you two. We have a dinner reservation to make." Her dad's voice penetrated Kelsey's foggy brain.

Kelsey stepped out of Jimmy's embrace, but he put an arm around her waist in a protective gesture as they approached Grady and Maria.

Grady gazed at Kelsey. "You should've seen your face when Jimmy stepped out of the car. I was glad he was there to catch you. I thought you might faint."

"That makes three of us." Kelsey sighed with relief.

"Make that four." Maria raised a hand. "The color

drained from your face."

"Well, all is good now that Jimmy is here and I've gotten over my shock." Kelsey smiled at her dad. "This is the best surprise you've ever given me. I never imagined this."

"I'm glad I could make you happy." Grady motioned toward the entrance of the restaurant. "Let's go inside."

Kelsey followed her dad into the restaurant as Jimmy held the door open for her. She wasn't sure whether she was happy. Part of her was overjoyed that he was here, the heart that was wishing for love. The practical part, the brain that was concerned about making this work, was worried. She would have to share a bedroom with him again. There was no getting out of it.

After they were seated at their table, Kelsey looked over at Jimmy. "How long have you known about this?"

Jimmy gazed down at her. "Since Tuesday night. It was hard to keep it a secret when we were doing our video calls."

"You told me you were going to your mother's for Easter." Kelsey frowned.

Jimmy's eyes twinkled with laughter. "When you asked, I said my mom was having Easter dinner at her house. I didn't say anything about going myself."

Kelsey thought back over their conversation. "You're right. You're sneaky, making me believe you were going to your mom's."

"You have to listen carefully to what people say." Jimmy grinned.

"Yes, I do." Kelsey couldn't forget how Brandon's smooth talk had fooled her. She couldn't let that happen with Jimmy. But Jimmy wasn't Brandon. She knew just where she stood with Jimmy.

For the rest of the meal, Kelsey listened as her dad and Jimmy talked business. She learned about his meeting with a supplier here. She took note that her dad seemed impressed with Jimmy's knowledge. She hoped that boded well for her dad putting the stamp of approval on her husband.

During the ride home, as Kelsey sat in the backseat with Jimmy, Grady pumped Jimmy for information about his family and schooling. He answered calmly, as if he'd expected the inquisition. Kelsey wanted to tell her dad to lay off, but when Jimmy reached over and squeezed her hand, she stifled her comment.

For the rest of the trip, she continued to hold Jimmy's hand. She drew comfort from his presence, but his presence also confused her. His kindness and willingness to protect her from her own mistakes made her feel guilty. They would go through that same discussion that occurred every time they were confronted with having to share a bed. Every time it came up, she considered going along with his wish to consummate the marriage, but every time she dismissed it. She wanted love, not an arrangement.

CHAPTER TWELVE

Jimmy brought in Kelsey's luggage and his own as Grady showed him to Kelsey's room. He set the bags on the floor and took in the white furniture, including a desk, bookshelves, and a queen-sized bed with a white comforter covered in polka-dots in several shades of blue. Matching curtains hung on the windows, and the pale-blue walls sported a poster of a big wooly dog. Did that mean Kelsey loved dogs? She'd certainly loved taking care of Dolly.

"It's a little girly, but at least it's not pink like it was when we first moved into this house." Grady motioned around the room. "Kelsey redecorated after Amanda left for college."

"I suppose that means she might do some redecorating when she moves into my place." Jimmy hoped she'd make his home her own. He wouldn't mind at all if she wanted to change things to her liking. That might mean she was investing in their future. Would she decorate a nursery?

Grady pointed to his left. "There's a Jack-and-Jill bath through that door. Amanda and Kelsey shared that bathroom. Now Amanda's old bedroom is the nursery. Noah usually sleeps through the night now, but occasionally he wakes up. So you might hear him because of the connecting bathroom."

"I'm a pretty sound sleeper." Jimmy wondered how

he'd sleep after Kelsey's baby was born.

"Good." Grady turned toward the door. "Maria and Kelsey should be back soon from picking up Noah."

"It's great that your brother and his wife are able to babysit for you." Jimmy followed Grady out to the kitchen and sat on one of the stools at the bar.

"You'll have a chance to meet them. They're coming over for Easter. If the weather is good, we'll have an Easter egg hunt in the yard for their two kids." Grady opened one of the medium-brown cabinets and brought out a glass. "Can I get you something to drink?"

Jimmy shook his head, thinking how he was going to miss his own family. Is that how Kelsey would feel once she moved to Pineydale, or would having Amanda nearby make things easier? "I'm good right now. Still full from supper."

"I hope you're not too full. Maria has a dessert for us when she gets back."

"I'll probably have room by that time." Jimmy patted his stomach.

Grady set out more glasses and some plates on the multicolored granite countertop with veins of brown and tan. He grew silent, and Jimmy worried that the man would ask about their marriage. So far, most of Grady's questions were about Jimmy's job, background, and schooling. He could tell Kelsey had grown agitated as her father asked more and more questions. Jimmy wondered whether she was worried, as he was, that her dad would figure out that all wasn't quite what it seemed when it came to their marriage.

While Jimmy stewed, Kelsey came through the door, carrying her little brother. Jimmy could only imagine her carrying her own child in a year's time. She was going to make a great mother.

She immediately came over to him. "Noah, I want you to meet your brother-in-law, Jimmy."

Jimmy stuck out his finger for the baby to grab, and the baby cooed. "I think he likes me, but I never thought about having a baby for a brother-in-law."

Grady chuckled. "The Reynolds have some different family dynamics. Over a dozen years ago, my brother, Clay, married a single mom who had a sixteen-year-old son, Max, whom Clay adopted. Now Clay has two elementary school-aged children as well. You may have met Max and his wife, Heather, at Amanda's wedding."

Jimmy nodded. "I remember Max and Heather. He's the one who's a cancer survivor."

"That's a lot to cheer for in this family." Maria opened the refrigerator and brought out what looked like some kind of cake.

"Then there's Maria and me. I was a widower when she moved to Pinecrest, and not interested in finding another wife, but my girls had a different idea." Grady went over and gave Maria a peck on the cheek, then hugged Kelsey. "I'm glad they did. Now I'm a father again when I should be a grandfather, but it's all good."

"It's great when things work out, even when we're not expecting it." Jimmy wondered if Grady would feel the same way when he found out in a couple of months that he *was* going to be a grandfather.

Jimmy gazed at Kelsey as a conspiratorial look passed between them. She smiled back at him, but her eyes held a concerned look. Was she worried about their marriage? The baby? The sleeping arrangements for this weekend?

He was such a chicken. He wouldn't ask her about any of those things because he might not like her answer.

After Maria served a cheesecake, they sat around the big oak kitchen table and talked about the plans for the weekend. Grady suggested that they take a drive the next day and show Jimmy some of the sights in the area. Gratitude welled up inside Jimmy. He felt accepted as Grady's son-in-law, one that he wanted for his daughter. Jimmy even imagined that he could find another father figure in his father-in-law, but that depended on how his relationship with Kelsey grew.

Kelsey stretched her arms over her head, then stood. "It's been a long week, and I'm tired."

"Me, too." Jimmy joined her, then looked at Maria. "Thanks for the delicious dessert."

"You're welcome." Maria put the leftover cake in the fridge. "If you want more, just help yourselves."

"Good night, you two." Grady grinned. "You can sleep as late as you like tomorrow."

Jimmy put an arm around Kelsey's shoulders as they left the kitchen. "I believe your dad thinks we're not going to the bedroom to sleep."

Kelsey frowned as she scooted through the doorway, but she didn't respond to his remark. "If you don't mind, I'll use the bathroom first."

"Sure." Jimmy berated himself for the comment.

With a heavy sigh, he flopped onto the bed. He laced his hands behind his head and stared at the ceiling. Maybe she'd make him sleep on the floor. He'd felt like part of this family tonight. Grady had welcomed Jimmy, and he couldn't help but think of his dad. James Cunningham would have liked Grady Reynolds. Jimmy hoped he could have a good relationship with his father-in-law, but first Jimmy had to have a good relationship with Kelsey. Was that even possible?

Yes. Video calls. Getting the house ready for her. Flying across the country when he hated to fly. He was being the best pretend husband he could be. That was easy because there was nothing pretend about his love for Kelsey.

"Jimmy, you can have the bathroom."

He sat up like a jack-in-the-box and hopped off the bed as if it were on fire. He stared at Kelsey, who wore those same cat pajamas she'd worn on their wedding night. "Sure. Thanks."

She didn't say another thing, just turned down the covers on the bed and slipped in. She didn't give him a clue as to where she expected him to sleep. Was she upset with him because he'd joked about the nighttime activities that wouldn't happen? He'd made a complete mess of the evening that had started so well.

He grabbed his stuff and hurried into the bathroom. While he brushed his teeth, he tried to think of some way to apologize. Everything he rehearsed in his mind seemed lame. He was probably better off not to mention it. Besides, she might already be asleep when he finished. Would he find her wall of pillows in the bed? What if he didn't?

Staring at himself in the mirror, he ran a hand over his day-old growth of beard. He liked the popular scruffy look and had often gone several days without shaving when he'd been painting houses. Now he had to shave every morning and put on a suit and tie. Some days when that tie felt like a noose around his neck, he wished he was back painting again.

He'd been voted best looking in high school, and Kelsey's roommate called him Mr. Eye Candy. But what did Kelsey think? The question was juvenile. What she thought about his looks didn't matter. Yeah, he wanted her to think he was handsome, but more than that, he wanted her to think he was a good man, a man she could trust and love. What she felt about him as a person mattered the most. Could she ever love him?

Jimmy opened the bathroom door a crack and peered into the darkness. Kelsey must have turned out the lights after he'd gone into the bathroom. He groped his way across the room until he bumped into the bed and cracked his knee on the footboard. He stifled a yelp as he grabbed his knee and rubbed it.

Slowly his eyes adjusted until he could see the outline of Kelsey's body underneath the covers. He stood there for a moment and gazed at her. He swallowed hard as he looked at the empty space on the other side of the bed. His space? There were no pillows to create a divide. Would he ever fall asleep if he had to lie that close to her and not touch her?

One way to find out. Jimmy eased his way into the bed and turned his back to her. Closing his eyes, he prayed God would give him the wisdom to make the right choices when it came to Kelsey.

Jimmy feared he had pushed her into this for his own selfish reasons, and that made him no better than Brandon. No. Kelsey had agreed to marry him in order to keep her father from finding out about Brandon and to give her baby a dad. But sometimes guilt still ate at Jimmy. He drove himself crazy with his thoughts going over the same territory again and again with no new solution in sight.

After what seemed like hours of wakefulness, Jimmy finally drifted off to sleep. He dreamed Kelsey was walking beside him along a cliff that dropped off to the rocks far, far below. A strange man confronted them and threatened to push them over the cliff. Jimmy tried to protect Kelsey, but the man grabbed her arm. Jimmy struggled to hold on to Kelsey while the man battered Jimmy's face. Kelsey slipped from his grip and fell into the nothingness, a scream filling the air.

Jimmy sat straight up in bed. The screams weren't only in his dreams. Kelsey was screaming in her sleep, her arms flailing. Then he realized his nose was bleeding. Had Kelsey actually punched him?

"Kelsey." He gently shook her. "Kelsey, wake up."

She quit thrashing about as her eyes fluttered open. "Jimmy?"

"I'm here. You were having a bad dream" They'd both had bad dreams.

"Jimmy." She grabbed on to him. "You're okay."

"Of course I'm okay." At least, he thought he was. He felt his nose. He hadn't been fighting with the strange assailant in his dream. He'd been fighting off Kelsey. "Are *you* okay? You were screaming in your sleep."

Closing her eyes, she placed a hand over heart. "I had a terrible dream. I'd already had the baby, and a man with a horrid mask and Brandon's voice was trying to take the baby from me. You were there and tried to stop him, but he stabbed you. I was trying to fight him off and take back the baby."

"That was a nightmare." Jimmy decided there was no point in telling her about his dream. "And I think I've borne the brunt of your dream."

"What happened?"

Jimmy swiped a hand under his nose. "You gave me a bloody nose."

"I did?"

"Yeah. You have a good punch." Jimmy touched his cheek under his right eye. "I think I might have a black eye tomorrow."

"Oh no. What will my dad say?"

"Let me clean up my face, and we'll worry about that later." Jimmy headed toward the bathroom.

"Let me help. I'll turn on the night-light so we aren't blinded by the bright overhead lights." Kelsey reached around him and flipped a switch.

A dim light along the bottom of the mirror created a soft glow in the room. Jimmy looked at his reflection. His nose was still bleeding, and a smear of blood stained his cheek where he had wiped blood away.

Kelsey looked at him. "I'm so sorry. I told you I'm not used to sleeping with someone."

Jimmy laughed. "I didn't know you meant you punched people in your sleep. I kind of liked waking up and finding you in my arms, not punching me in the nose."

Kelsey didn't respond to his comment. Had he done it again? Upset her? Why couldn't he keep his wishes to himself? She was already feeling bad about whacking him in the nose. He didn't need to upset her further.

"Sit on this stool." Kelsey pulled a little padded stool out of the knee hole in the counter.

Jimmy wasn't going to argue. "What are you going to do?"

"Clean up your face."

"I can do that."

"I know, but I also know where to find everything in here." She opened a narrow door and pulled out a washcloth and a towel.

In short order she was gently wiping the blood from his face. He definitely wasn't going to argue now. He liked having her tend to his wounds, even if she was the one who caused them.

"I didn't break your nose, did I?"

Jimmy reached up and wiggled his nose. "It hurts, but I don't think it's broken. I hope not. You also gave me a fat lip. What will Brianna say when she finds out you've messed up Mr. Eye Candy's face?"

Kelsey giggled, then covered her mouth with her fingers for a second. "I think you look handsome even if you do have a bloody nose and a fat lip."

"I'm glad you didn't ruin my face." Swallowing hard, he gripped the edges of the stool as she leaned closer and ran the damp washcloth across his face again.

Her assessment of his looks boosted his ego. Over the years, lots of people had told him he was handsome, but Kelsey's praise was all he wanted. Her proximity made it difficult not to pull her into his arms and kiss her, even though his lip was busted. He would recover from these physical wounds, but would he recover from the emotional wounds if she never came to love him?

Kelsey opened the medicine cabinet and moved several bottles and finally brought out one and held it up. "You should take some ibuprofen. That should help keep the swelling down."

"Yes, Nurse Kelsey. Whatever you say." He held out a hand, and she shook a couple of tablets into it.

She plucked a small plastic cup from a holder on the counter and filled it with water. "Here."

Their fingers brushed as he took the cup. A spark of awareness jumped between them. She'd been touching him as she washed his face, but the simple brushing of their fingers made his pulse race.

"I'm going to get some ice." She nearly sprinted out of the room.

Her actions told Jimmy she had felt the spark, too. He took a deep breath and expelled it in a loud whoosh. He looked at himself in the mirror and wiggled his nose. It didn't look crooked. It was sore, but not as sore as the time Mitch had punched him because of Whitney. He closed his eyes, trying to rid himself of those thoughts. Why did he have to think about her at a time like this? Maybe as a reminder not to do something stupid again.

In a minute Kelsey padded back into the bathroom, carrying an ice pack wrapped in a towel. "Here. Put this on your nose and eye. Maybe if you're lucky, you won't have a black eye in the morning."

"Lucky for you, too, if I don't have a black eye. And look what you did to my shirt. Blood all over it." Trying hard to keep a serious expression, he put the ice pack on his face. "What will people say when they find you gave me a black eye after I traveled all this way to see you?"

A little pucker formed between Kelsey's eyebrows as she stared at him. "I was asleep. I didn't know what I was doing."

A smile escaped as Jimmy looked at Kelsey. "I was just kidding."

"Haven't I asked you not to tease me?"

"You have, but I don't always obey orders." Jimmy

took a chance and reached for her hand with his free hand. When she didn't resist, he laced his fingers through hers and stared into her eyes. "You're easy to tease, and you might as well learn that my family is full of teasers. If you don't get teased in my family, you should be worried. We only tease the people we like."

Her blue eyes opened wide as she extracted her hand from his. "We don't do much teasing in my family. Guess 'cause my dad's a pretty serious guy. So I'm anxious about what he'll think."

"We just tell him the truth. He raised a daughter with a good left hook."

Kelsey put her hands on her hips and tried to glare at him, but she couldn't keep a straight face. Another giggle escaped as she glanced toward the door to the nursery. "Now that we have your face cleaned up, we probably should go into the bedroom. Good thing my screaming didn't wake anyone but you."

Jimmy opened his mouth to tease her again, but he clamped it shut. He would honor her request. Kelsey turned on the bedside lamp. It illuminated the tangled blankets, sheets, and the blood.

Jimmy pointed to the bed. "Looks like we have a mess here."

Kelsey hurried over to straighten the covers. "The blood will come out in the wash."

"And my wounds will fade in time."

Worry wrinkled Kelsey's brow. "Are you really okay?"

"Yeah. Let's try to get some sleep."

"Okay." Kelsey slid into bed and turned off the light.

Still holding the cold pack on his nose and eye, Jimmy

joined her. He lay on his back and stared into the darkness. He'd glanced at the clock. Three thirty. It had taken him nearly two hours to fall asleep in the first place. How long would he lie here awake this time?

"Jimmy?"

"Yeah."

"I'm really, really sorry."

"I know you are, Kelsey. It's okay. Maybe I should buy one of those catcher's masks to wear to bed."

"I thought you weren't going to tease me."

"Who's teasing? I need to protect my pretty face."

She poked him in the ribs. He poked back. She poked him again. He tickled her ribs. In the next instant Jimmy let the cool pack fall away, and they were in each other's arms. His pulse pounding, he used every ounce of his willpower to hold perfectly still.

"Kelsey? You know where this is going to lead."

She scooted out of his arms as quickly as she had fallen into them. With her face in her hands, she sat on the side of the bed. Jimmy scrambled to sit beside her without touching her, even though he wanted to hold her in his arms and comfort her. He waited as her shoulders shook in a silent cry.

Finally she dropped her hands and sat up straight as she sniffled. "I'm sorry. I'm really a sorry mess. You're not the tease. I am."

"It's okay."

"No it's not. You want this to be a real marriage, and for a few moments there, I let you think it could be." The little pucker reappeared between her eyebrows. "I don't want this to be about a physical attraction. I want this to be about love."

The vise of her words squeezed Jimmy's heart. She was attracted to him, but she didn't love him. Why had he let his stupid heart race into love without a second thought? What was that expression? *Fools rush in where angels fear to tread.* That described him perfectly.

What would it take to win Kelsey's love? He'd fallen for her as quickly as a hound chased a rabbit. That was the problem. Maybe he needed to start from the beginning with her.

He looked at her, wishing he could be the man she loved. "So what would you like me to do? Sleep on the floor?"

"No. No." She glanced at the bed. "Unless you want to."

Jimmy chuckled. "Who wants to sleep on the floor?"

"Nobody." She picked up the abandoned ice pack and placed it gently on his face. "You came here on demand because of my dad and your uncle. You shouldn't have to sleep on the floor."

"Thanks." Jimmy took over holding the ice pack and wished he had some words of wisdom to share with her. What if he told her how he felt? No. That was crazy. Then she'd feel awkward, pressured, or even sorry she'd ever agreed to marry him.

"You should lie back down with that ice pack on your face."

Was that her way of telling him to go to his own side of the bed and stay there? Still holding the ice pack, he got up and went around the bed. He lay down while she still sat there, her back to him. "Kelsey, what are you doing?"

"Praying."

That was what he should've been doing. He got up

again. "May I join you?"

"You mean pray together?"

"Yeah, we should do that."

She turned on the little lamp on the nightstand. "I'm not used to sharing prayers with someone. Lately, I haven't been sure about praying."

"Why?"

Kelsey lowered her gaze as he sat beside her. "Because of us."

Her statement dampened his spirit. "You're sorry you married me?"

She jerked her head up and looked right at him. "No. No. You've been my lifeline."

"Then what?" He peered at her as the little lamp cast shadows on her face.

She twisted her hands in her lap as she lowered her gaze again. "I feel awful because I can't give you what you want."

Jimmy let her confession settle around his heart, the heart that wanted her love, not just the physical aspects of marriage. "We're in this together. I agreed to your requirements."

She gazed at him. "But I can't forget that we did this to hide my pregnancy. How can God bless that? How can he answer my prayers?"

"But you were still praying?"

"Asking for forgiveness." Pain painted her features. "But can forgiveness come when I'm still living a lie?"

Jimmy held out his hands to her, and thankfully she placed hers in his. "That's been your issue from the beginning. I've been troubled with the same thought, but I don't have an answer. Can you share what you were saying in your prayer?"

"I was just pleading for forgiveness, even though I'm not sure I'll be forgiven."

"What do you want to do? Do you want to tell your dad the truth? Will that take away your guilt?" Jimmy squeezed her hands. "If you want to do that, I'll stand with you."

"Everything with my dad is so black and white. He'll blame you for helping me hide my pregnancy, and you don't deserve that. And he'll go after Brandon. I can't have that." Misery reflected in her eyes. "I've made a mess of everything. Just everything."

"Then maybe we just need to pray that God can clean up our mess."

"It's more my mess than yours."

"Don't forget. We're in this together."

"My emotions have been on a hormonal roller-coaster ride. But there's one thing I know for sure. It's kind of weird. I haven't known you very long, but I feel like you're my best friend."

Her earlier words had crushed him, but these words planted hope in his mind—hope that she would come to love him. Good marriages were built on friendship. That was a start. "Let's just pray."

"Will you say the prayer?"

"I will."

Without another word, she bowed her head.

Jumbled thoughts filled Jimmy's mind. Could he voice a coherent prayer? What was that verse about the Spirit groaning when a person didn't know how to pray? That was what needed to happen now.

Jimmy cleared his throat. "Lord God, Kelsey and I

come thanking you for the privilege of prayer. Thank You for listening to our pleas. We know we've done things that don't please You. Please forgive us. We've made a commitment to each other, and we pray You will help us keep that commitment. Give us wisdom going forward. In Jesus's name. Amen."

Kelsey still held his hands. "Thank you. That's just what I needed. You reminded me of the commitment we made to each other."

Jimmy hopped up from the bed and went to the dresser. He grabbed his wallet and pulled out a folded note card, then returned to sit beside Kelsey.

"What's that?"

He unfolded it. "Our vows."

"You carry those in your wallet?"

"I stuck them there on our wedding day and never took them out." He gazed into her eyes. "I actually forgot they were there until just now."

"Can we say them again?" Uncertainty radiated from her eyes.

Her question lightened his thoughts. "Sure."

"Should we read them together?"

"Okay, but these are mine." He pointed to the *I, Jimmy* on the card.

"I can put in the appropriate ones for me." She took one side of the note card as she looked at him with expectation.

"Okay."

Together they read the vows they had said on their wedding day. After they finished, Kelsey gazed at him, tears welling in her eyes. "Thank you for being my best friend."

Jimmy swallowed a lump in his throat. That was what he had to do. Be her best friend. He had to look at starting with this friendship and building on it. "As your friend, I'd like to know the boundaries. I know it's something we should've discussed before."

"Boundaries? Like what?"

"We've been playacting, but I'm not sure where that leaves us when we aren't."

"Oh." Her brow wrinkled. "I'm not sure what to say."

Jimmy wished he'd thought this through better. He didn't want this to come out sounding stupid. "We've been kissing and hugging for the benefit of the people watching. What's appropriate when people aren't watching? Are you okay with me putting my arm around you, holding your hand, hugging you? What's not to your liking?"

Her mouth parted slightly. She stared at him. Her eyes grew wide like a deer in the headlights. "I'm not sure. Maybe you should be the one to set the boundaries. Like tonight when you stopped and let me know what could happen if we continued our playfulness."

"Or maybe we both have to set the boundaries."

"And we can't be afraid to say what we're feeling when it comes to them." Jimmy didn't miss the irony of his own statement. Here he was telling her not to be afraid when he was exactly that. He was afraid to tell her he loved her. But maybe he could start with something. "Are you willing to go on a date with me?"

She looked at him, a shy smile on her lips. "Are you asking me out?"

"I am." Jimmy grinned. "I've wanted to do that ever since we met last October, but you lived too far away."

"I'd love to go on a date with you."

"Any good suggestions on where to go on a date around here?"

Kelsey motioned toward the clock on the nightstand. "Jimmy, do you realize it's nearly four thirty. I think we can discuss the date tomorrow. We need to get some sleep."

"Okay, but your dad did say we could sleep in."

Annoyance captured her look. "I'd poke you again, but I've learned my lesson in that regard."

Sighing, Jimmy got up and walked to the other side of the bed. "I don't know whether to say good night or good morning."

"How about sweet dreams?"

"Yeah. Maybe that way you won't pummel me in my sleep."

"You can always sleep on the floor." Kelsey lay down and pulled the covers up under her chin without another word.

A sinking sensation in his gut, Jimmy did the same. Why did he always open his mouth and undo the goodwill he had created? But he would follow through with this date plan even if it meant a candlelight dinner in his own kitchen when she finally moved to Pineydale. They needed a rewind, a chance to get to know each other for real.

CHAPTER THIRTEEN

The next morning Kelsey awakened once again in Jimmy's arms. Talk about not observing the boundaries. Did he wear some kind of magnet that drew her to him? Maybe it was just the warmth of another body in the bed that she gravitated toward. At least this time he was still asleep.

Hoping not to wake him, she slowly extracted herself from his embrace. Success. She lay on her side of the bed and watched him sleep. His nose wasn't swollen, but she couldn't mistake the black eye or the slight discoloration on his lower lip. Her heart fluttered as his chest rose and fell with each breath.

Whenever she was around him, she was in a constant state of confusion. He was funny, charming, and handsome. He made her pulse race with a wink. Was that love or something else? After her experience with Brandon, she couldn't trust her own instincts. She barely knew Jimmy, so how could she love him?

After this weekend she would have a month of nightly video calls in which to get to know him without his physical presence getting in the way. Then again, how could she get to know someone with a few minutes of video calls? She chided herself. She didn't have to know all the answers now. They had time to get to know each other before the baby came.

Jimmy opened his eyes and looked at her. "Hey, Rocky, did you get enough sleep?"

"You just can't help yourself when it comes to teasing me, can you?" Kelsey tried not to smile, but she couldn't help herself.

He chuckled. "Like I said, you're so easy to tease. What time is it?"

Kelsey sat up on the edge of the bed and pointed to the clock on the bedside table. "After nine. I'm pretty sure everyone else is up. Noah gets up pretty early."

"Guess we did sleep in. Your folks won't mind, will they?"

"Dad did say we could sleep in."

"Then I guess we're okay." Jimmy grinned. "How do I look this morning?"

"Not bad for a guy with a black eye and a fat lip."

Jimmy frowned. "I have a black eye?"

Kelsey reached over to touch his face, then withdrew her hand. "Okay to touch you?"

"As long as you don't poke it."

"Your face is a little purple right here under your eye." Kelsey barely brushed a finger above his cheekbone. "Did that hurt?"

"No, it's okay." He cocked his head as he stared at her. "You're good this morning? No morning sickness?"

"I'm good." Better than good.

She liked being here with him. He made her feel safe. Did that mean love? So what if it did, but he didn't love her? She didn't have to figure any of this out today. She should enjoy this weekend with Jimmy. After all, he was her best friend. She would enjoy that aspect of their relationship and figure the rest out later.

"Do you mind if I use the bathroom first?"

He gestured across the room. "Ladies first."

"Thanks." Kelsey hopped out of bed.

She glanced at herself in the mirror as she went into the bathroom. She ran her fingers through her hair. She had bed head, and she'd looked like that when she'd been sitting there talking to Jimmy. Not the way to impress your husband.

After she showered and put on a light coral ribbed-knit sweater and a pair of jeans, she padded back into the bedroom as she fluffed her still-damp hair. Jimmy lay on the bed as he read something on his phone. She wanted to ask what he was reading, but she didn't want him to think she was nosy. Would he care or not? More stuff to figure out.

"The bathroom's yours." Her heart fluttered when he looked her way. She swallowed hard.

"Great." Laying his phone on the bedside table, he got up. He grabbed his things and disappeared into the bathroom.

Wondering about Jimmy's non-talkative mood, Kelsey fretted that he was wounded in more ways than the physical. She should learn to take his teasing as he meant it. All in fun. This was part of getting to know each other. The scary part was having done everything backward. But then she'd been more afraid of living with her father's disappointment and condemnation than marrying a man she barely knew.

She wandered into the kitchen and found Maria making Noah laugh while she made funny faces at him. Every time Kelsey was around her little brother, she couldn't help thinking about her own baby. Would it be a boy or a girl? Now that the nausea had subsided substantially, Kelsey often forgot she was pregnant. Everything was normal until that nausea occasionally hit her unexpectedly.

"Hi, Noah."

Both the baby and Maria looked in Kelsey's direction.

"Well, you're finally up." Maria smiled.

"Yeah. It was nice to sleep in. I don't get to do that much at school."

"Did you sleep well?"

Kelsey nodded but wondered whether Maria thought the newlyweds hadn't done a lot of sleeping. "When did Noah wake up?"

Maria laughed. "We all slept in, even this little guy. Your dad's gone to the bakery to get those fabulous cinnamon rolls for breakfast."

"Yum. I haven't had those since Christmas."

"Where's Jimmy? Still sleeping?"

"No. He's getting dressed."

Maria picked up Noah and put him on a mat in the adjoining family room. "It's tummy time."

"He's getting so big." Kelsey sat on the barstool and watched her little brother.

Maria poured herself a cup of tea. "Would you like some?"

Kelsey shook her head. "I'll wait for the cinnamon rolls and have a glass of milk."

"You don't usually drink milk." Maria gave Kelsey a questioning look.

"I just like it with cinnamon rolls." Kelsey definitely wasn't ready to tell anyone she was pregnant. She didn't intend to say anything until she had moved to Pineydale, and even then she wasn't sure when she would make it known.

Maria patted Kelsey on the arm. "I just wanted to tell you how happy your dad is that you and Jimmy are here to share the holiday with us. I know he wouldn't tell you himself."

"I'm glad Jimmy is here, too." Kelsey realized how much she meant that. She had missed him when she didn't even know it. She wondered whether her dad had said anything about Jimmy or their marriage. What would her dad say when he saw Jimmy's black eye?

Maria smiled. "You know your dad was the one who arranged for Jimmy to come, don't you?"

"It was such a shock when he showed up, but a nice surprise." Kelsey had to admit that every part of her statement was true. Having Jimmy by her side brightened her life. "I was shocked because Dad didn't seem too pleased when we called him and told him we'd gotten married."

"He wasn't. He ranted around the house for days. He wanted to check out this guy who had married his little girl." Maria took a sip of her tea, then set the cup on the counter.

Kelsey swallowed hard. "Has Dad said anything more about our marriage since Jimmy's been here?"

"Not much, but I think he sees how much you love each other. He's coming around a little, but he probably won't tell you that either."

So her dad thought she and Jimmy were in love. That was a good thing. "Yeah, I know Dad. He's pretty tight lipped when it comes to stuff like that. Thanks for letting me know."

Maria hugged Kelsey. "Anytime. I need to tell you and Amanda more often how much you mean to me."

"And you to us." Kelsey hugged Maria back. "The best part is the way you made our family whole again."

"I believe that was God's doing. He brought us together."

Jimmy roamed into the room, his hair still wet from his shower. His appearance made Kelsey's heart trip.

"What happened to you?" Maria frowned.

Jimmy looked at Kelsey. "You didn't warn them about your left hook?"

Maria's gaze darted between Jimmy and Kelsey. "What's he talking about?"

"He's teasing me because I had a nightmare and accidentally gave him a black eye, a bloody nose, and a fat lip."

"That must've been some dream!" Maria gazed at Jimmy. "Do you need anything for those wounds?"

Chuckling, Jimmy shook his head. "No. Kelsey doctored me last night."

Before anyone could comment further, the sound of the garage door opening let them know Grady was home.

Kelsey hurried toward the door leading from the garage to the kitchen. "I can smell the cinnamon rolls already."

Grady walked through the door, a box in his hands. He stopped for a second and gave Kelsey a peck on the cheek. "Good morning, sleepyhead. Did you sleep well?"

"Obviously not." Maria gestured toward Jimmy. "I just found out she was beating up Jimmy in the night."

Grady set the box on the counter and looked Jimmy's

way. "What?"

Grimacing, Jimmy glanced at Kelsey. "You want to tell your dad about your famous left hook?"

Kelsey glared at Jimmy as she put her hands on her hips. "Will you quit teasing about that?"

Jimmy put an arm around her waist and pulled her close for a quick kiss. "You know how I love to tease you."

"Yes, I do."

"So would someone like to explain?" Grady asked.

Kelsey turned to her dad. "I had a really bad dream last night. In the dream I was trying to beat up a guy who stabbed Jimmy. Instead, I was actually waving my arms around in my sleep and whacked Jimmy in the face."

"So you were beating up on your husband when you thought you were beating up the guy in your dream?"

Kelsey nodded as she held her breath.

Grady burst out laughing as he ran a hand through the air. "I can just see the headline now. Wife beats up husband after mistaking him for the bad guy in her dream."

Kelsey frowned and glared at her dad, then Jimmy. "Okay, you two, quit teasing me."

Jimmy put an arm around her shoulders. "I thought you told me your dad doesn't tease."

"He doesn't." Kelsey frowned at her dad. "You never do that."

Grady was still grinning. "Sorry, honey. I just remember the last time you did that."

"What?" Kelsey's frown deepened.

"Yeah, when you were about five, not long after your mother died, you had a nightmare. You came crying into my room. I held you and rubbed your little back until you quit crying. You were afraid to go back to your room, so I let you stay there with me. I planned to take you back to your bed as soon as you fell asleep, but I fell asleep, too, and the next thing I knew, you were thrashing about and clocked me in the eye, then my nose."

"How come I don't remember this?" Kelsey asked.

"Because you were five. It was probably something you didn't want to remember, and neither did I." Grady turned to Jimmy. "So you're not the first guy she's beat up."

Jimmy glance at her sideways. "Do I dare laugh?"

Kelsey waved a hand at her dad and Jimmy. "Okay. Go ahead and laugh at my expense."

"Ah, Kelsey, you know we love you." Grady enveloped Kelsey in his arms. "You just have a bad habit of beating up people in your sleep. I won't laugh anymore."

"I love you, too." Kelsey hugged her dad back and wondered if Jimmy would take a clue and hug her, too.

As soon as she stepped out of her dad's embrace, Jimmy drew closer, a question in his eyes. "Do you forgive me for teasing you too much?"

Smiling, Kelsey nodded.

"Good. Your dad's right. We love you." Jimmy gently pulled her into his arms and kissed her.

Kelsey melted into his embrace, his arms giving her comfort, his kiss curling her toes. If only it weren't for show. If only those words about love were for her and not a ruse for her dad and Maria. When Jimmy ended the kiss, Kelsey stepped away, her legs shaky.

She stared at Jimmy as her previous thought ran through her mind. *If only those words about love were for her and not a ruse.* Did that mean she wanted his love because she loved him? Was that why she didn't want his kisses to end or why she wound up next to him in the bed whenever they slept together? In her confusion she couldn't answer that question.

"Let's dig into those cinnamon rolls." Trying to forget Jimmy's kindness and his kisses, Kelsey opened the box. "These look so good."

Maria quickly passed out plates, and soon they were eating and laughing. Kelsey couldn't remember when her dad had seemed so relaxed. She could tell he liked Jimmy. They were two very different men, but they seemed to get along. She liked that Jimmy fit into her family just as she had fit into his.

How would she feel when she moved to Pineydale? Unlike Amanda, Kelsey had never been far from home. She attended Washington State University a little more than two hours away. Would she be homesick, or would having Amanda nearby keep that from happening? Kelsey glanced at Jimmy, and he winked at her. She knew at that moment he would be the reason she wouldn't be homesick.

***

On Monday as Jimmy packed his suitcase, he thought about the weekend that had gone faster than he'd ever thought possible. Saturday they'd spent the day on a sightseeing trip through Pend Oreille County. That evening they'd had dinner at a restaurant somewhere along the way. Jimmy hadn't been exactly sure where, but because Grady had insisted on eating there, Jimmy had no chance to take Kelsey on a date.

Easter Sunday had given Jimmy the opportunity to

meet the folks at the church that Kelsey had attended since she'd moved to Pinecrest when she was eight years old. After church Grady's brother, Clay, and his wife, Beth, and their two kids, Alex and Abby, had come over for Easter dinner. That evening had been filled with games, conversation, and laughter. As Jimmy had interacted with Kelsey's friends and relatives, he'd wondered how she felt about leaving this community behind.

He hated the idea of leaving Kelsey and wished he could take her back with him. This time with her only served to remind him that he was in love with his wife, but she only saw him as her best friend. Best friend. Boy next door. Buddy.

Could he live with that? He had to. He didn't have a choice.

"Hey, Jimmy."

Jimmy looked up to find Grady standing in the doorway to the bedroom. "If you're done packing, I'd like a word with you while the women are gone."

"Just about done." Jimmy didn't miss the serious expression on Grady's face. What did that mean? Things had gone well with his father-in-law, but maybe that was only wishful thinking, too.

"When you're finished, come out back to the deck."

"Sure." Jimmy wasn't sure what his father-in-law wanted, but the expression on the man's face didn't give Jimmy a good feeling. Had he read things wrong this weekend? Or had Grady somehow guessed the marriage was a sham?

As Jimmy made his way toward the deck, he wished Kelsey were here. She had volunteered to accompany Maria to the store. What if Grady started asking questions that would reveal the reason for their marriage?

Despite the chill in Jimmy's heart, the spring sunshine warmed the deck.

Grady sat on one of the deck chairs as Jimmy approached. "Jimmy, have a seat. It's a nice spring day."

"It is, sir." Jimmy sat on the nearby chair. "Thank you for having me in your home."

"You're welcome." Grady sat there and didn't say anything for what seemed like a long time.

Birds chirped in the nearby pine trees. A sure sign of spring. Jimmy wished Grady would say something. Good, bad, or indifferent.

Finally Grady cleared his throat. "I'd like to be completely honest with you. As you might recall, I wasn't exactly happy when you and Kelsey got married. I thought it was a foolish thing."

"Yes, sir. I understand." Jimmy swallowed hard.

"You don't understand everything." Grady eyed him. "You see, when I married Kelsey's mother, we were very young, and we didn't know what love was, and I worried that you and Kelsey were following in our footsteps. I've never told either of my girls the things I'm about to tell you, and I don't want you to repeat it to anyone. I trust you to do that."

"Yes, sir."

"I just want you to understand where I'm coming from."

Jimmy had no idea what Grady was going to say, but it didn't sound good. "Okay."

"Before my wife Nina was killed in an auto accident, our marriage was troubled. Mostly my fault. I spent too much time at work and not enough time with my family."

Jimmy wondered where this confession was going. Why was his father-in-law saying things to him that he'd never said to his own daughters? Jimmy wished Kelsey were here to rescue him.

"I see the way you are with Kelsey, and that sets my mind at ease. You love her, but don't forget to spend time with her once she gets to Pineydale. I understand you're taking college classes as well as working for a very demanding boss." Grady raised his eyebrows. "Don't do what I did. Don't neglect time with Kelsey. Take care of my little girl. I want her to be as happy years down the road as she is now."

Jimmy swallowed hard, knowing only half of Grady's assessment was true. "Yes, sir. I will do my best to make Kelsey happy. I love her very much."

"I don't doubt it. Loving each other is good, but it also takes hard work to make a marriage last. It's not always sunshine and roses. There are storms, and those roses have thorns." Grady stood. "Be prepared to deal with those, too."

"I lost my dad a number of years ago, so I appreciate the advice." Jimmy stood and extended his hand.

Grady shook Jimmy's hand. "Any time you need a sounding board, feel free to call on me. Women can be a puzzle, but I hope you can learn from my mistakes."

Jimmy motioned toward the garage. "I think I hear a car."

"You do." Grady glanced at his watch. "The ladies have returned, and it's about time for Kelsey to take you to the airport. We'd better head inside and see if they need any help with the groceries."

While they brought in the grocery bags, Jimmy kept

thinking how good it had felt to declare his love for Kelsey to her father, but Jimmy couldn't tell her. Not until she was ready to hear it.

After the groceries were put away, Kelsey looked at Jimmy. "I've got my stuff to take back to Pullman, and I'm ready to take you to the airport."

"I'm packed. All I have to do is put my bag in your car."

Maria walked into the room. "And Noah has awakened from his morning nap just in time to say goodbye."

Kelsey went over and took Noah from Maria's arms. "You be good for your mommy, little man."

Noah cooed, and Kelsey snuggled her little brother. Jimmy thought ahead to when Kelsey would have her own baby to snuggle. He would be that child's father, not biologically but in every other sense. He would do that for Kelsey.

Jimmy held out a finger to Noah, and the baby grabbed hold. "You got a good grip there, buddy."

Kelsey stuck out her lower lip. "I'm going to miss seeing this little guy when I move to Tennessee."

"We can always do video calls." Maria hugged Kelsey. "I know you do those with Jimmy."

Kelsey nodded. "It does keep us in touch when we're apart."

Jimmy put himself in Kelsey's place as he saw what she would leave behind when she came to Pineydale. He felt the real responsibility of giving her a place to call her own. His father-in-law's words echoed in Jimmy's mind. He'd let his father down with reckless behavior. Jimmy vowed not to disappoint his father-in-law.

After hugs, kisses, and handshakes, Kelsey and Jimmy

were on their way. For the first few minutes of the drive, she didn't say anything. His desire to please her made him a chicken when it came to talking to her. He didn't want to say the wrong thing or ask the wrong question. Could he summon the cocky, assured Jimmy Cunningham, or was it better to just remain silent?

The coward in him chose silence as he pulled some work-related material from his carry-on bag. He tried to study it, but he couldn't concentrate. All he could think about was Kelsey.

As they neared the airport in Spokane, Kelsey glanced his way, then returned her attention to the road. "So we survived the weekend. How does it feel?"

Sad because he hated to leave her. Did she want to hear that? "Good now that my fat lip has gone back to normal."

She tried to glare at him, but a smile emerged instead. "You couldn't resist, could you?"

"No." Jimmy grinned as he stowed his reading material in his backpack. He loved that smile. Teasing her was the only way he could keep himself from telling her how much he loved her. What would he do when she shared his house?

"That's okay. I'm kind of getting used to it. I'll miss your teasing."

The bigger question: Would she miss him? "I'll be sure to think of some things to tease you about when we have our video calls."

"Yeah. I wouldn't want you to get out of practice." Kelsey gave him another sideways glance. "You and my dad seemed to get along pretty well."

"That's what I thought. I was sweating bullets about meeting your dad, but it turned out better than I imagined it would." Jimmy remembered her father's advice about giving Kelsey the attention she deserved.

"What did you guys talk about while we were gone?"

"Just guy stuff." Jimmy changed the subject. "Are you missing classes today?"

"Yeah, but I got a couple of friends to get the assignments, and they'll let me look over their notes. When do you start classes?"

"Since I'm working, I'm going to be doing a lot of those online. I have one that starts in May and goes through the summer. The rest start in the fall."

"So we'll both be studying next fall."

"And you'll be having a baby."

Kelsey didn't respond to his statement. He didn't know what to think of her silence. "Do you have a due date?"

Kelsey shook her head. "I haven't seen a doctor yet."

"Why?"

"I don't see the point when I'll be leaving." She averted her gaze. "I'll see someone after I move to Pineydale. I'll have to find a doctor there anyway."

"Okay." Jimmy wasn't sure what to make of her reluctance to see a doctor. "My sisters can give you the name of their doctor."

"You don't have to worry about it. I'll figure that out when I get there." Kelsey gripped the steering wheel until her knuckles turned white. "I'm not ready to tell people I'm pregnant. Okay?"

"Okay. I just want to make sure you take care of yourself."

"I will."

"When my sisters were pregnant, they had to take special vitamins and supplements."

"It's okay, Jimmy. You don't have to worry. It's not your baby anyway."

That was harsh. He'd never heard her talk like that. When he thought back over their conversations, he realized she rarely talked about her pregnancy unless she couldn't avoid it. She obviously didn't want to talk about it now, and she didn't want his advice.

Her reticence stumped him. She was married now. No one would question the fact that she was pregnant. Why didn't she want to discuss it with him? It wasn't like he was going to tell anyone her secret.

Kelsey drove onto the road leading to the airport. When she stopped the car in the departures area, she finally looked his way. Tears welled in her eyes.

"Kelsey, what's wrong?"

She pressed her lips together. She blinked, and a tear rolled down each cheek.

Jimmy reached over and wiped them away with his thumbs. "Talk to me. Tell me what's wrong."

Her breath hitched. "Everything. Just everything. I don't want to have this baby."

Jimmy stared at her. Did that mean she didn't want to be married to him either? "Are you sorry we got married?"

"I don't know." She sniffled. "This weekend was hard. All that pretending. I'm just thinking about how things will be in Pineydale. More and more pretending. It was hard enough getting through a few days, how can I keep doing…" She covered her mouth with her hand.

Her unfinished sentence socked him in the gut. He didn't understand. She had seemed relatively happy this weekend. Had he said or done something to make things worse? He couldn't come up with any words of encouragement. Everything he thought of sounded trite or meaningless.

Helpless. The word pounded in his brain.

She hung her head as she continued to grip the steering wheel. They couldn't stay parked here for long.

"Kelsey?"

She looked over at him, her eyes still welling with tears. She swiped a hand across her face but didn't say anything, just stared at him.

He was tempted to get his bags and just walk into the airport and out of her life. But he loved her. He had promised to struggle alongside her, cry with her, and support her dreams. He remembered Grady's comment about marriage being work. But what if she was considering an abortion again? He couldn't support that.

He glanced at his phone. He still had plenty of time before he had to go through security. He had to find out what was going through her mind. This was no time to be a coward.

"Kelsey, I'd like to park the car somewhere and talk before I leave. I need to understand why you're so upset. If you don't want to, I'll get out now and walk away. I won't bother you anymore, and you can do with this marriage what you'd like. I won't fight you."

She jerked her head in his direction, her eyes wide. "Don't leave me."

Her plea lightened Jimmy's heart, but at the same time, he heard her pain. At least she didn't tell him to go. "Will you please park the car in the parking garage?"

She nodded and took the road that led back to the garage. After taking a ticket, she pulled into a spot and shut off the engine. She didn't look at him, just sat there holding the steering wheel as she had done when they were parked in front of the terminal.

Jimmy rubbed the back of his neck and tried to figure out what he wanted to say. He wished he'd managed to figure that out while they'd been driving around to the garage, but he couldn't corral his thoughts. They were scattered like cattle over the range.

"Will you tell me how you're feeling?"

She encircled the steering wheel with her arms and laid her head there. "I told you. I don't want this baby. I don't want to pretend that our marriage is real."

"So what do you want to do about that?"

She lifted her head and looked at him, misery covering her face. "I can't do what I want to do. It wouldn't be right."

"Are you saying you wish you could have an abortion?" Jimmy's heart hammered as he waited for her answer.

She nodded and immediately looked away. "I know I shouldn't be thinking that. It's wrong. I think that's why I keep putting off seeing a doctor. A doctor will confirm my pregnancy. Right now I keep wishing it isn't real. That there's no baby. But if I see the ultrasound and hear the heartbeat, I won't be able to deny it."

Jimmy wanted to take Kelsey in his arms and make everything right, but he couldn't. He didn't know what it was like to be as troubled and torn as she was, not even when he'd been living a life of debauchery. He'd seen pretty clearly he was on the wrong path, and once he'd made a change, he never once thought of going back.

Even though they were married, she was fighting with herself over what to do about this baby. If Jimmy ever came face to face with Brandon, Jimmy was afraid of what he might be tempted to do. This weekend he'd seen the young woman he remembered from last fall, not the tortured soul sitting in this car with him.

"Can you tell me what's changed since you told me I'm your best friend? What's changed since we read our vows together and prayed together the other night?"

She appeared to be fighting back more tears as she blinked. "I was sitting in church yesterday listening to the Easter sermon and was reminded of Jesus's sacrifice. And here I am living a lie."

Kelsey was like a dog chasing its tail. She was going around and around in circles and making no progress. He'd come to grips with this marriage, pretense and all. He was ready to fight for it, but then he was in love with her. Obviously, she didn't feel the same way about him, and that was the problem. She had no emotional investment.

Jimmy sighed, her unhappiness chipping away at his emotions. "You continue to be troubled with the same things. You have to make a decision one way or the other. You're either going to go forward with this marriage and live with the decisions we've made about it and this baby. Or you can call it quits and do whatever you'd like. I won't stand in your way."

Agony marred her pretty face. "I'm afraid. Afraid of having this baby. Afraid I can't keep up the pretense. Afraid I'll bring you down with me."

Jimmy thought of one or two Scriptures that might be helpful. Like the one about being able to do things through Christ's strength or the one about Jesus never forsaking you. Who would have ever thought Jimmy Cunningham would be contemplating the use of Bible verses when dishing out advice?

He was sure Kelsey didn't want him to preach to her. He could pray—pray that she wouldn't do something she'd regret, something that would only add to her guilt and render their marriage useless.

"I thought we had a good time this weekend. I thought things between us were good. That we were going to work on our relationship with a look toward the future." He had thought she was making progress, but today she was right back at the starting line.

She buried her face in her hands and sat like that for several moments. When she looked at him, there were no tears, no expression, and no life in her eyes. His heart sank, taking his dreams with it.

"Remember—you told me I was your best friend. Best friends are there for you to lean on. I'm here to help you with whatever you're going through." Even though he'd thought about walking away, he wouldn't. He would live up to the vows he'd taken, even if they didn't include love.

"I feel sorry for you. Now my mess is your mess."

"I'm not sorry about marrying you." He wanted more than anything to tell her how much he loved her, but in her frame of mind, he was afraid it would be the worst thing he could do. He didn't know how he could leave her in the state she was in, but he had a job in Pineydale. She had college classes to attend.

He glanced at his phone. "Kelsey, I have to catch my flight. Please promise me you won't do anything without talking to me first. Please."

She took a deep breath and let it out slowly as she stared at him. "Okay. Call me when you get home."

"You can count on it." Her request took away some of

his worry. "Just remember. I'm your best friend, and I want the best for you."

"I know you do." She shook her head. "I'm sorry I'm such a blubbering mess of crazy roller-coaster emotions. You've been so patient with me. You deserve a medal."

"What I deserve is a hug, and you need one, too."

A little smile escaped as she looked at him. "That might be just what we both need."

"Good." Jimmy opened the car door and stepped out. "I'm coming to collect that hug after I get my bag."

As he pulled his suitcase out of the trunk, Kelsey met him at the back of the car. He set his bag on the ground, then slammed the trunk shut. He prayed Kelsey wouldn't slam the door shut on their marriage. He wanted a chance to give her the love she deserved.

Jimmy held out his arms and breathed a sigh of relief when she stepped into them. She wrapped her arms around his waist and held him tight, as if he was a lifesaver in the storm of her life's chaos. He wanted to be her lifesaver, but God was the one who could truly help her. Jimmy would pray that she would see that truth and cling to it.

Finally she stepped away and gazed up at him. "Thank you for putting up with my crazy mood swings."

"That's what I'm here for." Jimmy hoped that was all this was. Pregnancy mood swings. But he didn't want them to lead her down a path of regret. More than ever he wished she were going back with him now, not in four weeks.

"I don't think you signed on for this."

"I signed on for whatever this marriage brings."

Kelsey didn't say another word, just threw her arms around him again. "You are too good to be true."

This hug was real. There was no audience to convince, no one here to pretend for. She clung to him as if she didn't want to let go. He would take the feel of her arms around him all the way back to Pineydale. He would remember this hug every day and pray for more just like it.

CHAPTER FOURTEEN

As the plane taxied to the gate, Kelsey stared at the text on her phone. Her heart swam in a sea of disappointment. Jimmy wouldn't be here to pick her up. Amanda was coming. Would she think it strange that a husband wouldn't be here to greet the wife he'd been separated from for over a month? Kelsey guessed Jimmy didn't care. Could she blame him after the way they had parted at Easter?

Even though they'd had nightly video calls, Kelsey sensed his withdrawal. He always asked about her classes and made subtle references to her health in case Brianna was listening in. He didn't tease or joke. He didn't seem like his normal cocky self.

She had missed Jimmy. She wasn't sure what that meant, but now that her hormones had leveled out and she wasn't the moody, weepy woman he'd left behind, maybe she could figure that out.

Was he still interested in going out on those dates and looking to the future of their relationship, or had she completely killed any hope of that? He never mentioned it. Their conversations had consisted of polite questions and short answers. Nothing truly personal passed between them. She wasn't sure what to expect now, especially since he hadn't met her at the airport.

As soon as Kelsey got off the plane, she headed to the baggage claim. While she watched for her two large bags, Amanda called Kelsey's name.

Kelsey turned toward the sound. Amanda waved and hurried toward the baggage claim. She enveloped Kelsey in a hug, but she was wishing the arms around her were Jimmy's.

Amanda stepped back. "I'm so glad you're here now. Jimmy is eager to see you."

Kelsey manufactured a smile. *So why isn't he here?* The question sat on the tip of her tongue, but she didn't dare ask it. "I can hardly wait to see him."

"I'm sure you can't." Amanda stepped toward the spot where the baggage was coming out. "How many bags do you have?"

"Two. They're red with big yellow tags."

"Those should be easy to spot."

"Do you know if the boxes I shipped have arrived?"

Amanda shook her head. "Jimmy never mentioned that when I've been around. He's been working, working, working."

Worry clouded Kelsey's mind. She didn't want Jimmy to be like her dad when she was growing up. He worked all the time and never had time for them. Things were better after he married Maria, but Kelsey never forgot the times he'd promised to come to a school or church function but didn't show because of work. But she wouldn't voice her concern to Amanda. Kelsey didn't want her sister to have any hint that something might be wrong. Kelsey would put on a happy face and pretend that everything was perfect. She was getting too good at pretending.

"I see one of your bags." Amanda ran over and

grabbed a suitcase. "And there's the other one."

Kelsey retrieved it, then glanced at Amanda. "Are you parked close?"

"Yeah. Let's go." Amanda pulled up the handle of the suitcase and headed for the door. "Follow me."

Within minutes, they were on the road to Pineydale. Kelsey's stomach churned with a mix of anticipation and nerves. She didn't know what to expect when she saw Jimmy. At least she wasn't feeling nausea from her pregnancy anymore.

Amanda glanced Kelsey's way. "You're awfully quiet."

"I'm tired." Kelsey blew out a puff of air. "It was a long flight."

"Yeah. You lose three hours."

"I've been up since three thirty this morning. Two layovers later, I'm finally here. I don't want to have to make that trip again anytime soon."

"Yeah, that's what Jimmy said when he came back after Easter." Amanda eyed Kelsey. "That man must really love you, because he hates to fly."

"He never told me that." That he hated to fly or that he loved her.

"I don't think Jimmy intended to tell anyone, but we were helping him work on the house one weekend. He inadvertently said he hated to fly because of his experiences while he was in the service."

Kelsey didn't put much stock in Amanda's assessment of Jimmy's feelings of love. He pretty much had to fly out to Spokane because of his job. Everyone just thought he was eager to visit her. She supposed that was a good thing.

"I hope you're hungry, because I do believe your

hubby has supper planned for you."

Kelsey raised her eyebrows as she stared at Amanda. "You mean Jimmy cooked? He doesn't cook."

Amanda laughed. "I didn't say he cooked. I just said he has supper ready for you."

"That makes sense." Kelsey thought about their idea to learn to cook together. Did he still have those plans?

"So are you hungry?"

"Maybe." She glanced at her phone. "It's only three o'clock back home."

"But you've been up since three thirty. That's nearly twelve hours. And besides, Pineydale is home now."

Home with Jimmy. The thought gave Kelsey a sinking sensation. "Yeah, but I'll have to get used to it. What's the best part of living in Pineydale?"

"Mitch."

Kelsey giggled. "That was a stupid question, wasn't it?"

"Yeah."

"Besides Mitch."

"You're just trying to get me to admit I like small-town living now, aren't you?"

"Could be."

"I know what's going to be the best thing besides Mitch. It's having my sister living nearby."

Kelsey smiled. "Thanks. I feel the same way."

"We wouldn't have thought that a few years ago."

"But we've both changed a lot since then." Kelsey had had to grow up too fast. Sure she was an adult, but she should be looking forward to her senior year in college, dating, having fun with friends, and going to football games. Instead, she was married and having a baby. In a few months she'd be a mother. Those things still didn't seem real.

Where was the rewind button for her life? It didn't exist.

"You're almost home." Amanda motioned toward the side of the highway as the sign for the exit to Pineydale came into view.

Home. When would Pineydale feel like home? What was she going to do when she arrived at Jimmy's house? Would he come out to greet her? Would they have to make a big show of their reunion for Amanda's sake? Kelsey's stomach churned.

As Amanda took the exit and drove through town, Kelsey's insides turned into a jumble of nerves. For a few minutes she thought she might hyperventilate.

"You getting excited?" Amanda turned onto Jimmy's street.

Kelsey nodded. Excited. Apprehensive. Uptight.

Jimmy's house came into view, and Kelsey's pulse raced. They passed by several cars parked on the street. As Amanda pulled into the driveway, Kelsey took in the freshly mowed lawn and the pink and white petunias growing in the baskets hanging around the wide front porch. It looked even more inviting than it had the first time she'd seen it. Kelsey's insides were a tangle of nerves as she opened the car door.

Before she could get out, Jimmy came out the front door and ran to greet her. Their greeting had to satisfy an audience again, even if it was only an audience of one.

Kelsey thought she'd prepared herself for the obligatory hugs and kisses, but when Jimmy pulled her into his arms, she lost all sense of time and space. Being in his arms did feel like home. She clung to him much like the day when he'd left Spokane. She'd been a jumble of confused emotions then, but he'd stood by her and encouraged her to do the right thing. She had to admit she didn't know where she would be without him.

As he held her close, he whispered in her ear. "I missed you, and that isn't pretend."

Kelsey swallowed the lump in her throat. She wanted to say she missed him, too, but the words stuck in her throat. Fear of building false expectations kept her from saying anything.

As she gazed up at him, she realized he was going to kiss her. She also realized she wanted his kiss, and that scared her. He pulled her close, and their lips met. Nothing existed except this one man. Her heart spun around like a twirling ballerina until it felt as though it would fly right out of her chest.

"Ahem."

The sound of Amanda clearing her throat made Kelsey jump out of Jimmy's embrace. She had forgotten her sister's presence. Kelsey grinned sheepishly.

"I hate to break up you two lovers." Amanda grinned back. "I just didn't want you to forget I'm here."

Jimmy took hold of Kelsey's hand. "Let's go inside, and I'll show you the house. The main part of the house is done except one room I still have to get furniture for. I only have the basement to work on now." Jimmy glanced back at Amanda as he started up the walk. "And I had a whole lot of help. Amanda, Mitch, and Jeremy were my big helpers, but my mom and my sisters and their husbands pitched in, too."

"I'm excited to see what you've done."

"She's got luggage." Amanda opened the trunk of the car.

"I wasn't thinking about luggage." Not letting go of Kelsey's hand, Jimmy walked to the back of the car. "Let me get those out."

Amanda giggled as she helped Jimmy pull the suitcases out of the trunk. "I bet you weren't."

Kelsey listened to her sister joke with Jimmy. What had he been thinking about? He'd missed her. He'd also said that when he visited her at Easter. She'd missed him, but she was afraid to say it.

"We'll take these inside. Then I'll give you the tour." Jimmy pulled the suitcases up the front walk and lifted them onto the porch.

Kelsey wondered where she was going to put her stuff. "That sounds good. Have you received any of the things I shipped?"

Jimmy gestured toward the house. "The boxes are in the room without furniture. I didn't open them. I figured you would know more about where you want to put your things than I would."

Amanda patted Jimmy on the back. "Smart man."

"Amanda, will you check the stuff I have on the grill while I show Kelsey the rest of the house?"

"Got it." Saluting, Amanda waggled her eyebrows as she hurried away.

Kelsey looked at him. "You're making supper on the grill?"

"I've been practicing while you've been gone."

A little pout appeared on Kelsey's face as she frowned. "Now you're way ahead of me in the cooking department."

"You'll catch up in no time." He once again took

Kelsey's hand. "Let's get this tour started. Kitchen, dining room, and great room are mostly the same."

"Except the new TV and chair," Kelsey said.

Jimmy smiled. "You noticed."

Kelsey wasn't sure why that surprised him. Maybe because she hadn't spent much time in this house before she'd gone back to school. "I like the new additions."

"I hope you like the rest." Jimmy led the way down the hall and stepped aside as they reached the first doorway. "The newly redone bathroom."

Kelsey poked her head around the corner. "Oh wow! I love the double sinks. You made the cabinet they're in, right?"

Jimmy pointed ahead. "I put in a rain shower and soaker tub because I remembered how you liked the ones in the master suite."

So this was going to be her bathroom. "Thanks."

"Let's go across the hall." He leaned closer. "To your room."

"Okay." Little prickles raced up and down her spine. Her physical response to his presence was alive and well. From the moment he'd raced out the door to greet her, every nerve reacted to his company.

Jimmy turned the doorknob and let the door swing open. "This is the room you helped decorate when you were on video call."

Kelsey took in the pale-blue walls, the walnut furniture, and the blue-and-white paisley comforter on the queen-sized bed. "I love it."

"You helped pick it out."

"But it looks so much better in person."

"I knew you'd like it after I saw your room in

Pinecrest. You do like blue."

"I used to love pink."

"I know."

"You do? How?"

"Your dad told me. He said your room used to be pink."

Kelsey laughed. "Oh, it was sooo pink. Pink everywhere."

"So if you have a little girl, you won't do her room in pink?"

Kelsey stared at Jimmy. She had avoided thinking about her baby, whether it would be a boy or girl. She had gotten through this past month by shutting down thoughts of her pregnancy as soon as they popped into her mind. Although she was in the second trimester, her pregnancy still didn't show. But it wouldn't be long before that baby bump would be obvious.

Shaking her head, Kelsey bit her bottom lip. "I try not to think about it."

"You mean think about the sex of your baby or not think about it at all?"

Kelsey turned toward the window that looked out on the front porch. "Both. The thought of this baby generates no good feelings. I know that sounds terrible, but this pregnancy just makes me sad, angry, and scared."

"Would you like a hug?" Jimmy's eyes held a question as he stepped closer.

Without a second thought, she stepped into his arms. She let the warmth of his embrace soothe her troubled mind. If only Jimmy were the father of her baby. Oh wow! Had she just thought that? Were crazy pregnancy hormones at work again? Her emotions had settled over the last couple of weeks, but being with Jimmy had them twisted in knots again. He made her feel safe, but he also made her wonder if she should be the real wife he wanted. That was dangerous thinking. Why did he make her feel safety and danger at the same time?

She couldn't let misguided emotions lead her astray again. She had to make decisions based on rational, sensible thinking, not her pounding pulse, zinging nerves, or a racing heart.

"Kelsey, you don't know how glad I am that you came back." Jimmy tightened his hold on her. "I was so worried about you."

Taking a shaky breath, she gave him a quick hug, then stepped away and hung her head. "I'm so sorry I was terrible at Easter. I don't know why you even wanted me to come back after the way I was when you left."

"I wanted you to come back because I…I…" His voice trailed away as he left the sentence unfinished.

Kelsey licked her lips and watched some undefined emotion play across his face. Why couldn't or why wouldn't he finish his statement? Probably because he was too kind to remind her of the wrong-headed decision she had almost made. "Thank you for not giving up on me. Because of you I went to see a doctor after I got back to school."

"You did? Why didn't you tell me?"

Kelsey shrugged. "I should've let you know, but Brianna was always hanging around. I was afraid she'd start asking questions."

"Look at the bright side. Now you don't have to put up with a nosy roommate." Jimmy chuckled. "Just a messy one."

"So far I haven't noticed that you're messy."

"That's because you haven't lived with me long enough. I was trying to put my best foot forward so you'd marry me." Jimmy raised his eyebrows. "Do you have a due date?"

"November eighth. It seems a long ways away."

"It'll be here before you know it."

"That's what the non-pregnant people say." Kelsey laughed. "They don't have to do the waiting or feel like a blimp while they're waiting."

Jimmy wrinkled his brow. "You don't look pregnant yet."

"Yet. That's the optimum word. It'll be soon enough." Kelsey sighed. "I don't know when I'll be ready to share about this baby."

"We'll figure it out together." Jimmy squeezed her shoulders. "I just want to tell you I'm proud of you for not giving up on yourself or knuckling under to your worries. You're strong. This will all work out."

"It'll work out because you're beside me." Kelsey knew that to be more than true. "Whenever things seemed impossible, I remembered you were praying for me."

"Yes, I was." Jimmy smiled. "Okay. I've got one more room to show you, but I'm not sure you want to see it."

Kelsey frowned. "Why wouldn't I?"

"It's the room I planned for the nursery."

Nursery. The word hit her in the gut as Kelsey looked toward the hallway. More reality to face. "Do you have it furnished already?"

Jimmy leaned closer. "That would've given away our secret, but I've got some things I've been working on out in the shop that I'll show you later. But I still want to show you the room now."

"Okay." Seeing the nursery would make things even more real than hearing her baby's heartbeat—a heartbeat she had considered ending.

After they stepped into the room, Kelsey threw her arms around Jimmy and held him tight. He had saved her from making a grave mistake.

Jimmy held her in the circle of his arms, making her feel treasured. He didn't say anything. They just stood there together in the silence of the empty room.

"Are you okay?" Jimmy tightened his arms around her.

Kelsey nodded. "I just needed a little courage to think about this room."

"Always glad to help. I like holding you." He took a step back, his hands still on her arms. "I hope that's okay."

"It's okay." Kelsey's heart thudded. She wanted it to be okay, but she didn't want to give him the wrong idea.

The look in his eyes told her if she'd given him any encouragement, he would've kissed her. She was walking through a perilous jungle of emotions. His and hers.

Stepping away from Jimmy, Kelsey surveyed the room, its pale-yellow walls contrasting with the dark wood flooring. He shouldn't have to worry about his interaction with her, but he obviously did because she was still his wife in name only. She wanted to be in love with her husband, but she couldn't manufacture feelings.

She liked Jimmy a lot. A lot a lot, but was that love? How could she know? She thought she'd been in love with Brandon, but that wasn't love. It was stupidity. Torturing herself over her feelings wouldn't help either.

"So are you ready to discuss this room, or should we wait?"

Before Kelsey could answer, Amanda appeared in the doorway. "The food's ready."

Amanda rushed away, leaving Jimmy and Kelsey alone again.

"We'd better go." Kelsey headed for the door.

"You're right." Jimmy hurried to catch up to her and put a hand to her back as they left the future nursery.

"Is Mitch here?" Kelsey asked as they walked into the kitchen.

"Yeah."

"So you invited Amanda and Mitch over for supper?"

"I did." Jimmy ushered Kelsey to the back door. "In fact, there are a lot of people here. Come outside with me."

Kelsey wrinkled her brow. A lot of people. What was he talking about?

As they reached the door, Jimmy let Kelsey go ahead of him. "Ladies first."

Kelsey stepped onto the back deck and came face to face with a crowd of people.

"Welcome home, Kelsey!" The loud shout rose from the yard, where numerous tables covered in white tablecloths were scattered over the lawn.

Overwhelmed with emotion, Kelsey put a hand to her mouth as tears flowed down her cheeks. She looked up at Jimmy as she blinked back the tears. "You planned this?"

Putting an arm around Kelsey's waist, Jimmy grinned as he pulled her close. "My mom helped."

Kelsey wiped her cheeks and waved. "Thanks, everyone, for the welcome."

Mary rushed onto the deck and hugged Kelsey. "Jimmy wanted to throw a big party for your homecoming. He has missed you so much."

"It's good to be back." That statement was for real. Kelsey didn't have to pretend to like these people and their little town. Now she just had to figure out her feelings for her husband.

Jimmy stepped forward and banged a big spoon on the bottom of a pot. "Let's pray so we can eat."

A chorus of agreement rose from the group as folks gathered around the deck where Jimmy and Kelsey stood.

Jimmy reached for Kelsey's hand as he bowed his head. "Dear Lord, we thank you for this wonderful day, and I especially thank you for bringing Kelsey home safely. We thank you for this food and friends and family. Please bless this gathering. Amen."

"Guest of honor goes first." Mary nudged Kelsey toward the table on the deck loaded with food.

Kelsey helped herself to small portions. Although she wasn't suffering from pregnancy nausea, her stomach was tied in knots for a whole different reason. She liked these people. Her sister and Mitch, Jimmy's family, Charlotte, and Mitch's parents. Jimmy had even invited the Judge and Shirley. These folks had come to wish her and Jimmy well. She didn't want to lie to them, but that was what she'd be doing every day.

Jimmy leaned closer as he filled his plate, his voice barely a whisper. "You need to take more than that. You're eating for two."

Kelsey whipped around and glared at him. "I hope no one heard that besides me."

"Don't worry. They didn't. They're too busy talking to each other. No one is listening in on our conversation."

"You better be right."

"I am." Jimmy led the way down the steps to the table

closest to the deck and pulled out a chair for Kelsey. "Enjoy."

"I could do that a lot better if you didn't tease." Kelsey stabbed her fork into her salad.

Jimmy grinned. "I thought you'd gotten used to my teasing."

"You haven't done that for a while. So I'm out of practice putting up defenses."

"Let me understand this. You want me to tease you so you can work on your defense?"

Kelsey shook her head as she let out a helpless laugh. "I can't win with you."

"But you can." Jimmy waggled his eyebrows and whispered, "After these people leave, I can show you just what I mean. I miss sleeping with you. I like the way you cuddle."

Kelsey stared at him. Was he still teasing, or was he serious? "Do you also like the way I punch?"

Jimmy laughed. "You are going to keep me on my toes."

"I hope so."

"You two keeping secrets?" Amanda set her plate on the table, then sat down.

Amanda's question made Kelsey's stomach flip-flop. What would Amanda say if she knew the secrets they were keeping?

Kelsey grinned at her sister. "Just joking with each other. I'm still getting used to his teasing."

"Yes, he's quite the jokester. I learned that when I worked for him." Amanda motioned for Mitch to join them.

Soon the guys were talking baseball and Jimmy's job

while Kelsey and Amanda discussed the decorating for their houses.

As they ate, folks wandered over and congratulated Jimmy and Kelsey and wished them the best for the future. Kelsey wasn't sure what the future held for them. Real marriages held an uncertain future, too. But the arrangement she and Jimmy had made could spell disaster if they never fell in love.

Maybe the answer came in the determination to love Jimmy in whatever form that took. After all, they weren't the first couple to marry for reasons other than love. She wanted to make this work, not only for Jimmy but to not let down all these people who had come to wish them well.

***

The stars twinkled in the black sky, reminding Jimmy that God had put the world in place and He had the power to help in all kinds of circumstances. Like Kelsey, Jimmy feared that God wasn't pleased with the decision they'd made. Jimmy didn't have a clue how to make things right. Every time he thought there was hope for this marriage, Kelsey's actions told him something else.

A dog barked in the distance as Jimmy sat on the back deck and tried to sort out his feelings. Everything from the party was cleaned up and put away. The party itself had been a success, but his relationship with Kelsey wasn't. She had put on a happy face for their audience, but as soon as the last guest left, she had begged off looking at the things he was making for the nursery.

She had claimed she was tired. That could be. She'd had a long flight, and pregnancy often made women tired.

He'd learned that when his sisters were pregnant. But was he trying to rationalize her behavior to soothe his wounded ego? He didn't know whether she didn't want to deal with furnishing the nursery or whether she didn't want to deal with him.

He'd been so sure marrying Kelsey was the solution to both of their problems. He'd made his plans and persuaded Kelsey that they would work. Maybe he was like Sarah in the Bible who made her own plans to give Abraham a son, but her plans weren't God's plans. Just like Sarah couldn't undo her misguided plans, Jimmy couldn't undo his without causing a whole lot of heartache.

When Jimmy entered the house, quiet greeted him. The small lamp in the corner of the living room cast shadows across the floor. He glanced down the hall. Was Kelsey already asleep, or had she just gone into her bedroom to hide?

He grabbed a work folder from a drawer in the kitchen, then went into the living room and turned off the light. He stood there a moment and let his eyes adjust to the darkness. A light shone out from under Kelsey's door. He traipsed down the hall and stopped. He stared at the barrier between him and his wife.

He knocked lightly. "Kelsey?"

Silence. If she was awake, she wasn't answering. What did that mean?

The silence coming from the other side of the door poked a hole in his heart. He shouldn't have said he missed her. He shouldn't have said anything about liking to hold her. He shouldn't have almost kissed her for no reason. But he had a reason. He loved her, but he couldn't tell her. She didn't share his feelings. He wouldn't rush her.

Don't rush. Be patient. Love her with actions, not words. The commands rolled through his mind as he went into his room. He tossed the folder on the bed and stared at himself in the mirror on the dresser. A day's worth of stubble covered his chin. He rubbed a hand over it.

What did Kelsey see when she looked at him? Her husband or just a friend? She'd told him he was her best friend, and sometimes that seemed like enough for now. But their month's separation had done nothing to enhance that friendship. She had seemed more a stranger tonight than ever before.

What would tomorrow bring? What would happen in the next weeks and months? He had to prepare himself for the worst and hope for the best. He was up for a challenge. Jimmy Cunningham wasn't a quitter.

CHAPTER FIFTEEN

B acon sizzled in the pan. Coffee gurgled through the coffeemaker. Cinnamon rolls baked in the oven. Jimmy set two plates on the table along with napkins and utensils. He'd even picked some kind of pink flowers from the yard and put them in a vase to decorate the table. Now all he needed was Kelsey.

He hadn't heard a sound out of her room since he'd gotten up this morning. Was she still tired from last night's party? He glanced at the clock on the stove. Nine. It was still six o'clock back in Washington. He didn't know how early she usually got up for school.

As he stood there turning the bacon, he realized he didn't know a lot about Kelsey's habits. During the little bit of time they had actually spent together, they hadn't established any kind of routine. Is this how all newlyweds felt or just the ones who had a crazy marriage like theirs?

The timer went off, signaling the cinnamon rolls were done. He put on the hot mitt and opened the oven door. A burst of steam hit him in the face. He stepped back for a second, then grabbed hold of the pan.

"This is a domestic scene."

Kelsey's voice made Jimmy jump, and he lost hold of the pan of cinnamon rolls. Without thinking, he reached out with his unprotected hand to keep the pan from landing on the floor. That move resulted in excruciating pain. The pan clattered to the floor as he raced to the sink and turned on the cold water.

Kelsey rushed to his side. "Can I help?"

"Ice."

"No ice. Just keep your hand under the cold water." She glanced around the kitchen. "Where are your bowls?"

"First cupboard on the left. Why no ice?"

"I'll explain in a minute. Let me take care of your hand for now." Kelsey grabbed a bowl and filled it with water from the dispenser in the refrigerator door.

Jimmy glanced her way. "What now?"

Kelsey set the bowl on the table. "Go to the table and hold your hand in the bowl."

"Thanks." Jimmy did as she instructed, his pain subsiding just because of her presence.

"I'm so, so sorry I startled you."

"It's not your fault." Jimmy grimaced. "I shouldn't be so clumsy. Guess I have some work to do to impress you with my cooking skills. I was trying to surprise you."

"Instead, I'm the one who surprised you." Kelsey joined him at the table. "Let me see."

Jimmy lifted his hand out of the water. Her touch made it better, or at least made him forget the pain. "I'll survive, but I'm not sure about the cinnamon rolls."

Kelsey glanced at the floor, then at the stove. "Oh no. Your bacon's burning."

"Take it off the burner." Jimmy motioned toward the stove with his good hand.

Kelsey jumped up and raced to the stove. She removed the smoking pan from the burner just as the smoke alarm screamed. She looked at Jimmy. "How do I turn that thing off?"

"Open the back door and a window." Jimmy got up and tried to fan the smoke away from the alarm with a plastic cutting sheet he'd grabbed from the counter. As the smoke alarm went quiet, Jimmy looked a Kelsey with a sheepish grin. "This has not been one of my finer moments."

"But it was a sweet thought." Kelsey kissed him on the cheek. "Sit down again and put that hand back in the water. I'll take care of the mess."

"You don't have to clean up my mess." Sitting at the table, Jimmy wished she would forget about the disarray in the kitchen and just give him another kiss. That was wishful thinking, for sure. It had been nothing other than a friendly peck on the cheek, but for Jimmy it was so much better than the way she had hidden in her room last night. He cautioned himself not to read anything into her actions. If he did, he would be asking for trouble.

"I know, but I want to." Kelsey took the bacon out of the pan and put it on a paper towel. Then she retrieved the pan of cinnamon rolls from the floor. "Some of them stayed on the pan, so they're still good. I'll toss the rest."

"I had planned to scramble some eggs."

"I'll give it a shot, but first let's doctor your hand."

"You mean the cold water isn't enough?"

Kelsey shook her head. "You can't sit around with your hand in a bowl of water all day."

"I suppose not." Jimmy eyed her. "What do you plan to do?"

"Do you have honey?"

Jimmy nodded. "Yeah, but if you'd asked me that a week ago, I would've said no. My mom came over last week and went through my cupboards and made me a shopping list. She was appalled that I had nothing in it."

"I'll have to thank your mom, but she doesn't know the kitchen in my apartment at school was probably just as bad as yours."

"I know you said you didn't know how to cook, but you've never cooked at all?"

"I mostly ate protein shakes or breakfast bars for breakfast. The rest of the time I ate frozen meals or takeout. I was too busy to cook. I'm an expert on using a microwave." Kelsey tapped the door of the microwave.

"Yeah, a microwave is definitely my go-to appliance." Jimmy chuckled. "I know you told me before that you didn't cook, but I honestly didn't think you were as clueless as me."

"Well, I am." Kelsey wrinkled her brow. "I know I need to eat better because of the baby. The doctor I saw back home gave me vitamins and supplements to take."

Jimmy wondered whether she had thought about a doctor here. When would she consider this home? The last time he'd mentioned her seeing a doctor, she had shut the discussion down. Maybe she was more open to that now. At least she was thinking about taking care of herself and her baby. He prayed she was in a better place in regard to this baby than she was when he'd left her at Easter.

"So have you thought about a doctor here?"

She nodded. "I have the name of one over in Johnson City. I'll call and make an appointment on Monday."

"Good." Lifting his hand out of the bowl, Jimmy decided not to bug her. "So what are you going to do with honey?"

"Put it on your hand." She glanced back at the

cupboards. "Where would I find it?"

"In the pantry."

"And do you have gauze and medical tape?"

"Maybe in my bathroom. Is Nurse Kelsey going to treat my hand? She did a good job with my black eye."

Kelsey frowned at him. "You know I did nothing to help your black eye."

"Sure you did. You got ice. You are very good at getting ice." Jimmy's heart hammered as he gazed at her.

A little smile lifted the corner of her mouth. "You will soon learn that I'm very good at a lot of things."

"I think I already knew that." She was good at keeping him off balance. One minute he thought she didn't want to be around him. The next she planned to doctor his hand.

Kelsey disappeared down the hall and soon returned. "You have just what I need. Hold out your hand."

Jimmy followed instructions, trying not to let her see how her touch affected him. "Where did you learn all this?"

"From nurses who worked at the nursing home my dad manages. That's why I know ice isn't the solution for a burn. They taught me all kinds of neat things when I worked there." Kelsey smiled, but her eyes were sad.

Jimmy wondered whether she was thinking of Brandon, because she'd met him while working at the nursing home. Jimmy didn't want to think about the despicable man, but he came unbidden to Jimmy's mind. He hoped Kelsey would have a little girl, one who looked like her. He didn't want to think about her having a boy that looked like his father. Jimmy chased the troubling thoughts away. He made a vow to love Kelsey's child no matter what.

Kelsey finished holding the gauze in place with the medical tape. "You're all set. Just don't get it wet."

"Looks like you'll be doing dishes." He winked. "But the good news is I'm right handed."

"Yeah, but we'd better eat first. Guess I should make those scrambled eggs."

"You can't do worse than me in the cooking department."

"I am impressed that you made cinnamon rolls."

"They're just out of a can, but I wanted your first breakfast here to be a good one. Instead, it turned into a disaster."

Kelsey smiled at him. "It's not a disaster. We still have good cinnamon rolls, and the bacon is only slightly burned. I like my bacon crisp."

"You're being too nice."

"You're the one who's nice for making me breakfast." Kelsey took the frying pan that Jimmy had sitting on the counter. "Okay, let's see if I can scramble these eggs."

"I have confidence in you." Jimmy motioned toward the refrigerator. "By the way, there's a little bowl in there with some shredded cheese in it. Put that in with the eggs. My mom's suggestion."

"Sure. Sounds good." The egg mixture sizzled as Kelsey poured it into the pan. She stirred it. "So when the eggs aren't runny anymore, I should take the pan off the burner?"

"Sounds like a plan to me." Jimmy nodded. "We're quite the team in the kitchen."

"We are a team. You made the mess. I'm cleaning it up."

Jimmy laughed out loud. "Guess I'm not the only one

who likes to tease."

"I had a very good teacher." Kelsey took the pan from the stove and set it on a trivet.

"Yes, you did." Jimmy liked that she felt comfortable enough to tease him. Hope for their marriage filled his thoughts.

Kelsey came over to the table and picked up Jimmy's plate. "I'll zap the bacon and cinnamon rolls in the microwave to heat them up. That's my specialty."

Jimmy laughed again. "Go for it."

After the microwave beeped, Kelsey put bacon, eggs, and a cinnamon roll on Jimmy's plate, then her own and set the plates on the table. "What would you like to drink?"

"Coffee."

Kelsey poured him a cup of coffee and a glass of milk for herself, then joined him at the table. "How's your hand?"

"I'll live. Let's eat before our food gets cold."

"Okay."

"I'll give thanks for the food." Jimmy bowed his head and said a short prayer, hoping their camaraderie would last. When Jimmy raised his head, Kelsey was looking at him, anxiety in her eyes. "Is something wrong?"

Kelsey shrugged. "I'm just waiting for you to take the first bite."

"Although I don't cook, I'm almost certain you can't mess up scrambled eggs." Jimmy dug his fork into the fluffy mound of yellow on his plate and took a bite. "Delicious."

"You're not just saying that, are you?"

"No." Smiling, he shook his head. "Taste them for yourself."

Kelsey took a bite of her eggs, then looked at him. "They are good. Wow! I can make scrambled eggs."

"I knew you could do it." Jimmy took another bite.

Kelsey set her fork on her plate. "Was your burnt hand a ploy to get me to do all the cooking?"

Jimmy snapped the fingers on his good hand. "You found me out."

Kelsey laughed. "Hopefully, with my doctoring, your hand will be as good as new in no time."

"I'm sure it will." Jimmy stabbed at his eggs and took a big bite. Would this be a good time to ask about the nursery furniture? Would the goodwill between them end if he did? His tiptoeing around the subject wouldn't help anything. "After we eat, would you let me show you what I've been working on for the nursery?"

Kelsey took another bite of eggs, and chewed slowly. Finally she looked at him. "I can't pretend I'm not having a baby. So yes."

"Great!"

They ate in silence. Jimmy's thoughts wandered all over the place. He thought about the nursery and his plans. Maybe he should've consulted Kelsey about the nursery rather than rushing ahead and making furniture she might not like. When would she be willing to tell people she was pregnant? What was it going to be like to have her in this house every day and every night? Would she ever learn to love him? Mother's Day was next weekend. Being a mom-to-be should be something Kelsey wanted to celebrate, but he was pretty sure she wouldn't.

He had to let things go. Be patient. Let things play out in their own time. He shouldn't borrow trouble from the future.

Kelsey finished the last of the food on her plate, then folded her napkin on the table. "Thank you for breakfast, Mr. Cunningham."

"You're welcome, Mrs. Cunningham. We make a good team."

She gave him a little smile. "We do."

Jimmy smiled, his heart full as well as his stomach. He got up and took both their plates to the sink. "Even if I can't wash, I can clear."

Kelsey brought over the remaining dishes. "I'll rinse these off and put them in the dishwasher."

"You rinse, and I can put them in." Jimmy held up his right hand. "I've still got one good hand."

In minutes they had the dishes loaded in the dishwasher, and Kelsey washed the pots and pans while Jimmy wiped. This felt good. This felt right. This felt like everything he had ever wanted.

As he laid the dish towel on the countertop, he looked over at Kelsey. "Ready to go to the workshop?"

She nodded, but uncertainty radiated from her eyes. "Seeing baby furniture is just one more thing that reminds me that this pregnancy is real. Now that the morning sickness is over, I often forget, or maybe I just want to forget."

"I understand." But did he? How could he begin to put himself in her place? "Let's go."

Jimmy opened the back door for Kelsey. They walked through the yard together. He unlocked his workshop and let her in.

She glanced around the area. "So what are you working on?"

"In the corner." Jimmy pointed as he wove his way

across the cavernous space through numerous projects and machinery. Hoping these things would meet her approval, he lifted a cover to reveal a crib, armoire, changing table, and dresser made of dark cherry. "What do you think?"

Kelsey let out a little gasp. "Jimmy, they're gorgeous. When did you have time to do this?"

"At night after work." He ran a hand over the top of the dresser. "It was a much-needed break from the business world. I like creating things."

"Have you ever considered making this a full-time job?" Kelsey gestured around the shop.

"I'd have to have enough clients to make money." Jimmy shrugged. "This is just something I enjoy. Something to get my mind off the work I do to make money. This is pleasure, not work."

"But if you let more people know about this, you would have clients."

Jimmy ran a hand along the top of the dresser. "If I make this work, I might lose the pleasure of creating."

Kelsey opened the drawers and doors. "You do such beautiful work. More people should see it."

"I'd like to move the furniture into the nursery, but that would mean letting people know you're pregnant." Jimmy raised his eyebrows as he gazed at Kelsey. "When do you plan to do that?"

Kelsey didn't say anything, just continued to look over the furniture. Finally she turned to him. "I'm not ready yet."

"Okay, I'll leave it up to you, but I'd really like to get this out of my workshop and into the house. Everything gets so dusty out here."

"How do you do that without telling someone? You

can't move this by yourself."

"Jeremy could help me."

"And you think Jeremy will keep our secret?"

Jimmy shook his head. "But he can help me move the armoire and chest. Those are the big pieces. I can move the changing table and crib myself, especially the crib since I would take it apart and reassemble it."

Kelsey shrugged. "Do what you want, but just make sure Jeremy doesn't see the crib or changing table."

"I'll make sure he doesn't see them." Jimmy raised his hand as if taking a pledge. "I'll have him help me when we take the curio cabinet over to Mom's house on Mother's Day."

"Your mom is going to love that. Your creations are so beautiful. People really need to see them and find out what a fabulous craftsman you are. I love the furniture you made for the nursery. Thank you."

"I just want you and your baby to have the best."

She looked up at him with a little smile. "I have the best. I have you."

Jimmy's heart thundered. When she said stuff like that, he wanted to tell her how much he loved her. But their relationship seemed so fragile that he feared doing anything to disrupt the good feelings. Patience. Patience would serve him well.

Jimmy put an arm around her shoulders. "We have each other, and that's the most important thing right now."

She nodded, but her silence made him think he'd said too much again. He didn't know how to read her moods. He had so much to learn about his wife. He had to learn how to be a good husband. He had to learn patience most of all.

***

Kelsey opened the nursery door and peered inside. Over two weeks had gone by since Jimmy and Jeremy had moved the armoire and chest into the room on Mother's Day. Jeremy had raved about the beautiful pieces, and Kelsey had joined in the praise of Jimmy's work.

Mary had been thrilled with her surprise gift, and the day had been filled with love and laughter. Kelsey had enjoyed the family gathering and considered herself lucky that she'd been welcomed into Jimmy's family. She and Jimmy had shared in a video call to wish Maria "Happy Mother's Day."

The entire day reminded Kelsey that she was a mother-to-be, but she still couldn't bring herself to find joy in that situation. She only found worry, fear, and sadness.

She stepped into the room and walked over to the crib that now sat along the wall. She ran a hand along the intricate carving on the railing at the back of the crib. She moved to the armoire and opened the doors and then the little drawers at the bottom. Everything was perfect. Jimmy's talent amazed Kelsey every time she looked at these pieces.

Staring at the empty walls and crib, she wondered about the sex of her child. What kinds of decorations would eventually fill the empty spaces? She placed a hand over the little bump that made her pants tight. She had started wearing her loose tops. They were in style and raised no questions when she wore them. How long before she would have to reveal her pregnancy? She wanted to wait as long as possible before telling anyone.

Maybe after her next doctor's visit in a couple of weeks she'd be ready to share her news. The doctor had said she should bring her husband to the next appointment, but Kelsey wasn't sure how Jimmy would feel about that. She didn't want him to have to pretend an interest in a baby that wasn't his. But maybe she needed to include him. He was interested enough to make this furniture.

"Hey, what brings you into this room?"

Kelsey turned at the sound of Jimmy's voice. "Just looking at your beautiful work. What are you doing home so early?"

"Graham's sending me on another trip, so I'm home to pack my bag." Jimmy leaned against the doorjamb. "That means I'll be gone again this weekend and into the beginning of next week. I'm sorry I have to be away."

"That's okay." Kelsey was sure her smile looked forced. "It's your job. That's what you do. You can't help it when your boss sends you away. It'll be okay. I'll visit with your mom, Amanda, and Charlotte while you're gone."

"Come talk to me while I pack." Jimmy waved for her to follow him.

Kelsey traipsed down the hall to his bedroom. She rarely came in here, and she felt strange watching him pack. In the three weeks since she'd moved to Pineydale, she and Jimmy shared a house but little else. They lived like college roommates sharing a living space.

"Where are you going?"

"Atlanta." He stopped for a moment and looked at her. "Would you like to go with me?"

Why was he asking that? He spent very little time alone with her. "What would I do while you're working?"

He shrugged. "Yeah. You're right. You'd be bored, and Graham might keep me working late. Forget that I mentioned it."

Kelsey still didn't understand why Jimmy had issued the invitation. He was always up early and out the door almost before she got up in the morning. Graham had Jimmy working late almost every night. He came home and fixed his own meal or ate Kelsey's leftovers. Even on the nights when he was home early, they didn't spend time together because he was either studying for his college courses or some work-related information. He always seemed to have his head buried in paperwork of some kind. He hadn't even had time to spend in his workshop.

Kelsey worried that Jimmy would be like her dad. He had worked all the time and hardly spent time with his family. She didn't want that kind of life. But what could she expect when she wasn't willing to make this a real marriage?

Jimmy had said they would go out on dates to get to know each other better, but every weekend someone invited them over. His mom, his sisters, Amanda and Mitch, even Charlotte. They hadn't had a chance to go out alone. That wasn't Jimmy's fault, but he'd still fallen into the same pattern as her dad. No time for a personal life. It all spelled nothing good for this marriage.

Kelsey's emotions ran hot and cold. One second happiness over the invitation flooded her heart, but the next second she was concerned about Jimmy's expectations if she went. But shouldn't she at least give things a chance to blossom between them? "If you really want me to go, I could."

Jimmy zipped his suitcase shut. "That's okay. It was a

very impractical idea. Too last minute. I wasn't thinking of the time it would take you to get ready and pack. We need to take a little trip when I don't have to work. That would be better."

"Yeah, you're probably right." Kelsey's heart sank. She had the feeling that little trip would never materialize. There would always be a reason to put it off, cancel it, or never plan it in the first place. She'd learned that all too well from her dad.

Jimmy pulled up the handle on his suitcase. "I'm sorry to rush off, but I need to get to the airport."

"I understand." Kelsey understood all right. She knew what it meant when a man spent more time with his job than with his family.

She shouldn't blame Jimmy. This wasn't a real marriage. It was an arrangement that had nothing to do with love. Why couldn't she remember that? She needed to find something to do with herself besides care for the little garden she had planted. She really couldn't look for a job because she'd be going back to school in the fall. Maybe she could find an online class to take that would fill her time.

"Walk with me to the car." Jimmy wheeled his suitcase through the great room.

"Okay." Kelsey followed, disappointment dogging every step. She didn't know why she had this feeling. She didn't have the right to have expectations about their marriage other than Jimmy's commitment to be a friend to her and a father to her child. "When will you get there?"

"My flight lands at around nine o'clock." Jimmy opened the front door. "I'll call you when I land, because I'm not sure how long it'll take to get to the hotel. I don't want to call too late."

"Sure. I'll be waiting." Kelsey feigned a smile.

She walked to the car with Jimmy. He loaded his suitcase into the trunk, then went to the driver's side. She stood beside him as he opened the car door. Were any of his neighbors watching? Should she give him a hug and a kiss goodbye?

Stepping closer, Kelsey gazed up at him. "Do you have nosy neighbors?"

Jimmy wrinkled his brow. "Why?"

"Would they expect us to kiss goodbye?"

Jimmy closed the small gap between them. He put his arms around her waist and stared into her eyes. "Mrs. Cunningham, is this an invitation to kiss you goodbye?"

Swallowing the lump in her throat, Kelsey nodded, not trusting herself to speak. She was afraid her voice would come out in a squeak. Her pulse raced as she anticipated his kiss.

He grinned. "That's good because I never turn down a chance to kiss my wife. She has the sweetest kisses this side of the Appalachian Mountains."

Kelsey stood on her tiptoes and put her arms around Jimmy's neck. He leaned in and brushed his lips against hers. That was not enough. What was she thinking? She wasn't thinking. She was only feeling. Feeling lightheaded and completely entranced by her husband. She pressed her lips to his, asking for more. He deepened the kiss, and Kelsey was sure she might float away.

When Jimmy ended the kiss, he held her tight. "If I don't go now, I may never go. Save these kisses for when I get home."

Kelsey stepped back and covered her mouth with her

hands. She'd done it again. She looked up at Jimmy as she dropped her hands to her sides and shook her head "I don't know what gets into me. I'm always giving you the wrong signals."

"Must be my irresistible kisses." Jimmy gave her a peck on the cheek, then grinned. "I'd better get going."

"Okay." She pressed her lips together as she looked at her pink tennis shoes. Her cheeks probably matched them as a blush heated her face. Did he really think she had the sweetest kisses? What difference did it make when they didn't love each other?

Jimmy lifted her chin with a finger until their gazes met. "It's okay, Kelsey. You eventually let me know where things stand. I won't cross any line you set."

She flung her arms around his waist and buried her face against his chest. She could hear his heartbeat. "You're too good to me."

"Never good enough." Jimmy released her and got into the car, then leaned out the open window. "Don't have too much fun while I'm gone."

Kelsey just waved as he backed out of the driveway. How could she have fun when worry was her constant companion? She worried about actually having a baby and all that entailed. She worried that if she spent too much time visiting her mother-in-law, Amanda, or Charlotte, they might guess her condition. She worried about never being right with God again.

Jimmy was the only constant in her life, and she worried that he would eventually get tired of being the good husband and getting nothing in return.

CHAPTER SIXTEEN

Since their first breakfast at his home, she had taken to cooking and loved to try all the recipes his mom had given them. Unfortunately, out-of-town trips or late hours at the office relegated him to leftovers, but even Kelsey's leftovers tasted great.

He stood in the doorway between the laundry room and the kitchen and watched as she bobbed and shuffled to the music and sang a little off key. "Sweet Talkin' Woman," a song by Electric Light Orchestra, had been one of his dad's favorites. Every time Jimmy heard it, he thought of his dad. Now Kelsey was making more memories. She did not have her sister's singing voice, but Jimmy loved every off-key note Kelsey sang. He loved her. Why couldn't she love him?

Jimmy didn't know whether he should interrupt her little performance or just sneak into the house and back to his room. He didn't know how to deal with Kelsey anymore. Had he ever known how? Probably not. She'd been here just over five weeks, and little had changed in their relationship. Every time he thought they might be drawing closer, she withdrew.

She was his wife. He should be able to walk up behind her, pull her close, plant little kisses up and down her neck, and put his hand over her growing belly. But ever since that day she'd gotten carried away with kissing him goodbye in the driveway, she had kept her distance.

He hoped the lyrics to this song weren't a predictor of his future with Kelsey. Was he on a dead end street with her?

Graham's demands at work gave Jimmy an excuse not to spend time at home. It was almost a relief not to be around Kelsey. Every day he found it harder and harder to be so close to her and not want the marriage to be real. The trips away from home and the long office hours when he was home kept him from going crazy in his own house, and he always found solace in his workshop.

At the same time, he recognized the folly in chasing after this job. He wasn't happy with his employment situation either, but he had made these choices. Now he had to live with them. He couldn't be a failure again.

Tonight he looked forward to an evening with his wife and her newly learned cooking skills. Yet he was a man torn about spending time with his wife, knowing that time would make him miserable with wanting her love.

With a sigh, he picked up his satchel and slung it over his shoulder. He made his way through the kitchen while Kelsey continued to sing and chop. Just as he reached the hallway, the music stopped.

"Jimmy Cunningham, are you sneaking into this house without even saying hello?"

Jimmy hesitated before he turned to face her. "Yeah, I didn't want to disturb an artist at work."

She narrowed her gaze. "Are you making fun of me?"

"No." Sadness settled over Jimmy, and he didn't feel like teasing her or joking. "I'm being truthful. I didn't want to disturb you."

"Oh. Okay." A puzzled expression crept across her face. "Are you okay?"

"I'm just tired. It's been a long day, and I still have work to do." He turned to go to his room.

"Jimmy, are you going to eat the dinner I'm preparing?"

He stopped and looked at her again. "Sure. I'll be working. Let me know when it's ready."

"It won't be long," she called after him.

When Jimmy got to his bedroom, he slung his satchel. It landed with a thud on the bed. That was what he'd like to do with his job. At least he'd had sense enough to throw the satchel on the bed and not the floor, or he might be looking at a ruined computer.

Why had he ever thought the business world was for him?

Then there was Kelsey. Maybe he just needed to lay it all on the line. Tell her that he loved her and deal with the consequences. Things couldn't go on this way indefinitely. What had ever made him think a marriage like this would last?

Selfish ambition had led him down this path. He'd wanted to prove to everyone that he was a big shot with a prestigious job and a pretty wife. He'd wanted people in this town to see beyond the guy who had frittered away a scholarship and hurt people with his reckless living. Now the only person he wanted to impress was Kelsey, but she didn't care. And he was afraid he'd wind up hurting her just as he'd done with Whitney.

Jimmy sat on the bed with his head in his hands. *Lord God, only You can help me out of this mess. Please give me wisdom. I give this all over to You. Help me not to try to take it back.*

With his head still bowed as he sat there, Jimmy hoped his prayer made it beyond the ceiling. Despite the prayer, misery gripped him. He'd wanted to pray that Kelsey would love him, but that was selfish, too. He couldn't bring himself to say that prayer because he feared the answer was no, but he had to accept whatever God wanted.

"Jimmy." Kelsey stood in the doorway, a concerned look on her face. "I've been calling you. The food's ready."

Jimmy stood. "Great. I'm hungry. What did you fix?"

She leaned against the door, an impish smile on her face. "Something your mom told me you really like."

"What's that?" Jimmy wondered whether it was a good sign that Kelsey had fixed one of his favorite dishes.

"Fried chicken, mashed potatoes, and green beans."

"All my favorites. What were you chopping?" Jimmy stepped into the hallway.

"Fixings for the salad." Kelsey glanced back at him as she made her way into the kitchen. "Your mom told me I should feed you more vegetables because you're bad about eating healthy, but she did say you liked bacon in your beans."

"And you always listen to my mom?" Jimmy stood next to the kitchen counter.

"Yeah. I think it's a good thing to listen to my mother-in-law." Kelsey grinned. "She also showed me how to make real sweet tea."

"Now that's something you'd better know how to make if you live in the South." Jimmy laughed. "At least she told you to put bacon in my green beans."

"I'm happy to listen to your mom. Mothers are

important people to listen to. I wish I could've known my mom better. I love Maria, but I missed…"

As Kelsey's voice hitched and tears welled in her eyes, Jimmy put an arm around her shoulders and pulled her close. He wanted to wrap her in his arms and never let her go.

"It's hard to lose a parent. I know how much it hurt when I lost my dad, but I can't imagine how awful it was to lose your mom when you were so young."

Kelsey wiped at her eyes. "I didn't mean to cry. This is supposed to be a happy occasion."

"And that happy occasion is what? Are we celebrating something?"

"Yes. Our three-month anniversary."

Jimmy stared at her. Was this something he should've remembered? Did women think of these kinds of things, when men were clueless? "Am I in trouble because I didn't remember this?"

Kelsey laughed. "No, I just realized it myself while I was using my phone for the recipe for the carrot cake."

"Carrot cake?"

"Yes. Another thing your mom said you love."

"Then this is a celebration!" Jimmy wanted to grab Kelsey around the waist and twirl her around the room, do a little dance to that song she'd been singing, then kiss her until she couldn't think straight.

But that wasn't going to happen. Too many times he'd made the mistake of thinking things had changed between them only to have Kelsey back away, leaving him wondering what he'd done wrong. This time he wouldn't make that mistake. He shouldn't read anything into her celebration.

"And we're celebrating my cooking." She looked up at him with a satisfied smile.

Despite the lecture he'd just given himself, Jimmy took in this information with hope. He couldn't help himself. Is that what love did to a person? Made them senseless?

"I like that we're celebrating our anniversary with your cooking. It should be good since you've had all that practice."

"I hope so." She placed a hand over her heart. "Let's eat."

Jimmy glanced at the table, which Kelsey had set with placemats and matching napkins his mom had given them. "Would you like me to help you serve?"

"You can get the beans and salad. I'll take care of the chicken and mashed potatoes."

He set the beans and salad on the table. "Don't forget the gravy."

"I'll get that while you get dressing for the salad."

When everything was on the table, Jimmy pulled out a chair for Kelsey, and she looked up at him with a smile. He swallowed hard, his emotions on overload. If this could only translate into hope for the future of their life together.

He joined her at the table and said a prayer of thanksgiving for the food. When he looked up, she stared at him, worry in her eyes. He hoped it all tasted as good as it looked. He stabbed a piece of chicken from the platter and put it on his plate, then added the potatoes, gravy, and green beans.

"Don't forget your salad."

Jimmy laughed. "You're determined to make me eat vegetables."

"Besides, you told me you like radishes. They're good

for you."

"I do." *You're good for me.*

"So what do you think?"

"I haven't tasted anything yet. Do you want me to start with the salad?"

"Start with whatever you want."

"That's easy. The chicken." Jimmy took a bite. Perfect. Just like Kelsey.

"Well?" Worry lines appeared between her eyebrows.

"Don't tell my mom, but this is better than hers." Jimmy took another bite.

Relief wiped away Kelsey's fretful expression. "Just so you like it. That's all that matters."

So much more mattered than whether he liked her fried chicken. He wished he could start over and do this thing right with Kelsey, but that wouldn't have happened. She would've gone back to school, and he wouldn't have seen her again. This way, even if it started all wrong, he at least had a chance to win her love. Patience. Why couldn't he generate the patience he needed?

Jimmy tried everything else, and it was all delicious. "You know what this means?"

"What?" Kelsey's anxious look reappeared.

"You're the better cook, so you win the job."

Kelsey grinned. "I'll gladly take it. That way you can have all the time you need to do your work."

"I don't mean for you to get stuck doing the cooking all the time."

"Really. I don't mind at all. It gives me something to do."

Was she bored with her life here? "Have you visited Charlotte lately?"

Kelsey shook her head. "I've been keeping to myself the past couple of weeks. I'm afraid my pregnancy is beginning to show."

Jimmy wished she wasn't so concerned about people knowing she was pregnant. At this point, he didn't understand her reluctance to share the news. What could he say to encourage her? Would she get upset if he told her she should quit hiding out? The evening had gone well so far, and he didn't want to ruin it. Maybe he just had to take charge. Could he come up with the right words while he ate?

After he finished eating, he leaned back in his chair. "That was a fabulous meal."

"Thank you." Kelsey beamed.

Jimmy waved a hand over his empty plate. "I ate everything, even the salad. Do I get carrot cake now?"

Kelsey laughed. "Yes, after we clean up."

After they made quick work of the dishes, Kelsey cut two pieces of cake and put them on plates. "I'm going to watch a movie and eat my cake. Would you like to join me?"

Jimmy stared at her. This was a chance to connect with Kelsey, but he had work to do. He gave himself a mental shaking. What was he thinking? Work or wife? That was a simple choice. Wife.

"What are we watching?"

"*Overboard*, the original version. Amanda and I used to watch it when we were kids. Maria introduced it to us. She watched it when she was a kid."

"What's it about?"

"This woman falls off her yacht and winds up getting amnesia, and this guy pretends to be her husband, but I don't want to ruin the story for you."

Sounded like a chick flick, but he'd watch it because it was a chance to be with Kelsey. "So this movie appeals to a multigenerational crowd?"

"I guess you could say that." Kelsey got out two forks. "Here's a fork. Grab your plate, and we can eat our cake on the couch while we watch the movie."

"Sure." As Jimmy made his way to the couch, he wondered how close he should sit to her. If this were a real marriage, he'd sit right next to her with one arm around her. But Kelsey was his wife in name only. That fact ate at him day and night.

"All set?"

"Yeah." As set as he'd ever be.

Why was he such a chicken? He could turn to her right now and tell her he loved her, but he couldn't find the words, the right words that wouldn't make her back away. She was here with him, and he didn't want to ruin that. All his plans to take charge withered away.

She started the movie, then sat just close enough to him on the couch that he could be tempted to scoot over and put his arm around her. His brain was a mass of indecision. *Eat your cake, watch the movie, and don't do anything stupid.*

He finished his cake and set his plate on the coffee table. He leaned closer, but not too close. "The cake was delicious. I'm glad there's more."

A smile tilted her mouth. "Thank you."

"You're welcome." Every nerve in his body zinged. He could lean still closer and kiss her sweet lips, but he squashed that thought as if it were a pesky mosquito. He focused his attention on the movie and tried not to think about the fact that she sat just inches away.

The story unfolded, and Jimmy found that he actually enjoyed the movie, as well as sitting close to Kelsey. The room grew dimmer as the sun set. The only light came from the TV. He felt like a teenage kid planning his move to put an arm around his date during the movie. He had a one-track mind. Better get it on another track.

Kelsey's laughter made Jimmy realize he hadn't been paying attention to the movie for the last few minutes. She drew his attention like a bug to the light. But she was like one of those bug zappers. If he got too close, he would be sorry later.

While the last scene played and the two main characters kissed, Jimmy fought with all his brainpower not to think about kissing Kelsey. While he battled with his runaway thoughts, the sound of sniffles floated through the air. He glanced at Kelsey. She was blowing her nose and wiping her eyes.

He glanced her way, grinning. "Are you crying over this movie?"

Pressing her lips together, she nodded.

"How many times have you seen this?"

Kelsey held up both hands.

"Ten times?"

"More." Her voice came out in a blubber. "I always have tissues nearby when I watch it. I'm a sucker for happy endings."

Jimmy decided he was, too. He wanted a happy ending with Kelsey in the worst way. He'd gone around and around on how to accomplish that. He'd told himself to be patient, but patience never came. They'd been married for only three months, and over half of that time they hadn't even lived together. Love was making him crazy. He had to get out of here.

Jimmy stood. "Thanks for supper and the movie, but I've got work to do. See you in the morning."

"Don't work too hard."

"I have to if I want to do the job right." This job was more than he'd bargained for. He should've listened to Mitch's warning, but like with so many things, Jimmy had just barged ahead without considering what the future might hold.

"Okay. See you tomorrow."

Jimmy trudged down the hallway to his bedroom. Had he heard a little regret in Kelsey's voice? Hopefully, work would take his mind off her. That was probably wishful thinking, too.

He sat at the desk he'd set up in his room and opened the laptop computer. He brought up the files and combed through the spreadsheets. After a while the numbers swam before his eyes, but he wasn't done. He had to create a presentation for tomorrow, so he had to know this material backward and forward. He leaned back in his chair and ran his fingers through his hair. He'd been sitting here too long.

That carrot cake called to him from the kitchen. He smiled as he walked across the room. Kelsey had been so proud of the meal she'd fixed for him. She had done something special for their three-month anniversary. He shouldn't dismiss that, but he should temper his thoughts with patience. He had to remind himself of that every day, every hour, and every minute.

Darkness greeted him as he stepped into the hallway. Kelsey's door was shut. Not even the faintest light shone out from under her door. She must be asleep. He tiptoed to the kitchen and turned on the light over the stove. After getting another piece of cake, he went back to his room.

While he worked, he ate the cake. With every bite he thought about Kelsey. He tried to concentrate on the files and his presentation, but her smile flashed through his mind. He shook his head. This report had to get done even if he had to stay up all night.

Finally at one in the morning, Jimmy fell into bed exhausted. He had to get up early in the morning. He hoped he could function on a few hours of rest. Visions of Kelsey filled his mind as he drifted into sleep.

"Jimmy?"

Her voice made Jimmy sit straight up. His heart hammering, he looked at her silhouetted against the hall light as she stood in the doorway. Her face was in the shadow, and he couldn't read her expression. What was she doing here? "Kelsey?"

"Jimmy." Her voice cracked. "Something's wrong. Really wrong."

He jumped out of bed and ran to her side. "What do you mean?"

"I…think…I've…lost…the…baby." Each word came out between sobs.

The bedside clock read two fifteen as shock took over Jimmy's thoughts. He didn't know what to do or say. "What happened?"

"I don't know. These really bad cramps woke me up, and I went into the bathroom. There was all this blood and clots and pain." Her words came out in a strangled cry.

Jimmy's pulse pounded in his head. He had to be calm even though his mind was a mess. "I should take you to the emergency room."

"I don't know."

"We're going. Better safe than sorry." Jimmy took charge. Kelsey wasn't sure what was happening, and he certainly didn't know. They needed a professional opinion. "Just let me take you."

Kelsey looked down at herself. "I can't go like this."

"You don't need to change." Helplessness inundated him. He wasn't sure that was wise advice, but what did he know?

"But I want to. I just need to clean up."

"Okay. I'll put some towels in the backseat so you can lie down while I drive. Then I'll come back and get you."

Without bothering to change out of the work-out clothes he'd worn to bed, Jimmy drove to the nearest hospital. The car lights beamed into the darkness as he pressed his foot to the gas pedal. He didn't pay attention to how fast he was going.

When they reached the hospital, the emergency room was relatively empty. A nurse put Kelsey's information into her computer, then took her back to a room. Jimmy followed, feeling completely helpless. He waited there with her, neither of them saying anything. When a doctor arrived to examine Kelsey, Jimmy stepped out into the waiting area.

Pacing back and forth, Jimmy prayed. He prayed that Kelsey would be okay. If this was a miscarriage, how would she feel? How did he feel? Even though the baby wasn't his, he had kind of gotten used to the idea of being a dad. He loved kids. How would Kelsey react, since she hadn't wanted this baby in the first place?

Then there was the whole issue of their marriage. Kelsey didn't love him. She only married him to save herself from an impossible situation and to give her baby a father. If there was no baby, would she stay? The thought of her leaving was like a large stone pressing down on his chest. Would she stay if she knew he loved her?

Every time he thought it was a good time to confess his love, something happened to make him think twice. Kelsey's emotional state would be unsettled after this. He couldn't spring his love on her now.

While Jimmy continued to pace, the doctor came out of the room. "Mr. Cunningham, you can see your wife now. She wanted me to tell you that she had a miscarriage. I'm sorry."

Jimmy's heart sank, his emotions in a jumble. "That's what we suspected. Thank you for taking care of her."

"I've already told her, but she needs to see her regular doctor as soon as possible. Make sure she does. I'm sending her home with instructions and information about what to expect." The doctor shook Jimmy's hand, then hurried away to tend to another emergency patient.

Jimmy stood outside the room and prayed he would say and do the right things. He pushed the door open. Kelsey was already dressed in her gym shorts and T-shirt. He stood there for a minute, his brain not engaging his tongue.

"Kelsey, I…I don't know what to say."

"Neither do I."

"How do you feel?"

"Empty."

He wasn't going to ask. He would just hug her. He stepped closer and gathered her into his arms. "It'll be okay."

"I know it will. Maria had several miscarriages."

Kelsey's words were muffled into his chest.

"Maybe you should talk to her."

Kelsey shook her head against his chest. "No. Nobody needs to know I was pregnant. This is just between you and me."

"Okay." Jimmy didn't have a good feeling about that approach, but he'd keep his opinions to himself. It wouldn't be good for Kelsey to keep this all bottled up inside. Even if she hadn't wanted this baby, the emotional trauma had to be hard, and it had to be dealt with.

Kelsey extracted herself from his arms. "Let's go home."

"Sure."

On the drive back to Pineydale, Kelsey sat in silence. Jimmy took a clue from her and didn't say anything. He didn't know what to say anyway. *Powerless.* That one word described everything about this situation. It described him especially.

When they finally arrived at home, Jimmy parked the car in the garage, then turned to Kelsey. "How are you feeling?"

"Tired."

"Do you need to change your bedding?"

Kelsey shook her head. "There was no mess until I got to the bathroom."

"I'll take care of cleaning that up."

"You don't need to. It's mostly clean. I did that before we left." Kelsey didn't wait for him to respond as she went inside.

Wanting to say she shouldn't have done that, Jimmy hurried behind her. He wished she would talk to him, tell him how she was feeling emotionally, not just physically.

"I'm just going to bed." She stopped in the doorway to her room.

Jimmy frowned. "Are you sure you're going to be okay?"

Her expression solemn, she nodded. "I'll see my doctor tomorrow."

"Do you want me to take you?"

Her lips pressed together, she shook her head. "I'll be fine to drive myself. You have work, and I'm sorry I kept you up."

"You don't have to be sorry. Just get some sleep. If you need anything, don't be afraid to come and get me."

"Okay." Kelsey took in a ragged breath, her expression still vacant. "Thank you for taking care of me."

"That's what I'm here for. No thanks needed." Jimmy hated to leave her alone, but he had to go along with her wishes.

"I don't know what I'd do without you." Kelsey flung her arms around him and looked up at him, her eyes swimming with tears. "Will you stay with me? I don't want to be alone."

Nodding, Jimmy swallowed hard and gathered her into his arms again. He hoped she would continue to feel that way, because he didn't know what he'd do without her. "I'll stay as long as you want."

Kelsey took his hand and led him to her bed. Still in her gym shorts and T-shirt, she slipped under the covers. He joined her as he put his arm over her in the spoon position. Her body shook as sobs sounded in the quiet room. Sadness imprisoned his thoughts as he pulled her closer. While he held her, the sobs subsided, and she lay still in his arms. He wanted to take away her sorrow and her pain. Most of all he wanted to tell her he loved her. Finally, Jimmy fell asleep, Kelsey filling his arms and hope for their future filling his dreams.

CHAPTER SEVENTEEN

The obstetrician's instructions tumbled through Kelsey's mind as she drove home. Two weeks had passed since the miscarriage, and the doctor said everything looked fine, and she was free to try to get pregnant again after she had a period. She had just nodded and tried not to think about her loss. Trying to get pregnant again was the last thing on her mind.

He had reassured her several times that the miscarriage wasn't her fault. *Wasn't her fault.* The words echoed in her brain. But how could it not be her fault? She had wished her baby away a thousand times. Her terrible wish had come true.

Kelsey pulled her car into the parking lot of the local grocery store. She sat there for a few minutes and tried to settle her heart and mind. Jimmy's support had gotten her through that horrible experience. He had made sure she was okay before he left for work every morning. That first morning after it had happened and she had spent the night in his arms, he'd offered not to go to work, but she wouldn't let him jeopardize his job. She knew what a taskmaster Graham Cunningham was.

Jimmy never talked about his work, but she had a feeling he was trying too hard to please his uncle. But what reason did Jimmy have to rush home at night other than his workshop? Certainly he didn't rush home to see her. She wasn't sure why that made her sad.

Now everything was different. She had no baby on the way. Did Jimmy feel trapped in this marriage? She wanted to talk to him about it, but she didn't know how to bring it up or what to say. He still needed a wife. A divorce wouldn't look good to his uncle. She wished she knew what Jimmy wanted. She wished she knew what she wanted. Her emotions floundered in a sea of confusion.

Shaking away all the troubling thoughts, Kelsey got out of the car. Jimmy would be home tonight after another out-of-town trip. She wanted to buy some groceries to make him a special supper to celebrate his return. She had surprised herself at how much she enjoyed cooking. Besides fried chicken, Mary had told Kelsey that he loved steak and baked potatoes. That should be easy to fix, if she could figure out how to light the grill.

Kelsey grabbed a shopping cart and pushed it into the store. She headed for the produce department in search of the perfect baking potatoes. After she selected two, one large and one small, she spied the apples. Did she dare try to make an apple pie, another one of Jimmy's favorites? She would try.

After she selected the apples, she moved on to the large display of cheeses. Jimmy loved cheese in the sandwiches he often took in his lunch, and she wanted to get him something special. While she perused the cheeses, she heard two women talking as they stood on the opposite side of the display. The mention of Jimmy's name caught her attention.

"Do you know who's back in town?" asked one woman, not waiting for the other woman to respond.

"Whitney Hamilton."

"She hasn't been back in years, even to visit. Why is she back?"

"Her dad's health has really declined in the last six months. I think her mom begged her to come home to help."

"I wonder what she thinks about both Mitch and Jimmy being married."

"I don't think she cares that much about Mitch. She always had her sights set on Jimmy. He was the one she was in love with, even when she dumped him for Mitch." The woman sighed. "Jimmy Cunningham can sure turn some heads with those good looks of his."

"Yeah, but then he runs off and marries some young thing that he barely knew."

"Someone told me they thought she was pregnant, a one-night stand that resulted in a rush to get married."

"I heard they don't even live together. Is that true?"

"I don't know, but it wouldn't surprise me, if Whitney has her way, that Jimmy won't be married for long. Those two couldn't stay away from each other even when she was engaged to Mitch."

Kelsey wanted to run out of the store. If those women saw her, would they know who she was, or were they just talking about some nameless, faceless woman who was part of the small town's rumor mill? She would forget the cheese, grab the steaks, and get out of this store.

Hoping the women couldn't see her, Kelsey kept her face turned away as she found her way to the meat department. Hurriedly she looked over the steaks and grabbed a couple of packages and threw them into her cart and barreled down the aisle toward the checkout lane.

When Kelsey finally reached her car, she tossed the plastic bags containing her purchase on the passenger seat as she slid behind the wheel. While she drove home, she let those women's comments replay in her mind. Had people guessed about her pregnancy? Well, now there was no baby.

Kelsey's heart twisted, and the tears flowed. She wasn't even sure she knew why she was crying. The loss of her baby. All the pretending. The thought of losing Jimmy. Maybe all of it pressed down on her spirit. What had happened to the cheerful college student she'd been last fall when she'd first met Jimmy?

In the last three months she'd cried more than she'd probably cried in her whole life. Her mind replayed the conversation from the grocery store again and again as she drove into the garage. She kept hearing what the one woman had said. *Those two couldn't stay away from each other.* Did Jimmy still love Whitney? Did she still love Jimmy and intend to go after him even though he was married, as those women had surmised?

That conversation was all speculation and rumor, wasn't it? That was what happened with gossip. It turned into half-truths. The women didn't even have all the details right. She and Jimmy did live together now. At least they shared the same house. And beyond that, he was a good husband, sharing her secret and her pain.

With an overwhelming sense of loss, Kelsey took the groceries into the kitchen and put the steaks in the refrigerator. She glanced at the clock on the microwave. Three thirty. Jimmy would be home from the airport around six. She had time to make the apple pie and figure out how to light the grill.

By five o'clock she had managed with great difficulty to bake a pie. It looked good as it sat cooling on the counter, but she could only hope it tasted good. She put the potatoes in the oven, then searched through the kitchen until she found one of those long lighters to use on the grill. She wandered out to the back deck and looked at the grill. She turned the knob and held the lighter on the place where she thought the flame would start. Nothing happened. She tried again. Still nothing.

With a sigh, she went back into the house. The steaks would have to wait until Jimmy got home and turned on the grill. She made a salad. While she cut up the radishes from her garden, she thought about the time he'd teased her about planting radishes when she was a kid. Jimmy hadn't done much teasing lately. He didn't seem like the man she'd first married. Maybe he was unhappy being married to her. The only thing that kept them together was his stupid job, the job that kept him away from home too much.

Even when he was home, he was either studying for work or some class or out in the shop. He avoided her at every turn. With the news she'd learned today, she wondered about that trip to Atlanta. Had he seen Whitney there? Is that why the woman had suddenly showed up in town?

Even if Jimmy had seen Whitney, he wouldn't cheat on his wife. He wasn't that kind of man. But then he'd had no trouble messing around with Whitney when she' been Mitch's fiancée. No. No. Kelsey shook her head. That was not who Jimmy was anymore. But then why was he so unhappy?

Forcing herself not to think about those gossipy

women, Kelsey headed for her room to change into something special for Jimmy. On the way, she went by the nursery. The door was closed, and it had been closed since Jimmy had put the crib and changing table in there. He had said it would stay closed until she decided to announce her pregnancy. Thankfully, she had never done so.

Maybe it was time to face her loss in a concrete way.

She stood at the door with her fingers on the handle as she drummed up the courage to go in. Taking a deep breath, she pushed on the lever. The door swung open. She stared at the empty space across from her. The chest and the armoire still stood against one wall, but the crib and changing table were gone. Had Jimmy taken them away? He must have done it when she wasn't there and never told her. Did he think it would help her if those pieces weren't in the room?

He was only trying to be helpful, but the empty spaces in the room matched the empty space in her heart. She went over to the armoire and opened the door just to look at Jimmy's handiwork. Lying on the shelf was something white. She picked it up. She held a tiny sleeper with an attached cap. Something for a newborn with an inscription on the front. *Welcome to the world.*

A crushing sensation hit Kelsey in the chest as she held the baby clothing. Jimmy must've bought this for her baby. She sank onto the floor and covered her face with the sleeper as tears soaked the material. She'd lost her baby. She couldn't lose Jimmy, too.

The silent tears turned to sobs as she cried, the ache in her heart so great she thought she might explode from the pain.

"Kelsey. Kelsey. What's wrong?"

She uncovered her face and discovered Jimmy sitting next to her on the floor. She held up the sleeper, but she couldn't say anything coherent between the sobs.

Jimmy gathered her into his arms and rocked back and forth with her as he patted her back as if she were a small child. He smoothed her hair. Kelsey clung to him, her sniffles eventually fading away. Even after she stopped crying, she remained in his arms. Neither of them said a thing as they stayed together on the floor.

Finally, Kelsey looked up at him. "I'm sorry I blubbered all over you again. I seem to do that a lot. I'm so sorry. I want to be my old self again. Happy Kelsey, not this…this woman who has a crying jag every time she turns around."

"You can't expect not to grieve over your loss."

Kelsey sighed. "I guess I expected not to be sad. After all, you know very well I didn't want the baby. I've been so confused about my feelings."

"I won't argue with you there."

Kelsey smiled. "And you've put up with it all. Thank you."

"Maybe you need to talk to someone about it besides me. Talk to Amanda, talk to Charlotte, talk to somebody. Go to a counselor."

Kelsey shook her head. "I'll be fine. I'll get through this."

"I wish you'd reconsider."

"I know I'll be fine." *As long as you don't leave me.* At that moment, Kelsey looked at Jimmy and realized what she'd been denying for too long. She loved him, and that was the real reasons she didn't want to lose him.

Did he know Whitney was back in town? If he didn't,

what would he do when he found out? When he saw her again after all this time, would those old feelings resurface? Kelsey thought about what the doctor had said today. She could resume sexual relations with her husband. Is that what she needed to do?

Sex wouldn't keep him in this marriage. She ought to know that for sure. Love would.

Kelsey held up the little sleeper to put her mind on a different track. "Did you buy this?"

A solemn look crossed Jimmy's face. "I saw it on one of my trips. It seemed perfect. I'm sorry it caused you pain."

"It's okay." She wanted to say she'd save it for when they had a baby of their own, but she wanted Jimmy to love her first. Was she making an impossible wish?

She'd been so wrapped up in subterfuge, guilt, and fear of being hurt again that she had squashed her feelings for him as soon as they'd surfaced. Not anymore. The awareness bubbled up like a fresh spring popping up from deep in the earth. She loved him. But how could she make him love her? She couldn't. Love had to grow. Hers had. It had just taken her a while to recognize it.

***

The following Sunday morning, Kelsey awakened to delicious aromas. She lay in bed and smiled. Jimmy must be making breakfast. Hopefully, this time he wouldn't burn his hand. She'd be sure not to startle him.

After taking a shower and getting dressed, she made her way to the kitchen. She intentionally made enough noise along the way to warn him of her presence. When she stepped into the great room, he was already sitting at the table with a cup of coffee in his hand.

"Good morning. How are you?"

Moving into the kitchen, Kelsey wondered if he was referring to last night. "I'm good, and how are you?"

"Good. Now that...that you're here."

His hesitation made Kelsey wonder what was behind his statement, but she wasn't going to ask or read anything into it. "You have breakfast already on the table."

He motioned to the chair opposite him. "Just sit down and enjoy, but I wasn't sure what you want to drink."

Kelsey smiled as she went to the cupboard. "I'll make myself some hot tea. I'm not much of a coffee drinker."

"I'll remember that for future reference."

Taking his talk of the future as a good sign, Kelsey made her tea—but she still couldn't forget Whitney.

"I'm going to church this morning. I'd like you to go with me."

Was this a command or an invite? Kelsey had always attended church regularly, even in college when most of her friends chose to sleep in on Sunday mornings. But since she'd moved to Pineydale, she had found an excuse almost every Sunday not to go, especially on the weekends when Jimmy was out of town. Mother's Day and the Sunday before Memorial Day were the only two Sundays that had found her in church.

She'd been pretty much a hermit, refusing invitations from everyone, especially in the last weeks before the miscarriage. She had lived in fear that someone would see that she was pregnant, especially her sister. Amanda had been the hardest to avoid, but thankfully she'd had meetings with her mentor, country superstar Willow

Childs, in Nashville and had been gone for nearly three weeks right before Kelsey's miscarriage.

"Well?" Jimmy raised his eyebrows as he stared at her.

"I'll go." Kelsey would go because Jimmy asked. It was a chance to spend time with the man she loved, but she would still sit there with guilt swirling all around her. The baby was gone, but the guilt wasn't.

"Great." Jimmy reached across the table and captured one of her hands. "I know it'll be hard right now, but it'll get better."

She wasn't sure whether he was talking about the loss of her baby or the loss of honesty in her life. "I'll change into something different after we eat."

"You don't have to change. What you're wearing is fine."

Kelsey wasn't going to argue. Did he really think it was fine, or did he just not care that much? She wanted him to care. She just wanted him to love her.

"Thanks for cooking breakfast."

"You're welcome. It's about time I did some cooking." He took a gulp of his coffee, then set the cup on the table.

"You helped finish the meal the other night."

"Yeah, but you did most of the work. That apple pie was the best I've had in a long time." Jimmy grinned. "You're becoming a great cook, Mrs. Cunningham."

Kelsey smiled. "Thank you. It's fun."

"Is your online class fun?"

Kelsey shrugged. "It's okay. I have to get used to that kind of thing. How do you like taking classes that way?"

"I love it. I can do it at my own pace in my own time."

"How's work?"

"It's work." Jimmy took a big bite of his eggs, shutting

down the conversation.

Was Jimmy not thrilled with his job, or was it just her imagination? He just seemed so much more happy doing his woodworking. Or was that just because it was a hobby? She was thankful for one thing. This was one of the best conversations they'd had in a long time. One of the few where she wasn't crying over something. She could only hope they would have more like this. She wanted him to see her as a happy person again.

An hour later they stood on the steps of the church where Amanda and Mitch had gotten married. Jimmy put a hand to Kelsey's back as he escorted her into the building.

As soon as she stepped into the foyer, Mary rushed over to greet them. "It's so good to see you two here this morning."

Kelsey hugged her mother-in-law.

"Kelsey's been little under the weather, but she's better now." Jimmy hugged his mom.

Kelsey just smiled. That was an understatement. Everything about her life was under the weather. Everything except Jimmy. He was the sunshine in her life. She just hoped she could be a bright spot in his. "Jimmy's been taking care of me."

"We've missed you at the family gatherings." Mary looked at Jimmy. "I wish you didn't have to travel so much. I think I'm going to have to talk to your uncle about that."

Jimmy put a hand on his mother's shoulder. "Please don't."

Mary chuckled. "I was just kidding, but it does seem like he's always sending you out of town."

"That's part of the job." Jimmy nudged Kelsey. "We'd

better find our seats."

As they walked into the sanctuary, Amanda raced over to Kelsey. "You're here. I was beginning to think you were mad at me or had moved back to Pinecrest. I never see you."

"She's been under the weather." Jimmy repeated his little speech.

Before they could find a seat, Charlotte joined the group. "Well, well, well. If it isn't the long-lost newlyweds. You know being newlyweds isn't an excuse for skipping church."

"I know." Jimmy hugged Charlotte.

Kelsey prepared to hear his speech again as she also hugged Charlotte.

"And it isn't an excuse for never coming to see me." Charlotte wagged her index finger at them.

"We've been busy settling in. We promise to come visit you this week. We'll invite ourselves over to watch the Fourth of July parade from your porch," Jimmy said.

Charlotte wagged a finger at them again. "I'm counting on that."

"We'll be there." Jimmy looked over at Amanda. "Where you guys sitting?"

"Our usual place." Amanda motioned to a pew on the left side. "See Mitch?"

Jimmy took a step in that direction, but before he got any closer, a tall blonde sashayed down the aisle toward him. Kelsey saw the woman before he did. Kelsey had a pretty good idea who had eyes on her husband.

"Jimmy, hi." The blonde made her way by a couple of other people standing in the aisle.

The color drained from Jimmy's face. "Whitney, what

are you doing here?"

She laughed as she slipped an arm through his. "Pineydale is my hometown and where my parents live."

Jimmy's Adam's apple bobbed as he looked at the woman. "But you haven't been back in years."

"I know." A pout formed on her lips. "My dad's health is not good, and Mom wanted me to come home. So I'm here to help. And it looks like we'll be working together."

Jimmy's eyes grew wide. "Working together?"

"Yeah. You didn't hear? Graham has hired me to do IT work at his company."

"That's good that you could get work so you can help your mom." Jimmy extracted his arm from Whitney's and turned to Kelsey. "I want you to meet my wife, Kelsey."

"Hi, Kelly. It's nice to meet you."

"It's Kelsey."

"Sorry, Kelsey. Nice to meet the woman who finally tamed Jimmy Cunningham." Whitney smiled.

Smiling back, Kelsey wondered if her smile was as disingenuous as Whitney's. Did this woman have designs on Jimmy?

Kelsey had a sick feeling in the pit of her stomach. How could she compete with the tall blonde who looked like a fashion model? Kelsey wished she'd gone with her instinct to change into something nicer. Her skinny navy pants, the blousy sleeveless top, and her old standby pink tennis shoes looked frumpy next to Whitney's colorful sundress and strappy wedge sandals.

Jimmy and Whitney made a handsome couple. Her blue eyes sparkled as she gazed at him. They were both tall and beautiful. Kelsey swallowed a lump in her throat. Jealousy joined guilt in a tormenting dance through

Kelsey's mind. She did the only thing she could think of. She slipped her arm through Jimmy's just as Whitney had done a few minutes before. Only Kelsey didn't stand in the aisle—she tugged on her husband as she led him to the pew where Mitch sat.

When they were seated, Jimmy leaned across her. "Hey, Mitch, did you talk to Whitney?"

"Yeah. Her appearance is quite a surprise and the talk of the town."

"Did you know she's going to work for your dad?"

Mitch's eyes grew wide. "You've got to be kidding me."

Jimmy shook his head. "She told me herself. I can't believe it either, especially after your dad reminded me of"—Jimmy made air quotes with his fingers—"'the debacle with Whitney.' Now we're going to be working together."

Mitch chortled. "Better you than me. Glad I work at my own garage."

Kelsey didn't know what to make of Jimmy and Mitch's conversation. Why had Graham reminded Jimmy of the so-called debacle with Whitney?

The conversation came to an end as the praise band leader stepped to the microphone and said an opening prayer. As the congregation stood for the first song, Kelsey prepared herself to feel the same pressing weight of guilt that had plagued her for weeks. Instead the words of the song reminded her that nothing was too big for God's forgiveness, but as soon as the song was over Kelsey snatched back her guilt. She couldn't feel the forgiveness while she still carried her secret sin. Confession was the only thing that would free her, and she couldn't bring herself to do that.

Kelsey sat through the sermon with the same message as the song. The pastor read Psalm 86:15. "But you, Lord, are a compassionate and gracious God, slow to anger, abounding in love and faithfulness."

Jimmy reached over and squeezed her hand as if he knew what she was struggling with. Maybe he was struggling too, because they both shared her secret. He held her hand until they stood for the closing prayer and song. Her worry about Jimmy had dissipated until Whitney made an appearance again as they walked to the back of the church.

Amanda grabbed hold of Kelsey's arm and pulled her aside in the foyer. "Hey, it's been so long since we've had a good visit. You guys come over to our place for lunch. We're just going to grill some burgers."

"I'll see what Jimmy has to say. He might have plans." Kelsey glanced toward the other side of the foyer where Whitney had commandeered Jimmy. "Let me check with him."

"I'll go with you." Amanda leaned closer. "Is that the infamous Whitney?"

"She's a whirlwind." Kelsey had some other names that might be more appropriate, but she didn't want Amanda to have the first inkling that Kelsey might be jealous.

"I've got some things I want to run by you on Monday," Whitney said as Kelsey and Amanda approached.

"Sure." Jimmy saluted.

Kelsey wanted to believe her husband wasn't thrilled with the prospect of working with Whitney, but she couldn't forget what those women in the grocery store had said. Was it true that Jimmy couldn't stay away from Whitney? Would her constant presence in their office be too much of a temptation for him to resist?

Kelsey tried not to think about it as she slipped her arm through Jimmy's and smiled up at him. "We have an invitation for lunch over at Mitch and Amanda's."

"Great." Jimmy smiled down at her, then turned back to Whitney. "See you Monday."

Whitney batted her eyes. "It'll be like old times."

Jimmy didn't say anything, just escorted Kelsey out the door.

Mitch caught up to Jimmy. "That was awkward. I want to be a fly on the wall in my dad's office on Monday."

"No you don't." Jimmy frowned. "I don't know where she's coming from, but I kind of feel sorry for her."

Kelsey took in the conversation with uncertainty. Jimmy didn't seem the least bit interested in his old girlfriend, so why did she flirt unmercifully with him in front of his wife? Kelsey would like to ask, but the less said about Whitney, the better.

Lunch with Amanda and Mitch reminded Kelsey about the importance of family. Jimmy might not love her, but her sister did. She should never have shut herself off from Amanda, but Kelsey still wasn't brave enough to share everything with her sister. Maybe that would come in time, but for now Kelsey would enjoy their day together and try not to think about the woman who could spell trouble for her marriage.

CHAPTER EIGHTEEN

"Jimmy, I'd like to see you in my office immediately. Bring those latest reports with you." The tone of Graham's voice didn't spell good news.

"I'll be right there." Jimmy ended the call and sat at his desk for a moment to gather his thoughts. Was this going to be another late night?

Jimmy collected the folders on his desk, then trudged down the hall toward Graham's office. The door stood wide open, and Whitney sat in one of the chairs in front of Graham's desk. Not Whitney again. He'd spent more waking hours with her than he had with Kelsey. If it weren't for the fact that he and Whitney had a tumultuous history, he might jokingly call her his work wife. But it was no joking matter.

If Jimmy didn't know better, he might suspect his uncle and Whitney had conspired together to make Jimmy's life miserable. Since coming back to work after his day off on the Fourth of July, he'd spent every weeknight for over a month working late with Whitney as they went over websites, sales figures, and supply chain management stats.

When he arrived home at night, Kelsey was already in bed, and he was gone in the morning before she got up. If it weren't for the weekends, he would never see her. She never complained or said anything about his late nights. But then maybe she didn't care because she didn't love him. They were housemates, and that was about it.

During these meetings, Whitney was at his side constantly, almost as if she knew his wife had married him for reasons other than love. Whitney had no trouble making her interest in him known. He'd fallen for her ploy once before, but this time he was a married man. Even if that marriage was in name only, Whitney didn't have any business acting this way. What was she thinking?

Graham motioned toward the empty chair next to Whitney. "Jimmy, have a seat. We've got a lot to discuss."

"Yes, sir." Without looking Whitney's way, Jimmy took a seat. "What's on your mind?"

"You two have done a great job moving things forward. Sales are up, and I like that. But I think we can do even more." Graham walked to the front of his desk and handed them each a brochure. "Look this over."

Jimmy opened the shiny trifold brochure and glanced at the information. A weeklong conference in Denver, Colorado, near the end of next month. Was Graham wanting Jimmy to go? He didn't want to ask and put ideas in Graham's mind, but Jimmy figured that was the intent of passing out the brochures.

"This sounds like a very good conference." Whitney looked Jimmy's way. "Don't you agree, Jimmy?"

"I think you should go." That would get her out of his hair for a week.

Graham motioned with his index finger. "I do, too, and Jimmy, you should also go. You two make an excellent team."

Jimmy didn't say anything. Would Kelsey go with

him? No, she couldn't. She started classes that week. Would he have to skip his own classes in order to please Graham?

"We do," Whitney piped up as she waved the brochure in the air. "And I think we could learn a lot from this."

"When do we have to make a decision?" Jimmy sat forward in his chair and wished he could discuss this with Graham alone.

Graham made a wide gesture with his hand. "I think it's already been decided. You two are going. I'll have my assistant make the arrangements."

"Okay. I'll be in my office if you need me for anything." Jimmy stood and shook Graham's hand, then left the room before Whitney could waylay him.

Jimmy entered his office and closed the door. He sat at his desk and stared out the window as he leaned back in his chair with his fingers laced behind his head. He didn't want to go, especially if Whitney was going. He wanted to stay home with Kelsey. How was he ever going to make something of their marriage if he was never home, never had a chance to interact with her?

What would happen if he refused to go? Only one way to find out. Jimmy headed back to Graham's office, making sure to avoid Whitney on the way.

Jimmy knocked on Graham's door.

"Come in."

Jimmy entered the office and found Graham studying something at his desk. "I need to talk to you about this conference."

"Sure." Graham motioned for Jimmy to sit.

"I don't need to sit down. This won't take long."

"What's on your mind?" Graham came around the

desk.

"I'm not going."

Graham frowned. "What do you mean you're not going?"

Jimmy eyed his uncle. "Just what I said. I don't need to go to this thing. Sending Whitney will be good enough. We both don't need to attend."

"I disagree."

"You want me to get my degree. My classes start that week, and besides, I have a wife, at your urging, and she likes to see her husband occasionally. I haven't been home much lately." Jimmy wasn't sure whether Kelsey actually wanted him around, but it didn't hurt his cause to mention her.

Graham rubbed his chin as he paced back and forth in front of his desk. When he stopped, his expression made Jimmy's insides curdle.

"You took this job knowing that there would be huge demands on your time. If you want to get ahead, you have to make some choices, and they're not always choices that make your family happy. So here's the bottom line. You can go to the conference, or you can pack up your things and collect your severance."

Wow! Jimmy knew his uncle was hard-nosed when it came to business, but he didn't know to what extent. Jimmy didn't want to make any rash statements. He had to think this over. "I'll let you know what I decide before I go home today."

"I'll be waiting."

Jimmy strode back to his office. This time he paced back and forth. What was he going to do? If he was honest with himself, he'd say he hated this job. He'd been unhappy for weeks. The only thing that made him smile was Kelsey, but too many times she made him sad because she didn't love him, at least not the way he loved her. She liked him. She'd told him he was her best friend. He clung to that.

How was he supposed to support a wife without a job, but how was he supposed to have a family life if he was never home? He remembered the conversation he'd had with Kelsey's dad. He'd told Jimmy not to make the mistakes he'd made when he'd put his job before his family. That was what Graham was demanding. Job before family—ironic, since he'd insisted Jimmy have a family of his own.

Jimmy pounded his fist on his desk, then plopped down on his chair. He had two rotten choices. A job and no time to spend with Kelsey, or no job and no way to earn an income and support a wife, a wife who had college tuition to pay. He supposed he could go back to work for Jeremy and paint houses.

Jimmy didn't want to be a failure again. He should've stuck with painting houses in the first place. He had promised Kelsey's dad that he would take care of her and be a good husband, one who spent time with her. Without a job he'd have plenty of time to spend with her, but how would he put food on the table?

He put his hands behind his head and stared at the ceiling. Maybe he ought to pray, but he didn't know what to pray for. "Lord, just don't let me do something stupid."

Before the last word was out of his mouth, Whitney barged into his office. "You're thinking of quitting. You can't do that."

Jimmy just sat there and stared at her. "Says who?"

"Me."

"And why should I listen to you?"

"Because you know me, Jimmy. Our relationship goes way back, and I think this trip could rekindle things for us."

Jimmy couldn't believe what he was hearing. "What are you trying to rekindle?"

"Whatever you want." She batted her eyelashes at him.

Jimmy stood and pointed to the door. "I want you to leave. I'm a married man."

"But not happily married."

"Who says?"

"It's the word around town." Whitney stared at him, challenging him to deny it.

"I love Kelsey. That's all you need to know."

"Suit yourself, but if you ever change your mind, I'll be around."

As Whitney left the room, Jimmy sat on the edge of his desk and wondered if he'd just awakened from a bad dream. He rubbed a hand down his face. Had the Lord just given Jimmy an answer to his prayer? Yeah. He needed to run from Whitney just as Joseph had run from Potiphar's wife.

Jimmy typed up a letter of resignation, printed it out, and then cleaned out his desk, stuffing his things into his satchel. He looked around the office. He'd learned a lot about himself in the time he'd worked here. At least this experience wouldn't go to waste. He knew now he wasn't cut out for this kind of work, but what was his calling? Would the whole town look at him as a failure again? Is that the way Kelsey would view him?

With a heavy sigh, Jimmy made his way to Graham's

office and knocked on the door.

"Enter."

"Hello, Uncle Graham." Jimmy shifted the satchel on his shoulder and laid the paper on the desk. "Here's my resignation letter."

With a grim expression, Graham picked it up. "I'm sorry it has come to this. You were doing a good job."

"Thank you, but I've realized this isn't for me."

"That's a good thing to learn." Graham held out his hand. "I wish you the best in whatever you decide to do."

"I appreciate that." Jimmy shook his uncle's hand. "I'll see you around town."

"Give my best to Kelsey."

"I will, sir."

"And if you ever change your mind, feel free to come around."

"I don't see that happening."

Trying to figure out what he was going to say to Kelsey, Jimmy walked out of the building. He drove home with a feeling of dread in the pit of his stomach.

His grandmother's words played through his mind. *What a tangled web we weave when we first practice to deceive.* That was the quote he'd heard over and over from her after he'd told a lie. That was the way his marriage to Kelsey had started—with a deception. Now both Kelsey and he were unhappy. He wanted a real marriage, and all she wanted was to live up to her side of the bargain. Since there was no job, did that end the bargain?

If he let Kelsey go, would she be happy again? Or was that playing into Whitney's hands? He didn't want anything to do with Whitney. He just wanted his wife to love him.

No baby. No job. The two things that had precipitated their marriage no longer existed. Even though he loved Kelsey, had the time come to put an end to the charade?

When Jimmy reached home, he discovered an empty house. Kelsey wasn't here. Where was she? Should he call her, or would she think he was checking up on her? He wouldn't have these questions if theirs was a real marriage.

Jimmy dumped his stuff on the kitchen counter and went out to his workshop. The smell of wood and varnish greeted him. He loved that smell. He glanced around at his handiwork. This is what he enjoyed doing, but it wouldn't pay the bills. Or could it?

Lifting the cover from the crib, he ran a hand along the smooth wood that made up the railing. He'd gotten it out of the house as soon as he could after Kelsey's miscarriage, but that empty room was still a reminder of what Kelsey had lost. He didn't know how to comfort her. He'd failed again. He failed at the job. He'd failed to win her love. He'd come up short in every category. He'd put this nursery together before she was ready, and now there was no baby. He had made things worse.

Maybe he just needed to get away and do some soul searching. He could go up to his grandpa's cabin and spend some time alone and figure out what he was going to do with his future, with Kelsey. He wanted her to be a part of his life, but he wasn't sure that was what she wanted, especially now.

He packed a bag and took it out to the car. He looked back at the house. Should he leave a note for Kelsey? No. She might not see a note. He'd send her a text. *Kelsey, I'm going away for a couple of days. I just need some time alone to think some things over.*

As Jimmy drove to the cabin about an hour's drive from Pineydale, he wondered how he'd managed to make such a mess of his life. Envy. He'd always envied Mitch and his family's wealth, but had it come at a price? He'd never been close with his uncle Graham, so Jimmy didn't know about their family life. Maybe Mitch had chosen the garage over his dad's company because he didn't want to be tied to a job like a ball and chain.

Then there was pride. Jimmy had been too full of himself after Uncle Graham had made the job offer. Jimmy remembered that Proverb. *Pride goes before destruction.* He'd been too sure of himself. He'd planned to make a lot of money and be someone important in town, but instead he'd been chasing his tail, like Mitch's dog.

After Jimmy arrived at the cabin nestled in the forest, he took his things inside and opened up the windows to air out the place. Since his dad had died, visits to the cabin were infrequent. The place needed a good cleaning. He could think while he cleaned, and he needed to pray for God's help and wisdom to turn the circumstances of his life around.

***

Clouds danced around the sun as it rode on the treetops while Kelsey moseyed down the sidewalk after her visit with Charlotte. Kelsey loved being able to walk from place to place in the small town. As she neared the corner where she would turn toward home, she looked straight ahead. Jimmy was at work just a few blocks away. What would he do if she dropped by his office?

Would she find him working with Whitney? Kelsey

had never asked about the other woman's presence at his job, but Kelsey couldn't help thinking about Whitney. Jealousy lurked in Kelsey's mind, but she shoved it away. She would not let that destructive emotion win, even when her weeknights were spent alone while Jimmy worked.

Jealousy might not win, but worry might. The only thing that saved her from going crazy was the weekend. They spent Friday and Saturday nights with Mitch and Amanda, either going out to eat or playing cards and sharing a take-out meal or something Mitch and Jimmy cooked on the grill. Kelsey tried to capture those happy times to sustain her during the lonely week.

Jimmy never talked about his job, and Kelsey never asked. Maybe she should. So today she would stop by and let him know they had an invitation to Janelle's house for supper instead of going to Mitch and Amanda's.

When Kelsey reached the building with the redbrick facade, she stopped in the parking lot. Did Jimmy like surprises? She didn't know that about her husband, and she should. Maybe she should call first.

She fished her phone out of her pocket and punched Jimmy's name in her contact list. The phone rang and rang and rang. Finally she got his voicemail, but she didn't see any point in leaving a message. She was here, so she might as well go in. She opened the door and stepped inside.

Kelsey headed to the receptionist's desk. A middle-aged woman, whom Kelsey didn't know, smiled. "May I help you?"

"Yes, I'm Jimmy Cunningham's wife. Could you point me toward his office?"

"Certainly. It's the third door on the right, down that hallway." The woman pointed to her left.

"Thanks." Excited to see where Jimmy worked, Kelsey made her way down the quiet hallway.

As she approached the second doorway, two women were talking, and one of them mentioned Jimmy.

"I've heard plenty of rumors that Jimmy isn't happy with that drab little wife of his. I don't know what he's thinking, but I wouldn't be surprised if Whitney doesn't have designs on him just like she did before she left town. She thought she wanted to marry Mitch, but she always finds her way back to Jimmy."

"Yeah, they both left work early today. I wonder what's going on."

Kelsey slunk back down the hallway until she was nearly back in the reception area. Hoping no one would see her besides the receptionist, Kelsey raced out the front door, her heart aching. How could she compete with Whitney?

Sprinting down the block, Kelsey tried not to cry. She would not let that woman make her cry. When Kelsey reached the end of the block, her phone dinged. A message. She grabbed her phone. From Jimmy. Her heart raced as she read it.

Where had he gone? Was he with Whitney? She swallowed the lump in her throat as she stared at her phone. He was thinking things over. Was he trying to decide whether to end their marriage? Was Whitney going to win?

Kelsey stood on the corner and closed her eyes. She had to think. She had to come up with a plan. She couldn't lose Jimmy. But she didn't have anything to offer him except her love, and what if that wasn't enough?

Her whole world was crumbling around her, but it had

been crumbling since she'd given in to Brandon. Maybe this was what she deserved. Would Amanda understand? Whether she would or not, Kelsey had to talk to someone.

When Kelsey reached Amanda's house, she rang the doorbell. Dolly barked, and in a second Amanda opened the door.

"Kelsey, what are you doing here?"

"Walking." Despite trying to put on a happy face, her eyes welled with tears.

"Kelsey, what's wrong?" Amanda took Kelsey's arm and pulled her over to the couch.

"Jimmy." Kelsey buried her face in her hands.

"Jimmy? Is he sick, injured, in an accident?"

Kelsey shook her head. "I'm afraid he's going to leave me for Whitney."

"That's ridiculous." Amanda raised her voice. "Look at me."

Sniffling, Kelsey looked at Amanda. "No, it's not."

Amanda eyed Kelsey with a no-nonsense look. "Tell me what's going on."

Kelsey pressed her lips together, then handed her phone to Amanda. "Read the message."

Amanda looked down at the phone. "So he's going to take some time to think things over. Do you know what things?"

"Not for sure, but I can guess." Kelsey went on to tell Amanda what she had heard from the women at the grocery store and also the women at Jimmy's office. "Now do you understand why I say that?"

Amanda frowned. "But Jimmy loves you, and I could tell he was annoyed at Whitney that Sunday right after she moved back here."

"He might've been annoyed then, but they've been working together day and night for the past month. Jimmy doesn't get home until after I go to bed at night during the week."

"And you know for a fact that he's working with Whitney?"

Kelsey nodded. "Every Sunday at church, she has corralled Jimmy and told him how great it is to work with him, even though they have to keep late hours. It seemed to me that she was just making sure I knew how much time they were spending together."

"Has Jimmy said anything about it?"

Kelsey twisted her hands in her lap. "No, he never talks about work."

"But you guys seem so happy together when you're with us."

"It's all a charade."

Amanda frowned again. "How so?"

"You know how you were so shocked and upset when we got married?"

"Yeah."

"Well, it was all pretend."

"You mean you're not really married?"

"Oh, we're married, but in name only." Kelsey let out a harsh breath.

"Why?"

"I'll explain, but please don't judge me." Those were the same words she'd said to Jimmy that night at the reception.

"Why would I judge you?"

Kelsey swallowed hard. "Because I've done some awful things."

"Like what?"

Kelsey lowered her gaze. She didn't want to see the disappointment in Amanda's eyes. Her voice cracking, Kelsey explained everything. Brandon. Jimmy's job requirement. The agreement to get married. The pretending. The miscarriage. Jimmy's constant kindness through it all. And how she finally realized she loved him. "But he doesn't love me."

"How do you know he doesn't? It sure sounds like he cares a lot about you. Maybe he's fallen in love with you just like you've fallen in love with him."

Kelsey frowned. "But he's never said so."

"You haven't either."

Amanda scooted closer and hugged Kelsey. "I'm so sorry you've gone through all this. You should've told me."

Kelsey sat back. "I was afraid. Afraid you would think less of me."

Amanda raised her eyebrows. "Really? I was the queen of misbehavior."

"That's the whole point. No one would expect me to get into this mess."

"We all make mistakes, but I know I thought you were crazy for marrying Jimmy like you did, but now I don't think it was a mistake. You have to tell him how you feel."

"But what if he doesn't feel the same way?"

"What do you have to lose? You want to fight for him, don't you? Have you called him?"

"Yeah, but I just get his voicemail. Maybe he doesn't want to talk to me."

"Try again."

Kelsey poked at the screen on her phone. When she got

Jimmy's voicemail again, she looked at Amanda. "Still voicemail. And I don't know where he is. For all I know, Whitney could be meeting him."

"I don't believe that for a minute." Amanda reached for her phone. "Let me call Mitch and see if he has any idea where Jimmy could be."

Kelsey wrinkled her brow. "Don't tell Mitch why I'm looking for Jimmy. Please keep this between you and me. Tell him I need to find him because his sister has invited us over for supper. That's true."

Amanda put the phone to her ear as she squeezed Kelsey's hand and mouthed, *Between you and me.* Amanda motioned toward the kitchen. "There's a pencil and pad in the desk drawer. Get them for me."

A spark of hope pushed Kelsey's worry aside for a moment. She returned with the pencil and pad. Amanda scribbled something on the pad, then ended the call.

Amanda handed the paper to Kelsey. "Instructions to the cabin that used to belong to Jimmy's grandpa. Mitch thinks Jimmy is probably there."

"But what if he's not?" Kelsey took the paper, remembering how Jimmy had said the mantel on the fireplace came from his grandpa's cabin.

"Let's believe you'll find him there."

"Okay." Kelsey stood.

Amanda hugged Kelsey. "Let's say a prayer before you go."

Amanda and Kelsey held hands as they bowed their heads. Amanda prayed for a safe trip for Kelsey and that she would find Jimmy and a good outcome.

"Thank you." Kelsey hugged Amanda again. "I forgot I walked."

"I'll drive you home so you can get your car."

Minutes later, Kelsey was on her way out of town, headed toward the mountains. As she took the first turn off the highway, her heart raced. What if he wasn't there? What if he was there and he didn't want to talk to her? What if he was there and Whitney was, too?

Kelsey pushed all the negative questions aside and took the last turn on the instructions. The road snaked through the deciduous forest where ferns grew along the ground and Queen Anne's lace created a blanket of white near the roadside.

A red reflector on a post signaled the entrance to a driveway. Kelsey slowed the car to read the number on the dilapidated mailbox. This was the place. She turned down the gravel road. Just around the corner, she spied a log cabin with a big front porch and a view of the mountains. Jimmy's car was parked at the end of the drive. No other cars were in sight. Did that mean no Whitney, or did it mean they had come together?

After parking behind Jimmy, Kelsey exited her car and breathed the fresh mountain air. A creek babbled just beyond the cabin. Another sound floated her way. *Thwak, thwak, thwak.* She couldn't figure out what it was, but it was coming from somewhere beyond the cabin.

While Kelsey climbed the steps to the porch, nerves curdled her stomach. She approached the door. *Please, Lord, don't let this be a mistake.* She knocked. No answer. Now what? Should she try the door? What would she find on the other side? Jimmy and Whitney locked in each other's arms, or worse?

She knocked again, louder. Still no answer. Jimmy's car was here, so he had to be here somewhere. She turned the knob, and the door swung open, squeaking on its hinges. Not a soul in sight.

The large open room contained a blue-and-red plaid sofa and a matching overstuffed blue chair. A small flat-screen TV hung on the wall above the fireplace. A round oak table surrounded by four ladder-back chairs separated the living area from the tiny kitchen. On the far wall, there was a closed door. She recognized Jimmy's bag lying on top of the table. A smaller bag lay next to it. Whitney's?

Kelsey closed her eyes against the thought. "Jimmy? Jimmy, are you here?"

No answer. Kelsey wasn't sure whether to be happy or suspicious. Was someone behind that closed door? She might as well find out. She knocked and called out his name again. Still nothing. She turned the knob and opened the door just a crack and peered into the dim room. When she saw that no one was there, she released the breath she'd been holding.

As she opened the door wider, she caught a glimpse of movement from somewhere. No one was in the room, so what had she seen? She stepped into the space that contained a queen-sized bed covered in a patriotic quilt featuring red, white, and blue squares and stars. A large window looked out onto the forest and mountains beyond.

As she stood there, she discovered the movement she'd seen just before she stepped into the room was a reflection of the sun off something outside. She stepped closer to the window. Her stomach took a nosedive as she spied Jimmy standing shirtless while he swung a maul over his head and split a log. Pieces of the log flew in two different directions. He stopped and wiped his brow with his forearm. He readied another log and repeated the action, his muscles rippling in the sunshine. Kelsey swallowed hard as she watched her handsome husband.

Her husband. She didn't want to lose him.

She had to talk to him.

Kelsey made her way outside and around to the back of the cabin. She stood at the corner and watched him.

"Jimmy." She held her breath.

He looked up as he let the head of the maul hit the ground. He leaned on the handle as he looked her way. "How did you find me here?"

"Mitch."

Jimmy smiled wryly. "That cousin of mine can't stay out of my business."

"It's not Mitch's fault. I asked where I could find you, and he guessed here. I'm glad he was right."

"So why are you here?"

Jimmy's questions didn't inspire Kelsey's confidence. "I needed to let you know Janelle has invited us to supper tonight."

"Did you get my text?"

Kelsey nodded. He obviously didn't want her here. But she wouldn't give up. She was here, and she was going to tell him how she felt.

"Then you know I want to be alone. Why didn't you just text me back?"

"I wanted to make sure you got the message."

"Well, either way, I wouldn't have gotten it. No cell service up here." Jimmy stared at her and stayed right where he was. "So you came all the way up here to tell me we're invited to my sister's for supper?"

Her heart pumping so fast she thought it might beat right out of her chest, Kelsey shook her head. "I came because I have something I want to tell you."

Jimmy stepped closer, dragging the maul with him. "I have something I have to tell you first."

"Okay." Kelsey swallowed hard. Was he going to tell her he was expecting Whitney?

He lowered his gaze as he rubbed the back of his neck. "I quit my job today."

"Why?"

"Because it was consuming my life, and I hated it." He looked up at her as he let out a halfhearted laugh. "Here I thought it was what I wanted. Instead, it turned out to be a nightmare. So there's no job anymore that requires a wife, and you don't have a baby that requires a father. If you want, we can call this bargain marriage quits." Shrugging, he lowered his gaze again. "Your call."

Her call. Kelsey didn't want to keep him trapped in this marriage if he wanted out, but first he had to know how she felt, even if he rejected her. She licked her lips and summoned all her courage as she took several steps closer until she was standing directly in front of him. She wanted to look into those gray eyes when she declared her love.

"I don't want to call it quits for one reason. If you want Whitney instead of me, I understand, but I want you to know this one thing before you walk away. I love you, Jimmy Cunningham."

The maul fell at Jimmy's feet as he closed the gap between them. He put his arms around her waist and whirled her around. "That's the best thing you've said since you told me I was your best friend."

Kelsey's head spun. "It is?"

Jimmy set her on her feet and continued to hold her around the waist as he pressed his forehead to hers. "Yes.

I've loved you for months, but it never seemed the right time to tell you. I thought your emotions were always in a fragile state because of your pregnancy, then the miscarriage. I kept waiting for the right time to tell you, but—"

Kelsey pressed her lips to his, cutting off whatever he had planned to say. She didn't need any more explanations. He loved her, and that was all she needed to know.

When the kiss ended, Jimmy stepped back, holding her at arm's length. "Mrs. Cunningham, I have no idea how I'm going to help put food on the table without a job, but I'll support you with all my love."

"We'll figure that out. That's the last thing I'm thinking about right now."

Jimmy grinned. "Does this mean you'd like to make our marriage real in every sense?"

Kelsey nodded.

"Then I'd better shower. I'm pretty sweaty."

"I'll be happy to wash your back." She giggled.

"I'll take you up on that offer." Jimmy grabbed her hand.

They raced to the cabin.

"What about your sister?"

"Later we'll walk down the road until we get a signal and let her know we're not coming." Jimmy chuckled as he lifted Kelsey up into his arms and carried her over the threshold. "The honeymoon begins."

EPILOGUE

....

The following Christmas Eve

Colorful lights twinkled on the Christmas tree in the corner of Jimmy's living room. A fire crackled in the fireplace as his family and Kelsey's family gathered in the room. Laughter and conversation floated through the air. The children played in a corner near the kitchen, while the adults occupied the couch and chairs in the living room and dining room. Kelsey figured the jovial gathering would turn dour after she and Jimmy told the truth about their marriage.

They could go just the way they were with only Amanda knowing the truth, but Kelsey had decided she wouldn't free herself of the guilt if she continued to harbor that secret part of her life. Although she knew God had forgiven her, she had to forgive herself. Part of that forgiveness was confession.

Jimmy rang a little bell sitting on the mantel to get everyone's attention as he took Kelsey's hand. "Thanks, everyone, for coming to share our first Christmas Eve as a married couple. It's especially wonderful to have Grady, Maria, and Noah here to celebrate."

"And we're glad to be here with Amanda and Kelsey." Grady waved a hand in the air.

"I want to thank everyone who has given their support as Kelsey and I worked to get my woodworking business off the ground. I've got almost more orders than I can handle, so I'm looking to hiring some help in the new year."

Applause filled the room until Jimmy held up his hands.

Kelsey took the Bible from the hearth and opened it, then looked out at these people she loved. She prayed they would accept what she was about to tell them with open hearts, forgiveness, and prayers. "Besides having you all here to share Christmas Eve, Jimmy and I want you here to share with us as we renew our marriage vows."

As a murmur went through the gathering, Jimmy put an arm around Kelsey's waist and drew her close. "I know this is unusual because most couples don't renew vows except to celebrate an anniversary, but Kelsey and I want to do this because we didn't get to share this with you when we got married last March. Kelsey has something she'd like to say before we do that."

Kelsey swallowed the lump in her throat as she looked down at the Bible. "First, I want to read James 5:16. 'Therefore confess your sins to each other and pray for each other so that you may be healed. The prayer of a righteous person is powerful and effective.'" She looked up and shared a smile with Amanda. "As the verse says, I have something to confess."

"We both do." Jimmy looked at Kelsey with a nod.

Kelsey leaned into Jimmy as she told her story, with Jimmy chiming in on occasion. When she was finished, she smiled through her tears as Jimmy kissed the top of her head. "We had not only been pretending for you but pretending for each other, pretending that we didn't care because we were afraid of getting hurt. But there's no more pretending, only love. And we want to share that tonight as we put love into our vows."

"And we have special guests with us tonight, Davis and Shirley." Jimmy motioned for Davis to come forward. "Davis married us, and we asked him if he would do that again."

Davis joined Jimmy and Kelsey in front of the fireplace. "As you know, I'm a retired judge and occasionally marry people. Although I'm not a preacher, I still like to include some Scripture as long as the couple has no objection. I also pray for all the couples I marry. I especially prayed for Jimmy and his new bride because I remember him as a little tyke running around my yard. I'm glad the Lord brought them through a troubled time so they could find love.

"So let's join Jimmy and Kelsey as they repeat their vows in a celebration of their love for each other."

While their family looked on, Jimmy and Kelsey repeated their original vows in unison but added a pledge to love each other.

"I, Kelsey, Jimmy, accept you, Jimmy, Kelsey, as you are. You are my friend. I will respect you as a person, a partner, and an equal. I will listen to you with kindness and empathy, and give encouragement. I promise to rejoice with you in good times and struggle alongside you in bad times. I promise to laugh with you, cry with you, and grow with you, even as time and life change us both. I promise to learn with you, to support your dreams, and to understand our differences. I take you to be my husband, wife, my companion, and the friend of my life. With these words, I marry you and bind my life to yours.

"I take you as my one true love. I will cherish our union and love you more each day than I did the day before. I give you my hand, my heart, and my love from this day forward for as long as we both shall live."

After they finished, Davis said a simple prayer, then Jimmy and Kelsey were enveloped with hugs and congratulations.

Jimmy once again held up his hand. "We've got one more thing we'd like to announce. I'll let Kelsey do the announcing."

Kelsey smiled up at Jimmy. "We're looking forward to having a baby of our own sometime near the end of May next year. A boy."

As the room erupted with applause and congratulations, Amanda ran over and hugged Kelsey. "This is so exciting. We have news to share, too. Mitch and I are also having a boy around the same time. I was going to wait until tomorrow to announce it. I have this little package for dad telling him he's going to be a grandpa."

Kelsey laughed. "He's going to be a grandpa twice."

"Two boy cousins. We'll have to make sure they grow up friends rather than rivals." Mitch shook Jimmy's hand.

Jimmy nodded. "For sure."

Corey, Janelle's oldest, looked up at Jimmy. "I think you forgot something."

Jimmy hunkered down next to his nephew. "What?"

Corey wrinkled his nose. "You forgot to kiss her."

Standing, Jimmy and the rest of the adults erupted with laughter.

"I'll have to remedy that." Jimmy motioned for Kelsey to come over to him.

All smiles, Kelsey put her arms around Jimmy's neck as she stood on her tiptoes. "Mr. Cunningham, please do kiss me."

"Absolutely, Mrs. Cunningham." Jimmy pulled her closer and kissed her while applause swirled around them. When the kiss ended, Jimmy looked into her eyes. "There's only one word for that. Perfect."

Dear Readers,

Thank you for reading A Baby to Call Ours. I hope Jimmy and Kelsey's story touched your heart and brought you a lesson about God's forgiveness and not being afraid to confess our sins to the One who loves us. Both Jimmy and Kelsey are characters who struggle with a huge lie, but they learn how to seek God's will and not their own plans for their lives.

I would love for you to write a review and let other readers know what you think about *A Baby to Call Ours.*

Please check out the other books in the Front Porch Promises series, *A Place to Call Home, A Love to Call Mine, A Family to Call Ours,* and *A Song to Call Ours*. If you would like to get information on my upcoming books, please sign up for my newsletter by visiting my website www.merrilleewhren.com.

Merrillee Whren

ABOUT THE AUTHOR

Merrillee Whren is an award-winning and a *USA Today* bestselling author who writes inspirational romance. She is the winner of the 2003 Golden Heart Award for best inspirational romance manuscript presented by Romance Writers of America. She has also been the recipient of the RT Reviewers' Choice Award and the Inspirational Reader's Choice Award. She is married to her own personal hero, her husband of forty plus years, and has two grown daughters. She has lived in Atlanta, Boston, Dallas, Chicago and Florida but now makes her home in the Arizona desert. She spends her free time playing tennis or walking while she does the plotting for her novels. Please visit her website, www.merrilleewhren.com or connect with her on social media sites.

https://twitter.com/MerrilleeWhren
https://www.facebook.com/MerrilleeWhren.Author/

Made in the USA
San Bernardino, CA
09 January 2019